About the

Maya Blake's writing dream started at thirteen. She eventually realised her dream when she received The Call in 2012. Maya lives in England with her husband, kids and an endless supply of books. Contact Maya: mayabauthor.blogspot.com, on X @mayablake and Facebook @maya.blake.94

Andie Brock started inventing imaginary friends around the age of four and is still doing that today; only now the sparkly fairies have made way for spirited heroines and sexy heroes. Thankfully she now has some real friends, as well as a husband and three children, plus a grumpy but lovable cat. Andie lives in Bristol and when not actually writing, could well be plotting her next passionate romance story.

Nina Milne has loved Mills & Boon, since as a child she discovered stacks of Mills & Boon books 'hidden' in the airing cupboard so is thrilled to now write for them. Nina spent her childhood in England, US and France. Since then she has acquired an English degree, one hero-husband, three gorgeous children and a house in Brighton where she plans to stay. After all she can now transport herself via her characters to anywhere in the world whilst sitting in pyjamas in her study. Bliss!

Princess Brides

Princess Brides: A Marriage of Convenience

MAYA BLAKE

ANDIE BROCK

NINA MILNE

MILLS & BOON

First Published in Great Britain 2025
by Mills & Boon, an imprint of HarperCollins*Publishers* Ltd
1 London Bridge Street, London, SE1 9GF

www.harpercollins.co.uk

HarperCollins*Publishers*
Macken House, 39/40 Mayor Street Upper,
Dublin 1, D01 C9W8, Ireland

ISBN: 978-0-263-39782-6

MIX
Paper | Supporting
responsible forestry
FSC™ C007454

CROWN PRINCE'S BOUGHT BRIDE

MAYA BLAKE

CHAPTER ONE

REMIREZ ALEXANDER MONTEGOVA, Crown Prince of the Kingdom of Montegova, paused before the imposing double doors, his raised fist as frozen as the rest of his body.

It didn't escape him that anyone who knew him would be shocked by this uncharacteristic display of hesitancy. Since infancy he'd been lauded as a fearless, valiant visionary who would one day steer his people to greater heights than any of his forebears had imagined.

But here he was, cowed by a set of doors.

Granted, they weren't just any doors. They were the portals to his final destiny. As pretentious as the words sounded, that didn't make them any less true.

He'd been dreading this day.

The simple truth was he didn't want to go inside. Didn't want to face his mother the Queen. Every instinct warned him that he wouldn't emerge the same person.

When had that ever mattered? He'd never belonged to himself. He belonged to history. To the destiny forged by countless Mongetovan warriors who'd fought bloody battles to carve out this Western Mediterranean kingdom with their bare hands.

For as long as he drew breath he would belong to the people of Montegova. Duty and destiny. Two words branded with indelible ink into his skin.

Like twin weights they settled like a heavy cloak over his shoulders, making his next breath a torturous chore.

'Your Highness?' his senior aide prompted nervously but firmly from behind him. 'Her Majesty is waiting.'

One voice in many that peppered his daily life. One that

cajoled and coaxed and, when he closed himself off to that, as he'd mastered doing, prodded and pushed.

The morning's summons, however, had been absolute.

His mother requested his presence at nine o'clock sharp. The solid gold antique clock standing proudly in one of the many marbled and hallowed hallways of the Grand Palace of Montegova solemnly announced that he was five seconds from being late.

With a resigned breath, he unfroze his fist, rapped sharply on the gold-leaf-framed doors and awaited the command to enter.

It arrived, brisk and firm, yet wrapped in a layer of unmistakable warmth.

The voice accurately reflected the woman seated in the throne-like chair beneath the grand coat of arms that spelled out her royal status in Latin, her flint-grey gaze tracking him across the vast office.

She nodded approvingly when he executed a respectful bow before taking his seat before her.

'I was wondering how long you'd remain behind the door. Am I really so frightful?' she mused with a trace of sadness in her eyes.

That sadness grated, but Remi refused to let it show.

He was used to people wearing that expression in his presence. He was used to several more expressions, yet sorrow and pity chafed the worst. But he supposed it was better than being treated as if he were made of fragile glass.

He ignored the emotion and searched her face for signs that, just this once, his instincts were wrong. But from her perfectly coiffed hair and flawless make-up, to the classic Chanel suit she favoured for official duties, and the diamond and emerald brooch made in the image of the Montegovan flag, Remi was left in no doubt that this meeting was exactly what he'd suspected it to be.

The axe was truly about to fall.

'Not frightful, no. But I suspect the reason for this summoning will leave one of us less than thrilled.'

His mother's lips pursed momentarily before she rose. A tall, striking woman, she would have commanded attention with effortless ease even if she hadn't been the reigning Montegovan monarch. Long before she'd become Queen she'd won three beauty pageants across the world. When she deigned to bestow it on the deserving her smile could stop a grown man in his tracks—Remi had seen it first-hand. The hair that had turned silver almost overnight ten years ago, after his father's death, had once been as dark as his own, but she'd owned that very visible sign of pain and grief with the same stalwart strength that had stopped her kingdom from descending into chaos at the sudden death of its King and the scandal that had followed. At twenty-three, Remi had been deemed too young to take the throne so his mother had taken his place as interim ruler. He was supposed to take the throne on his thirtieth birthday. But then further tragedy had struck.

His mother was the strongest woman he knew. Which was why everything inside him tightened when, after several minutes examining the spectacular view from her office window, she returned to her desk, planted her palms on the polished antique cherry wood and locked eyes with him.

'It's time, Remirez.'

His gut clenched tighter. She very rarely used his full first name. As a child that had never boded well for him or his hide. As a grown man of thirty-two it still commanded his attention.

Unable to remain seated in the foreboding of impending fate, he stood and paced in front of her desk. 'How much time are we talking, here? Weeks? Months?'

It wouldn't be years. She'd already given him two years. And lately she'd indicated, without cruelty, that it was time to set his own grief aside.

'I would like to make the announcement that I'm stepping down at the next Solstice Festival.'

The third week in June.

'That's…three months away.' The reality of it hit him like a cold wave in the face.

'Yes,' she replied firmly. 'Which means time is of the essence. We must put our house in order before we begin to make the announcements.'

'Announcements?' he echoed. 'Plural?'

His mother's gaze dropped momentarily to her desk. 'I'm not just stepping down, Remi. I'm also taking extended leave from all official duties.'

Isadora Montegova wasn't just the ruling monarch, she was also an active member of parliament.

'You're resigning? Why?'

Her lips compressed—a sign that she didn't like to admit whatever it was she was about to say. 'The past few years have been difficult for both of us. I need a little…time away from everything.'

She wouldn't stoop so low as to call it *me time*, the way others might, but if anyone had earned the right to retreat and regroup it was his mother.

Not only had she borne the unexpected death of her husband with unwavering strength, she'd weathered the subsequent scandal unleashed by the discovery of her husband's decades-long secret with remarkable dignity and poise.

Behind closed doors, though, Remi had caught glimpses of the true toll it had taken on her. He himself had barely been able to hold back his fury at discovering that the father he'd held in such high esteem had proved to be faithless. Over the years his rage had boiled down to a simmering resentment, but it had never dissipated. Because not only had his father caused his mother untold hardship by his actions, he'd also thrown the kingdom into turmoil for years. Years which had taken a brutal toll on his mother. On him and on Zak, his younger brother.

Secrets and lies. It was a cliché until it happened on your doorstep and was played out for the world to see.

He tamped down on his fury as his mother reached out.

'Which brings me to the next housekeeping problem.' She opened a slim folder and slid it across the desk.

And there, displayed in full Technicolor, was the latest source of his mother's angst.

Jules Montegova.

The surly half-brother who'd been presented to them moments after his father's burial. The twenty-eight-year-old whose paternity had been proven via a discreet DNA test, to be royal, courtesy of an illicit affair his father had indulged in when he had briefly been stationed in Paris on diplomatic duty.

Jules was the scandal that had nearly unsettled the kingdom. The paparazzi had gone on a feeding frenzy for months, prising open every closet they could find in the hope of unearthing more skeletons.

It would have been easier to stomach had Jules not proved to be nothing but a thorn in their sides from the moment he'd arrived in Montegova ten years ago.

Remi scanned the picture, his jaw clenching as he noted the glassy eyes, the dishevelment, the slurred expression of drunkenness. 'What has he done now?' he bit out.

Queen Isadora's mouth twisted. 'A less aggravating question would be what *hasn't* he done? Three weeks ago it was reckless gambling in Monte Carlo, then he flew to Paris and carried on gambling for another four days. The royal bursar was apoplectic when he received the bill. Ten days ago he turned up in Barcelona and gatecrashed a private party Duke Armando was throwing for his niece. Since then he's been in London, and in the past few days in *this* woman's company,' she said, sliding aside the first picture to reveal several more.

They all showed variations of the same woman. Dark blonde. Leggy. Bright green eyes and a figure designed to stop traffic. She was striking. And her smile would win a contest against a thousand-watt bulb.

But she was a dime a dozen in Remi's world. All flash and no substance.

Hell, in one picture she was literally flashing her underwear, uncaring that the world could see her lacy thong as she threw her arms around his half-brother's neck. In all of the pictures her clothes barely covered her admittedly remarkable assets, and the camera's glare threw every curve and dip into high-definition exposure.

Remi examined her carefully, searching for weaknesses. His gaze tracked her pert little nose, her wide, sensual mouth, cheekbones sculpted by a master craftsman and a delicate jawline designed to be worshipped with fingers and lips.

The sleek line of her neck dropped to slender, lightly tanned shoulders. Her collarbones were revealed by a sleeveless top, drawing attention to her soft throat and the impressive swell of her breasts. A flat, toned stomach, rounded hips and those endless legs completed the package.

She was flawless. Physically, at least. He had very little doubt that she would be severely lacking in other areas. Except maybe in the—

'Who is she?' he snapped, intensely annoyed with the direction of his thoughts. Who cared how the trollop was in bed?

His mother resumed her seat, her gaze meeting his. 'Her details are on the last page. The rest is still sketchy, but I've seen more than enough to know she presents a potential problem. For one thing, Jules never usually stays in one place more than a few days. He's been in London for almost two weeks. And, unfortunately, these are the least offensive pictures. Whatever is going on between them needs to end. *Now.* The royal transition must be as smooth as possible. So far he's refused my summons for him to return to Montegova. Short of having his bodyguards forcibly put him on a plane—and risk a kidnapping charge—I have to find a way to bring him to heel.'

Remi's gaze was drawn, against his will, back to the pictures. He flipped to the last page. The woman his half-brother had taken up with was summed up in four lines.

Madeleine Myers
Waitress
Twenty-four years old
College dropout

Distaste filled his mouth. 'You want me to take care of it?' For the sake of his kingdom's reputation, his half-brother's antics needed to be curbed before they attracted unwanted attention.

Queen Isadora linked her fingers and placed them on the desk. 'Jules may not have any interest in behaving like a Montegovan except when it eases his way into casinos and parties, but this cannot be allowed to continue. He pretends otherwise, but he's a little in awe of you. I dare say you scare him a little too. He'll listen to you. And you're the only one I trust to handle this discreetly.' She cleared her throat. 'With the news of my stepping down and your ascension to the throne we can't afford another scandal now. Especially when you announce that you'll be taking a wife at the end of the summer.'

Icy shock gushed through his veins, rendering him speechless for one stunned second. 'I will be *what*?' he demanded when he found his tongue.

'Don't look so shocked. Surely this doesn't come as a surprise? You were all set to do so two years ago.'

Different emotions surged high—a peculiar mingling of pain, futile anger, bitterness and guilt. The first was natural—the pain of a cherished one lost never went away. Although lately the pain had been less and the other emotions more pronounced.

His anger stemmed from a life cut far too short. From all the plans made that would never come to fruition. And the bitterness was aimed squarely at fate and the cruelty of time.

The fact that his fiancée had been on her way to her doctor when the tragedy had struck was irony itself.

Which brought him to the guilt. The culmination of events had been his fault and his alone. For that he had to bear the crushing weight on his soul.

'You would be king and married by now if we hadn't lost Celeste,' his mother said, gentle but firm.

His teeth clenched at the unnecessary reminder. 'I'm well aware of that.' Just as he was well aware that his voice now echoed the chill weaving through his bloodstream. 'But tell me, Mother, where exactly am I to conjure a bride from in three months?'

If he'd hoped to cow her with his caustic tone, he should have known better.

Without missing a beat she opened a tiny drawer directly in front of her chair and took out a single piece of paper. 'The list of candidates we put together for you five years ago is still viable—save for one. She married a count and is already pregnant with her second child.'

The trace of wistfulness in her voice further aggravated Remi, but he kept his emotions on a tight leash, saved his verbal dexterity for the noose caressing his throat.

'I didn't stoop to plucking my future wife from a list put together by faceless advisers five years ago and I'm not about to do that now.'

Queen Isadora slapped the piece of paper down on the desk. 'Well, that's too bad. This time you don't have the luxury of time or indulgence. Perhaps this is the best way forward. I married for love. You were about to marry the woman of your heart. Look where *that* got us both!'

Remi stiffened. His mother froze in her chair, her eyes widening in shock at her own outburst. Thick silence slammed between them as Remi examined her closer, noted the pallor beneath the make-up, the lines of stress bracketing her eyes.

He'd absorbed more of her duties this past year, but he could still see the strain of office on her face.

Heavy really *was* the head that wore the crown, temporary or not.

A crown that was soon to be placed upon his own head.

Before he could comment she gathered herself with regal poise, her spine ramrod straight as she speared him with a glare.

'Let me be clear, Remirez. I will not sit by and watch all that I've painstakingly rebuilt these past ten years fall to ruin again because your sensibilities won't allow it. You'll go to London, separate your half-brother from this piece of bad news and bring him home. Then you'll pick a bride and announce your betrothal one week before the Solstice Festival. At the festival we'll give an official date for your wedding, which will be three months after your engagement. That gives you six months to get used to the idea of marriage. I'll make myself available to help with preparations if you need me to. Otherwise, I look forward to being the lucky mother of the groom come September.'

She closed the folder and nudged it an extra inch towards him, before straightening the specially engraved pens which had belonged to his father.

When she was done, she looked him straight in the eye. 'It's time to take your true place as head of this kingdom. I know you won't let me down.'

One minute later, Remi walked out. And, as he'd rightly predicted, everything had changed.

Five more weeks.

Maddie Myers resisted the urge to check her phone for the exact hour and minute before this nightmare was over.

She should never have agreed to this preposterous proposition. So far every second had been hellish.

But then her choices were severely limited. And when a Lamborghini sideswiping you compounded those woes by knocking the grocery shopping paid for with your last tenner out of your hands, you needed to take a moment to accept that things *were* truly awful.

With luck in very limited supply in her world, she'd thanked every star she could name for escaping that horrifying incident with just a few unpleasant-looking bruises, the occasional twinge in her ribs that made it difficult to take a full breath and a sore arm.

To be honest, Maddie was sure it was the shock of being nearly run over that had made her agree to Jules Montagne's scheme in the first place. But by the time she'd downed that second restorative brandy she'd been in the darkest pit of despair, one that not even expensive booze could lift her from. So when the owner of the Lamborghini of Death had offered her a solution to her problems…

Truth be told, at that point she'd been seriously considering the logistics of how to sell one of her kidneys, so a rich assaulter with money to burn had seemed the answer to her prayers.

Nevertheless, it had taken her forty-eight hours to accept his deal. Probably because he'd been cagey about why he needed her in the first place. If Maddie had learned one thing in life, it was to look before she leapt. Blind trust was no longer a flaw that would tarnish her.

She'd trusted her mother to stay and help the family she'd helped break apart. She'd trusted her father every time he'd told her he had his addiction under control. And Greg… He'd been the worst culprit of all.

So when Jules had delivered that stony-faced *ask no questions* ultimatum her first instinct had been to walk out of the fancy wine bar he'd taken her to after nearly running her over, and never look back.

But no matter how many times she'd checked her meagre bank account, or riffled through her belongings in the hope of finding something pawn-worthy, the balance had fallen far too short.

With time running out for her father, she'd had no choice but to return Jules Montagne's phone call.

Of course his help hadn't come for free. Hence her being once again dressed like a high-class escort, listening to him hold court among his circle of trustfundistas and minor royals in another VIP lounge as they guzzled thousands of pounds' worth of champagne.

She'd long since passed the *life is so unfair* and *why me?* stage. And after her mother's shocking desertion Maddie had shrugged off *there's always hope* too.

'Hey, Maddie, smile! The way you're staring into your glass, you'd think somebody's died.'

She plastered on a fake smile while the urge to scream burned through her gullet. True, no one had died. But the man who'd once been a strong, supportive father—a man now sadly broken by his failures—most definitely would, unless she pulled off this performance successfully and collected the payment due to her.

Seventy-five thousand pounds.

The exact amount needed for her father's private kidney operation and aftercare in France.

The exact amount Jules had agreed to pay her if she pretended to be his girlfriend for six weeks.

She raised her gaze from her glass and connected with the gunmetal eyes of her pretend boyfriend. The man who barely spoke to her once they were away from the prying eyes of the paparazzi who dogged his every movement.

'Smile, *cherie*,' he insisted, with a hard, fierce light in his eyes.

She tried again, aiming for authenticity this time. She must have succeeded. He gave a brisk nod and raised his glass to her before swinging back into whatever joke he'd interrupted himself in.

Maddie breathed in relief, winced as her ribs protested,

then went back to wondering just how long she could survive down this rabbit hole.

The first time they'd gone out she'd heard one tabloid hack shout a question about Jules's family—specifically how the queen felt about his behaviour. Maddie had asked him about it. He'd shut her down with a snapped response she was sure had been a lie, and reminded her of the *ask no questions* rule.

The possibility that she'd struck a bargain with a minor royal had triggered unease. Media attention was the last thing she wanted.

Despite needing the money desperately, she'd voiced her concerns. Jules's suggestion that she wear headphones with the music turned up high to avoid the paparazzi's questions, and keep her head down to avoid the camera's flash had worked a treat. After all, she couldn't answer questions she couldn't hear.

Maddie was sure that her perceived rudeness had earned her a disparaging label on social media. But the great thing about selling your laptop so you could buy food and using your phone only for emergency calls to avoid expensive bills was the blessed absence of the burden of social media.

So here she was, firmly ensconced in Wonderland, with no inkling of why she was playing pretend girlfriend to a handsome, spoilt, maybe minor royal who travelled with two bodyguards.

She watched him beckon one of them. Jules whispered in his ear, then loudly ordered another half-dozen bottles of Dom Perignon as the young guard headed to the back of the nightclub.

In the gleeful melee that followed the arrival of more booze, very few people noticed Jules following his bodyguard.

The sudden realisation that she'd aligned herself with a man who was headed down the same path of addiction as her father was enough to propel Maddie to her feet. She wasn't sure exactly how she would deal with Jules Montagne if she caught him taking drugs, but her burning anger and anxiety couldn't be contained.

She was halfway across the floor when a commotion by the front doors caught her attention.

Except it wasn't a commotion. It was more a force of nature invading the onyx-and-chrome interior of the Soho nightclub.

Two bodyguards, taller, sharper and burlier than the ones who followed Jules around, parted the crowd.

The man who sauntered forward and paused under a golden spotlight nearly caused Maddie to swallow her tongue.

Frozen in place, she stared unashamedly, certain that the faint tendrils of artificial smoke and strobe lighting were causing her to hallucinate the sheer magnificence of the god-like creature before her.

But no.

He was flesh.

The quiet fury and electric energy blanketing him clearly transmitted through the muscle ticking in his jaw.

He was blood.

Royal blood, if the arrogant, regal authority with which he carried himself and the further four bodyguards who formed a semi-circular barrier around him were any indication.

There was something vaguely familiar about him, although where she could possibly have caught a glimpse before of that square, rugged jaw, those haughty cut-glass cheekbones or those sinfully sensual lips eluded her.

Eyes like polished silver gleamed beneath slashed dark brows, scanning the crowd as he continued to prowl through the semi-dark space.

As he drew closer Maddie knew she should look away. Not out of shame or discomfort, but out of sheer self-preservation. He radiated enough sensual volatility to urge her to avoid direct eye contact. To take herself out of his mag-netising orbit before she was swallowed up in his vortex.

And yet she couldn't make her feet move. In fact she was fairly sure her lungs had stopped working too, now she was witnessing the way he moved. Like a jungle cat on the prowl… Each step a symphony of grace and sym-metry and power.

Utterly absorbing.

Infinitely hypnotic.

She was unashamedly gawking when his eyes locked on her. For a fistful of heartbeats he stared.

Hard. Intense. Ice-hot.

Then with long strides he zeroed in on her. His scent invaded her senses as powerfully as the man himself. He smelled of ice and earth, elemental to the core and so ut-terly unique she could have stood there breathing him in for an eternity, her sore ribs be damned.

'Where is he?' he breathed, and the sound was electri-fying enough to send skitters of stinging awareness over her skin.

Whether by some silent command, or simply because everyone in the room knew they were in the presence of greatness, the volume of the music had dropped. That was the reason she heard him and knew that his voice was deep and accented, resulting in sensually wrapped words that triggered a yearning to hear him speak again just for the hell of it.

Maddie knew that would never happen. When this man spoke it was for immediate and masterful effect, no extra-neous words necessary.

Seconds passed. His nostrils flared slightly. She realised she hadn't answered.

'I…' She swallowed hard. 'Where is…? Who do you mean?'

'The man you're here with. Jules—'

'What are *you* doing here?'

The snapped question from Jules held anger, panic and defiance, slicing through Maddie's comprehension that the stranger—whoever he was—knew *her*, knew she was with Jules.

He didn't answer immediately. Instead he studied Jules from head to toe, causing him to fidget and adjust his ruffled clothes.

'What did you think would happen when you refused to answer your summons?' he asked icily. 'Did you think your activities would be allowed to continue unchecked?'

Jules opened his mouth, but the other man stopped him with a wave of his elegant hand that would have been poetic had it not been filled with foreboding.

'I will not have this conversation with you here, while you're in this state. Come to my hotel tomorrow morning. We will have breakfast together.'

Each statement was a stern directive, permitting neither disagreement nor disobedience.

It rubbed Jules the wrong way. His chin jutted out. '*Pas possible*. I have plans in the morning.'

Low thunder rumbled across the stranger's face. 'According to your assistant, the only thing you have scheduled is sleeping off your hangover. You will be present, in my suite, at 9:00 a.m. sharp. Is that understood?'

They faced off for less than ten seconds, but it felt like an hour.

Jules's abrupt nod bordered on the insolent, but at the piercing, relentless regard directed towards him his head dropped the way a dog's might when confronted with its disobedience by its master.

The older man stared down at him for another long stretch before his eyes slid sideways to the usually raucous group Jules partied with, who were now respectfully, watchfully silent.

Then his gaze switched to Maddie. He took his time

scrutinising her, from the loose knot of her thick hair to the painted toes peeping through her stilettoes.

Every inch of bare skin his gaze touched—and unfortunately there was a lot of it—blazed with an alien, thrilling fire, even the tips of her fingers. She wanted to recoil. Retreat. But there was something weirdly hypnotic about his eyes on her that held her in place, made her struggle to catch even a shallow breath.

Jules followed his line of sight and his eyes widened a touch when he spotted Maddie. Clearly he'd forgotten she existed. He hastily rearranged his expression and reached for her arm. '*Viens, mon amour*, let's go home.'

Maddie stiffened, suppressing another wince.

Even with her limited French, she understood the endearment. In all the time they'd been playing pretence Jules had never called her that. Nor had he invited her to his place. Their routine once they left a club or restaurant and the paparazzi lost interest was for one of his bodyguards to put her in a taxi.

Before she could respond, the stranger shook his head.

'It's 2:00 a.m. You've partied enough for one night. Go home. I'll see to it that Miss Myers makes it to wherever she's going safely.'

Jules's eyes flashed with anger. 'You're assuming she isn't going back to my place. You're assuming she's not my live-in girlfriend.'

'Is she?' Without waiting for an answer he turned sharply to her, silver eyes pinning her to the spot. 'Are you?'

The two words were bullet-sharp.

'That's not the point,' Jules interjected aggressively.

'Either she is or she isn't. Answer the question,' he demanded, without taking his eyes off her.

Very much aware that she had no clue what was going on, Maddie went with the truth. 'No, we're not living together.'

Jules's jaw clenched, but she shrugged it off. If he wanted

to give the impression that they were more serious he should have told her. She was uncomfortable enough about the subterfuge as it was.

'Your driver will take you to your hotel, Jules,' the stranger said, glancing pointedly at the hand Jules had on her arm.

Jules muttered a very rude, very French curse. One he intended the man to hear. One that produced a flash of anger in his silver eyes before his expression was ruthlessly blanked.

Without warning Jules yanked her close, cupped the back of her head before slamming his mouth down on hers.

The kiss was over in seconds, but the shocking violation kept Maddie frozen for longer. Stunned, and more than a little incensed, she watched Jules leave without a backward glance, strongly resisting the urge to swipe her hand across her mouth.

She knew he'd kissed her for effect, to annoy the domineering man standing before her, whose gaze was now a darker silver as it swept over cheeks gone pale before returning to her mouth. And she knew, despite the burning urge to rub off the last trace of that kiss, it would be a dead giveaway that might cost her a lot in the long run.

So she raised her chin, met eyes that blazed with a fierce light she couldn't fathom.

'Come,' he said abruptly. Then, like Jules, he turned and walked out.

Maddie shook her head once to clear it. When nothing altered the sensation of having just experienced a furious electric storm, she stumbled back on shaky legs to her seat.

She had no intention of following that arrogant, dangerously compelling man anywhere. The only place she was headed was home, to the flat she shared with her father. To the safety and discomfort of her single bed.

Excited chatter and camera phones aimed her way hastened her movements. She still had no clear idea what had transpired a few minutes ago, but she wasn't sticking around to be the cynosure of all eyes.

She'd have enough to deal with come morning anyway. For one, she had to ensure her father got through another day without succumbing to the addiction that had decimated not just *his* life but the relatively carefree family life she'd taken for granted.

She pushed harrowing thoughts of her father's addiction and her mother's desertion aside, stood up—and was met with a wall of muscle.

'Miss? Come with me, please.'

It was one of the superior bodyguards. Far from assuming the stranger had accepted she had no intention of following, he'd left a minder behind to ensure she obeyed his command.

The chatter was rising. Curious looks and pointing fingers were aimed at her as she scrambled to find a way around her dilemma.

Stay here and deal with the gossip-hungry pack, or go outside and deal with the even more dangerous predator who had made every nerve in her body zing to life?

'Oh, my God, did you actually see him?'

'He's like...a god!'

'I could actually drop dead from how drop-dead gorgeous he is!'

'Who is she, *anyway?'*

That last question propelled her feet forward, fuelled by the distinct impression that the bodyguard wasn't above physically bundling her up and delivering her to his master.

Outside, the sleekest, shiniest black limousine idled at the kerb. The shiver that lanced through her when she spotted it had nothing to do with the chilled late-March air.

As she drew closer the driver, standing to attention, swung the back door open.

The interior light was off, so all Maddie saw with the aid of the streetlights were long, trouser-clad masculine legs and polished shoes.

'Get in, Miss Myers.' The instruction was deep, resolute and throbbed with impatience.

She was a few dozen yards from Soho's bustling main street. Her legs were strong enough to outrun the bodyguards...

'Take my advice and don't bother.' The suggestion was an arrogant drawl, wrapped in steel.

With every fibre of her being Maddie wanted to refuse. But she knew it would be futile. Whoever he was, unmistakable power and authority oozed from him. Plus, his bodyguards were in prime condition.

So, with a snatched breath, she climbed in. The earlier she got this over and done with, the quicker she could go home, she told herself. She needed to be at work in a few short hours.

The moment she slid into the car, the door shut behind her.

For tense seconds she withstood those eerie eyes glinting at her, withstood the need to glance at him and pretended interest in the luxury interior and the long, soft leather bench seat. But inevitably her gaze was drawn to him, like an unwitting moth to a flame. Again his gaze dropped to her mouth before rising to meet hers, leaving her shaky and tingling all over again.

Enough of this.

'Who are you and how do you know who I am?' she demanded, when it became clear he was just going to stare at her with those electric eyes.

The question seemed to startle him. Then his head went back in a manner that could only be termed *exceptionally regal*.

'My name is Remirez Alexander Montegova, Crown Prince of the Kingdom of Montegova. I know who you are because I have an excellent team of private investigators who make it their job to furnish me with that kind of information. Now you will tell *me* how much it will take for you walk away from my brother.'

CHAPTER TWO

'YOUR BROTHER?' MADDIE cringed at the squeak in her voice.

'Technically, half-brother. We share the same father.' His voice was coated in dark ice.

She shook her head, confused. 'But…but his name is Jules Montagne. And he's French.'

Whereas this man's accent was an enthralling mix of Italian, French and Spanish.

Crown Prince Remirez…*oh, my God*…shrugged one rugged shoulder. 'He's French on his mother's side. And the name he uses is a ruse, I suspect, to throw people off the scent.'

'Off the scent of what?' she asked, grappling with the alarming disclosure and the fact that everything about the man lounging like a resting panther finally made sense. As did the fact that the resemblance she'd noted was to Jules.

He remained silent, then a tiny interior light was illuminated above his head. Once again he was bathed in golden light. He seemed even larger against the dark backdrop of the car, his jet-black hair glinting, the shoulders beneath his bespoke suit broader and even more imposing.

'Off the scent of his true identity. Off the scent of gold-diggers, con artists and hangers-on,' he replied with icy-cold condemnation.

There was little doubt the accusation was aimed at her. And it deeply irked Maddie that even that couldn't stop her body's hyper-awareness of him. Couldn't stop her noticing her clammy hands or the elevated temperature between her thighs.

'Right. I see.'

'I'm sure you do,' he replied wryly.

She leaned closer to the window and flinched as her arm protested. She dragged her gaze from the view of Waterloo Bridge. 'Where are you taking me?'

'Where I said I would deliver you. To your home,' he answered simply. 'What's wrong with your arm?'

'Excuse me?'

His gaze dropped.

She followed it and realised she was rubbing her lower arm. She hastily dropped her hand. 'Nothing. I'm fine. You know where I live?'

His gaze stayed on her arm for another handful of seconds before he replied, 'Yes. I also know where you work, where you went to school and who your dentist is.'

Apprehension fizzled inside her. 'Is that some sort of threat?'

'I've merely armed myself with knowledge. After all, it is power, is it not? Did you not get into this car to do the same?'

'I got into this car because you sent your supersized bodyguard after me.'

'He didn't touch you.' The finality behind the words indicated she hadn't been touched because he'd wished it to be so.

She forced a laugh, despite the surge of energy thrumming through her belly. 'Oh, wow, I'll consider myself lucky, then.'

He knew everything about her. Did he know about her father? Her mother? Greg? Was he aware of the shameful secret that dogged her every wakeful moment and followed her into her nightmares?

'You haven't answered my question,' he said.

She swallowed the pulse of anger in her throat. 'And I'm not going to. It's insulting. I don't know you from Adam and yet you think you can just throw money at me and I'll do your bidding?'

He didn't respond immediately. Not until the limo stopped at a set of traffic lights a mile from her flat. 'I haven't done any throwing since you haven't given me your price. How long have you known Jules?'

Unease ramped up the vibrations in her belly. 'I don't see how that's relevant—'

'You've known him a little over a week. You've been out with him almost every night and yet you've never returned to his apartment with him.'

The depth of his knowledge sent a sheet of ice gliding over her skin. 'That doesn't mean anything.'

'On the contrary, that leads me to conclude you're holding out for something. What is it, Miss Myers?'

She smiled. 'Sex, drugs and rock and roll—what else?'

Her dripping sarcasm went straight over his head as he threw a disdainful glance out of the window.

'Jules wouldn't be caught dead in this neighbourhood. So, unless you've been copulating somewhere other than his apartment, I highly doubt it's sex. And I know for a fact that it's not drugs.'

'That's ridiculous. How would you know that?' she threw back.

Slightly narrowed eyes were the only indication that he found her questioning insolent. 'Because it's a condition of his remaining in my royal bursar's good graces that he stays clean. In return for his generous allowance, he's tested for drugs on a regular basis.'

Although the information allayed her earlier fears, Maddie was still disturbed by the revelations. 'Tested? You're saying that you *pay* him to stay off drugs?'

Prince Remirez's lashes swept down. 'Among many other things,' he murmured.

Curiosity ramped high. 'Really? Like what?' she asked, telling herself it really was time she found out more about the man who'd promised to pay her to pretend to be his girlfriend.

'Like things that are none of your concern,' Prince Remirez returned chillingly. 'And, just in case you're inclined to peddle what I've just told you, know that I'll sue you for everything you own if any of this makes it into tomorrow's papers.'

'Yeah, good luck with that,' she replied waspishly, before she could help herself.

'You think my caution is idle?' he mused coolly, his stance relaxed in a way that said he found her in no way threatening.

She shook her head, smiling with more than a little relief when the limo pulled into her street.

'Not at all. I meant good luck finding anything of value to sue me for.'

The moment the words left her lips she wanted to snatch them back. But it was too late.

Eyes like laser beams latched onto the truth. 'You're destitute,' he declared after a taut pause.

Shame crawled over Maddie's skin. Followed instantaneously by searing anger. 'What I am is none of your business. We're strangers to one another. So *I* won't jump to the conclusion that you're a rich, pompous royal bastard who looks down his aristocratic nose at the less fortunate, if *you* don't assume I'm some worthless gold-digger who's just itching to jump straight out of your car and into a paparazzo's pocket.'

'I don't have proof that you're a worthless gold-digger, but I'm growing certain that you're a shameless exhibitionist,' he replied in that charismatically accented voice that threw her for a second before his meaning sank in.

'*Excuse me?* What gives you the right—?' She glanced down sharply and gasped as flames of embarrassment shot into her face.

Oh, God.

The hem of her dress had crept up almost to her crotch, and somehow one creamy slope of a breast was exposed in the gaping neckline of her halter top. The wardrobe Jules had provided for their outings was one of the many things she'd baulked at. One of the many things he'd stated were deal-breakers.

'I suggest you pull yourself together before that notion becomes concrete,' he advised, with a new husk in his voice and a banked blaze in his eyes that directed the flamed inward, singeing low in her belly and then lower, in places she didn't want to acknowledge.

She hurriedly pulled down her hem and adjusted her neckline, aware that his gaze tracked her every movement. Aware she'd been judged and found severely lacking.

When she was as adequately covered as she could be, she fixed her eyes on the door handle. 'Are we done here?'

He sat back, master of everything he surveyed—which eerily felt as if it included her—and crossed one leg over the other. 'That depends,' he drawled.

'On what?' she asked, still unable to look him in the eye.

He didn't respond.

More than a little unnerved at the racing of her heart, she lifted her gaze to his. 'On *what*?' she repeated.

A slow, predatory smile lifted the corners of his lips. Beneath the light his eyes gleamed, taking on an unnerving, hypnotising colour that made her believe he could see right to the heart of her. To the sensual vibrations stroking her nerve-endings. To the unsettling licks of fire in her belly.

Her fingers tightened around her bag, and she was about to demand he answer her when he gave a brisk nod to someone out of sight. The door immediately sprang open.

'You'll find out in due course. Goodnight, Miss Myers.'

Maddie's nights since she had been forced to abandon her child psychology courses at university and return home to care for her father had been plagued with worrying about finding a way to keep the roof over their heads and her father from the pit of addiction. Sleeplessness had become the norm, the creaking of the cheap slats beneath her mattress the discordant accompaniment to her anxiety.

Tonight, however, other thoughts and images reeled through her mind, and agitation drove her fingers into her worn duvet as a plethora of emotions eroded any hope of sleep.

Disbelief—she'd met a true-life, drop-dead gorgeous crown prince who might have stepped off the silver screen.

Anger—he'd blatantly stated that he was threatening her because he suspected she was after something from his brother. Technically true, but still…

Arousal? No, she wasn't going to touch that.

And anxiety—*'You will find out in due course.'*

Did he mean the agreement she'd made with Jules? If so, how?

It was clear he held a great deal of sway over his younger half-brother, despite Jules's defiant attitude. Would he stoop to denying her what Jules had promised her?

That last thought kept her awake for the rest of the night until, giving up on sleep, she dragged herself out of bed just before her alarm went off at six.

Her father was already up, although not dressed, when she reached the kitchen. Maddie paused in the doorway, breath held, and examined him. His gauntness was even more pronounced than it had been a month ago—the result of his failing kidneys on top of the strong painkillers he'd become addicted to when his thriving property business had failed in the crash a decade ago.

He'd hidden his addiction for years, in a misguided attempt to keep up appearances and hang on to a wife who had made no bones about the fact that she expected to live a certain lifestyle and demanded her husband provide it.

A near overdose had brought everything to light three years ago, showing the shocking damage Henry Myers had done to his body. It had also been the start of many promises to get clean that had resulted time and again in relapse, and the raiding of their meagre finances to seek help for him that had pulled them deeper into destitution.

Eventually the fall from affluent lifestyle to nursing an addict in a tiny flat in one of the poorest neighbourhoods in London had become too much for her mother.

Once upon a time her father had been healthy, outgoing, a pillar of a man his peers had looked up to. Maddie's childhood had been pampered and carefree, if a little emotionally unrewarding. She'd learned not to complain early on, when she'd realised her father loved her but was always busy and her mother was more preoccupied with retail therapy than her daughter's emotional well-being. Even when the distance between her and her mother had widened, Maddie had been secure in her father's abstract affection.

All of that had ended with Priscilla Myers's three-minute phone call to Maddie at university. She'd had enough. Maddie needed to come home and take care of her father because she wasn't prepared to live in poverty and disgrace. Any guilt about abandoning the husband she'd promised to stand by in sickness and in health hadn't been reflected in her voice. She'd walked away without a backward glance or a forwarding address.

Maddie bottled up the still ravaging anguish now as she fully entered the kitchen. 'You're up early.' She kept her voice light and airy.

Her father shrugged half-heartedly. 'Couldn't sleep,' he muttered.

'Do you want breakfast? Toast and tea?' she asked hopefully.

He shook his head. 'I'm not hungry. Maybe later.'

He was avoiding her gaze—a sure sign that the demons of addiction were snapping at his heels again. Her heart dropped. Had she owned more than the couple of hundred pounds she kept for emergencies in her bank account she would have taken the day off and stayed home to offer the support he baulked at but clearly needed.

Pushing back the despair, she pinned a smile on her face.

'Mrs Jennings will look in on you later. She'll fix you lunch if you're hungry. There's food in the fridge.'

His mouth compressed but he didn't reply. Maddie pushed past the bite of guilt. Although her father suspected it, she hadn't confirmed that desperation had driven her to pay their next-door neighbour a small sum to look in on him a few times a day.

After he had been bumped from the transplant list twice after relapsing, she'd resorted to desperate ways of keeping an eye on him. The last barrage of tests had revealed he was weeks away from full renal failure.

The doctors had advised that they wouldn't sanction her father's operation unless he remained clean for at least six months. He'd waved away her worries when she'd talked to him about it but so far he'd stayed clean.

All she needed to do was come through with the funds required for his operation. Funds entirely dependent on whether she finished her stint with Jules Montagne. Correction: Jules Montegova. Half-brother to Crown Prince Remirez Alexander Montegova.

The latter's image rose up, large and imposing, dragging a small shiver down her spine as she finished her breakfast.

By the time she was done with the morning rush hour customers at the café where she worked near Oxford Street, the seed of worry that had taken root in the small hours had grown into a bramble bush.

Jules normally sent her a text in the early hours before he went to bed, telling her where and when to meet for their next 'date'. When midday came and went without a word from him, her worry escalated to full-blown anxiety.

She didn't want to waste her precious phone minutes calling him, but the inkling that something was wrong wouldn't ease. Too much hinged on finishing what she'd started with Jules for her to prevaricate about this. She decided she would call him during her break.

The café was quieter, but still half full. Besides her, two

other waitresses were busy delivering dishes to customers, with a third, Di, cleaning the table next to where Maddie was sorting cutlery.

'Holy cow, it's Prince Remirez!' Di screeched.

Maddie almost jumped out of her skin, nearly dropping the two dozen forks in her hands. 'What?'

Di pointed, wide-eyed, at the window.

Heart slamming against her ribs, Maddie turned and watched the man she'd spent far too many precious hours thinking about examining the café sign and the pavement with the same dripping disdain he'd shown for her neighbourhood last night.

The late March sun burst through the clouds in that moment, outlining his upturned haughty face in jaw-dropping relief.

Last night, in the dark nightclub and darker limo, she'd thought his breathtaking male beauty too good to be true. Now, with the sun caressing every spectacular feature, Maddie was left in no doubt that from head to toe the man next in line to the throne of Montegova was a magnificent male specimen.

She managed to drag her gaze from that rugged jaw and captivating face long enough to glance at her colleague. 'You know who he is?'

Di rolled her eyes. '*Duh!* Every female with a pulse over the age of fourteen knows who he is. His brother Zak is equally hot. I wonder what the Crown Prince is doing here, though. I would've thought Bond Street was more his speed if he's shopping. Hey, don't royals have minions to do that sort of—? *Oh, my God*, he's coming in *here*!'

Maddie turned away, praying Di was wrong. He wasn't here for her. *He couldn't be.* In the dark of a nightclub, in the midst of minor celebrities and royalty, it was easy to explain away a crown prince's fleeting interest in her—even to herself.

Here, among the cheap plastic furniture and even cheaper

food of a street corner café, it was difficult to rationalise why *the hottest man alive* would seek her out.

But what were the chances that he was here on some other mission?

Di continued to chatter away. Maddie kept her back to the door, despite the mocking voice that said she was burying her head in the sand.

Moments later she heard the hush in the café, heard the firm, confident footfalls of a man who believed he owned the very ground he walked on—right before she felt the mildly earth-shaking vibrations of his presence behind her.

'Miss Myers.'

Dear God, she hadn't imagined the impact of that voice. Nor had she imagined its pulse-destroying effect on her.

She tried fruitlessly to fight the shivers coursing through her as she turned around. And promptly lost her grip on the forks in her hand.

The clatter was astounding.

Face flaming, Maddie dropped to her knees, furiously scrambling for the forks. Before her, a pair of polished hand-stitched shoes remained planted. Unmoving. She refused to look up, refused to acknowledge the existence of the man clad in an expensive, dark navy pinstriped suit that probably cost more than her year's salary. She crawled around him, snatching up the utensils as her face grew hotter. When she had them all she sat back on her heels, prepared to rise.

'Miss Myers?'

Maddie bit her lip, knowing she couldn't avoid looking at him. She tilted her head, her breath strangling all over again when her eyes clashed with his silver-grey ones. They were ferociously intense, even as one eyebrow slowly lifted mockingly and he examined her flushed face.

'Um…yes?' She was sure embarrassment was what had rendered her voice a husky mess, *not* the charged volts shooting through her pelvis and the stinging awareness that she was at eye level with his crotch.

She blinked, her brain emptying of everything but one single, breath-stealing erotic image.

'You missed one.'

A throat cleared. Hastily she glanced down, saw one cheap scratched fork held between his long, neatly tapered fingers.

She snatched it from him. 'Thank you.'

Still on her knees, she placed the forks on the nearest table, then froze when Prince Remirez extended one elegant hand towards her.

Her heart leapt into her throat as she considered the many ways she could refuse his assistance without causing offence.

There were none.

So she placed her hand in his, felt his fingers glide across her palm on their way to gripping hers. She'd once read a novel in which the heroine described feeling pure electricity when she touched the man of her dreams. Maddie had rolled her eyes then.

Now she sent a silent apology to the maligned character.

Crown Prince Remirez would never be the man of her dreams, and she wasn't going to waste her time counting the many ways why, but the reality that singed and branded and claimed that small portion of her body promised that she would never shake another hand without remembering this captivating moment.

Her insides liquefied as he tightened his grip and tugged her to her feet. The slight tautening of his face and the flare in his eyes told her he wasn't completely unaffected by what was happening. Nor did he miss her wince as her arm twinged in pain.

The moment she felt steady on her feet she tried to snatch her hand from his. He kept hold of her for a moment longer before he released her.

When she could breathe again Maddie threw a furtive glance around her. As suspected, every single gaze in the café was fixed on her, including her boss's—although his curiosity was beginning to dissolve into annoyance.

'Would…would you like a table, um… Your Highness?' Was that the correct form of address? Or was it Your Grace? 'You can pick any one you like. I'll be with you as soon as I finish putting—'

'I'm not here to dine, Miss Myers.' He cut across her, not bothering to keep his voice down. Or the disdain out of it.

She reminded herself that she needed this job and therefore couldn't afford to be rude to patrons or non-patrons. 'In that case I can't really help you, since I'm working. Maybe we can—'

'It's in your interest to make time. Now.'

About to refuse, because her heart rate didn't seem interested in slowing down, and because he really was a little too potent to her senses, she paused. Something in his voice warned her against it.

Belatedly she remembered that he'd summoned Jules to breakfast this morning. Had Jules divulged their connection? Was that why he was here?

She searched his face and came away with nothing but further evidence of his heart-stopping gorgeousness.

A quick glance at the clock showed it was a quarter past eleven. The lunchtime rush hour wouldn't start for another half hour. 'Jim, can I take my break now? I'll make it up later.'

The head chef, who also happened to be the café's owner, glanced from her to Prince Remirez and then, barely hiding his irritation, nodded. 'I s'pose so.'

She flashed him a grateful smile, then dived into the small cubicle that doubled up as a changing and break room to get her bag. Slinging it crossways over her shoulder, she hurried through the café and out onto the pavement.

Where a small crowd had gathered, their camera phones ready to capture the image of the most captivating man on earth.

'We'll have more privacy in the car,' Prince Remirez pronounced smoothly, a second before his hand arrived at her waist and nudged her firmly in the direction of the open back door of a limo.

Maddie entered, immediately noting the different configuration of the seats from last night's car. There was no bench seat on the far side behind the driver. Which left her no choice but shuffle along the seat as Prince Remirez slid in after her.

The door shut behind him and instantly the atmosphere closed in around them. The push of air wrapped his scent around her, triggering that insane urge to bury her face in his neck and drown herself in his scent.

Whether it came from a bottle or it was a specially branded scent, it was lethal enough to be seriously addictive to women.

Addictive.

The word brought her up short, flinging her foolish ruminations into harsh reality. 'Okay, Your Highness. You have fifteen minutes.'

He adjusted his cuffs, rested his elegant hands on his thighs before fixing his ferocious eyes on her. 'Your business with Jules is over,' he stated bluntly.

Maddie tried not to panic, but fear raced up her spine and threatened to paralyse her all the same.

After forcing herself to take a few slow, rib-bruising breaths, she pulled her phone from her pocket. 'With all due respect, I want to hear it from him.'

Prince Remirez glanced at her phone. 'He's already on a plane to Montegova. You won't see him or talk to him again. Your number has been blocked from his phone permanently so save yourself the trouble.'

A cold shiver ploughed through her. 'Why are you doing this?'

He reached into his breast pocket and extracted a dark burgundy card with sleek gold numbers embossed on the front and back. 'I came here to tell you that if you wish to salvage anything from this I am prepared to hear you out.' He nodded at the card. 'My address and private number are on the back. You have twenty-four hours to use it. Then I too will be out of your reach.'

CHAPTER THREE

LAST NIGHT, SEEING her in real life for the first time, Remi had thought her beauty exceptional.

Right now, watching the muted light from the sun-roof bathe her in a soft glow, she was even more exquisite.

Maddie Myers's beauty was like nothing he'd ever seen. For starters, he couldn't put his finger on why she would look so magnificent in a cheap, drab waitress's uniform when last night she'd been dressed in finer, albeit more risqué, attire.

The other puzzling thing was that Remi had dated women who were equally beautiful. And yet something about this woman, whose beauty oozed from her very pores, triggered a stark, cloying hunger within him that he hadn't quite been able to get a handle on.

That hunger had roared to life the moment he'd walked into that dismal café, and intensified when she'd dropped to her knees before him. Even now base images reeled through his mind. Images he had no business accommodating in public.

Years spent perfecting the art of schooling his expression had saved him from blatantly telegraphing his reaction. But those images were etched clearly in his brain, gaining lurid purchase as her plump lips part in shock.

'Jules is really gone?' she demanded huskily.

Remi gritted his teeth, finding the chore of discussing his half-brother with this woman intensely unsatisfactory. 'Yes.'

Brows two shades darker than her honey-gold hair bunched together in confusion. 'But… I don't understand.'

'What's there to understand? He's finally decided to grow up and make a meaningful contribution to the kingdom.'

'Just like that?' she asked sceptically.

'Of course not. It's taken a considerable amount of time to make him accept his responsibilities.'

'And you came here to get him to do that?'

Remi shrugged. 'It was past time someone did.' He watched her carefully for signs that whatever had been going on between her and Jules was more than a light dalliance.

Her eyelashes swept down, shielding her expression from him. He fisted his hand on his thigh to curb the urge to cup her chin and expose her gaze to him.

After a moment, she swiped the tip of her tongue over her bottom lip. 'Did he…did he say anything about me?' she enquired gruffly.

His irritation grew. 'Should he have?'

Her long lashes flew up, jade-green eyes flashing at him before she turned to stare blindly out of the window.

Remi continued to study her. Although her fingers twisted the handle of her bag in agitation, her expression didn't reflect the forlorn anguish of a discarded lover. No, Maddie Myers's demeanour betrayed a different sort of torment. One of panicked frustration.

Jules had been an important cog in the wheel of her plans. A thwarted plan she was now furiously reassessing.

Still, he needed to be sure. 'You didn't kiss him back.'

Her head whipped towards him, her eyes widening. 'What?'

'Last night your supposed lover kissed you goodnight. You didn't kiss him back. In fact you seemed disturbingly apathetic.'

Remi was certain that had been one of the reasons he hadn't acted on his visceral need to separate them. The other had been because he hadn't wanted to attract even more attention than his presence in that seedy nightclub had already garnered.

Maddie Myers schooled her features in a way that would

have made his childhood deportment instructors proud. 'Didn't I? You must be mistaken.'

'I was not. Why were you with Jules?' The question was beginning to grate, like a tiny stone in his shoe.

'According to you, he's several thousand miles away. Therefore why we were together no longer matters, does it?'

Her gaze dropped to her phone, and there was a contemplative look in her eyes.

'It matters if you're planning to contact him the moment you're out of my sight. If you are, I seriously advise against it.'

Defiant eyes met his. 'I fail to see how you're going to stop me, since the minute I step out of this vehicle I intend never to see you again.'

'You delude yourself if you think you'll be free of me that easily.'

'And you delude *your*self with…with whatever you think this interrogation is. I owe you nothing. Getting into this car with you was a courtesy. One you've outworn. So, if you'll excuse me, I'm going back to work now before I annoy my boss.'

She reached for the handle to the door that would open onto the street.

He darted forward and seized her wrist, quiet fury laced with something that felt alarmingly close to dread fizzing through his bloodstream. 'Are you always this careless with your safety?' he demanded, aware his voice was harsh and gruff.

He told himself it had nothing to do with the guilt fused into his being. Or the breathtaking smoothness of the skin stretched over her racing pulse.

For some reason she found his question amusing, although her thousand-watt smile barely made an appearance before it was extinguished again. 'Did you not ask your brother how we met?'

All he'd wanted from Jules this morning was his agreement to board the royal plane back to Montegova, and a promise that he would cease contact with Maddie Myers immediately. Discussions of duty and responsibility had been shelved when he'd realised his brother was severely hungover.

'The subject didn't come up.'

'Well, he nearly ran me over with his supercar. And, no, I wasn't being reckless. The signal to cross was still green when he hit me.'

Remi's blood went deathly cold. Over the last two years he'd lived with an unending torrent of might-have-beens. All the things he might have done to alter events. The image of Maddie Myers lying lifeless on a filthy pavement awoke demons he'd fought hard and failed to conquer.

'Jules hit you with his car?' He was aware his voice was a thin, icy blade. But it was only when she flinched that his gaze dropped to the hold he had on her.

He loosened his grip as other things began to fall into place. The wincing she tried to hide. The flash of pain across her face last night in the car and when he'd touched her in the café.

Rage rose to mingle with the guilt. 'How badly were you hurt?' The gravel-rough demand seared his throat.

Her head dipped and her gaze fell to her lap. 'Besides my pride and a few bruises and scratches, I'd say the groceries that met their end on Camberwell New Road came off worse.'

Ice-cold fingers gripped his nape. 'Don't be flippant about it.'

His harsh rebuttal made her flinch. When her eyes darted to his fists, Remi realised he'd clenched them so hard the knuckles were bloodless.

'I… It wasn't a big deal,' she whispered.

He slowly unfurled his hands. Sucked in one long breath. 'Was that when you struck this secret bargain between the two of you?'

A flash of alarm crossed her face, then evaporated to leave faint pink spots on her cheeks. Without answering she turned resolutely to the door. 'This conversation is over. Goodbye, Your Highness.'

Remi had no intention of letting her get away. Not until he'd delved into these new revelations. Revelations that had him secretly reeling.

'I've changed my mind. You no longer have twenty-four hours.'

He picked up the card she'd dropped on the seat between them and slid it back into his pocket.

He nodded abruptly. And a moment later his car had left the kerb and the café behind.

Her shocked gaze swung to the window, then back to him. 'What the hell do you think you're doing?'

'We're going to talk. In one hour you'll either have decided you don't work at that café any more or your boss will be adequately compensated for your absence and you can return to work tomorrow morning. Either way, neither of you will lose. Put your seatbelt on.'

'No! I don't know how things work in your country, but here what you're doing is called kidnapping!'

Remi caught her arm just beneath the short sleeve of her cheap shirt, again noting the satin-smoothness of her skin and the sizzle of miniature fireworks that transmitted from her skin to his.

Back in the café, when he'd first touched her, he mocked himself for over-exaggerating the sensation. Now he knew for sure as the blood heated in his veins.

Her breath hitched and her alluring eyes dropped to where he held her before she jerked away from him. 'Please don't touch me.'

Reluctantly, he released her. She gave a tiny shake of her head, as if she found the sizzling, unwanted chemistry as confounding as he did. That knowledge only intensified the urgency rampaging through him.

'You will tell me why you're anxious to get in touch with Jules. After you tell me in detail about your first meeting.' He frowned as his memory came up blank on that part of Maddie Myers's recent history. 'Why isn't there a record of the accident or a hospital visit?'

Sparks flared in her eyes. 'Because there wasn't one. And in case I didn't get around to mentioning it last night, it's loathsome of you to pry into my life the way you blithely believe you have a right to.'

'Why wasn't there one?' he demanded.

'Because your brother didn't take me to hospital, that's why.'

This time he couldn't contain his curse, the fury that tripled his heartbeat or the churning alarm that underpinned all his emotions. 'He nearly ran you over and you didn't demand to be taken to a hospital?'

Her expression closed and she avoided his gaze. 'I told you—'

'You're trying to hide the fact that you're favouring your right arm and yet you flinch and grow pale with every contact. Either you're truly intent on deluding yourself that your injury is no big deal…' he paused as a deeper bolt of emotion, a protectiveness he didn't welcome, kicked him in the gut '…or there's another reason you're burying your head in the sand.'

He hit the intercom and instructed his driver on a different destination.

'Either way, it has nothing to do with you,' she replied stiffly.

'That's where you're wrong, Miss Myers.'

Wary eyes blinked at him. 'What's that supposed to mean?'

'It means it's my duty to ensure that nothing a member of my family does comes back to bite us when we least expect it. And now I have a better idea of what went on between you and Jules we can get down to the bottom line. But not until I find out what I'm dealing with.'

'I... I don't understand.'

'I'm taking you to the hospital, Madeleine. You can protest if you wish, but know this: the earlier you deal with me, the earlier we can be rid of each other.' He waited a beat, despite the volatile emotions churning through his bloodstream. 'So will you come with me of your own free will?'

Green eyes flew to his and again he caught the faint alarm in the bronze-flecked depths. Her lightly glossed lips parted and she sucked in a slow breath. After a moment, she nodded. 'Yes.'

The churning subsided a touch. 'Good.'

Reaching over her shoulder, he drew the seat belt across her body, forcing his gaze not to linger on her breasts as he secured her in place.

'This isn't a hospital! This is—'

'My private physician.'

'At a private clinic in Harley Street?'

Remi frowned at the accusation. 'Other than pointing out the geographical location, do you have a point?'

'Yes. I have a point. I can't afford a private doctor.'

Agitation charged her movements and he caught her wince as she freed herself from the seatbelt.

'*Dio*, calm down before you aggravate your injury.'

'First of all, we don't even know if I *have* an injury. Secondly, please stop ordering me about.'

He took a sustaining breath and reminded himself why he was doing this. For his family.

For reasons he intended to get to the bottom of before the day was out, neither Jules nor his bodyguards had seen fit to report the incident with Maddie. Remi shuddered to imagine what the press would do if it got out.

He wasn't out of the woods yet. He needed to play this

right to prevent any possibility of a scandal further down the line.

But beyond that he knew there was another reason. The unquenchable need to make sure history didn't repeat itself. That he didn't spend more nights racked with guilt about someone else—even if that person was this stunningly gorgeous but aggravating blonde who looked nothing like his Celeste but who nevertheless evoked astounding, groin-stirring sensations within him.

He ruthlessly pushed the hot throb of lust aside and nodded to his driver to open the door. 'I value my time and my privacy. I'm assured of both here. And you insult me by suggesting that I would expect you to pay for medical attention necessitated through my brother's actions. Now, do you have any further objections?'

Plump lips he found far too tempting stayed shut for a long moment before she exited the vehicle. He followed, telling himself the tingle in his fingers *wasn't* from the desire to touch her again, to place his hand on that delicate waist and guide her into the clinic.

In fact, he made sure to keep his distance from her as they were checked in and Maddie was escorted into a suite where a barrage of scans were lined up.

Fifty minutes later he stared out of the window, jaw clenched, as they were driven away from Harley Street towards his hotel.

'You pushed for those tests and now you're not going to say anything?' Maddie asked testily from beside him.

He kept his gaze on the passing view. He deemed it much safer, because something about the sling around Maddie's arm agitated his every last demon and fired a level of fury he'd never known before.

'A hairline fracture on your ulna. Two more on your ribs. Bone-deep bruises on your left hip that will take two more weeks to heal.' The words fell from his lips like shards of glass.

'I know what the doctor said. I was there too, remember?'

He rounded on her, knowing his rage was misguided but unable to stop himself nevertheless. He speared his fingers in her hair, ignoring her hot gasp as he dropped his face to hers.

'I don't know who I'm more furious at—you for not insisting on seeing a doctor or Jules for being a blind, selfish idiot and landing me in this situation,' he breathed against her mouth.

She gasped, and the sound transmitted straight to the core of his roiling emotions. To her credit she said nothing, for once choosing the wise course. But her silence meant that other sensations rose to the fore—her closeness, her unsteady breathing, the warmth of her delicate jaw beneath his fingers, the wild pulse racing at her throat. The velvety smoothness of her lips.

Against his better judgement he glided his thumb over her lower lip, then suppressed a thick groan as her lips parted.

The gentle rocking of the car jerked him to his senses. Just as shame and guilt slammed into him.

Celeste.

Every moment in this woman's presence, behaving like a base animal, betrayed his late fiancée's memory. And dragged him deeper into a quagmire he was beginning to fear he would never be free of.

The top floor of the Four Seasons hotel was on permanent reservation to the Montegovan royal family since they were frequent visitors to England. And perhaps its most valued asset was the discreet private access it granted to its VIP guests.

Remi was grateful for the entrance now, not only because it shielded him from prying eyes, but also because it was secure enough not to require his bodyguards' presence.

He didn't need witnesses to his agitated state, nor did

he need indiscreet enquiries as to why he was escorting a woman wearing a waitress's uniform and a sling to his suite.

A gorgeous, dangerous woman with lips as soft as silk.

He shoved his balled fists into his pockets, cursing his libido's atrocious timing and the instrument responsible for its reawakening.

Despite the revelations of the last two hours, he hadn't changed his initial assessment of Madeleine Myers. A typical gold-digger out to capitalise on an unfortunate incident. Except now she had a solid basis from where to launch her attack.

His mind froze as the horror of it replayed itself. *Dio*, Jules had nearly run her over. Had she been petrified? Or had shock numbed her?

Unbidden, the stark script of Celeste's last few days tumbled through his mind, reminding him of life's fragility with a punch in the gut.

He sucked in a deep breath and slowly loosened his fists. The circumstances of his fiancée's death and Maddie's accident were miles apart. Yet that underlying helplessness against fate remained.

'Has no one ever told you it's rude to stare so openly?' she demanded waspishly as the lift arrived.

His gaze flickered over her brazenly defiant face. 'Not if they risked a flogging, no,' he answered drolly, and silently cursed Jules again.

But it wasn't his brother's fault he was caught in the loop of his past. The conversation in his mother's office had also raked up a subject he didn't want to think about, never mind act on it.

Nonetheless it was an issue he needed to tackle.

He gestured Maddie forward. With another wary glance at him she preceded him into the lift that would take them directly to his penthouse suite.

When they exited, seconds later, she surprised him by neither glancing around at the luxurious decor or at the priceless Montegovan paintings and artefacts that lined the hallway. Without fail, every visitor granted access to this private floor was bowled over by the opulence and grandeur his mother had spared no expense in commissioning five years ago.

Still, Remi didn't doubt Maddie Myers's motives for one minute. She was definitely after something. And he was determined to find out what.

The moment they entered the suite, she faced him across the space of the vast living room. 'I'm here now. Can we get this over with so I can return to my life?'

'Is that what you'll do once you leave here? Return to your life and forget all about Jules and my family?'

She frowned. 'Of course. What else do you think I plan to do?'

His mouth twisted. 'I abhor liars, Madeleine.'

'And *I* don't like bullies, so I guess we're one for one.'

'Sit down.'

She stared at him for several seconds before swivelling to glance around the room. For some reason her expression tightened as she finally took in its elegance.

'No, thank you. I don't plan on being here that long.'

'You'll stay for as long as I wish you to.'

'Or for as long as it takes me to call the authorities. I came here of my own volition. I have a right to leave when I wish.'

'We seem to be going around in circles.'

'Then I suggest you cut to the chase.'

Such fire. He would have been impressed if it hadn't been for the desperation he sensed in her.

'Very well. I want you to strike a new bargain with me.'

She froze, her eyes widening. 'Excuse me?'

'Jules is gone. Whatever deal you had with him now belongs to me.'

Her eyes narrowed. 'What is this? Some sick game of Pass the Parcel? You don't even know what the deal was.'

'Whatever it is, you didn't get it. If you had, you wouldn't have been distressed when I told you he'd left.'

Her chin lifted, tugging up the sling. Fire. Vulnerability. Remi didn't want to be touched by either but he was explicably drawn to both.

'You're assuming a lot, aren't you?' she said.

'Am I?'

She remained silent but her defiance abated.

'Shall I call your bluff and show you the door?' he pressed.

Uncertainty flickered in her eyes before her long lashes swept down, hiding her expression yet again. 'You really came here to bring Jules back?'

'That was the main purpose of my trip, yes.'

'Then why aren't you following him? Earlier you said you'd be gone in twenty-four hours.'

'No, I said I'd be available to you for twenty-four hours. That was how long I was prepared to wait to hear your side of the story. When I made plans to come here I anticipated meeting some resistance from my brother. I gave myself ample time to get the job done.'

'You managed to dispatch him in twelve hours. So you want me to do what? Fill up your free time like a court jester?' she demanded, with an hauteur that would have impressed his etiquette instructors.

'Was that the role you agreed to play for Jules?'

Her lips pursed and her gaze fixed warily on him. 'I… I'm—'

'Spend the evening with me.'

He froze. Those weren't the words he'd intended to say, but now they were out there he didn't take them back.

She was shaking her head. 'I can't. I'm…busy,' she said, her free hand rising to cradle her arm.

He dragged his gaze from that little helpless gesture, fought that bolt of protectiveness. 'Cancel your plans.' He hardened his voice. 'Didn't you have a similar arrangement with Jules?'

'No. I didn't meet him till ten—sometimes eleven.'

He despised the fact that his curiosity swelled even larger. 'That's too late. I wish to see you earlier. And you should come prepared to grant me certain assurances.'

She frowned. 'What kind of assurances?'

'The kind that require you to sign a confidentiality agreement.'

'And if I don't?'

'Then be prepared to have your life turned upside down until I'm satisfied you mean my family no harm.'

She inhaled sharply. 'Harm? Why would I…? I never meant them any harm in the first place!' she exclaimed hotly.

The affront in her tone would have reassured Remi had he not been taught a cruel lesson never to take anyone at face value. For decades he'd trusted every word that fell from his father's lips, had blindly followed where he led, right up until his true character had been revealed.

And even after that cruel betrayal he'd trusted Jules when he'd given his word that he would help protect the family legacy in danger of being ripped apart following the revelation of his father's infidelity.

Bruised and devastated from one betrayal, he'd been too grief-blind to mitigate against the possibility that he was being played again.

Jules had shown his true colours within days of being accepted into the Montegovan royal family. And then the final blow had come when he'd least expected it. All those assurances that Celeste was safe…that the worst wouldn't happen. False promises and betrayal. They had pitted his life, eroding trust until it wasn't a commodity available to him any more.

This woman, with a body that would tempt even the staunchest saint, wasn't going to sway him from what needed to be done.

'How much did Jules promise you?' he asked, in a voice spiked with ice.

The moment she inhaled sharply, he knew he'd guessed accurately. *Money*. His insides twisted with distaste. 'Tell me how much and I'll triple it.'

Her wariness increased. 'Why?'

'I'm privy to Jules's financial status. I assure you my resources are considerably more substantial. Moreover, I can't risk you changing your mind at a later date, no matter how noble you're purporting to be right now. What better way to mitigate that than by making you a serious offer?'

She gasped. 'God, you're not just rude, you're also offensive.'

'I'm doing what it takes to ensure my family isn't held to ransom by anyone.'

The past must have bled through into his voice because her gaze sharpened. 'That happens often, does it?'

'Your insolence isn't getting us very far, Madeleine.'

A telling little expression flitted over her face at his use of her name. One that flamed the lingering heat in his body. For several moments all he could think about was whether those lips would taste as sublime as they looked, how the plump curves would feel between his teeth.

With an inward curse, he reined himself in. 'I don't have all day.'

She cleared her throat. 'I agreed to be his girlfriend in return for—'

'*Be* his girlfriend or *play* his girlfriend?' he interrupted sharply.

She swallowed. 'Play his girlfriend.'

He exhaled as a knot unravelled in his gut. 'In return for?'

'For…seventy-five thousand pounds.'

The words were hushed but the look in her eyes dared him to denigrate her. He shoved his hands into his pockets and fought for control, but the attempt to curb his emotions wasn't as easy as he'd anticipated.

'You look as if you're ready to chew rocks, Your Eminence, but before you spit out any more insults, please know that I don't really care what you think of me.'

'It's *Your Highness*, or *Crown Prince*. Or whatever I give you permission to use at some point in the future,' he replied tightly.

'Well, whatever you call yourself, spare me that condescending look.'

'It's not condescension you see on my face, Miss Myers. It's puzzlement as to why you would sell yourself so cheaply.' The offensively paltry sum wasn't the main reason for his disgruntlement, but Remi didn't want to examine why.

She went a shade paler, and then her alluring eyes sparkled with rekindled anger. 'Excuse me?'

He allowed his gaze to drift down her body, taking in her elegant neck, her trim, tiny waist, the feminine flare of her hips and the long, shapely legs currently encased in cheap stockings.

'With the right amount of polish you could be exquisite. And I don't mean dressed in those distasteful clothes you were wearing last night. Unless you suffer from a debilitating case of low self-esteem, I believe you know this. So why sell yourself so cheaply?'

'First of all, I resent the assumption that I *sold* myself. I didn't. I agreed to play a role in return for payment. I may not be professionally trained, but I believe that's what actors and actresses do all the time. Secondly, you suggesting that I use my looks to land a better deal is frankly distasteful. I *know* what I'm worth, Your Highness, and it has nothing to do with the configuration of my genes. Now, if you're done insulting me, I'm going to leave this place and forget you exist.'

He strolled towards her, drawn to her inner fire despite himself. 'Great speech, but I'm afraid it's not going to be as easy as that.'

'Watch me,' she returned, right before she tightened her grip on her handbag and headed for the door.

Wrapping his arm around her waist as she walked past him felt natural. Almost *too* natural. He'd only meant to detain her, but once her body was plastered to his, once he felt her warm, vibrant skin through the cotton of her shirt, his intentions altered. Not even the bolt of guilt that slammed into him made him drop his arms.

'A quarter of a million pounds,' he rasped.

Her mouth dropped open. 'W-what?' she stuttered.

'You heard me.'

She shifted in his hold, one hand rising to rest on his chest. 'You...you can't. That's too much.'

He tensed. 'Too much for what?'

Her gaze dropped from his. 'Nothing.'

He nudged her head up with a finger under her chin. 'There has to be a basis of truthfulness between us before this goes forward.'

The hand on his chest bunched, then pushed him away. Reluctantly, he released her.

'You assume something *is* going to happen between us,' she said.

'Drop the pretence. You're still as destitute now as you were this morning.'

She glided a nervous tongue-tip over her lower lip, dragging his attention again to that enticing part of her body that was chiselling away at his composure.

Perhaps his mother was right and it was time to look beyond his life of strict official duty and responsibility to the crown.

His gut tightened. From as long as he could remember, there'd been no one else for him but Celeste. He'd been satisfied with the projection of a life with her based on affection, mutual respect and dedication to his kingdom.

There'd been no over-exuberant displays of affection, but the sex had been satisfying—if a little underwhelming with the passage of time. But that had been acceptable in light of his father's extramarital affair and the claim that he'd had no control over himself.

Remi had sneered at that weakness.

He welcomed a life devoid of such emotional entanglements, and *if* his body was done with the self-imposed celibacy he'd placed upon it since Celeste's death, *if* the time had come when he could move beyond the heavy fog of guilt to the semblance of a future, he would decide with his head and not with the sharp, fevered passion that saw some men make fools of themselves. Not with the stark, blazing hunger that currently clawed at him, courtesy of the siren in front of him.

His mother had called him this morning, demanding to know who he'd selected from her list. The unspoken suggestion that there must be some sort of deadline on the guilt and grief that shrouded him had triggered a bolt of fury. His terse response had strained their conversation. But he'd hung up knowing he needed to make a decision, and soon.

But not before he'd dealt with the powder keg Jules had left behind.

'A quarter of a million pounds is much more than the seventy-five thousand you bargained for. That and a signed confidentiality agreement means you'll get to walk away with more money than you dreamed of,' he said.

'You make me sound like a cold-hearted gold-digger,' she muttered, her words wrapped in a thin layer of something close to anguish.

But he'd seen her last night. Like in those pictures palace security had dug up, she'd been dressed for maximum effect, the wisps of nothing she wore designed to captivate any red-blooded male within her radius.

He didn't like to admit it, but the thrumming of his blood insisted he wasn't altogether immune to Madeleine Myers.

'Time is up. Yes or no?'

CHAPTER FOUR

A QUARTER OF a million pounds.

Enough for the operation her father desperately needed with plenty left over for a better place for him to live after his procedure. Surely the prospect of a brighter future would end the cycle of depression her father couldn't seem to break? It might even stretch to hiring a carer for him so she could return to university to finish her studies.

The possibilities of what that money might do staggered her for a minute, momentarily lightening the heavy weight of despair. She took a deep, relieved breath for the first time in what felt like for ever.

And then she looked into the formidable eyes watching her with thinly veiled distaste.

Relief turned to shame. A powerful need to toss his offer in his face ploughed through her. It would be immensely satisfying to walk away, prove that she wasn't the cheap little gold-digger he'd branded her. She wasn't her mother, she wanted to tell him. She didn't value her relationships based exclusively on the size of a man's bank account.

Surely he would look at her with less damning eyes if he knew the money was for her father?

A stark reminder whisked away that foolish notion.

How could she have forgotten about Greg? Friendly, cheeky Greg, who at fourteen had been one of her closest friends, part of the gang at their country club. Greg, whose wealthy parents had bred horses and looked down their noses at anyone whose personal portfolio didn't include three homes in exotic locations...

She'd been too blinded by desperation to see his true colours when she'd turned to him for support when her world had turned grey. He'd hidden his distaste well. Had fooled her with his false sympathy when she'd told him about her father. In the bleak, uncertain landscape of her new reality Greg had been her only shelter, and she'd unashamedly leaned on him in the months after her mother's desertion when the unvarnished truth of her father's addiction had come to light.

For months Maddie had trusted him with everything.

Right up until he'd hit her with the callous truth.

Greg's betrayal had decimated not just her heart but her trust. Her only consolation was that she'd never given him her body. That would have been the final humiliation.

She looked at Remi Montegova and was grateful her tongue hadn't run away with her. Men like him judged a person's worth by their prestige and status. Right from the start he'd shown his disdain at her destitution, believed she would stoop to the lowest level to achieve her avaricious ends. Even now, just like Greg, he was staring down his nose at her, demanding to know what her price was.

If she agreed to Remi's proposal she would do so with her secrets intact.

If?

In her dire position she had very little choice. She was pretty sure the window for returning to her job at the café had closed.

She licked her dry lips, felt something hot and dark and forbidding zinging through her stomach when he followed the action. 'If I agree to this, what exactly would it entail?'

His eyes glinted momentarily, but it faded before she could decipher its meaning.

'For starters, you won't leave my sight until the confidentiality agreement is signed. After that you'll stay here in the hotel with me. I've accepted an invitation to a charity gala tonight. You'll accompany me. On Sunday you'll return with me to Montegova and stay there until I'm sure you won't change your mind and capitalise on your circumstances.'

Her stomach dropped in shock. 'What? I'm not... I can't just pick up sticks and leave!'

Silver-grey eyes narrowed. 'Why not?' he demanded. 'Perhaps because you have other commitments you're not divulging?'

The sensation in her belly intensified. 'And what if I do?'

An eerie stillness settled over him, his body becoming statue-still. Eyes the colour of threatening thunderclouds locked on her as a muscle ticked in his jaw.

'I'm not Jules, Miss Myers. I won't deal with you while you have a lover hovering in the background, ready to throw a spanner in the works.'

He walked stiff and imposing towards the door, his broad shoulders unyielding.

'Wait!'

He stilled, but didn't turn around.

'I don't have a lover. But I do have responsibilities.'

He swivelled in a smooth, regal move, those incisive eyes piercing into hers once more. 'Explain—and be quick about it.'

My God, he really was insufferable. But then weren't most people with power and authority? As much as she loved him, hadn't her father displayed a fraction of Remi's arrogance once upon a time, when he'd believed himself infallible?

'It's my father. I live with my father. I can't just...leave him.'

A fraction of that chill dissipated from his eyes, and then they grew contemplative.

'You work long hours. You're away from him for a considerable part of the day—which means that he's either able-bodied and can look after himself or he has someone else to take care of him.'

His deductions set out in clipped tones, he waited, his gaze probing hers as if daring her to refute them.

'He's able-bodied,' she said, cringing at the half-lie. 'But that doesn't mean I want to leave home for however long you intend this to be.'

He strolled with measured steps, like a predator stalking his prey, back to where she stood, frozen. 'How did your father take your liaison with Jules?'

He'd barely noticed her absence. And that was the problem. He barely noticed anything any more.

Pained wrenched at her heart. She breathed through it. 'I'm a grown woman.'

As if she'd issued an invitation his gaze swept over her body, firing charged volts everywhere it touched. By the time he returned his gaze to hers she was acutely aware of every pounding heartbeat, every unsteady breath she took.

'This thing happens only on *my* terms, Madeleine,' he stated ruthlessly.

She knew the truth behind that statement. She wasn't from his circle so he didn't trust her. What better way to keep her in check than to keep her close? Exercise his perceived right to treat her with contempt the way Greg had treated her when he'd learned the full circumstances of her fall from privilege?

But she couldn't leave her father to his own devices for long stretches. That would most certainly see him relapse before she could get him the help he needed. Unfortunately, that outcome depended on acceding to this man's wishes.

Still...

'I... I can't just pack my bags and go to Montegova with you,' she said a little desperately.

His shrug said her dilemma wasn't his concern. 'Take the next few hours to consider my offer. My driver and one of my bodyguards will take you home. You'll be brought back here at seven and you'll give me your answer then.'

Maddie took a deep breath that went nowhere near dispersing the apprehension rolling through her.

From the bodyguards and the limo to the ultra-VIP entrance to the suite she suspected was reserved for royalty, to the luxurious decadence of these rooms, everything about Remi Montegova screamed privilege and undiluted entitlement. Maddie knew that even if she walked out of here this second, she wouldn't be free of him unless he wished it.

He had determined that she was a threat to his family. One that could be neutralised by opening his wallet and keeping her prisoner for however long he pleased.

As shameful as that ultimate slur was, when it came right down to it his offer was staggeringly life-changing. All she had to do was negotiate shrewdly.

She ignored the little voice in her head that told her this performance wouldn't be straightforward—not when she couldn't look into those eyes without wild heat invading her belly. Not when she didn't even need to close her eyes to recall how it had felt to be pressed up against his hard, hot body.

But, unlike Jules's mercurial behaviour, she knew where she stood with the Crown Prince. His disdain for her was evident in every word he spoke.

Why not use that disdain as a barrier? Insulate herself in it until she got what she wanted?

With another deep breath, she forced herself to meet his gaze, even though it felt as if he was trying to strip off a layer of her skin, burrow underneath and root all her secrets.

'Okay.'

'No, Miss Myers. I want to hear the words.'

'Yes, I'll come back tonight and give you my answer.'

He stared down at her for a taut spell, an indecipherable gleam in his eyes. Then he veered away, striding over to an antique desk to pick up the phone. He relayed instructions in that curious mix of languages before replacing the handset. Minutes later, a knock came on the door.

A rake-thin man whose uniform announced his butler status appeared out of nowhere, gave a stiff bow and opened the door. The same bodyguard who'd escorted her from the nightclub last night entered the room.

'This is Antonio. He'll make sure you get where you need to go.'

In other words he'd be her shadow for the foreseeable future. It was pointless to protest.

She walked to where she'd dropped her bag earlier and picked it up. When she turned, Remi stood behind her. Antonio and the butler stood at a discreet distance.

'Um…is there something else?'

Remi's gaze flicked to her hair and then slowly dragged down her body again. Dear God, the man could strip the thoughts from her head with just the look in his eyes.

'I'll have my stylist deliver appropriate clothes to you.'

She nearly choked on her tongue. 'Excuse me?'

'You expect to attend a charity gala dressed as a waitress?'

Maddie looked down at her uniform, at her threadbare tights, the worn flats.

'Of course not. But I have a perfectly adequate wardrobe.' It was a white lie. She had one classic black gown. The rest of the designer labels her mother had pushed upon her over the years had been sold off long ago to pay the bills.

His face grew taut. 'If you intend to wear the clothes my brother furnished you with, think again.'

'I don't,' she retorted, wondering at the relationship between Remi and Jules.

She met his gaze and something within the intense depths told her it would be wise not to ask. She shivered as he continued to look at her with an intense, almost possessive gaze.

Maddie lowered her eyes, certain she was imagining things. Jules hadn't owned her. Remi most definitely didn't want to. He couldn't have made that clearer with his attitude. Nevertheless, there was something unsettling in his eyes. Something that made her breasts tingle and her belly flip-flop.

A phone rang in the background, dragging them out of the thickening sensual bubble.

Remi took a single step back. 'Good. I expect you back here at seven. Don't be late,' he said, then walked away.

Maddie didn't take a full breath until she'd shut the door of her flat behind her half an hour later. Free of Remi's disturbing vortex, the enormity of what she was contemplating overwhelmed her.

On shaky legs she entered the living room, found it empty, and approached her father's room. The door was ajar. She nudged it wider and was half relieved, half disappointed to find him asleep.

Had he been awake, what would she have said? That she'd negotiated a deal with one brother to act as his girlfriend and was now on the brink of negotiating with another for a higher sum because he believed she was a shameless, blackmailing gold-digger?

Silently, she retreated to her room, knowing that come seven tonight she would have no choice but to accept Remi's proposition or risk losing her father.

Maddie curled her fingers around the leather bound document and tried to ignore the two other people in the room. An impossible feat, of course. Everything about what she was doing evoked industrial strength butterflies in her stomach that were impossible to dismiss.

To his credit the butler, tutored in diplomacy to within an inch of his life, remained unobtrusive. Not so much his employer, the Crown Prince of Montegova, who prowled lazily in front of her as she attempted to read the fine print of the agreement.

She wanted to snap at him to be still. To be less distracting. To be less drop-dead gorgeous. Less...*everything*. But she bit her tongue. She'd agreed to this and there was no going back. Nor was there any point in denying that Remi's effect on her was shockingly visceral enough to stop her breath every time he crossed her vision.

It would wear off. It had to. No one could carry off that level of saturated charisma and power indefinitely!

She'd ignore him, just as she had all the unwanted attention that had come her way in the café. She snorted under her breath, wondering what Remi would think of being compared to the greasy construction workers and overly familiar salesman who patronised her workplace.

Her *ex*-workplace.

The inescapable reminder that she was now jobless and temporarily relocated to Remi's hotel rammed home. Her fingers shook as she recalled her conversation with her father. He'd barely responded to her carefully constructed explanation of why she would be away for two days, his absent nods when she told him that Mrs Jennings would be staying over to keep him company the only indication that he'd heard her.

For an unguarded moment Maddie wished she had a close friend to confide in. Then she wouldn't feel so dammed alone. But all her so-called friends had deserted her the moment the Myers family had fallen on hard times.

Greg had taken it a step further and kicked her in the most brutal way when she was down. His betrayal had eroded her trust to nothing and ensured she had nothing in reserve to offer anyone else when he'd coaxed her into emptying her bank account and shrugged off the risky investment that had lost her everything under the banner of 'it happens'.

Her bitter thoughts scattered when Remi approached, impatience stamped on his face. He'd given her fifteen minutes to read the confidentiality agreement, with the offer of an independent lawyer should she need it. That time had passed five minutes ago.

If she played her cards right her father could be on his way to surgery in a matter of days.

'Are you ready to sign?' Remi asked.

Her eyes jerked to his face, as seemed to happen automatically whenever he spoke. It was as if his whole body was a powerful magnet, drawing her to him. And once she was drawn, it was impossible to look away.

God, was it normal for one man to be graced with such good looks? Sculpted cheekbones, ruggedly cut jaw and glossy hair notwithstanding, it was that aura of raw masculinity that triggered the wild fluttering in her belly. She watched, enthralled against her will, as one eyebrow slowly lifted, his expression growing mocking at her unashamed perusal.

Face flaming, she dropped her gaze and grimaced inwardly when she saw he was holding out a pen to her.

The moment of truth. 'Um…'

'Percy has other duties to attend to. If you'd be so kind as to express yourself better I can ask him to stay or leave.'

She snatched the pen from him, flipped the document to the last page and signed it. Within a minute it had been signed by Remi and witnessed by Percy the butler.

When the door shut behind Percy her gaze swung to the man who effectively, according to their agreement, owned her for the next six weeks.

He was watching her too, but after a moment his gaze dropped to travel over her body, taking in her new attire.

An hour after she returned home she'd answered her door to be handed a large package by Antonio.

She couldn't help but glance down at herself. The bodice and straps of the peach-coloured gown were layered in a bandage design that clung to her shoulders, torso and hips in an intimate caress before the silky material fell to her ankles.

She didn't want to recall the heat she'd glimpsed in Remi's eyes when he'd first seen her, but the memory burned now as she withstood his scrutiny.

She wasn't going to get attached to any of this glitz and

glamour. Once this was behind her there would be no place in her life for social events that involved wearing five-thousand-pound dresses and shoes.

'Did you receive my email?' he demanded.

Along with the dress, he'd sent her a new phone—one with only one number programmed into it. *His*.

She'd barely had it for ten minutes before his email had arrived. It had contained details of the charity gala, including who would be in attendance, the reason behind the fundraiser and the menu that would be served. It wasn't clear whether this was royal protocol or Remi was a control freak. Most likely a bit of both.

'Yes, I did. All read and understood, Your Highness.' She couldn't quite help the hint of sarcasm in her tone.

His eyes gleamed. 'When we're alone you may call me Remi.'

'And you may call me Maddie.'

He inclined his head in a regal nod, then prowled towards her, his face set in uncompromising lines. 'All I ask, Madeleine, is that you apply a little bit of that polish you have exhibited on the outside to the inside too.'

The barb pricked, wedging itself firmly under her skin. 'You don't want the evening to start off with insults, do you?' she asked.

'I want the evening to start off by us not turning up late,' he rasped, before heading for the door. He threw it open and glanced pointedly at her.

Maddie followed, the body-skimming dress and the effects of walking in four-inch heels causing her hips to sway self-consciously.

She watched his gaze drop momentarily down her body before he looked away.

They left the suite and rode down in the lift in a charged silence she wasn't in the mood to disperse. She was heading for the private entrance when his hand snaked around her waist.

'Where are you going?' Remi asked.

The heat of his hand against her silk-covered skin rendered her speechless for a moment. 'I thought… Aren't you using your private access?'

'What's the point? I was seen with you last night—and this afternoon at your former workplace. Believe me, every angle has already been covered by the media. Evasion tactics are no longer necessary.'

She bit her lip. 'And you're okay with that?'

'Ultimately it's no one's business *what* you are to me, but if you're asked go with the truth. We met through Jules.'

She grimaced. 'And let them all think that I'm a slapper who's jumped from one brother to the other?'

'I find stating the truth, no matter how brutal, is better than ambivalence.'

Maddie wasn't given time to process his words. The moment they stepped through the revolving doors his fingers tightened around her waist, sending her sizzling senses into full-blown fireworks.

Her breath caught at the pulse-racing effect of such a simple gesture. But then nothing about this man was simple. Everything screamed complicated and mind-boggling excitement. The only thing lacking was the *Keep Off* signs that should have been stamped all over his impeccable tuxedo.

The sensation was only heightened when they slid into the dark interior of the limo, and even after quickly positioning herself as far away from him as possible she was immediately engulfed in his deep, intoxicating scent.

What on earth was wrong with her?

'How is your arm?' Remi asked.

She stared at him, stupefied, for a moment before his words sank in. The doctor had advised that as long as she didn't aggravate her arm she could go without the sling for short periods.

'It's fine.'

The intensity in his eyes didn't abate. 'Did you take your medication?'

His brusque concern threatened to wrap itself around the protected core inside her. But, like the intricate web of lies Greg had wrapped around her for his own twisted amusement, she knew the Crown Prince's guise was false too.

'Can we dispense with the pretence?'

Silver eyes hardened. 'Pretence?'

She nodded. 'You pretending to care about me. I'm a conniving little gold-digger, remember? And, while we're at it, I don't think you touching me in public is strictly necessary, so let's cut that false courtesy too.'

For the longest stretch he remained silent. 'I will touch you when I deem it necessary in public. And you will not object because you have signed an agreement that ties you to me for the next six weeks,' he stated, in a deep, imperious voice that drilled mercilessly into her senses.

The unshakeable knowledge that he could draw such a visceral, unfettered response from her any time he chose was shockingly unsettling.

Even more unnerving was the fact that a large part of her wasn't recoiling from that thrilling possibility.

'Then you won't mind if I reciprocate?' she dared, striving to ignore the anticipation firing her blood. 'A gold-digger needs to earn her money, after all.'

'It's a shame I'll never have the pleasure of seeing this insolence tamed out of you one day,' he mused dryly.

The reminder that he would be out of her life in a few short weeks silenced her. And when his phone rang, she listened as Remi conducted a conversation in a tense but lyrical mix of French and Italian.

Montegovan.

She stared at his proud, unforgiving profile, reflecting the genes passed down by his warrior ancestors.

Whatever was being discussed wasn't to his liking. His

rugged jaw clenched multiple times before he squeezed the bridge of his nose. Then the phone call ended abruptly.

Miles went by in silence. Silence that gave her too much time to make dangerous observations, like how his strong, elegant fingers rested on his taut thighs, or the shape of his Adam's apple as he swallowed. The decadent sensation she'd experienced when his fingers brushed her back.

She shifted in her seat as low heat intensified in her belly. 'Everything okay?' she asked.

He glanced her way and she almost wished she hadn't spoken. Those far too incisive eyes locked on hers in the semi-darkness. 'The challenges of family rearing their head again.'

She nodded. 'Your father?'

He blinked in surprise before his eyes turned a shade cooler. 'My father died ten years ago.'

Her heart lurched. 'Oh… I'm sorry for your loss.'

He acknowledged her sympathy with a regal tilt of his head.

Unwilling to let the dangerous silence return, she cleared her throat. 'So who was that?'

'That was my mother—the Queen. Doing what she does best,' he said, with the faintest trace of bitterness.

'Which is?'

'Issuing edicts and expecting me to fall in line,' he mused darkly.

Maddie hid a grimace. From their very first encounter she'd known that no one dictated to this man. Whatever was being asked of him, he would counter it with merciless determination.

'What of your own mother?' he asked.

She started in surprise. 'What?'

He shifted sideways and her mouth dried as the stunning perfection of the Crown Prince was fully focused on her. 'Your mother,' he repeated.

A vice tightened around her chest. 'She's no longer in the picture,' she replied, hoping he would drop the subject.

But he was an all-powerful prince, used to getting his way.

'Why not?'

She contemplated resisting—except he'd answered her question just now. 'We weren't always…destitute. My father used to own a thriving property business. Then the bottom fell out of the market. His business went under and we went from living in a ten-bedroom mansion in Surrey to a tiny flat in inner-city London.' Her shrug didn't quite hit the mark as painful reminders hit home hard. 'My mother didn't take the change of circumstances well. She left my father when I was in university.'

'She didn't just leave your father. She left you too,' he stated.

Her breath caught at the unexpected gruff gentleness in his voice. She'd expected a detached response, a callous dismissal of her pain, but his gaze didn't hold any censure.

'That's not all, is it?' he murmured, those eyes that saw too much boring into her.

She snatched in a breath, the urge to unburden herself swelling inside her. 'Does it matter?' she asked, attempting to reel herself in.

His answer was forestalled by their arrival. But not before he shot her a fierce glance.

Exiting the car, he turned to help her out.

The disquieting sensation increased as she stepped out to an explosion of flashbulbs. Rapid-fire questions flew at her.

'Who are you?'

'What are you to the Crown Prince?'

'How long have you two been together?'

She noticed the questions aimed at Remi were more subdued and a whole lot more respectful. Not that he answered any of them. He looked through the throng as if it didn't exist, and with a suave shift of his body shielded her injured arm and wrapped his hand around her waist again.

Nudged against the hard column of his body, she felt hers screech into awareness as they travelled along the red carpet.

After a few steps he glanced down at her for a long moment. There was a look in his eyes that tightened the muscles in her belly.

'Are you okay?'

She jerked out a nod, reminding herself sternly that it was all an act.

Still, it didn't calm the butterflies as she entered the impressive lobby of the five-star hotel hosting the gala.

According to his email, the fundraiser was in aid of establishing sports facilities for disabled children in half a dozen developing countries. When Remi introduced her to the chairwoman of the foundation, Maddie threw herself into finding out everything she could about the work of the charity, just so she could ignore the fact that she was the avid cynosure of incredulous gazes and whispers.

She raised her chin and tried to smile through it, striving for every ounce of poise hammered into her at the nose-bleedingly expensive private school her parents had enrolled her in when she was eleven.

As the evening progressed, she noticed Remi's speculative gaze straying increasingly towards her.

'Our meal hasn't been served yet, so I know I don't have spinach stuck on my teeth, or something similarly unseemly, so why are you are looking at me like that?'

He paused for a beat. 'I'm not a man who's easily surprised,' he murmured, his tone low and deep as conversation hummed around them.

That earlier sting returned. 'You think you have me precisely pegged, but you don't. My current circumstances may be deplorable to you, but perhaps you should make an effort to look beyond that. You might be surprised.'

His grey eyes grew more contemplative. 'Very well. Tell me why you dropped out of a top-level university after one term to anchor yourself to that tawdry little café.'

The unexpected question threw her enough to draw an unguarded gasp. 'It wasn't tawdry. It was…okay.'

'You almost sound as if you miss it.'

She shrugged. 'It wasn't so bad.' The hours had been a long slog, but they'd made her forget the bleakness of her existence. The free meals had helped too.

He leaned closer, bringing his heady scent deeper into her orbit. 'Tell me you're not harbouring notions of returning there at some point in the future?' he rasped with a definite bite.

'What do *you* care?'

'That place was beneath you,' he breathed.

'Careful, Your Highness, or you'll get a nosebleed up there in your high and mighty castle.'

'You're far too exquisite to be working in a place like that.'

A flare of pink rushed into her cheeks. 'You can't say things like that,' she said, aware that a few heads were turning their way.

Without warning he reached out, brushed a finger down her heated cheek. 'Why not? It's true.'

She knew the wisest choice would be to pull away, but every cell in her body wanted to lean closer into his touch, prolong that wicked thrill flowing through her bloodstream. 'Still, no one goes around talking like that.'

'Then I'm terribly lucky not to be no one,' he said.

'God, do you hear yourself? You sound—'

'Arrogant? Conceited? If it conveys my message that I prefer your silky skin to be perfumed with expensive scents rather than recycled cooking oil, then so be it.'

The melting sensation in her belly was saved from spreading to encompass her whole body by a discreet tap on a microphone.

With almost enervating relief she jerked back into her seat, her fingers clenched tight in her lap. After a moment Remi relaxed too, directing his attention to the podium.

Ignoring the chaotic emotions churning inside her, she redirected her thoughts to what he'd said earlier about her dropping out of university.

Just how much of her past had Remi dug into? She bit the inside of her lip. If he carried on it would only be a matter of time before he uncovered the truth about her father.

She waited until the speech was over and the guests had resumed their conversation before she turned to him. 'I thought you were going to stop digging into my past now that I've agreed to your little circus?' she whispered.

His eyes pierced hers, holding her captive. 'That information was in my preliminary report. Why *did* you drop out?' he asked again.

'Why are you interested?'

His gaze swept down to her lips and lingered. 'I think perhaps we should extend the parameters of our agreement.'

Heavy, charged heat bloomed in her belly. She grew intensely aware that she wasn't sitting very far back in her seat, that only a sparse inch of space separated them. The velvety firmness of his lips was tantalisingly close. One slight move and she could brush her mouth against his.

'Extend them…how?' she managed, aware that her voice had grown embarrassingly husky.

'The bare bones of your history will do.'

Disappointment lanced through her, almost making her gasp. When she had it under reasonable control, she answered. 'You already have that—whereas I know next to nothing about you. For instance, why is everyone here surprised that you brought a date with you?'

She was close enough to see the chill in his eyes before he abruptly drew back from her. 'Probably because I haven't been seen in public with a woman in two years,' he rasped.

Mild shock fizzed through her. Remi Montegova wasn't

a man who'd lack for female attention. She would bet her last tenner on it. 'May I ask why?'

The look he slanted her was filled with scepticism. 'You expect me to believe you don't *know*?'

Her breath caught at his frosted tone. 'Know what?'

'It's been almost twenty-four hours since we first met. Most people would've satisfied their curiosity about me by now.'

Maddie wasn't about to admit her disturbingly rabid interest in him. 'I don't own a laptop, Your Highness, nor do I bother with social media any more. Also, I've been busy dealing with other things today. So, no, I haven't had time to research you.'

He stared at her for half a minute before presenting her with his impressive profile. He wasn't going to answer. Clearly the extended parameters didn't include that particular question.

But after a moment he glanced back at her. 'You're a novelty to them because the last woman I dated was my fiancée,' he stated baldly.

Her lips parted, further shock unravelling through her. Questions stormed her mind. Why had the most eligible bachelor in Europe, perhaps even the world, not dated for two years? And who and where *was* the woman once promised to him?

Before she could ask, he added, 'And, no, that subject isn't up for discussion. It's purely for information purposes only.'

His statement didn't stop a dozen questions from storming her brain.

She cleared her throat, strove for a safer subject that didn't threaten to consume her whole. 'If you still want to know, I was studying child psychology at university.'

Surprise flared in his eyes.

Her laughter was tinged with bitterness. 'Is it really so shocking that I'd be interested in helping children?'

'You're putting words in my mouth.'

'Deny that you had preconceived notions about me,' she dared.

His outward demeanour didn't change, but she sensed his complete withdrawal even before he turned to strike up a conversation with another guest.

Her conviction that Remi Montegova's opinion of her wasn't about to change any time soon settled deeper, and jarred more than she wanted to accept, but she managed to wrestle herself under control and smile through the next hour.

By the time after-dinner drinks commenced and a four-piece band took their place near the dance floor she was in desperate need of reprieve. About to escape to the ladies' room, she froze as Remi turned to her. He sent the man she'd been conversing with a smile full of diplomacy that didn't make it any less stiff or dismissive.

'Your first dance is mine,' he stated.

The thought of her body close to his, moving in sync with his, sent a bolt of deep awareness through her. Dangerous, arousing awareness.

She should refuse. But she found herself rising, sliding her hand into his.

Fingers firmly gripping hers, he led her to the polished dance floor to the sound of a slow waltz. Her pulse raced faster and she fought to breathe as he gently raised her injured arm and laid it against his chest. Then one hand glided around her waist, resting there as his gaze speared hers.

She followed his lead, and strove not to react to his magnetic proximity as he started to move.

Of course the Crown Prince of Montegova danced with elegant, breathtaking sophistication.

Very much aware that even more gazes were fixed on them, she attempted to find another subject for hers. And ended up meeting those enigmatic silver-grey eyes again. Eyes that saw far too much.

'Why not just tell them you're not interested?' she asked, a little too unsettled to guard her tongue.

'Excuse me?'

'There seems to be some sort of competition going on about who can get your attention. If you're not interested, why not just let them know?'

As if on cue, a stunning redhead twirled by a few minutes later. Completely ignoring the man accompanying her, she sent Remi a sultry smile.

Spikes of irritation, and another emotion she staunchly rejected as being jealousy, impaled Maddie. 'It must be hard, having women throw themselves so blatantly at you.'

For some reason her tart observation amused him, and his sensual lips curved with the barest twitch.

'Something funny?'

'It seems I've offended you again. You didn't strike me as having delicate sensibilities before.'

'I don't,' she denied hotly, then attempted to pull herself from his arms.

'What do you think you're doing?'

'The waltz is over. Let me go, please.'

In contrast to her demand, his hand tightened on her waist. 'We're under scrutiny, Maddie. This isn't the time to make a scene.'

'Oh, really? I…'

Her words trailed off as his head dropped in a slow but inexorable descent that announced his intention to do precisely as he pleased.

She had time to move away…time to place a hand on that broad chest and stop him from doing something that she knew in her bones would intensify the cyclone tearing through her. She didn't do either.

Her breath strangled to nothing, she watched Remi Montegova's imperious head lower until his lips were a scant centimetre from hers. Her gaze locked on his and she waited, felt his breath wash over her face as he stretched out the moment until her every sense screamed with a rabid, alien hunger, before slanting his mouth over hers.

As kisses went, the hard but brief imprint of his mouth over hers shouldn't have made such a stomach-churning impact. It shouldn't have rooted her to the spot, made the music echoing in the ballroom or the people within its walls seem to disappear.

But the ferociously intense look in his eyes and the searing brand of his kiss made Maddie experience every nanosecond of it with a vividness that promised she wouldn't forget or dismiss it any time soon, and the eye contact he maintained as he delivered the searing kiss electrified her to her very toes.

As slowly as he'd commenced the thrilling assault he retreated, giving her time to absorb the shivers rolling through her, the flames flickering insistently in her belly and the wild tingling between her legs.

It was that last damning sensation that pulled her up short, helped her fill her lungs with much needed oxygen as she attempted to make sense of what had happened.

'What…what are you doing?' she whispered under her breath.

The overwhelmingly male figure before her smiled, and a hand she didn't recall releasing hers joined the other at her waist in a firm hold. 'Extending the parameters of our association,' he said.

'I don't recall agreeing to…this.'

He stepped back, his face tightening a touch. To everyone else the Crown Prince would be a picture of elegant royalty and sophistication. But she was catching glimpses of the man underneath. Beneath the façade there was ferocious determination. An iron will. And a dark anguish.

It was too overwhelming.

Before she could recover her thoughts, he settled his hand on the small of her back and led her out of the ballroom, not stopping until they were outside.

CHAPTER FIVE

OUTSIDE, A LIGHT DRIZZLE was falling, creating puddles on the pavement.

Maddie gathered the hem of her evening gown, preparing for a quick dash to the limo. But she froze as Remi stayed her with his hand, and watched, a little stunned, as he shrugged out of his tuxedo and draped it over her shoulders.

The enfolding warmth and intimacy of his body heat heightened the already surreal atmosphere, so when he stared down at her for a moment before laying a hand in the small of her back and nudging her gently towards the waiting limo, she didn't protest.

The driver hurried towards them with a large umbrella. Remi took it from him, holding it over her head as the drizzle intensified.

She attempted to tell herself the chivalrous act was for show, but the idea wouldn't stick. Unlike his half-brother, Remi exuded magnetic charm, as well as other larger-than-life characteristics, some of which set her teeth on edge. But every single one commanded attention, focused on the simple fact that he was head and shoulders above others. A man who did exactly as he pleased.

Which circled her racing thoughts back to the fiancée he'd mentioned. She was still attempting to throttle that curiosity when the limo pulled away.

The shift of air shrouded her in his scent once again. More than a little agitated, she sat up and started to shrug off his tuxedo. 'Take this back.'

He shook his head. 'No, keep it on. Your temperamental English weather is out in full force,' he quipped, nodding out of the window to where rain lashed the windows.

For a moment she watched the hypnotic diagrams the rainwater drew on the glass. For as long as she could remember she'd loved storms. She loved watching the rain wash the world clean. Now, ensconced in the limo with Remi, watching the rain fall felt almost too intimate.

She cleared her throat and turned to find him watching her. 'Can we talk about what happened? And, more importantly, can we agree that it'll never happen again?' she stressed, relieved when her voice emerged briskly.

His eyes gleamed in the dark. 'You find what I did so objectionable?'

There was a peculiar throb in his voice that sent tingles down her spine.

'I prefer to have a say in when advances like that are made on me,' she said.

'Did you have such an agreement with Jules?'

The question was fired at her.

'Excuse me?'

'You may not have responded when he kissed you, but you didn't protest either.' His intense gaze dropped to her lips. 'Did you agree that he could kiss you?'

'No! For your information, that kiss took me by surprise too. And frankly I'm done being manhandled by you and your kin. So shall we add that to the ground rules?'

'No.' His expression hardened before his gaze reconnected with hers. 'That will not be necessary because it won't happen again.'

Something irritatingly resembling disappointment pounded through her. From the moment she'd set eyes on him he'd messed with her equilibrium. The harder she tried to regain her footing, the faster she spun out of control. It needed to stop.

They pulled up to the hotel, under the thankfully wide awning erected at the front entrance. Remi didn't seem in a hurry to reclaim his jacket, and his hand returned to the small of her back the moment they stepped out of the vehicle.

Despite the stark admonition to herself to regain her equilibrium as soon as possible, she couldn't stop herself from inhaling his scent with every breath, nor halt the awareness flaring over her skin when they entered the lift.

In the mirror's reflection his shoulders looked broader beneath his pristine white shirt, the cut of his torso delineating a physique most men only dreamed about. She was so busy ogling his body she didn't notice the lift had arrived at his floor and the doors had slid open until she caught his hooded scrutiny through the mirror.

Heat flew into her cheeks, her mortification intensifying when his gaze turned chilly. But with twisted gratitude she absorbed the sharp rejection, let it throw off the haze that threatened to shroud her.

Stepping out of the lift, she shrugged off his jacket and held it out to him. 'I don't need this any more. Thank you.' Her voice was husky with hurt but she didn't care.

He took it, the brush of his fingers stimulating another shiver that set her teeth on edge. She needed to get her faculties back under control, because this was insane.

'Goodnight, Your Highness,' she threw over her shoulder as she marched towards her suite, conscious that he was watching her. Against her will, she hesitated with one hand on the door.

'Sleep well,' was all he said before he sauntered off, one finger hooked into his jacket and a supreme confidence in his swagger that made her want to keep staring at him.

In direct contravention of that need Maddie whirled away, entered the junior suite she'd been assigned by Percy, under Remi's instruction, and shut the door behind her.

The suite was a smaller version of Remi's but no less breathtaking. Her breath caught all over again as she looked around, scrutinised the paintings and objets d'art dotted around the room. Everywhere she looked she saw a reflection of royalty, power, prestige. There was even a photo of a monarch bearing a striking resemblance to Remi shaking hands with a president.

But not even the magnificence of her surroundings could curb the tiny tremors that continued to radiate through her body as she relived their kiss. Even now her fingers itched to trace her mouth, soothe the tingles that should have passed.

An hour later, Maddie tossed and turned for the umpteenth time, punched her pillow in a vain effort to settle, then with a start realised she hadn't thought of her father all evening. She'd been so absorbed by Remi she'd forgotten to make her check-in call.

Guilt flaying her, she eyed the clock. It was after midnight. If by some miracle he'd combatted his insomnia, all she'd be doing was disturbing his rest.

She sank into the pillow, praying for similar oblivion to take her thoughts from the man who'd captivated her senses.

Her prayer wasn't answered. The moment she closed her eyes, her mind veered back to Remi. To the dance. To that kiss.

The kiss she didn't want to happen again, she reiterated to herself.

She lived with the harsh consequences of trusting her emotions every day. Greg had used their childhood friendship to betray her. And, while her agreement with Remi was signed in indelible ink, both men were of the same ilk, judging and treating those less fortunate than themselves as unworthy.

She wasn't about to make the same mistake twice.

Against her better judgment, she reached for her phone and typed his name into an internet search engine. And there, in vivid Technicolor, lay the evidence she wasn't sure was wise to see.

Celeste Bastille had been stunning, in a gentle, doe-eyed way that showed she'd been born to be the perfect foil for a man like Remi. The daughter of French and Montegovan aristocracy, she exuded poise and charm in every picture

Maddie uncovered, her utter devotion to the man at her side clear in every look.

Maddie only managed to look at a few before she tossed her phone away. Remi still loved her, if that expression of guilt and anguish on his face early this evening was any indication.

Her heart lurched at the thought of what such loss would have done to a man living in the public eye. And not just any man. A crown prince with a duty to his kingdom and future throne. A crown prince who'd lost his princess.

No. Despite the fiery insanity of that kiss, she couldn't fool herself into thinking it was anything but a throwaway reaction for Remi. And henceforth her best course of action would be to have minimal, only strictly necessary contact with Remi, and keep her father at the forefront of her mind.

But as sleep took her she knew that task might be easier said than achieved.

Kissing her had been a mistake.

Remi grimaced as he swallowed a mouthful of cognac. The smooth heat did nothing to burn away the guilt riding him. Nor did it lessen the pounding arousal flooding his manhood.

To make matters worse, his desperate scramble to recall Celeste's voice, her laugh, her gentle manner, had failed him for a few shameful seconds. Replaced with vibrant green eyes, a husky laugh, a defiant chin and bee-stung lips.

He shouldn't have kissed her.

Telling himself he had done it for the cogent reason of freeing himself from unwanted attention so he could preserve Celeste's memory felt hollow in the aftermath of the savage hunger it had awakened in him.

He'd *enjoyed* the sensation of holding another woman in his arms. Tasting her warm, willing flesh. Hearing that hitch in her breathing that signalled an arousal that matched his.

Worst of all was his inability to wrestle that beast of

arousal under control. But what he'd done might have worked. No doubt there would now be a scramble to find out who the woman was who'd made Crown Prince Remi Montegova act so out of character.

Because even with Celeste he'd resisted even simple public displays of affection, never mind giving in to the ravaging lust that clawed through him.

His skin tightened with guilt as the silent promise he'd made to his dying fiancée returned to haunt him. His fingers tightened around his glass. He hadn't sinned yet. Hadn't taken another woman into his heart.

But you're thinking about taking another woman to your bed.

A necessity. For the sake of his kingdom.

Excuses.

The cold blanket of grief and guilt settled more heavily as his gaze skated over the view of night-time London. The simple truth was that he'd let Celeste down. She was dead because he'd failed her.

Remi veered away from his censorious reflection in the living room window.

His mother's second phone call this afternoon, questioning his motives, had riled him. He was already aware that his inability to fully control himself around Maddie Myers might reap unpalatable consequences. His mother pointing it out hadn't pleased him. Only his assurance that he was returning home in another day had appeased her.

As for her insistence that he choose a wife…

If he rid himself of his hunger with Maddie, then on his return home he could focus on the more rewarding task of governing Montegova.

Celeste had understood what sacrifice meant. Would she have understood this decision?

He headed for his bedroom, his every step dogged by duelling emotions of guilt and arousal. But through it all the thrill heating his blood only grew hotter.

It was still present the next morning as he flicked through the financial section of the morning paper. Sunrise had brought more coverage of him in the social pages and another call from his mother.

It had taken exactly one minute of examining the front page and its breathtaking picture of Maddie to stoke the fire in his groin and deepen the decision that had taken hold of him somewhere between dawn and sunrise.

She was a beautiful woman. There was no denying that. In his world, women like her were a dime a dozen. But there was something more about her that snagged his attention. Something that compelled his gaze now, as she approached the dining table. Something unsettling that wouldn't let him ignore the hypnotic sway of her hips and the proud rise of her breasts.

It was deeper than common lust and, whatever it was, it armed itself in preparation to battle his unrelenting guilt.

'Good morning,' she murmured when she reached him.

Remi folded the newspaper, took time to wrestle himself under control—because duty and loyalty demanded precedence over blind, red-hot lust—then took his time to assess her. She wore a blush-pink off-the-shoulder sweater that bared one creamy shoulder and a grey knee-length skirt that cradled her hips before flaring at the knees. Tasteful clothes, which somehow managed to look sinfully decadent on her body.

He shifted in his seat in a vain attempt to decrease the pressure behind his fly. 'You slept well, I hope?' he asked.

She sat down and smiled her thanks at the coffee-pouring Percy before deigning to glance his way. 'No, not really.'

He frowned at the bolt of concern that shot through him, wrestled it down until his butler had departed. 'Is it your arm? Do you need further medical attention?'

Her sling was back in place, but she shook her head. 'No. My insomnia had less to do with my injuries and more to do with missing my own bed.'

'Considering where you live, I find that hard to believe.'

Bright green eyes flicked to him. 'And here I was hoping the insults wouldn't start until I'd at least armed myself with caffeine.'

Remi's insides tightened. For some absurd reason, this woman burrowed beneath his skin with very little effort. It was aggravating. And peculiarly stimulating. 'Does my honesty offend you?'

'There's honesty and there's *brutal* honesty. I'm a firm believer in using the latter as a last resort,' she said, meeting his gaze with eyes filled with censure.

Remi felt a spark of surprise. Very few people dared to challenge him any more. Evidently this brave creature wanted to be one of the few. He didn't know whether to smile or put her in her place.

'Tell me why you didn't sleep well,' he found himself demanding as he buttered a piece of toast, placed it within reach of her left hand and did the same with a small platter of fruit.

'Thank you,' she murmured, her eyes dropping to her coffee cup. 'I promised to check in with my father last night and I forgot.'

'As you said yourself, you're a grown woman—not a teenager with a curfew.'

'Nevertheless, I made a promise and I didn't keep it.'

She was omitting an important fact. And, just like yesterday, his need to know grew to unacceptable proportions. 'You've yet to pack for Montegova. The driver will take you home this morning. Will that not suffice?'

Her gaze avoided his. 'Um…about that…' she murmured, a pinch of guilt on her face.

Foreboding and lust burned as she licked her lower lip. 'Whatever it is, spit it out,' he prompted.

'Is it…possible to have an advance on my payment?'

The stirring in his groin abated. 'Less than twenty-four

hours into our agreement and you're already demanding payment?'

'I know it's not strictly what we agreed, but—'

'You demand trust and yet hold back from telling me the whole truth about your circumstances.'

A spark of anger lit her green eyes. 'Are you saying the only way you'll agree is if I let you dig where you please into my life? You think that's fair?'

He shrugged, hardening himself against the angry hurt in her eyes. 'You're naïve if you ever thought we were on an equal footing.'

Her mouth compressed, and a rough exhalation flared her delicate nostrils. 'Is that a no to my request?'

He suppressed the need to question her further, to know everything about this woman. Why couldn't he stop thinking about her? Why, even now, did he want to lean across the table and fuse his mouth to hers?

'How much do you need?'

Again her tongue flicked over her bottom lip. 'Ten percent.'

Twenty-five thousand pounds. Not much in the grand scheme of things, but it could buy her a clean exit from his life. The urge to say no clambered through him. But a look into those stormy eyes told him she would stand her ground, fight for what she wanted.

Admiration flared through him again, but he throttled it back. He wasn't here to laud the few admirable qualities Maddie possessed. What he wanted was further leverage for his own purpose—because he had no intention of letting her get away.

'Very well. You will get what you need. In return, I have a condition of my own.'

Her eyes widened. 'What?'

He shook his head. 'We'll discuss it tonight. I have an appointment to get to.'

She worried at her lower lip with her teeth. It took a great deal of control for him not to stare.

'What if I don't like your condition?' she asked, with the tiniest quiver in her voice that Remi wanted to hear over and over again.

He stood before that battering temptation overwhelmed him. 'It's an offer of a lifetime. I'm confident you will agree. But if I'm wrong…' He shrugged. 'Then we'll revert to our previous agreement. The funds will be in your account within the hour.'

'I… Thank you.'

Against his will, his gaze moved over her face, her throat, the increased rise and fall of her breasts. The thought of tasting those lips again fired bolts of lightning through his bloodstream.

His blatant scrutiny made her colour heighten. He curled his fist against the need to trace her pink flesh.

'I trust you won't take my money and disappear?'

The challenging spark returned to her eyes as her chin lifted defiantly. 'I'm not going to keep proving myself to you. You can choose to trust me. Or not.'

Remi was still mulling over their conversation three hours later, as he sat down to lunch with his ambassador to the United Kingdom.

Maddie's fearless, plucky attitude would land her in hot water one day. Or make her irresistible to a man who was drawn to her fiery spirit. A man who would be free to kiss those intoxicating lips, mould her breathtaking curves…

He sucked in a breath, shifted as his manhood stirred to life.

Dio, what the hell was wrong with him?

He'd liked his life with Celeste. Had enjoyed her genteel nature, her generous acceptance of the challenges of being associated with a crown prince.

Nevertheless, hadn't he wished that on occasion that she

would challenge him more? Stand up for what she really wanted? Offer stimulating conversation instead of smilingly acceding to his wishes?

He stiffened, disgusted with himself for dishonouring her memory. His fiancée had been loved by everyone she'd come into contact with. He wouldn't sully her memory by comparing her to Maddie—a woman full of secrets. Full of fire. Full of hidden depths he wanted to explore.

With mounting frustration he snapped his napkin open, startling the ambassador. But, no matter how much he threw himself into their nitty-gritty discussion of geo-politics, he couldn't get the woman with the defiant green eyes and Cupid's bow lips out of his head.

Which was probably why he was still disgruntled when he returned to his hotel suite. His mood plummeted further when he found Maddie nowhere in sight.

He turned as Percy entered the room and subtly cleared his throat. 'Where is she?' he all but snapped.

'Miss Myers hasn't returned since she left this morning, Your Highness.'

Stomach-hollowing disappointment replaced his disgruntlement. 'She didn't return for lunch?' he asked sharply.

'No, Your Highness.'

She'd dared him to trust her. And he had. So much for thinking she was even a fraction of the woman Celeste had been.

Dismissing Percy, he plucked his phone from his pocket and dialled her number. Her husky voice directed him to leave a message.

Remi's mood blackened. He'd been well and truly duped. Considering she'd gone from being almost penniless to being twenty-five thousand pounds richer, courtesy of the wire transfer he'd approved, she could be anywhere by now.

The reason why she'd absconded with such a paltry sum when she could have been infinitely richer didn't even puzzle him. He'd seen her bank account, knew she'd been destitute. Desperately so. And he'd handed her the tools to leave him.

His jaw gritted. She wouldn't get away with it. They had an agreement.

About to summon his security chief, he froze at the sound of approaching footsteps.

She arrived on a whirlwind of silk and heels, her face flushed, a few wisps of hair escaping its sleek knot. Even flustered and flushed, she was a captivating sight. He stared, a fever sweeping through his veins.

'Where the hell have you been?' he snarled.

She screeched to a halt, her breathlessness drawing his gaze to her chest. 'Sorry, I—'

'And why did your phone go to voicemail?'

Her wide gaze dropped to the bag in her hand. 'Oh, no. I'm sorry. I forgot to turn it back on.'

His eyes narrowed. 'Back on? After what?' Again that spike of jealousy came from nowhere. 'Tell me where you've been, Maddie.'

She blinked, her face growing wary at his icy tone. 'I was with my father. He wasn't feeling well after...after we went to the estate agents to secure our new place.'

He frowned. 'You're moving house?'

She nodded. 'That's why I needed the money. For a down payment and to get the rental process started. Then I had to start packing. The whole thing took longer than I expected. I turned my phone off so I wouldn't be disturbed.'

'Considering I'm the only one supposed to have access to you, am I to assume you didn't want *me* to disturb you?'

'I just...needed to concentrate on my father, okay?'

'Why?'

She hesitated for a beat, then took a deep breath. 'My father isn't well. Everything took longer than I expected. But I'm here now...'

Wary green eyes met his. He loathed the wave of relief that swept through him. It strongly indicated something weighty he didn't want to acknowledge. Something compellingly close to possessiveness.

She shifted on her feet, commanding his attention.

'So are we okay? Or does that granite-hard jaw and the tight grip on your phone mean you're about to ask for your money back? If so, I won't be able to oblige. A good chunk of it is gone,' she informed him.

She was here now. He needed to let it go. But too many emotions still churned through him.

'If I'm not about to be summarily dismissed, can I ask a favour?' she asked.

'I suggest you quit while you're ahead. Or do you enjoy testing me?'

The merest hint of a smile curved lips glistening with whatever gloss she'd employed. With an elegant pirouette that wouldn't have been amiss in a ballet dancer, she turned away.

'Fine. I need help with my zip, but I'll ask Percy to give me a hand, shall I?' she asked, with a look over her shoulder.

His attention dropped to her bare shoulders and the silky-smooth expanse of her back. When he dragged his gaze back to her face she was staring at him with a hint of challenge in her eyes.

Dio, she could give the most notorious siren a run for her money.

She took a step towards the kitchen Percy had made his domain.

'Madeleine.'

Uttering her name was meant to be a warning. Instead it triggered something darker, more potent in the air. She stilled, her gaze widening as she watched him. 'Yes?'

'Stay.'

He approached without sensing his feet move. Her perfume filled his ravenous senses, stabbing him with a need to lower his head to that control-wrecking curve where her neck met her shoulder.

His not quite steady fingers found the zipper, slowly glided it upward while his hungry gaze roved over her light gold skin as the garment came together.

He barely heard her husky *thank you* over the loud drumming in his ears, and the sight of her cleavage when she turned to face him threatened to flay him.

Dio, this was getting out of hand.

'So, are we good?' she asked again.

'No,' he growled. 'We're late. And getting later by the second.'

She reached up to smooth back the wisp of hair that had escaped. When she dropped her arm she was the epitome of charm, poise and lethal temptation.

'Then what are waiting for?'

'This,' he muttered.

Like a starving man, he curled his hand over her nape and tugged her close. Wrapping his arm around her waist, he slanted his mouth over hers, his tongue delving between her lips as he attempted to slake his gutting hunger.

She froze against him for a single moment before her arms crept around his neck. Remi dragged her closer, slavish need sending him up in flames. When the weight of her firm breasts settled against his chest he groaned. His shaft thickened, his blood roiling as he tasted her deeply, heard her breathless whimper against his lips.

She was exquisite. Magnificent. And he wanted her more than he'd wanted anything for a long time.

They weren't going to make the first act of the opera. Their host would be disappointed but he would understand—because Remi was the Crown Prince of Montegova, after all. He would send ahead his apologies.

In a minute.

After he'd taken the edge off this insane hunger.

Maddie was barely aware of being lifted off her feet and carried out of the living room. Her senses attempted to return when Remi set her down next to a wide divan in the private living room attached to his bedroom.

Drunk on lust, she watched him tug off his tie and toss it away. Her skin grew tight, her whole body trembling in the peculiar fever only this man evoked. She curled her fingers in the soft expensive cloth for support.

'You know how phones work, Maddie. I expect you to pick up when I call. Understood?'

She blinked. 'Yes. In the future I will. But I've already apologised. Are you going to keep bullying me about it?'

Yes, she risked infuriating him further, but she couldn't seem to stop playing with fire where he was concerned. It wasn't surprising, therefore, when he prowled towards her, every masculine inch of him streamlined with purpose.

'I've never bullied anyone in my life. Whatever I've asked of you, you've given willingly, have you not? I don't intend that to change…especially in respect of our future liaisons,' he drawled.

She didn't want to know about those. She *really* didn't. 'Whatever you think they are, keep them to yourself. Why are we in here?' she asked breathlessly.

'Are you sure you don't know?' he taunted softly, staring down at her with single-minded purpose that made her senses jump.

His hands wrapped around her upper arms, sending sensual shockwaves rippling to her very toes.

'Remi, what are you doing?' Her voice was a panting rush.

'Seeing if I can free myself from this insanity,' he said darkly.

'What…what insanity?'

He didn't answer. Not vocally. He plastered her body against his hard length, searing her mouth in a kiss that erased her every last thought.

Every warning she'd armed herself with withered and died. With a helpless moan she wrapped her arms around his neck, jerking onto her tiptoes so she wouldn't miss a second of his kiss.

When he pushed her back onto the divan she went willingly, her senses on fire. He broke away abruptly, stared at her with eyes that glinted with a touch of bewilderment. Then he took her mouth again, kissing her with a wild, frenzied intensity as his hands roamed unapologetically over her body.

Maddie felt that same bewilderment flare through her, but it wasn't enough to stop the freight train of her desire. For now, the whys didn't matter. Especially not when he cupped her breast, moulded her yearning flesh for several teasing seconds before dragging his fingers over the tight peak.

She cried out, her own fingers digging beneath the lapels of his jacket to explore the tight muscles of his shoulders.

With an impatient growl, he levered himself off her, shrugged off the offending garment and tossed it away. Eyes glued to hers, he nudged her legs apart. Heat rushed into her face as his gaze slowly dropped to where her dress had ridden up her thighs.

One impatient hand pushed the material higher, exposing the tops of her garter belt and the lacy panties already growing damp with need.

He made a rough sound under his breath. Then he settled himself over her, the rigid column of his erection imprinting itself unashamedly against her damp centre as he fused his mouth to hers once more.

Time grew elastic. All Maddie knew was that she was at the point of screaming her need, of begging him to ease the terrible ache at her core when he reached between them and boldly cupped her sex.

He swallowed her hot gasp, his tongue flicking erotically against hers as his hand delved beneath the lace of her panties. Expert fingers grazed the swollen bundle of nerves and her whole body burned furnace-hot. She wasn't aware that her nails had dug into his shoulders until he flinched and raised his head.

For a taut moment, stormy eyes stared down at her. 'How are you doing this to me?' he muttered thickly, as another whisper of guilty bewilderment flickered over his face.

Her face flamed. 'I… I'm…'

He shook his head, denying her stuttered response. Still staring at her, he let his fingers explore, circling her slowly, erotically. Another whimper burst from her throat and, seeing the single-minded purpose on his face, she felt a tiny sliver of apprehension pierce through her desire.

He was touching her where no other man had.

Suddenly the virginity she'd pushed to one side in her fight for survival became a precious commodity she didn't want to throw away on a quick fumble. Certainly not with a man who looked at her with guilt-laden eyes.

She grabbed his wrist, halting the wicked onslaught between her thighs. 'Remi…'

He stilled, his eyes widening a fraction as he slowly exhaled. 'You want me to stop?' he breathed in quiet astonishment, as if he couldn't believe it.

She couldn't believe it either. 'I…' The denial that had surged so true in her head moments ago faltered.

His free hand spiked into her hair and his lips found the sensitive area beneath her ear. Delirium heightened and she fought to breathe.

'I don't know why I crave you like this. If you really want me to stop, say so,' he rasped in her ear.

She squeezed her eyes shut, absorbing the thrilling shiver that coursed through her before she attempted to find her voice again. 'I'm not stopping you… I'm… I don't know…' She paused, self-consciousness pummelling her. 'I'm a virgin,' she finally blurted.

He reared back as if he'd been shot, expelling a stunned breath as he stared down at her. With hectic colour staining his cheeks, and hair dishevelled from her frenzied exploration, he was the most spectacular sight she'd ever seen.

Maddie wanted to rise up, explore more of him before this thing inevitably ended. But then that skilful hand began to move again. Slowly. Tortuously.

'Tell me why you're twenty-four and still a virgin,' he demanded, his grey eyes almost black with stormy desire.

The pleasure strumming through her almost made her vision blur. 'Before you jump to conclusions—no, I haven't been waiting around for the perfect opportunity to hand my virginity to a crown prince. You're... You don't have the monopoly on emotional challenges. I was let down by someone I trusted. After that sex became...inconsequential.'

That wave of possessiveness washed over his face again, and then, his eyes still boring into hers, his touch intensified. There was something mind-melting about having him watch every whimper of pleasure he drew from her.

By the time he circled one finger at her entrance, she was a mindless wreck. She wasn't going to pass out. She refused to. She wanted to remember every second of this ride. Because it had to stop soon.

'Whoever he was, did he make you feel like this?' he rasped gruffly.

Her hair unravelled further as she shook her head. 'Never,' she whispered.

'Do you want me to stop?'

She swallowed. 'No...'

Pure male satisfaction flared over his face. Then, before she could wrestle back the last of her sanity and put a stop to this madness, his finger slid inside her. Slowly. Carefully. Ensuring she felt every breath-stealing second of invasion.

Her muscles clenched around him, greedily absorbing the giddy sensation. Then Remi touched the barrier of her innocence and the look on his face was transformed again, eclipsing all previous emotions.

Her heart lurched, thumped wildly against her ribs as

she deciphered it. Shock. Hunger. *Possessiveness.* Raw and unadulterated.

She shouldn't be feeling so exhilarated. Shouldn't be allowing that fever to rage even more fiercely through her bloodstream.

'Dio mio, veramente exquisitivo,' he breathed.

'Remi…'

'Be calm, my beautiful innocent. I'll safeguard your treasure,' he muttered thickly.

He didn't remove his touch. Instead he levered himself over her, that enthralling finger moving in and out of her as he started to kiss her again, his tongue mimicking the action of his finger.

Maddie had no warning, no way to prepare herself when bliss shattered what remained of her world. With her fingers buried in his hair, Maddie gave herself over to intoxicating sensation, a slave to the magic of his fingers as he sent her soaring high.

She was aware that a hoarse scream ripped from her but she didn't care. It was all she could do to hold on to him as her world exploded in fragments of colour.

When she came to, she was alone on the sofa. Remi stood framed between the two heavy drapes at the window, his gaze on the street below. Whether he was granting her time to compose herself or was once again caught in the grip of furious guilt—she suspected the latter—she was thankful for the reprieve.

Quickly she straightened her clothes, passed a shaky hand over her hair just as he turned around. For a full minute he simply looked at her, until a different, more self-conscious flame rushed over her skin.

'Why are you looking at me like that?' she asked, the shakiness racking her body infusing her voice.

'You're a beautiful and desirable woman.' His voice was heavy, gravel-rough.

Her skin burned hotter. 'That sounds like an accusation.'

His hand slashed the air. 'Perhaps I'm still trying to understand—'

'Look there's no great mystery, okay? I had a boyfriend—'

'A *boyfriend*?' He spat out the word as if it was poisonous, his eyebrows knotting in a thunderous frown.

'Yes, you know what those are, don't you?'

Her sarcasm bounced off him, his expression remaining the same as he slid his hands into his pockets. 'Tell me. I want to know.'

'Greg and I grew up together. I thought we were friends. We fell out of touch for a while, but when I needed a friend I called him. We grew…close. I thought I was in a trusting relationship with him. Until I found out my plight was fodder for his amusement with his rich friends. Not only that, turns out Greg makes a habit of seeking out women and talking them into taking risky financial ventures with his company. Unfortunately I was one of those naïve victims.'

Maddie couldn't disguise her bitterness, nor shake off the heavy weight of her own failure and Greg's betrayal. She'd trusted him enough to hand over the last of her father's savings, with his reassurance that his stockbroking firm would double her money within a few months, ensuring she would have enough for his rehabilitation, filling her with wild hope.

She'd lost everything.

Remi exhaled sharply. 'Did you report him to the authorities?'

She shrugged again. 'It was all above-board, apparently. Greg claimed I'd willingly signed on the dotted line and that I knew the high risk of the investments he was making on my behalf. There was just enough truth in his story and, using our history, he convinced the authorities that I was a bitter ex-girlfriend with a grudge. He got away with it. And I was left with nothing but the clothes on my back and, yes, my virginity.'

Remi walked towards her, his eyes fixed on her face. 'Is he the reason you're caught in this lifestyle?' he asked thinly.

'It would be easy to blame everything on him. But, no, he just happened to be one straw in the bundle that eventually broke me.'

One sleekly masculine eyebrow rose. 'You think yourself broken?'

She shrugged. 'I'm currently living with a strange man who likes to throw his weight about, berate me when I'm fifteen minutes late and is paying me for the privilege. What would you call that?'

'I call it negotiating for what you want without compromising what's important to you. And I'm not strange,' he tagged on.

Maddie bit her lip against the smile that wanted to escape. 'Careful, Remi, or I might think you respect me.'

The corner of his mouth twitched for half a second before that bewildered frown returned ten-fold and he turned away sharply.

'There you go, treating me like I'm a leper again.'

He froze. 'What are you talking about?'

She shook her head. 'What happened on the sofa wasn't planned, so if you're going to hate yourself for it could you please do it elsewhere?'

She wasn't completely sure that she wouldn't welcome a repeat, despite the polarising vibes now emanating from Remi. And just what did that say about her willpower?

'Maddie—'

'If we're not going out, I'd like to go to my suite now, please,' she interrupted, not sure she could take any more of that look on his face.

For another long moment he stared narrow-eyed at her, until stinging awareness grew into unbearable proportions. He opened his mouth, but before he could speak his phone burst to life.

He stared at the screen with a mixture of grim resolution and irritation. 'I need to take this call. Then we'll talk. Yes?'

Licking her lips, Maddie nodded, managing to hold herself together until he left the room. Then she hightailed it to her suite on embarrassingly shaky legs.

She was staring into space, her senses roiling out of control, when her own phone rang.

It was with trembling hands and an unfocused mind that she answered. It took a minute for Mrs Jennings's distressed tones to sink in. And as Maddie rushed for the door she was almost grateful for the distraction of this new bombshell that had been thrown into her life.

Because now she didn't have to dwell on the terrifying knowledge that what she'd just experienced with Remi Montegova had fundamentally changed her. And that there might be no going back.

CHAPTER SIX

REMI SUPPRESSED ANOTHER groan as he stepped out of his dressing room and headed back into his private living room. At the ringtone announcing his mother's call, part of him had relished the news he intended to give her, even though he knew she would resist it. But he'd already warned her he would do things his way.

With the charged tension between them, he'd been reluctant to leave Maddie, and he'd almost changed his mind on seeing the lingering arousal in her eyes. Remembering the taste of her. Her unfettered responses. Her tight innocence.

The cold shower he'd taken minutes ago, after cancelling his invitation to the opera, was rendered useless as his body surged in fiery recollection. He quickened his steps. And arrived in an empty room.

Maddie wasn't in the main living room. Or in her suite.

'Where is she?' He repeated his earlier question to Percy when he rushed into the kitchen. Only this time he instinctively knew he would like the answer even less than last time.

'She's gone, Your Highness. She requested a taxi fifteen minutes ago.'

Remi attempted to rein in his irritating alarm as he dialled Maddie's phone. The request to leave a message reminded him that she'd confessed to switching her phone off. They'd been distracted by other matters before she could turn it on again.

Anger rising, he picked up the suite's phone and dialled Raoul, his chief of security.

'Where is she?' he snapped for a third time.

'She's in a taxi heading south, Your Highness.'

'Why did she leave?' Remi despised the intensity of the disquieting sensation.

'She didn't say, Your Highness. She only said to tell you something came up.'

Remi took a long, deep breath, aware of his fraying control. 'Did something happen this afternoon? Something to indicate what was suddenly so urgent?' he breathed.

'I'm sorry, Your Highness. I don't know.'

Fury cut through his disquiet. But even that was unwelcome. He was far too wrapped up in Maddie Myers. And yet he couldn't locate an off switch. That cloying need to know everything about her smash through him again.

Dio, he was being irrational. The woman had a right to her secrets, whatever they were. But the sensation wouldn't go away. The discovery of her innocence had revealed another facet of her character that stunned him. But his admiration for Maddie for standing on her own two feet in the face of her challenges was also the reason he was annoyed with her now.

And, call him a chauvinist, but her streak of independence was beginning to grate as badly as her absence. After the pleasure he'd given her, after watching her come apart so spectacularly in his arms, would it hurt her to yield to him a little?

His mouth firmed even as his shaft stiffened at the reminder of what they'd shared on his sofa. He'd felt her innocence. Felt it and experienced a primitive urge to claim it.

He wasn't ashamed to admit the discovery had taken him completely by surprise, that even the thought that he would be betraying Celeste's memory hadn't been enough to dissipate the untamed hunger that prowled through him even now.

Last night, when a cold shower hadn't frozen the hunger or dispatched the guilt that had settled on his shoulders, he'd forced himself to take another path, to think rationally about the problem he faced.

The call with his mother had settled that once and for all.

He refocused. 'I'm coming downstairs. You know where she's headed. Take me to her.'

'Immediately, Your Highness,' Raoul replied.

He slammed the phone down and cursed Maddie's elusiveness.

Even though he'd never taken advantage of it, the privilege of his birth included never having to pursue a woman. Women of standing and gold-diggers alike made no bones about their willingness to fall into his bed at the slightest display of interest.

Barely an hour ago Maddie had succumbed to his caresses—then immediately dismissed him. He was finding that a…unique experience. One he didn't wish to repeat.

Irritation intensifying, he dialled her number again. For the third time her smoky tones directed him to leave a message. He tossed the phone away, his teeth meeting in a hard clench.

She'd better not to be with another man. *Or what?* The voice in his head taunted. *He'd go against all his breeding and make a scene?*

Why not? *She was his.*

Remi froze as the enormity of those three words hooked into him, unshakeable and real.

As he tried to breathe through the dizzying sensation his phone rang again. He snatched it up. Leaden disappointment seized his gut when he saw his mother's number displayed on the screen. For the first time in his life, Remi did something un-prince-like. He ignored the Queen's summons.

His mood hadn't improved one iota by the time they turned into the street he'd delivered Maddie to after their first meeting. He exited the vehicle and followed Raoul to the shabby, nondescript entrance to a tiny ground-floor flat. The door before him was thin and insubstantial, with peeling green paint.

Swallowing his distaste, he leaned on the bell, gratified when he heard a jangle of sound within. The sight of a dishevelled Maddie immediately reversed that sensation.

'What are you doing here?' she blurted, with a hasty look over her shoulder.

'You will let me in,' he instructed.

Her chin lifted. 'Will I?'

'Unless you want your neighbours to witness our conversation, yes.'

Her gaze darted past him to the six bodyguards stationed on the street and the sleek convoy of his motorcade, which was already drawing attention.

'Or you can just get back into your vehicle and leave?' she suggested hopefully.

His gut churned harder. 'I'm not leaving. This will go easier if you let me in.'

Her face paled a little but she stood her ground. 'I'd really rather not.'

'For both our sakes, I hope you didn't leave my bed to be with another man.' The very thought of it sent a spike of anger and jealousy through Remi.

Her eyes widened with shock, then anger. 'You think I left you to come to another man?'

He didn't—not completely. But the possessive beast holding him prisoner wouldn't let go, and nor would the thought that, having touched her innocence, she belonged to *him*, no matter how irrational both notions were.

He tried clinical reason. The decision he'd made would slake this unrelenting hunger within him so things could settle back to rationality. So he could focus on his duty and obligation to his crown. Where was the harm in that?

The harm is your betrayal.

The gentle voice in his head drew ice over his roiling emotions.

Remi exhaled and reasoned with it. It wasn't a betrayal if his kingdom needed him. He'd been tasked to find a solution. It was as simple as that.

He focused on Maddie's face. 'You left without telling me, after agreeing to stay. You'll pardon me if I don't have the fullest confidence in you right now.'

'I left because I had an emergency,' she replied hotly. 'I didn't think you'd appreciate me stomping into your bathroom to inform you.'

'What about using the phone I gave you?'

She mangled her lip again, drawing his attention to the swollen curve he'd kissed less than two hours ago. His groin tightened, and he felt that hot flash of lust flooding him again.

'I wasn't exactly thinking straight, all right?'

A rustle of noise from inside the flat made her tense. Nervous, she attempted to minimise the space between herself and the door.

'You have five seconds to let me in before I walk away, Maddie. You'll recall I had another proposition to discuss with you. But if I leave both our agreement and the new proposal will go away.'

She hesitated another moment before her gaze boldly met his. 'I'll let you in—but, for the record, I won't be judged. If I see so much as a trace of judgement on your face, this is over.'

The urge to remind her who she was talking to reared up, but Remi found himself nodding, agreeing to her terms of entry.

She released the door and stepped back to reveal a dank hallway with threadbare carpets and more peeling paint on the walls. It offended his every sensibility to know she lived in this appalling place. She didn't belong here. She belonged in a palace, among the finest things in life, draped in silks and sparkling jewellery, being fed the best gourmet meals and treats that would produce her thousand-watt smile.

Most of all she belonged in a world where that anxiety on her face was taken away for ever.

He wanted to be the one to do that for her.

Remi stiffened in shock at the direction of his thoughts, then assured himself that his reasoning dovetailed with his own goals.

'I guess you've changed your mind,' she said, a flicker of hurt mingling with disappointment at his reaction to her surroundings.

He blocked the door before she could shut it in his face, stepped inside and shut it firmly behind him. He stared down at her, breathing in the alluring perfume that still clung to her despite being in this dismal place. Her elegant throat moved in a swallow, her fingers fidgeting with the folds of her dress. He wanted to plaster her against that dirty wall, lose himself in her the way he'd craved to do in his suite.

Another rustle from inside reminded him they weren't alone.

Abruptly, she turned and hurried down the hall.

Remi followed, arriving in a shabby living room full of mismatched dilapidated furniture and packing boxes, to find her crouching over a shrunken figure.

'I think the water spilled on the floor,' the figure croaked.

'It's fine. I'll take care of it,' Maddie murmured softly.

Remi took in the scene. The man couldn't be more than fifty years old, although he looked much older and in an appalling state of health. Nevertheless, the familial resemblance was evident from the eyes that took him in for one unfocused moment before sliding away to Maddie.

'Who's this?' the man asked.

Remi stepped forward, extending his hand to the man wearing threadbare clothes that hung on his bony figure. 'I'm Remirez Montegova. You must be Maddie's father.'

The older man's lips twisted, his gaze resting heavily on his daughter. 'You would think *she* was the parent, the way she chivvies me. Perhaps you can talk some sense into her—get her to give me what I need.'

'What you need is rest,' she replied firmly, although Remi caught the slight wobble in her chin.

Remi took a closer look at the man, his gut tightening at the evidence of addiction.

'I'll get you some more water,' Maddie said.

She picked up a plastic cup and hurried out of the room. Remi followed.

The kitchen was in a worse state than the living room, but again he swallowed his distaste as Maddie turned around.

'Whatever you're going to say, save it.'

'Very well, I won't ask if you have the necessary health shots to survive living in a place like this. Instead I'll ask how long you think you can keep your father on that sofa when it's clear he needs advanced medical attention?'

Anger and frustration sparked fire in her eyes. 'You think I don't *know* what he needs?' She lifted a shaky hand to her temple. 'I had a system in place. It wasn't brilliant but it was working—until…'

'Until?' he bit out.

Despair replaced her anger. 'He's been so good,' she whispered. 'We were almost there.'

'He's relapsed?' Remi guessed accurately.

She nodded miserably. 'Now the hospital won't take him.'

'What hospital?'

'The one I was taking him to for a kidney transplant.' She shook her head and picked up the cup with a shaky hand. 'Why am I even telling you any of this?'

He stepped forward and took the cup from her before she dropped it. For one unguarded moment he basked in the added leverage he'd been granted. Then he was reminded of life's cruelties, and the wisdom of seizing opportunities when they arose. At some point between last night and this morning he'd decided this woman was the answer to his dilemma. He wasn't about to be swayed by softer feelings.

He set the cup down.

'What are you doing?' she demanded. 'I have to—'

'Your father doesn't need water. He needs urgent care.'

'Yes—the kind that requires money!'

His eyes narrowed. 'The money I'm paying you?'

'Of course. Why else would I subject myself to your presence?' she sniped.

Remi wanted to kiss those insolent lips, run his mouth, his tongue, his teeth over her flawless skin and keep going until he possessed her completely.

He suppressed the wild craving. Just as he suppressed the guilt. For whatever reason, this lust had a hold on him for now, but he knew the moment he had her the thrill would be over. For now he needed to concentrate on achieving his immediate goals.

'What I'm paying you will be nowhere near enough to give him the proper care he requires.'

She frowned. 'Of course it will. I spoke to the hospital myself. I know exactly what I need.'

'Does that include long-term after-care? Does it include a contingency plan if he rejects the organ? Or treating the myriad complications that could arise? What about now he's relapsed? How long was he to remain clean before they would perform the operation?'

'Six months,' she whispered, her face paler than before.

'So you're going sit around for another six months before you can reschedule?'

'Enough with the questions. I really don't need you to point out my problems to me.'

'Good. Then allow me to provide a solution.'

Wary blue eyes met his. 'What?'

He pushed his hands into his pockets, took a step back from her so he could think more clearly without the enthralling scent of her warm, perfumed skin fracturing his thoughts. 'There's a clinic in Switzerland, funded by my family. It's secluded, with state-of-the-art facilities, and most importantly discretion is guaranteed.'

'Don't tell me—it's where you royals go to dry out when you fall off your gilded wagons?'

Remi remained silent. He wasn't about to confirm that Jules had been the main reason for their association with the Swiss clinic.

'Why are you taunting me with this medical wonderland?' she asked guardedly, her arms around her middle.

A deep twinge lanced his chest. He ruthlessly suppressed it. He was providing an immediate solution to a dire problem. One that suited them both.

'It isn't a taunt. I can have your father there within the next twenty-four hours.'

She sucked a breath. 'Why are you helping me? My problems have nothing to do with you, and if I recall correctly I've agreed to do what I need to do to earn my keep.'

'Because I require your services for longer.'

Her eyes narrowed. 'How much longer?'

He hesitated, simply because he hadn't considered this. How long? Long enough to appease his people? His mother? His own desire for her?

The latter would scorch itself out sooner rather than later. The hotter the passion, the quicker it burned out, right? As for his mother—she'd come round to his idea too. As she'd said, they'd both been seduced by the idea of for ever, only to be disappointed by fate. This time he intended to use his head rather than his heart.

Which only left the well-being of his people. They'd been through one scandal in the recent past. Montegova required stability. Not stability that would cost him a lifetime but for the foreseeable future nevertheless.

'Remi? What sort of services?' There was apprehension in her voice, but also hope.

The twinge dissipated and he breathed more easily. 'I'll ensure your father receives the treatment he needs to get him back on his feet. You need never worry about him again.'

She took an unsteady breath. 'And in return…?' she pressed again.

'In return, I want you to marry me.'

Maddie had misheard him. This was cruel payback for her abrupt departure from the hotel. His irritation on arrival on her doorstep, her unwillingness to allow him in, his distaste at being subjected to the evidence of her destitution… All of it amounted to this…this humourless joke at her expense.

The fact that her heart had stopped for several exhilarating seconds, that she'd wanted to snatch the words from the air, hold them in her heart, was equally cruel.

Remi wanted her. She wasn't blind to that fact. But this… What he'd said…

She shook her head. 'The door is behind you, Remi. Feel free to use it.'

Brackets formed around his mouth as he stared her down with intense displeasure. 'Excuse me? Perhaps you didn't hear—'

'I heard you just fine. And I don't appreciate you wasting my time with your jokes—'

'You think my asking you to marry me is amusing?'

Laughter erupted from her throat before she could stop it. She regretted it almost immediately. In her defence, she needed a coping mechanism against the wild hope that surged when he'd said those words.

I want you to marry me.

Cold reality set in. She looked around the tattered grey kitchen that strained to contain the powerful, endlessly magnetic royal planted in the middle of it. There were no visible contaminants, so she wasn't hallucinating. No. Remi Montegova was in complete control of his faculties. And the force of his stare strongly suggested that he was awaiting her answer.

Dear God. 'You're not joking?'

His nostrils flared, a sure sign that he was offended by her response. 'I assure you I am not.'

'But…that doesn't make sense.'

Her words triggered a shift in his expression. An understanding, almost. He nodded. 'Perhaps I went about this the wrong way. I need to explain.'

'Please do,' she encouraged, still unable to believe her ears.

His gaze flicked to the grimy window before returning to her. 'After my father's death we uncovered his extramarital affairs and the existence of Jules. It caused a lot of instability within the kingdom. My marriage and coronation were supposed to allay that but then…' His jaw tightened. 'Then I lost Celeste and I had to put off taking the throne.'

'Why does that matter? Your people still love you, surely?'

Something flickered through his eyes, but his demeanour remained austere. 'My mother wants to step down from the throne,' he announced solemnly.

The unexpected revelation drew a gasp. 'That means you'll be…king.'

He nodded. 'It's not exactly news, but it seems there's a new urgency now.'

'Why?'

'The Montegovan people are forward-thinking in many ways, but they're also traditionalists. They would prefer a widowed monarch than an unmarried one.'

'You mean they think you're unsuitable because you're single?'

He shrugged. 'To them I may be king, but I'm also just a man, subject to the weaknesses of the flesh. They don't expect me to live a monk-like existence. And, as my father proved, even married monarchs aren't infallible.'

The idea of Remi with a faceless woman shot a dart of anguish through her. She struggled to keep it from showing. 'So to take the throne you need to be married?'

'In the face of the challenges my family is currently facing, yes.'

She snatched in another shaky breath. 'And you think choosing someone like me to be your...your *wife* is the answer?' Even saying the word left her a little dazed. 'Didn't I read somewhere that you have a handy list of potential brides to choose from?'

His features clenched. 'I won't be dictated to on who I choose as my wife and Queen.'

Her heart stuttered again. 'Are you telling me there aren't committees and meetings and strategising before royal marriages are arranged?'

He remained silent for a minute. The atmosphere throbbed with charged emotions before he spoke. 'Celeste and I met at a tea party thrown by the royal housekeeper for her grandson when I was six and she was three. My mother didn't believe in separating the staff's children from the royal children. Celeste could easily have been the granddaughter of the stable manager and we would still have been engaged to marry.'

'But she wasn't, was she? She was part of your world, approved by your mother,' she insisted.

'I didn't ask for her approval then. I am not asking for it now.'

The knot in Maddie's belly tightened as he spoke of his fiancée. She fought to see things from his point of view of cold rationality. They had mutual problems that demanded a solution. Still a cold breeze washed over her.

'It's that simple for you? That clinical?'

A grim smile twisted his lips. 'It's best if I approach this with my eyes wide open.'

As opposed to being in love? As opposed to swearing his undying devotion to the woman who was now six feet under and would probably hold his heart for ever?

The chill intensified within her and she shook her head. 'Even if I wanted to marry you—and I don't—all you would be doing would be inviting more speculation about you... about your choice of bride.'

His face slowly hardened. 'Is that your final answer?'

She opened her mouth to say no, it *wasn't* her final answer. She needed time to wrap her head around the shocking concept. To get herself on safe ground after the bombshell of his question.

Maddie closed her mouth again. With a deep breath, she looked deep into his eyes, searched his features. And with an unshakeable force she realised he truly meant it. Remi Montegova really was asking her to marry him.

She shook her head.

For several seconds he said nothing, those vivid eyes fixed on her face. When it got too much to bear, she dragged her gaze away. In the carefree days of her childhood, she'd daydreamed like most girls about that special moment when the man of her dreams would propose to her.

Not for a single second had she imagined it would be a clinical proposition from a real-life crown prince in the middle of a decrepit kitchen in a near-derelict flat.

'Maddie.' Her name was a burst of icy impatience.

She shook her head again. 'I'm sorry—'

The words were barely out of her mouth before he turned and strode purposefully out of the kitchen. She remained frozen in place, the shock of his abrupt departure holding her prisoner until the sound of a hacking cough ripped through the air.

She came to her senses with a gasp, the stark reminder of her father's condition and the growing dread that the only solution to his recovery was walking out the door galvanising her into movement.

Somewhere between rushing out of the kitchen and throwing herself against the front door to stop Remi from opening it, she wondered if she'd been struck with some sort of madness. But what choice did she have? Her father wouldn't make it for another six months.

So she placed herself before him, forced herself to look up into the stone-hard, brutally gorgeous face of Crown Prince Remi Montegova and said one word. 'Wait.'

One very regal, very haughty eyebrow lifted. 'You need to say more. I wish to hear the words, Maddie.'

'Are…are you sure this is what you want?'

Ruthless determination blazed through his eyes. 'I'm sure of what I want. Be sure of what *you* want and tell me.'

Maddie swallowed, and with the strongest notion that she was stepping into a dangerous abyss she whispered, 'I'll marry you.'

CHAPTER SEVEN

MADDIE CLENCHED HER jaw tight against the urge to take the words back, to step away from the precipice of the wild unknown upon which she somehow found herself poised. But an even greater power kept her rooted to the spot, kept her words locked in her throat as she stared up at the man she'd just agreed to marry.

In turn, he stared down at her, the light that gleamed in his eyes moments ago gone, and in its place a flat regard that set a whole new wave of anxiety blooming beneath her skin.

What had she done?

She finally managed to unglue her tongue, but before she could speak he stepped up to her. One hand rose, hovered next to her face before his fingers slowly brushed her cheek, her neck, rested on her shoulders.

'A word of advice before this thing goes forward, Maddie. This is merely a transaction—a marriage of convenience for the sake of Montegova and my people. It would be wise not to think any more of it.'

Something withered and died inside her—something she hadn't even known existed until she'd lost it. The yawing emptiness it left behind made her furiously regroup, tighten the reins around her scattered emotions.

'Are you warning me not to fall in love with you?' She infused her voice with as much haughtiness as she could and knew she'd struck the mark when his eyes narrowed.

'That is exactly what I'm saying,' he confirmed.

She inhaled shakily and for a moment was ashamed of her treacherous body and the weakness Remi evoked within her. Was it that same weakness Greg had seen in her and taken advantage of?

The thought straightened her spine. 'Thank you, but that somewhat presumptuous warning isn't necessary. I've already learned my lesson once before. You may be a great catch in your royal circles, but you're not exactly my type.'

His expression morphed from coldly forbidding into… something else. Something that removed the flatness from his eyes and replaced it with a gleam of challenge.

Maddie ignored the skitter of alarm and attempted to shrug off the hand that lay too close to the pulse hammering at her throat. His hold lightened, turned into more of a caress as it drifted down her arm to rest at her elbow.

'And what exactly is your type?'

Less charismatic. Less overwhelming. Less…everything.

She didn't voice the words. He was gorgeously imperious, irresistibly arrogant enough.

A round of deep coughing shattered the thick silence, dragging her attention from the enticing magic of his touch. When she darted away from him Remi dropped his hand, but he didn't step out of her way.

'I have to go and see to my father,' she said.

'We have further issues to discuss.'

She swallowed, the enormity of what she'd agreed to hovering like an electric storm. 'I know.'

He nodded. 'But first I'll make arrangements for your father to be moved from here in the next few hours.'

Surprised by the dizzying speed of his actions, she nodded. 'Thank you.'

'I'm merely facilitating your smooth transition into my life, Maddie.'

A transaction. Nothing more. 'I'm still grateful,' she replied.

Something shifted in his gaze, but he looked away before she could decipher it. With a hand on the door, he paused. 'I expect you back in the suite by six o'clock. Pack whatever you need from this place. You will not be returning.'

He was gone by the time the mild panic freezing her

vocal cords had receded. She looked around the soulless hallway, wondering if the last ten minutes had truly happened. Had she really just agreed to marry the future King of Montegova? A man who'd warned her not to fall in love with him?

The vice that had wrapped around her chest at the warning tightened. Breathing through it, she hurried into the living room. Her father had fallen into a light sleep, his chest rasping with every breath.

She'd been more frightened than shocked when she'd received Mrs Jennings's call. She had disposed of the painkillers she'd found after a frantic search, knowing full well it was already too late for her father's operation.

But it wasn't too late to save him. And if the answer was to marry Remi...

Even now she couldn't complete the overwhelming thought. Was this price too high to pay?

She stared down at her father and firmed her lips.

No price was too high.

But as she tucked a blanket around him and hurried to her room she knew that wasn't altogether true. There was a reason her instincts had warned her to stay away from Remi the first time she'd seen him in that nightclub. But, unlike her blind trust when she'd believed Greg, she was walking into this with her eyes wide open. Besides, Remi wasn't plying her with false promises.

That reassurance firmly in place, she fished out her suitcase.

Maddie took her most valued possessions—pictures and mementoes of her and her parents in happier times, the necklace they'd given her on her sixteenth birthday...

She was still locked in a semi-haze when a team of six medical staff arrived on her doorstep two hours later.

Their firm, efficient manner reassured Maddie that her father was in good hands. Her anxiety abated further when Henry accepted his new situation with surprising alacrity.

He even emerged from his stupor to return her grip when she held on to him for one last minute before he was loaded into the private ambulance.

Tears filled her eyes when he caressed her cheek. 'Be all right, Dad. You're all I have. Please be all right,' she whispered fervently.

He gave her a sad smile. 'I'll do my best, sweetheart.'

'Promise me,' she insisted, even though she knew she shouldn't.

He closed his eyes for a long second. Then he nodded. 'I promise.'

The doctor stepped forward, shattering the moment. 'We'll prep your father at our Chelsea clinic in preparation for his flight to Geneva tomorrow.'

Maddie swiped at her eyes and swallowed the lump in her throat. 'It's happening that quickly?'

The doctor nodded. 'We've been instructed to get your father on the road to recovery as soon as possible.'

Remi. All afternoon, despite being gone, his presence had lingered in the form of the gleaming SUV on the street and the two bodyguards within it.

They followed her to the clinic now, and one stood outside her father's room—ready, as he'd informed her, to escort her back to the hotel.

With her father hooked up to IV fluids and falling asleep, Maddie knew she couldn't linger. The moment she stepped into the hall the bodyguard fell in behind her, steering her out through a discreet entrance and into the SUV.

What felt like only minutes later they were back at the hotel. Her already shortened breath evaporated as Remi, tall and commanding, materialised before her when the lift doors parted. With an elegant hand, he gestured to his suite. She told herself it was no use baulking at the silent command. She was doing this with her eyes wide open.

'I trust everything is all right with your father?' he asked.

She nodded, her gaze flicking to him as she sensed his

repressed impatience. 'He was looking better even before I left.' She mentally crossed her fingers that it would continue.

'That's good. Sit down, Maddie.'

She sat. The quicker they got this discussion over with, the quicker she could retreat to her own suite, deal with the shock that hadn't quite abated.

Percy's arrival with a tray of drinks only added to the surreal sensation. She watched in silence as he uncorked a bottle of champagne, poured out two glasses and then with a respectful bow made himself scarce.

'Are we celebrating?'

Remi simply shrugged one shoulder. 'I'm aware that I may have appeared a little…clinical before.' He prowled over to her, one glass extended.

Maddie took it, unable to drag her gaze from his powerful leanness. 'So now you're trying to soften yourself towards me? Are you afraid I'm going to change my mind?'

'You've given me your word and I'm learning that you're a woman of your word.'

Before she'd fully absorbed that unexpected compliment, he continued.

'But I also wish to demonstrate that I will not be a complete ogre in our marriage.'

Marriage. The word still had the ability to churn her guts and rob her of breath. Which was probably why she simply bobbed her head.

'Shall we drink to that?'

There was a tightness in his voice she would have hazarded a guess was anxiety in any other man than the one standing before her. Whatever it was, it brought even more acute awareness when he lowered his body into the seat next to hers, suffusing her with his intoxicating scent.

She trembled as he clinked his glass against hers and as she took a sip of exquisite champagne, very much aware that his eyes were fixed on her face. 'What else did you want to discuss?'

He sipped his drink too, then placed his glass on the coffee table. 'It's imperative that we make this marriage work for the sake of my people. There has to be a smooth transition when my mother steps down. Which is why we need to expedite this. You father will soon be on his way to Geneva. Even if you weren't committed elsewhere you wouldn't be able to visit him. He'll be in isolation for the next eight weeks. If we are to marry in five weeks then—'

'Five *weeks*?'

He tensed. 'You object to that?'

'I thought… You're the Crown Prince, soon to be King. Doesn't a royal wedding take months…*years* to plan?'

'My mother has been waiting two years for me to be married. She's motivated to make it happen sooner rather than later.'

The reminder that his last wedding had been brutally thwarted by tragedy dropped like an anvil between them. A glance at his face showed that forbidding expression, blocking everything else out.

Maddie knew he was undertaking this marriage out of duty to his people alone. He'd even gone so far as to tell her not to fall in love with him because his heart was committed for ever to someone else.

She quickly averted her gaze, snatched in a breath when she spotted how close she was to spilling champagne all over herself, but when she started to shift away from him he stopped her with a hand on her arm.

'One last thing.'

She gritted her teeth. 'Yes?'

'Although this isn't a love match, I expect you to act a certain way when we're in public.'

Maddie couldn't stop a bitter laugh from spilling out. 'So I'm expected to fawn over you in public, am I?'

'Within reason and the appropriate comportment, yes.'

God, he was unbelievable. 'What about you? Do you

get a pass in the fawning department or is this a *quid pro quo* situation?'

He stiffened. 'Be assured I'll do my part,' he said.

Despite the weird somersaults in her tummy, she grimaced. 'Is all that really necessary?'

'It is. Part of your wedding preparation will be tutoring in the art of diplomacy.'

Unable to withstand his touch without giving away the sensations rampaging through her, Maddie rose. He remained seated, but his eyes stayed on her as she paced in front of the coffee table. When she opened her mouth, he stopped her with a commanding hand.

'If you're about to express reservations, you're wasting your time. Things may seem overwhelming at first, but I'm assured you'll rise to the occasion.'

'I'm glad one of us is confident.'

'You're twenty-four years old. You were little more than a child when the burden of taking care of your father fell on your shoulders. You turned your life inside out for him. I am confident our marriage will be far less challenging.'

Because he would never feel the wild, dizzying breadth of emotion for her that he'd felt for Celeste.

The churning inside her intensified as he rose and advanced towards her. When he cupped her cheeks, tilted her face up to his and angled his head towards hers, she stopped breathing.

Without speaking, he sealed his mouth over hers.

The kiss was thorough, deep and knee-buckling. Steel-like arms gripped her, plastering her body against his as he patiently, ruthlessly, explored her.

When it was over he raised his head. For several seconds they stared at one another as her pulse thundered in her ears.

'What…what was that for?' she eventually stuttered.

'Practice. For all the ways that count, Maddie, I expect this marriage to appear real.'

* * *

From that moment on the series of events that tripped into each other was exponentially overwhelming. Both in London and Montegova, the publicity ball was rolling forward, gathering furious momentum.

When they left the hotel for the airport the next morning, it was through the front doors, to find media interest triple the size of any they'd encountered hitherto.

'What's going on?' she asked.

'My press office have alerted the right people that my interest in you has become something…*more.*'

He didn't answer any of the media's frenzied questions, but his hold around her was proprietorial, the long look he sent her before they got into the limo possessive and sensual.

She was just reiterating to herself that this was all an act when they arrived at a private airport and she caught a glimpse of the jaw-dropping Montegovan royal jet.

Enough to accommodate several families comfortably, the two-deck plane was so opulent Maddie was afraid to touch any gleaming surface. Her sense of disquiet was intensified when, upon boarding, Remi swiftly disappeared with a clutch of officious-looking advisers.

When an elderly gentleman approached and introduced himself as a history professor, specialising in Montegovan history, Maddie was grateful for the chance not to dwell on the overwhelming things happening to her.

Over the next few hours she learnt that only Remi's direct ancestors or their queens had ruled Montegova.

Which brought a question screeching into her mind.

They hadn't discussed children or future heirs to the throne. But Remi's words from last night returned with a deeper, more frightening meaning.

'For all the ways that count, Maddie, I expect this marriage to appear real.'

Did that mean children? With her?

She was grappling with this disturbing new dynamic when Remi entered the cabin. His eyes narrowed on her as he casually dismissed the professor.

'What's wrong? You look as if you've seen a ghost.'

'I have a question,' she blurted, before she lost her nerve.

One imperious eyebrow lifted.

'I've just discovered that only your family have ruled Montegova.' She licked dry lips, attempted not to react when his gaze dropped to her mouth. 'That means you intend your own children to rule...'

Her words trailed off when a harsh, bleak look hardened his face. Something jagged slashed at her heart but she forced herself to keep breathing.

'I intended my children to take the throne one day, yes.'

Her next exhalation was decidedly shaky. 'But that means...'

'That means I'm required by law to consummate my marriage in order for it to be legitimately recognised. But when I take you to my bed on our wedding night it'll not be so you can bear my children.'

Why that only caused that wrenching ache in her heart to intensify, Maddie couldn't comprehend. It was clear that Remi needed time to come to terms with his new future. They were in the same boat.

But were they?

He was looking after his people's future, but in many ways he was stuck in the past with his dead fiancée.

The cold wave that washed over her was still present when they landed and were met by a sizeable delegation on the tarmac.

After a swathe of introductions and hearing names she would struggle to remember, they boarded a royal motorcade of sleek limos. Minutes later Maddie caught her first glimpse of the stunning capital city.

Just like everything Montegovan she'd encountered so far, Playagova was a stunning mixture of ancient and modern architecture, every corner pulsing with a rich history she was dying to explore.

But with each mile closer to the royal palace, Maddie's nerves grew tighter, until by the time they arrived at the stunningly magnificent building her pulse was racing and her fingers were a twisted mess in her lap.

Remi's long fingers reached for hers, triggering a whole new range of nerves. Ever since he'd mentioned their wedding night a deep, carnal ache had settled in her pelvis—one she couldn't suppress no matter how much she tried. And she was beginning to think it was useless to fight it any more.

She was wildly attracted to him. And he intended to possess her completely, if only for one night. Maddie shivered, then caught his sharp inhalation. Turning her head, she met his gaze full-on, unable to stop the wave of heat that engulfed her.

His eyes dropped to her lips and they parted automatically, responding to the hunger sparking between them. That hunger turned ashen when his jaw abruptly tightened and he removed his touch.

With the ghost of his fiancée placed solidly between them, Maddie was left with the distinct feeling that the non-turbulent future Remi had promised was less than certain—at least for her.

Unless she found a way to cage her emotions in this clinical marriage she'd agreed to, she risked exposing herself to a pain far greater than the pain she had suffered at Greg's hands.

She was reminding herself of that as she waited with Remi outside Queen Isadora's private dining room. Once again dressed impeccably in a bespoke suit, he was a jaw-dropping vision, with a presence that absorbed her to the exclusion of all else.

Butterflies took flight again as she cast a furtive glance

at his remote expression. 'Any tips on how to deal with this?' she attempted with forced levity.

His expression didn't change. 'Simply be yourself.'

'You mean my *charming* self, don't you?'

His response was to conduct a slow, thorough perusal of her body, taking in the orange gown a palace stylist had presented her with less than an hour ago. The capped sleeves and respectable neckline projected a classic elegance she desperately hoped for.

'You captivate whether you mean to or not, Maddie. You'll have no problems with my mother,' he rasped.

She wanted to hate him for leaving her tongue-tied once again. But she was still busy attempting to breathe as elegant double doors opened before them and a steward stepped forward.

'Her Majesty is ready to receive you,' the man announced.

The dining room held a table large enough for three dozen people. Seated at the head was the Queen of Montegova.

Eyes similar to Remi's tracked them until they reached her. Queen Isadora neither frowned nor smiled, but Maddie felt as if her every secret was displayed in bold scarlet letters above her head as she held the queen's gaze.

'Maman, it's good to see you.' Remi bowed and brushed kisses on her cheeks.

Queen Isadora ruthlessly assessed her son. 'Is it?'

'Let's not make this any more difficult than it needs to be,' Remi replied.

'I see we're dropping all semblance of diplomacy,' the queen responded, and then her gaze swung to Maddie as Remi pulled out a chair for her.

Maddie caught herself before she sat down, manners and what little she'd read of royal protocol kicking her into giving a curtsy. 'It's an honour to meet you, Your Majesty,' she murmured.

'She has manners. That's something, I suppose,' Queen Isadora quipped.

'Maman…' Remi's voice held a rumbling warning.

His mother turned sharply to him. 'This isn't how it is supposed to be. When I sent you to England to handle the Myers situation I pictured a lot more circumspection. Instead you've returned with this—'

'Your Majesty, I would be so very grateful if you wouldn't speak about me as if I'm not here.'

Two pairs of eyes turned to her, the male ones holding mocking amusement and the other a trace of shock.

Queen Isadora spoke first. 'You have fire. I'll give you that too.'

'What else will you give me, Your Majesty? If we're to be family, I'd like to know the best way to proceed without causing offence.'

Maddie caught the faintest twitch of her lips before the rigidness her son was so masterful at settled her features.

'Let's not be hasty. You are not quite family yet.'

'But she will be. I have made my decision,' Remi stated.

The implacable announcement made the queen exhale sharply. For several heartbeats silence reigned, her face paling slightly as she searched her son's face. Then something extraordinary happened.

Queen Isadora gave a deep sigh, her ramrod-straight spine relaxed and she nodded. 'Very well. If this is how it's going to be, I will accept it.'

Maddie hadn't been aware she was holding her breath until it rushed out. But then she discovered her ordeal was far from over.

For the next two hours, in between the presentation of mouthwatering dishes, the queen grilled her on everything from her childhood pets to her mother's desertion.

The discovery that Remi had kept nothing from his mother should have upset her, but having everything out in the open, a clean slate, was liberating. She was tired of carrying the burden of her family's shameful secrets.

But even as that old weight dropped away she knew she carried a newer, more devastating one. One she didn't want to give voice to yet. If ever.

Her gaze flicked to Remi as he escorted her to her suite. She intended to keep up a full emotional guard around him. Those same instincts that had screeched a warning the moment they'd met clamoured even louder now, telling her to heed his warning against falling for him. And for as long as this sham marriage lasted she intended to do just that.

CHAPTER EIGHT

MADDIE LOOKED UP from the report she was reading about her father as Remi walked into the large living room attached to her suite. As had happened increasingly alarmingly over her last five weeks in Montegova, she felt something wild and unfettered lurch in her chest at the raw masculinity that charged from him, his predatory prowl towards her sparking every nerve ending to life.

Comforting thoughts of her father's progress gave way to a tense shakiness inside her as those eyes fixed on her with the unnerving intensity she'd come to expect. As she searched his face, Maddie also recognised other expressions, those she kept hoping would be absent when he looked at her.

She breathed out, unable to avoid the hard-edged detachment, the rigid wall he'd erected around himself almost from the moment they'd landed in Montegova. And with every day she spent in the palace she was made aware of how much Remi had loved and cherished Celeste.

From the suite of rooms in the east wing that no one entered to the Lipizzaner mare lovingly groomed each day but which no one ever rode, Remi hadn't just erected a shrine to Celeste—he'd surrounded himself with reminders of his lost love.

Each discovery had triggered a bewildering ache to Maddie's own heart, an ache that intensified the more she attempted to deny its power over her. That power was very much present right now, threatening her with a runaway pulse and shortness of breath as Remi stopped in front of her, towering and powerful.

She set the report down. 'I didn't think I'd be seeing you again today.'

They'd performed the last of their day's engagements at midday. The charity rowing competition had been well-attended, and the crowds gathering outside the grounds of the royal lake had duly been introduced to Remi's new betrothed.

To say that wedding fever had taken hold of the country was an understatement. It had even eclipsed the queen's announcement that she was stepping down from the throne—an outcome that had brought a rare, wry smile to Queen Isadora's lips.

For the first week Maddie had been stunned by her ready acceptance by Remi's people, and the endless stream of gifts arriving from far and wide in celebration of their engagement.

But that euphoria had waned when, with each passing day, she'd realised the man she was marrying wasn't in the least bit affected by the excitement, that the charm and attention he lavished on his future bride when they were out in public was just an act.

Behind closed doors Remi couldn't get away from her fast enough.

Deep down she couldn't fault him for that. He'd warned her against developing any untoward emotion. The trouble was, Maddie was beginning to think that her heart and mind had differing plans.

'I came to give you this,' Remi said, producing a royal blue velvet box from his pocket.

'Another trinket?' she asked.

There'd been a steady procession of family heirlooms over the last week, presented to her as part of Montegovan tradition. One of several.

'Why are you doing this?' she blurted, unable to stop herself in the face of his rigid demeanour.

If anything, his expression grew even more remote. 'This belonged to my grandmother. She wore it on her wedding day.'

She waved him away. 'I don't mean whatever is in that box. Why are you marrying me if you're so unhappy about it?'

He stiffened. 'Do I need to rehash my reasons one more time?'

'I know you're doing it for your people, but surely a part of you must want this for yourself too?'

'You think I don't want this?'

'Yes, I do,' she replied boldly. 'I think you'd give almost anything for the person you're marrying—*me*—to be somebody else. Tell me I'm wrong.'

He lost a shade of colour—the first time she'd seen Remi less than in full control. A second later his jaw clenched tight.

'That line of reasoning is useless and a waste of time. The past cannot be changed.'

She rose to face him, even though their equal footing was an illusion. 'And yet you're letting it dictate your future. If you're truly not done with grieving over her then you should wait. I've met your people. They'll understand if you need to find someone else who...'

Her words fizzled away when he tossed the box onto the seat she'd just vacated and cupped her shoulders in a firm hold.

'We have an agreement. If this is your way of attempting to wriggle out of it, think again.'

'I'm trying...' She stopped and took a breath. 'No one will talk about her. Everyone whispers. They're scared of upsetting you by saying her name out loud.'

His eyes narrowed. 'What?'

'You heard me.'

His eyes burned into hers, warning her against pursuing a forbidden subject. 'You're prying into matters that don't concern you.'

She laughed—a bitter sound that scraped her throat. 'Don't concern me? Because this is supposed to be some sort of clinical transaction?'

'Precisely,' he snapped.

The ache in her heart grew. She rubbed at it with her clenched fist but it didn't dissipate. 'I'm not a robot without feelings. I can only keep up the charade for so long.'

'Is that a veiled threat?'

She sighed. 'No, it's not. It's a suggestion that you may be doing yourself and your people a disservice in the long run if this marriage they seem so happy about turns out not to be what they expect.'

His nostrils flared. 'You *dare* to tell me how to see to my own people's well-being?'

Maddie tried not to be distracted by the fingers still gripping her, branding her skin. 'I'm attempting to give you a new perspective. You shouldn't dismiss your mother's way of doing things out of hand. You never know—you may even find someone on her list you might grow to like eventually.'

'You think I don't *like* you?'

Her chest tightened. 'Do you really need me to answer that?'

He stared down at her for breathless seconds, and then with a harsh sound he yanked her close. Merciless lips seared hers, creating a path for lustful flames to consume her whole.

It had been five long weeks since that wild encounter in his suite back in London. With every touch and look he'd orchestrated in public, the hunger he'd incited in her had only intensified. And, try as she might to deny it, desire bore down on her tenfold now, rendering it impossible for her not to wrap her body around him, strain to get even closer.

One hand gripped his waist, the other spiked into his hair in a turbulent bid to intensify the kiss. He met her bold demand, thrusting his tongue into her mouth. For endless minutes they devoured each other, their hands almost frenzied in their wild caresses.

They were both panting when Remi eventually tore away from her. He didn't let go, or remove his gaze from her. 'I may not have conventional feelings towards you,' he rasped, 'but this unstoppable fever in my blood desires no one else but you. Do you understand *that*?'

With every cell in her body she wanted to claim those words, hold them close to that ache in her chest. But she couldn't. Because… 'That's just sex,' she said shakily.

'It's more than most people have.'

'And when that's gone…?'

His lips compressed. 'Then we'll find a way to co-exist in civility.'

'That can't be enough for you, surely?' she countered.

His hands dropped from her like leaden weights to fist at his sides. Maddie watched with sickening fascination as he reasserted absolute control of himself.

'For the sake of my kingdom, it has to be enough. For *your* sake, you'd better not renege on our agreement.'

She drew a breath, but before she could speak his gaze flicked to the report on the chair.

'Your father is making good progress, I understand?'

She nodded. 'Yes.'

'Let that be your defining goal, then.'

What about me? What about my heart? What about what I want?

The words remained stuck in her throat as he nodded at the velvet box. 'See you at the altar tomorrow, Madeleine. Wear the necklace. It will please me.'

He left the suite, taking the vibrancy and the oxygen out of the room. She subsided into her seat, her stomach hollowing out as she acknowledged just how much she'd wanted that conversation to go differently.

Had she really expected some indication that he'd one day get over his devastating loss? That the impenetrable fortress around his heart would crack open to let someone else in? Someone like her? How much warning did her foolish heart need? It was time to accept reality. To stop hoping for the impossible.

Hands clenched in her lap, she stared down at the velvet box. She wasn't sure whether she reached for it out of curiosity, to see what other priceless heirloom was being bestowed upon her, or whether it was because it was the last solid confirmation that come tomorrow she would be marrying Remi Montegova, as she'd promised.

For better or worse, and for however long it lasted, she was locked in this thing with Remi. Perhaps if at some point in the future his emotional detachment turned into physical detachment he might even let her go, spare them both the inconvenience of a loveless, sexless marriage.

Maddie ignored the further anguish that thought brought and stared down at the unopened box. She had to embrace this upcoming wedding wholeheartedly, put her best game face on and play her role.

Except that wasn't so easy the next morning as she stood before the bevy of attendants who'd arrived to prepare her for her wedding day.

For the last hour they'd gone about their duties with quiet efficiency, kind smiles and muted excitement, all carefully orchestrated to allay her jitters. Except the butterflies in her belly were in full kamikaze mode. No matter how she diced it, she was marrying the Crown Prince of Montegova—the man who in a few short weeks would be king.

Clinical undertaking or not, it was enough to steal the breath from her lungs—especially when her wedding gown was lowered over her head. She'd fallen in love with it on sight, picked it out of the vast selection three top Montegovan couturiers had presented her with five days after their engagement had been announced.

It was made of silk and lace, and the sweetheart neckline showed the barest hint of cleavage. The heavy material followed her form down to her knees in an elegant train of diamond-studded lace. Her arms were covered in the same lace pattern to her elbow, but at the back the design dipped in a deep vee, leaving her bare from nape to waist.

She'd been a little reticent about choosing the daring design, but her heavy lace veil would conceal the back of the dress, and for some reason she'd experienced a spark of delight at the thought of wearing this particular dress today.

Maddie suspected that the spark had come from the inadvertent discovery of Celeste's wedding dress on her one visit to the east wing. She knew she should have left the private suite that seemed suspended in time the moment she'd suspected what it was. But curiosity had overwhelmed her. And she'd known the second she'd spotted Celeste's demure heavy satin gown that she would choose differently for herself.

Perhaps that had been wrong, she pondered now as she slid nervous hands over her hips.

Whether Remi chose to acknowledge it or not, Maddie intended to stay true to herself in this marriage. In every way she intended to be her own woman—if only for the sake of her sanity.

With that affirmation, she attempted to smile as the head attendant presented her with the box that contained Remi's grandmother's wedding necklace. Awed gasps echoed in the chamber as the two-tiered diamond necklace was reverently placed around her throat and fastened. And with that final click, her time was up.

Maddie blinked hard at the tell-tale sheen in her eyes as she caught her reflection. She'd woken this morning to a profound loneliness that had left tears on her pillow. For far longer than she'd wanted she had wished her father or even her mother were by her side.

That feeling had only intensified during the long hours of preparation, until it was balled in a dull ache in her chest. So receiving a hand-delivered envelope, and opening it to see a note from her father, had drawn more heart-wrenching tears.

On one last whim she crossed to her bedside table, picked it up and re-read it.

My dear Maddie,
The past few years have been difficult for all of us,
but especially for you. I haven't been there for you
and I've let you down.
This note isn't about asking for forgiveness. It's
about expressing my unwavering pride in you, my
joy at your accomplishments and my awe at your
strength.
My only regret today is that I'm not there to walk
you down the aisle.
I wish you a long, happy and fruitful marriage,
my dear.
As for forgiveness...perhaps one day I'll ask for
it. When I'm strong enough and worthy to be called
your father again.
For now, with all my love,
Dad

She treasured the note, held it dear in her heart. But the truth was that she was in this alone. Her only relief was the fact that Remi had been insistent on coming clean about her family's circumstances to avoid further scandal, and had sent out a press release about her father being in rehab. The expected furore had accompanied the news, but had died down very quickly soon after. Her past was no longer a secret, and she could walk down the aisle with her head high.

Accepting she would so alone, Maddie was stunned when she arrived at the entrance to the west wing, where her wedding carriage awaited, to find a tall, dark tower of a man bearing a striking resemblance to Remi waiting for her.

With suave elegance, he took her hand and brushed a kiss over her knuckles. 'My brother told me you were walking down the aisle alone. I came to offer my services,' he said, in the same deep voice as Remi. 'I'm Zak, by the way.'

It took a moment to locate her voice. 'Zak… It's lovely to meet you, but you don't have to,' she managed shakily.

He shook his head. 'My offer isn't completely altruistic. I'm told I've been remiss in not getting involved in the wedding preparations. The least I can do is get to know my future sister-in-law before she actually marries my brother. So shall we?'

He held out his arm to her, much as his older brother had several times since she'd met him, but without the charming smile Zak displayed now.

Maddie took a deep breath and blinked back tears. 'Thank you.'

Within minutes of settling next to him in the car, she felt her nerves come back full force, then intensify as the sheer volume of the crowd gathered to witness the ceremony overwhelmed her.

To her eternal gratitude, Zak kept the conversation light as they progressed slowly towards Duomo Montegova, the sixteenth-century cathedral reserved for royal ceremonies.

Maddie waved and smiled, but attempted to blank her mind to what was actually happening. Ironically, it was Zak's presence, reminding her that she would be his brother's wife before the hour was out, that made it impossible to get away from the fact that she was risking certain heartbreak by tying herself to a man who would never love her.

She knew she'd gone beyond risk the moment her senses leapt at her first sight of Remi, poised at the altar.

His grey morning suit was impeccable, its bespoke design highlighting his towering frame to perfection. The sweet flower girls before her, the pageboys carrying her train, the stunning lighting inside the cathedral and the soft gasps from the guests all faded away as Remi became the sole focus of her attention.

Even Zak's slight stiffening when they reached the place

where a familiar-looking socialite sat with her daughters, and a brief glimpse of a young woman's pale face as she stared at Zak, didn't dilute the potency of her connection to Remi. It was a miracle that she managed to place one foot in front of the other and breathe in and out as she finally arrived in front of the man who would be her husband.

She barely heard Zak's murmured words as he handed her over to his brother. All she could feel above her thundering heartbeat was Remi's grip on hers, that intense determination in his eyes.

'You look breathtaking,' he murmured gruffly.

The words sounded sincere, but she couldn't help but wonder if he was wishing he'd said them to someone else. From behind her veil she searched his face—a futile task, but one she couldn't seem to stop herself from conducting.

Was this destined to be her life? Searching for signs that Remi felt something for her other than duty and obligation?

A delicate throat-clearing from the priest refocused her. Automatically, she repeated the words she'd practised for the last week. The knowledge that they were final and binding forced a lump into her throat.

After several seconds Remi turned his lithe, powerful body towards hers, in a less than subtle command for her to speak her vows.

'I take thee, Remirez Alexander Montegova, to be my… husband…'

An exhalation from the crowd confirmed that hers wasn't the only breath being held at that moment. A furtive glance at Remi showed his eyes burning deeply into her face. She quickly averted her gaze, focused on repeating the remaining vows that bound her irrevocably to him.

When his turn came he spoke his vows in deep, solemn tones, with no hesitation as he slipped the wedding band onto her finger. The last of her breath was strangled in her lungs when he lifted the veil off her face. With one finger tilting up her chin, his head descended, his intention to follow tradition an immutable certainty.

The kiss was firm, branding, but over in the briefest of seconds. Still, it drew gasps and sighs as he slid his arms around her and brought his mouth to her cheek.

'Bravo—you played the game admirably. And it wasn't such an ordeal, was it?'

She plastered on a smile but didn't respond—because she couldn't. The heavy weight of the platinum and diamond wedding ring on her finger kept her mute. But she managed to keep her smile in place as Remi walked her back down the aisle and throughout the elaborate banquet, the first dance and their ride through the streets.

By the time she re-entered her suite, to change her attire for the trip to the Amber Palace—the honeymoon residence passed down from Remi's grandfather to him—her smile was frozen in place.

She'd barely touched her food, had taken no more than a few sips of the vintage champagne during the reception. Luckily no one had commented on her lack of appetite. They'd been too busy absorbing the news that Remi had truly married *her*, a commoner with unsavoury baggage in the form of a drug addict father and an absentee mother.

'Is everything all right, Your Highness?'

Maddie started, the sound of the title automatically conferred upon her on marriage stealing her breath.

She managed a small nod. 'I'm fine, thank you.'

Just a little bit longer, she told herself. *Then there will be the night to deal with.*

A different set of nerves assailed her. And it had nothing to do with the impending hot air balloon ride with Remi— the last event of their wedding ceremony—although that was daunting in itself.

When she'd learned of that aspect of the ceremony, she'd experienced a childlike thrill—right up until the moment it had dawned on her that the ride would culminate at the palace where she'd spend her wedding night.

Maddie couldn't suppress the tremor that shook her. Remi desired her. Enough to overlook her complete inexperience? And for how long?

Pushing the questions out of her mind only worked until she once again came face to face with Remi.

He'd changed into a navy suit, with a pristine white shirt and a velvet bow tie. With his hair combed neatly, and a pass of the razor over his jaw, he was a sight to behold as he took her hand and led her across the immaculate lawn towards the giant hot air balloon emblazoned with the House of Montegova's royal crest.

With one hand holding up the hem of her pale gold evening gown, she joined Remi in waving to their guests before they headed down the red carpet to board the basket.

Her every sense flared into awareness in the enclosed space as Remi stepped in behind her and signalled to the balloon technician. In minutes they were soaring into the sky, vintage champagne in hand.

The scene below her was breathtaking. Only one thing could have made this moment more special. If the man next to her had been truly and completely hers.

That thunderbolt of an admission froze her in place as Remi closed the gap between them. Strong arms arrived on either side of her, caging her in, and helplessly she breathed him in, unable to stop a shiver as his scent pervaded every atom of her being.

Her action drew a frowning look. 'I'm sorry...' he murmured solemnly.

Startled, she snapped her gaze to his and was imprisoned by fiercely gleaming eyes. 'For what?'

'I never asked whether you were okay with heights. We can land and go by car if you prefer?'

Maddie shook her head, drawing her gaze from his hypnotising one to the carpet of lights twinkling beneath them as the sun began to set.

'I'm not afraid of heights. And it's beautiful up here,' she replied, taking a sip of champagne.

He merely nodded, but she felt his gaze resting on her.

'How long is the flight?' she asked, trying to dissipate the charged tension eddying around them.

'Under an hour.'

'I'm surprised you're allowed this mode of transport. Your bodyguards must be beside themselves.'

The rarest of smiles twitched his lips, and she burned with the need to see the full force of it.

'They're close by.'

She turned her head and met his gaze again. 'Really?'

His smile widened a touch as he nodded his head over his right shoulder. A glance in that direction only showed her a speck on the horizon. On closer inspection, though, she noticed it was a helicopter, flying out of sound range.

'Have you *ever* known true privacy?'

He shrugged. 'It's easier to just let them do their thing. They know when not to intrude.' His gaze slowly raked her, returning with a banked heat that enflamed her. 'That will be as close as they will get in the next five days.'

'You mean the Amber Palace has its own security?'

He lifted his glass and took a long sip before answering. 'Do you really wish to know?'

The butterflies somersaulted in her belly. 'Why else would I ask?'

'Perhaps you're trying to avoid discussing what's coming?'

She took another large gulp of champagne in a wild bid to steady her nerves, but the glass shook as she lowered it and read the look on his face. Remi wasn't attempting to hide his hunger for her.

'Is there any point in discussing it?' she asked, in a voice that emerged unsteadily.

He shook his head. 'No, only the absolute certainty that I will make you mine before the night is through.'

The deep timbre of his voice invaded her being, more intoxicating than the champagne in her hand. Another shiver rolled over her when his hand closed over hers, resting on the lip of the basket.

'It would please me to know that you're not attempting to get tipsy.'

'I'm not,' she said hurriedly.

'You barely touched your meal,' he stated.

'Are you trying to ruin my buzz?' she murmured.

His gaze raked her face and settled on her mouth. 'The only buzz I want you to experience is the sensation of having me buried deep inside you. I will accommodate no other.'

She swayed against him. An actual weak-at-the-knees sway that he halted with a firm hand on her waist. And there his hand stayed for the duration of their flight.

After she gave a helpless, unfettered moan.

After he leaned down and slowly, thoroughly, tasted her lips.

After she forgot about everything—including the technician whose back was discreetly turned to them as they continued to soar through the sky.

After it struck her hard that she was living the most exquisite moment of her life, with the last of the setting sun in front of her and the darkening of the capital city behind them.

Tears rose to her eyes as with their descent a boom of fireworks ripped through the sky, painting the darkening curtain of night with exhilarating colour.

She snatched in a stunned breath. 'God, it's wonderful!'

The hand branding her waist tightened and Remi pulled her close, until her back rested against his broad chest.

'Yes,' he said simply, before his lips brushed her temple.

They remained silent for the rest of the journey, until

the burnt gold spires that lent the Amber Palace its name rose into view.

Smaller in scale than the official seat of the monarchy, it was no less breathtaking. But as the basket touched down next to an elaborate lamp-lit maze, set to the east of the palace grounds, there was only one thing on Maddie's mind.

Her gaze slowly rose to meet Remi's. There was no going back. This was her wedding night, and if it was all she'd ever get—duty to the Montegovan crown or not—she would take it. Treasure the experience. She would give her virginity to her husband without trepidation or regret.

CHAPTER NINE

REMI ATTEMPTED TO moderate his pace to match his new bride's as they strode through his favourite palace. Despite her avid scrutiny of her surroundings, the tell-tale tremble of the fingers caught in his announced her trepidation. On the one hand he could hurry and get this over with, so she'd see there was nothing to worry about. Or…he could stay away from her altogether.

No.

The latter was out of the question. This marriage needed to be consummated. And he… He needed to have her before he went insane.

But she looked a little pale, so he slowed his steps further, led her from one opulent living space to the other.

'How long has this been in your family?' she asked once they'd circled back into the least formal of the living rooms.

He let her extricate her fingers and engage him in conversation instead of doing what he yearned to do—which was to sweep her off her feet and stride up the stairs into the master bedroom suite.

'My great-grandmother built this as a surprise wedding present for my great-grandfather.'

Her eyes widened as her head snapped down from where she'd been examining the murals on the ceiling. 'How long did it take to build and how on earth did she manage to keep it secret?'

Remi recalled the fond tale with a smile. 'Very carefully, with a lot of bribery and a few tantrums that ensured she would be left alone for when she needed to visit the site. She instructed the first stone to be laid the day after they were betrothed. They didn't marry for two years.'

'And did he like his surprise?'

'According to the historians, she left clues of secret passages and architectural delights that enticed him to stay for six months.'

Like the specialised jewels created in this part of his kingdom, the whole palace was decorated in different shades of amber, with expert lighting that gave the illusion of it being suspended in a field of dark gold.

'I'm not surprised he didn't want to leave. It's stunningly beautiful.'

He watched her touch the amber teardrop crystal on a nearby lamp and wanted those fingers on him.

Striding to her, he seized her hand again, lifted it to his lips. 'I will give you a fuller tour later,' he said, aware that his voice was deeper, rougher. 'Right now I have a more urgent need.'

When her lips parted on a soft pant he couldn't hold back any longer. He swept her into his arms, satisfaction oozing through him when her slim arms encircled his neck.

'What are you doing?' his sharp-clawed kitten demanded as he strode out and up the stairs. 'I… I can walk.'

He wrapped his arms tighter around her. 'I'm giving you the chance to tell your own story some day—one that doesn't include tripping over the stairs because your husband was too impatient with you.'

'Are…are you?' she asked, her voice tremulous, her gaze wary.

He paused long enough to drink his fill of her undeniable beauty before mounting the last step. But that pause also let in that little voice that said he needed to do *more*. He'd held her at arm's length because ever since her arrival he'd expected her to find a loophole, get out of their agreement. He'd issued veiled threats, left her to her own devices when he could have given her a little more of his time and attention.

He'd noted her hesitation before she'd said her vows.

That most of all had unsettled him. If he wanted this marriage to work, even on the basest level, he needed to do… *more*. He negotiated challenging trade deals, walked diplomatic tightropes all the time. So why did the idea of *more* unnerve him?

He took a breath, and went with the carnal truth. 'I want you, Maddie. More now than I did half an hour ago or the moment we first met.'

Her breath shuddered out, her eyes growing several shakes darker as she watched him.

'Would you like me to show you?'

Her nod was shy, a touch hesitant, but it still swept fire through his veins, lent further urgency to his steps.

Within a minute they were in his private chamber, the doors behind them firmly closed. Without setting her down, he lowered his head and took her mouth with his. Her soft moan set the blaze inside him higher, and when her tongue brushed timidly over his mouth Remi nearly lost his footing.

He'd barely lowered her down when he spiked his fingers into her bound hair. Then he dived deeper, unable to wait one more second for a taste of his wife.

His wife…

For the first time since tragedy had struck, the thought of anyone but Celeste as his wife didn't strike with oppressive pain.

Perhaps it was because the deed was done. Perhaps his physical craving for Maddie was dimming the guilt and pain. Whatever it was, he intended to take it—even if it was just for tonight.

He licked her soft, velvety lips, then stroked his tongue deeper into her mouth, absorbing her unfettered shudders as her arousal spiked to match his. He repeated the action a few times before gently nipping her tongue with his teeth. She whimpered.

'Do you like that, *piccola*?' he breathed against her lips.

'Mmm…yes.'

'Then you shall have more.'

Remi kissed her until she clung to him. Until they were both breathing hard. Until the pressure in his groin demanded further action.

He gently nudged her to the side of the bed. Then, dropping to his haunches, he tugged her shoes off. He glanced up, surprising a strange expression across her face.

'What?'

She bit her lip. 'You... Almost kneeling at my feet. Feels...weird.'

He brushed his thumb over her delicate anklebone. 'Weird good or bad?'

'Is it bad to say good?' she whispered.

Remi lifted her right foot and kissed her soft instep. A shiver raced up to engulf her whole body.

'Nothing that happens between us tonight in this room will be bad,' he responded.

Within his grasp her foot trembled, and her colour deepened. He slipped his hands beneath her gown, trailed his fingers up her legs without taking his eyes from her face.

'Why are you watching me like that?' she asked, again in the hushed whisper that had varnished her words since they entered his room.

'You're to be mine. I want to see what pleases you.'

Her flush deepened. 'Will I sound gauche if I say *everything*?'

His hands tightened convulsively on her knees as a sudden compulsive need to claim *everything* swept over him. But did he have a right to *everything* when he couldn't return the same? And why the sudden yearning for exactly that?

He shook the thoughts free, glided his hands higher up her silken flesh until he brushed the edge of her panties.

'I'll give you as much as you can take. Stand up and turn around, *piccola*.'

She obeyed. Still kneeling, he reached up and drew down her zip, exposing her supple back and delicate spine to his gaze. He kissed the base of her spine as he divested her of the dress and her bra. Then, hooking his fingers into her panties, he tugged the scrap of satin down her legs and tossed it away.

His mouth watered at the taste of her skin, the feel of her naked hips in his hands, the scent of her sex. Nudging her back around, he kissed his way up her belly to her luscious breasts as he parted her thighs and caressed his thumbs over her damp sex.

'Remi…' she moaned, her trembling intensifying as he licked and teased her nipples.

The clamouring grew too wild to resist and he drew back and pulled down the bedcovers. 'Lie down and open your legs for me. I want to taste your innocence one last time before I claim it.'

Her breathing truncated as she silently obeyed. With their gazes broken, Remi allowed himself another look at the magnificent landscape of her body, at the secret place between her thighs he intended to lay full and final claim to tonight.

Full and final?

This time the voice lingered even after he'd attempted to brush it away. Continued to linger as he nudged her slender legs high, kissed his way down her right knee, then the left. It lingered as he delivered the ultimate kiss, watched her back arch off the bed and her fingers scramble for purchase in the silk covers. It was still there when he tongued her clitoris and felt her body grow taut a moment before her climax ripped through her.

The satisfaction that mingled with his lust was unlike anything Remi had ever experienced before, and after caressing her through her release, when he rose to divest himself of his own clothes, the wild hunger rippling through him stunned him further.

He reached for a condom and was tugging it on when she slowly blinked her eyes open and sought his gaze.

'Remi...' she murmured.

Something shifted in his chest, and again his attempt to bat the sensation away felt woefully inadequate. Two steps brought him to her. He wrapped his arm beneath her and repositioned her on the pillows. Before she could speak he captured her mouth once again, eager to escape the worrisome sensations zinging through him.

He caressed her from nape to hip, with hands that weren't quite steady. When he grabbed her arms and hooked them behind his neck she immediately wrapped them around him, clung on tight.

That wild craving to have her there *always* pierced him. No doubt it was the newness of this, the novelty of her innocence. No doubt he would be rid of these absurd notions once he'd had her.

With that thought, which had more than a whiff of desperation attached to it, he slotted himself between her thighs and cupped her nape with one hand. Her lids slowly lifted, her alluring eyes meeting and clinging to his.

'Are you ready to be mine, Madeleine?'

A tremor shook through her, then she nodded. 'Yes.'

He positioned himself at her core. When her breath caught he lowered his head and delivered a gentle kiss. 'Relax, *ma petite*.'

She breathed out.

With a muted groan, Remi pushed himself inside her snug, exquisite heat.

The flash of pain that ripped through Maddie drew a scream. Mindlessly, she dug her nails into his shoulders. He flinched, and yet his next kiss was as gentle as the last.

'Be calm, Maddie. The worst is over.'

Wildly she shook her head, reluctant to breathe, reluctant to move. 'I...can't...'

'You can. You will. You're mine,' he breathed against her lips, and surged inside her once more.

Prepared for further pain, Maddie gasped as a different sensation arrived. And stayed with his next thrust.

On the sixth, bliss such as she'd never known flowed up her spine. She'd thought that night in London had opened her eyes to pleasure. And again just now, when he'd used his mouth, she had imagined she'd crested the very pinnacle of desire.

The phenomenon of Remi moving powerful and deep and relentless inside her robbed her of everything except hedonistic pleasure. His mouth at her lips, her throat, his hands holding her tight to him wrought magic. She'd asked for everything. *Everything* was turning her inside out with ecstasy.

'Oh… God!'

'Oui…si…'

She wouldn't have thought it possible, but the mixture of languages that formed Montegovan sounded sexier than ever, whispered in her ear by its crown prince. Her husband.

'Remi,' she gasped as he angled her hips and surged deeper.

'Dio mio, cosi exquisitivo. Dea…'

'Translate…please. I… I want to know…'

'You're exquisite…a goddess,' he breathed in her ear. 'I will teach you Montegovan, then you will understand…'

'Yes.' She wanted that too. *Everything.* And more.

Maybe it was foolish to ask. But she… Dear God, she was in love with him. She couldn't *not* be.

She opened her eyes, though she couldn't remember shutting them, to find his ferocious gaze fixed on her, ten times more intensely than he'd ever looked at her before. She couldn't have looked away if she'd wanted to. So she didn't.

She lost herself in his power and in their pleasure until the bough broke again. More spectacular. Vastly superior in sensation. Her scream this time was of pure ecstasy, and the fingers digging into his back pleaded for it never to cease.

He kept moving within her, kept up the sizzling tempo

until he gave a long, guttural groan. His magnificent body grew taut, and then convulsions rippled through him.

For the longest stretch of time, the only sound in the suite was their snatched breaths and racing hearts. When they calmed, he withdrew from her body. Maddie barely managed to curb a whimper, and watched in silence as he left the bed and entered the adjoining bathroom.

Boneless, she collapsed on the bed, her every sense still struck by the awe of what had just happened. Was it like this every time? How soon could it happen again?

She was still drifting on a sea of sated bliss when Remi returned and scooped her up.

'What…where are you taking me?'

The sound of a bath running and the scent of bath oil drifted through her senses, answered her question.

'A bath will do you good,' he said, before lowering her into warm, jasmine-scented water.

Maddie couldn't stop the blush that suffused her face as the water closed around her. Expecting him to leave her to it, she started in surprise when he nudged her gently forward and slid in behind her. She would have thought what they'd done in the bedroom was intimate enough, but having him share her bath introduced a whole new level of intimacy that wrapped itself around her heart—much as she wanted him to wrap his arms around her.

When he did just that, a moment later, all the barriers she'd attempted to erect around her heart crumbled. She wanted this. Wanted *him*. For ever.

The weight of that need terrified her—so much so that she stiffened.

The arms around her tightened. 'Is something wrong? Are you sore?'

She pulled her knees up to her chest, shook her head as another blush flared into her cheeks. 'I'm fine,' she blurted.

'You're not,' he countermanded smoothly as he nudged her head against his shoulder. 'It's okay to be overwhelmed.'

Maddie wanted to laugh, but feared it might morph into a sob. She wasn't fine. Far from it. She was hopelessly in love with a man who would never belong to her. Perhaps even now she was on a countdown to when he'd walk away from her.

The heart that had soared minutes ago in her new marriage bed dipped alarmingly, grey despair filling the empty spaces. Terrified of giving herself away, Maddie kept her head tucked into his shoulder, not protesting when he picked up a washcloth and began gliding it over her skin.

For one absurd moment she wanted to ask whether he'd done the same for Celeste. Thankfully that curiosity passed unuttered, but it did nothing to dissipate the knot of tension in her belly as she withstood his ministrations.

Perhaps it was the warmth of the water, his powerful but gentle hands, or the acceptance that she had truly passed the point of no return, but Maddie slowly began to relax as other sensations pushed themselves to the forefront of her consciousness.

She became acutely aware of Remi's solid body enfolding hers, the back-and-forth motions of the washcloth over her breasts and belly, the slight hitch in his breathing. She didn't know what prompted her to lift her head, glance up into his face. Once she did, she couldn't look away.

They stared at each other for an interminable minute before his gaze raked over her face to rest on her lips. Unable to stop herself, she lifted her hand to his taut cheek, wild need urging her to explore further. She smoothed her thumb over his lips, his faintly stubbled chin, the bridge of his patrician nose, the sleek wings of his eyebrows. He was perfection, and she wanted to weep with the heartrending knowledge that he would never be hers.

But he's here now. He's yours for now.

She felt his manhood stir against her hip and gasped at the renewed thrill in her veins. Seeing the fierce hunger in his eyes, she drew her hand down his neck, over his superbly honed chest and hard six-pack. There she hesitated, her face flaming all over again at the thought of touching him so intimately.

'Touch me, *dea*,' he encouraged thickly.

Goddess. That was what he'd said the word meant.

Her insides melted. It was dangerous to be this affected by the endearment, but it was already too late. The word flowed into her heart, joined all the other pieces of gentleness and desire and attention she'd received from him.

Like a miser tucking away precious gems, Maddie gathered every scrap and stored them in her heart. She would need them one day, maybe one day far too soon, when he turned away from her.

She slid her hand over his hot skin, beneath the water to his groin, her breath dissolving in her lungs as she grasped his thick girth.

His hiss of arousal made her flinch, but the look in his eyes encouraged her to continue on her path. Emboldened, she grasped him more firmly, explored his glorious length until he hissed again.

'Enough, *dea*,' he ground out.

She wasn't ready for this sensational moment to be over just yet. 'Please…' she whispered, even though she expected him to stop her.

His answer was to spike his fingers in her hair and angle her face up before plundering her lips with his. Time ceased to matter as he kissed her with a fierce thoroughness that left them both breathing hard when he abruptly ended the kiss and repositioned her over his lap.

Maddie clung tightly to his shoulders as his steely length nudged her core. Just as before, the first probe was gentle, insistent—and breathtaking. His gaze stayed on her face, absorbing her every reaction as he slowly penetrated her once more, strong hands gripping her hips for his possession.

Maddie gasped as all the sensations from before came

screaming back. And with no prospect of pain this time, the pleasure was tenfold.

Tears rose in her eyes as bliss suffused her. When he rocked her into movement, when she understood the advantage of her position, she began to move over him.

He grunted—a thick, masculine sound that filled her with feminine power. That power might be fleeting and feeble at best, but it still lent her enough impetus to take him deeper, to glide her fingers into his hair and notch his head up for the addictive kiss only he could provide.

Remi gave her what she wanted and more, one hand rising to cup her breast and torment its peak as he kissed and possessed her. Within minutes they were careening towards that unstoppable summit, scented water splashing around them as he introduced her to a whole new level of pleasure. Guttural Montegovan words fell from his lips as he edged her higher, and she opened her heart, letting his words spill into those greedy spaces.

Nirvana arrived in a thrilling rush that went on for ever. Beneath her, Remi gave a rough shout in the steamy space as he charged through his own climax.

She welcomed the strong arms that bound her and held her close, and as their heartbeats slowed she dared to hope that perhaps they had something to build on after all. Perhaps if they had this, in time they would have something more. Because surely he couldn't be this affected, this intimate with her, without considering handing over even a small piece of himself?

She would find a way to make him happy in any way she could. In the hope that one day he might truly see her, even love her.

That bleak little voice mocked her again, called her ten kinds of fool for attempting to compete with a ghost.

But surely there was a way for her to show Remi that, while she would never replace the woman he'd lost, she could be something meaningful to him eventually?

She was so absorbed with her frantic plans to make her new husband love her that she didn't realise he'd stiffened beneath her until a curse she didn't understand but knew for its harsh iciness ripped through the room.

She froze. 'Remi...?'

He rose from the water with her in his arms as if she weighed nothing. His face was turned away from her but she didn't need to look into his eyes to tell that something was terribly wrong. The clenched jaw, the tension bracketing his mouth and the thunderous, forbidding frown evidenced that something was definitely amiss.

It took all of three seconds for her to clue into what was wrong. 'Oh... God...'

'*Si,*' he hissed icily.

Stepping out of the bath, he disengaged from her and placed her back in the water. Unable to stomach the horror on his face, she hugged her knees.

They hadn't used protection. They'd been so caught up in the moment that crucial part of it had gone out of their minds. At least that was her suspicion.

A furtive glance showed his deepening horror. 'Remi...'

'No,' he breathed, spiking his fingers through his hair.

'What does *no* mean, exactly?' she asked.

He responded with a string of Montegovan words that meant nothing to her.

'Translate. Please.'

He strode across the room, snatched up a towel, wrapped it around his hips. Still with his back to her, he sucked in a tortured breath. 'How could I?'

'How could you what?' she asked tremulously.

He swivelled to face her. 'Be so damned careless.'

Her head dipped a fraction, her heart hammering at his bleak tone. 'We both were, Remi.'

His hand slashed the air. 'I don't mean *you*. I was careless with *her*. I promised myself I would never be careless again. And now I have done it again. With you.'

She flinched. 'You mean Celeste?' He was bringing his dead fiancée into *this*? She wasn't sure whether to be furious or desolate. She chose the former. 'It's our wedding night, Remi. It might not mean anything to you, but it means something to me. How can you bring her into this moment?'

'What?' His brows clamped together as if she was speaking an alien tongue.

Perhaps she was. Bitter laughter ripped from her throat. 'What was I thinking?' she murmured to herself. 'This is how our marriage is going to be, isn't it?'

His frown deepened. 'What are you talking about?'

'Don't pretend you don't know. How can you not know when she informs your every decision? How can you not know when you never stop thinking about her?'

Fierce eyes narrowed. 'Maddie—'

'No,' she interrupted, equally fiercely. With a strength she hadn't known she possessed, she rose out of the bath, her gaze fixed on his as she stepped out. 'How do you think it makes me feel when the first thing you think about when you're faced with a crisis is *her*?'

His head went back as if she'd struck him. For a moment she wished she had, if only to knock a little bit of sense into him.

'Calm down—'

'Why should I? You just dismissed me out of hand. Even though this is happening to *both* of us, you didn't even think about me.'

His expression grew even more arctic. 'If I hurt your feelings—'

'*If?* Look at me, Remi. Do you actually see me standing here in front of you?' she asked, in a voice that reflected the anguish tearing through her.

A muscle ticked in his jaw. 'Of course I do. Don't be absurd.'

'I'm being *absurd*, am I? Perhaps next you're going to

call me melodramatic for having feelings? For wanting a say in my own marriage?'

'Protecting you is my prerogative,' he replied tersely. 'My priority.'

Just like it was with Celeste. He didn't need to say the words.

She battled to keep the anguish from ripping her asunder. 'Can we talk about this like two rational human beings? *Please?*' she tacked on at the absolutely implacable look on his face.

He stared at her for a charged moment and then nodded brusquely.

About to speak, Maddie realised she was still stark naked. He realised it too, his gaze heatedly raking her body before, veering away sharply, he snagged a robe and held it out to her.

She started to reach for it.

The wave of dizziness came out of nowhere, snatching the strength from her knees and the air from her lungs.

With a shocked, guttural curse, Remi lunged for her, locking her into his arms as her body crumpled.

'Dio mio,' he cursed thickly. 'Are you okay?'

The dizziness dissipated as quickly as it had arrived, leaving her senses clear. 'Let me go. I'm fine.'

'No, you are not.' Robe discarded, he swept her up and strode back into the bedroom, placing her on the bed before stepping back. 'We will talk after you've had something to eat and rested.'

'No, I want to talk *now*.'

He seared her with a blistering, imperious gaze that reminded her that in everything but the coronation ceremony he was the King.

'Some things you have a say in, Maddie. The subject of your health and well-being, especially when you're neglecting them, isn't one of them. You barely ate anything all day long, and indulged in new experiences on top of that. If you wish for a rational discussion then you'll do as you're told.'

She tugged the sheets up to cover herself even as she raised her chin in defiance. 'Are you calling me irrational?'

His face closed up even more and he expelled a harsh breath. 'I'm recommending we talk when emotions are less heightened.'

With that he strode into his dressing room. He emerged five minutes later, dressed in the most casual attire she'd seen him in so far. Unbelievably, the dark cargo pants and polo shirt merely enhanced his attractiveness.

Thinking he was leaving, she caught her breath when he approached the bed. He stopped by the bedside table, snatched up the phone and calmly issued instructions before replacing the handset.

'A meal is being brought up to you,' he stated.

'Are you leaving?' she asked, and immediately wished back the needy words.

His gaze met hers for a moment before he turned away. 'It's better if I remove myself from here for now,' he rasped.

'Because you can't stand to be around me?'

He froze, then whirled towards her. 'Because our history of clashing tells me that we won't make it through a meal together without you voicing what's on your mind. Am I wrong?'

He wasn't. She wanted to discuss this *now*, get it out of the way, while he was intent on staging a diplomatic retreat. 'Even if you're not, I can't exactly stop you, can I?'

His nostrils flared. 'No, you can't. Rest, Maddie. I'll see you in a few hours.'

It's our wedding night, she wanted to scream. She swallowed the words. He didn't need to be reminded. That bleak look on his face told her he hadn't forgotten.

She watched him stride purposefully for the door, watched it shut with a decisive click behind him. Immediately Maddie felt as if a light switch had been thrown, plunging her world into darkness.

She'd made love to her husband on her wedding night without protection. And the first thing he had thought to mention was his dead fiancée. How clearer could it be that this marriage was doomed?

With shaking limbs, she sank back against the pillows, fighting for the breath that she couldn't catch properly in her lungs. She should never have agreed to marry him. She should never have agreed to this devil's bargain.

But then where would her father be?

Tears rose in her eyes as anvil weights of impossible choices pressed down on her.

She was still mired in despair when a soft knock sounded fifteen minutes later. The middle-aged woman who'd introduced herself as head housekeeper, when the staff had met them earlier, directed a younger maid, who pushed a silver trolley towards the bed.

Together they prepared a tray of food and a glass of pure Montegovan spring water and set it in Maddie's lap. Belatedly, she wished she'd thrown on the robe when she caught their subtle stares. She mentally shrugged. At least the palace gossip wouldn't include speculation on whether her marriage had been consummated or not. She even managed a blush when the housekeeper picked up her discarded gown and carefully laid it on the sofa.

She picked at the fruit, flat bread and cold meats, drank the juice and sipped at the water. She suspected Remi had instructed the housekeeper to ensure she ate, because the older woman found an excuse to linger until Maddie had finished most of her plate before, smiling and curtsying, she departed.

Left alone with her thoughts, she was aware that a single one had emerged from the churning quagmire. The consequences of their actions went beyond Celeste and a marriage that seemed doomed even before it had begun.

If fate chose a different path for her, she would emerge from her wedding night carrying the future heir to the Montegovan throne. And one thing was very clear. Her new husband couldn't have been less thrilled about that prospect if he'd tried.

Remi paced his study, a single lit lamp the only illumination in the darkness. He embraced the gloom, let it amplify the sheer magnitude of what he'd let happen. He deserved this.

His carelessness was breathtaking. How could he have let himself be so blinded by lust that he'd forgotten himself at the very first opportunity?

Sure, he hadn't planned on making love to her again that second time, but how was that an excuse when it had never happened before?

The truth was that he had lost himself.

Her beauty, her responsiveness, that tentative but determined exploration of her newly found sexuality...they'd all been a potent combination that had turned him on more than he would've believed possible before tonight.

He'd indulged himself, and in so doing had lost his mind. Spectacularly. And now he was faced with the possible consequences.

Maddie wasn't on birth control.

He'd read her medical report—knew a discussion had taken place with her new doctor for her to start after the wedding, in case she developed side effects.

The responsibility had therefore fallen squarely on him. How could he have failed so spectacularly?

There may be no consequences...

He wasn't reassured. He'd fallen at the first hurdle, just as he'd failed to come clean and admit that Celeste hadn't crossed his mind more than a handful of times since he'd returned to Montegova. That he'd been consumed with thinking about Maddie and finding ways to keep her to their agreement.

Because admitting it would have been too revealing?
Yes.

Was tonight's slip a subconscious effort on his part to ensure she remained at his side? Even after vowing never to be careless with another's health again?

That unnerving thought froze him in place until the next one arrived hard on its heels.

Fatherhood. His new wife might well be carrying the next king or queen of Montegova. *His child*.

The reality shook through him, and then confounded him further by staggering him with need and...*hope*.

No. He couldn't possibly *want* this. Not when it could come at such a cost.

The hands he dragged through his hair shook. The notion unsettled him deeply. He stared into the middle distance, attempting to recall Celeste's face, remind himself of why he'd chosen this path. But he saw only Maddie, her anguish as she'd hurled accusations at him.

He swallowed, then gritted his teeth.

This couldn't happen again. If any consequences came of this night he would do everything in his power to ensure Maddie's safety. If nothing came of it—if fate saw fit to give him a second chance—he would do the right thing going forward. The *only* thing.

She'd slipped beneath his guard and under his skin. If he couldn't think clearly around her then his options were severely limited.

Skirting his desk, he sank heavily into the chair behind it, not sure which scenario he preferred. Both settled iron vices around his chest, strangling him. But he had no choice. It was the safest option.

He dragged his hands down his face, prolonging the moment for as long as possible.

Then he picked up the phone.

CHAPTER TEN

THE SUN WAS creeping beneath heavy silk curtains when Maddie opened her eyes. Anxiety and despair, coupled with the long, emotional wedding day, had finally taken their toll and she'd tumbled into a dreamless sleep just after midnight.

Heart hammering, she jerked upright, a fist-sized stone settling in her chest when her fears were confirmed. Remi hadn't returned to the suite. Or if he had, he'd chosen not to wake her.

Deep down, she knew she'd slept alone. Her senses were too attuned to him not to have noticed his presence.

Willing calmness to her thudding heart, she dragged herself out of bed. A quick inspection after using the bathroom showed only Remi's clothes in the dressing room. The thought of wearing the evening gown Remi had peeled off her body last night made the knots inside her tighten harder, so she retrieved the robe she'd never got round to wearing last night and shrugged it on.

With a deep breath she left the suite—to find a young maidservant hovering in the stunning hallway that looked even more spectacular in daylight than it had last night.

The girl, a few years younger than Maddie, gave a deep curtsy. 'Your Highness, I'm to escort you to your suite and ready you for breakfast with His Highness.'

Relief fizzed deep inside Maddie. A part of her had been afraid Remi had left the palace altogether.

Murmuring her thanks, she followed the girl to the only other door in the vast hallway. It turned out to be the suite adjoining Remi's. And inside the decidedly more feminine suite, set out in similar but more delicate amber tones, she found a whole new wardrobe ready for her.

After a quick shower, she selected a pale lemon sundress, slipped her feet into stylish mules and brushed her hair out. Light blusher to disguise her pale cheeks and a quick dab of lip-gloss and she was ready.

Remi sat at the head of a banquet-like dining table made of polished cherry wood, his fresh clothes and neatly combed hair evidence that he'd slept and dressed somewhere else.

The rigid expression that greeted her further evidenced the unsurpassable chasm between them.

'Good morning, Maddie. Did you sleep well?' he enquired tonelessly.

She forced a shrug. 'I slept. Let's leave it at that.'

His gaze flickered, but he remained silent as a fully uniformed butler approached. She knew she'd meet the same resistance if she attempted a discussion on an empty stomach, so she forced herself to eat a slice of toast and scrambled eggs, washed down with a cup of tea.

The moment she set her cutlery down Remi rose. 'We'll talk in my study,' he stated.

Her heart hollowed as she followed him down several magnificently decorated hallways and into a room decked out on three sides with floor-to-ceiling bookshelves, some holding first edition books.

But she wasn't there to gawp at the contents of Remi's ancestral library. She was there to discuss—perhaps even battle for—her marriage.

She hid her flinch when he shut the door and paced steadily to the window, looking out for a moment before facing her.

'What happened last night can never happen again.'

The heart dropped to her stomach and she sank into the nearest seat. 'It's too late to seek an annulment, Remi,' she replied, striving for a jovial tone that fell far short.

His lips firmed. 'That isn't quite the course of action I intend to take.'

'Then by all means enlighten me.'

'I'm aware that you were thrown into the deep end with the expediency of our wedding preparations. Now that it's over we can throttle things down a notch.'

'Isn't that what a honeymoon is for?'

He gave a half-nod. 'I'm proposing you extend that for longer, if you wish, by remaining here at the Amber Palace. It's not exactly a new concept. My mother stayed here when she was pregnant with me.'

'You mean stay here on my own...when you return to the Grand Palace?' she asked, sick premonition crawling over her skin.

There was a tight clench of his jaw. 'Yes,' he replied.

'We haven't been married for even twenty-four hours and already you want a separation? Because, let's face it, that's what you're proposing, isn't it?'

'Madeleine—'

She held up a staying hand. 'Don't try and couch it in diplomatic terms. We made love without protection and now you're freaking out.'

He drew in a long, harsh breath, his chest expanding along with his aura until she could see nothing, feel nothing but his overwhelming presence.

'I'm putting safeguards in place.'

'By banishing me?' she asked shakily.

A shadow passed over his face but his iron will held. 'We will continue to see each other. We just won't live under the same roof.'

She jumped up, unable to sit still any longer. 'What the hell are you so afraid of, Remi?' she demanded through a throat dry with panic.

For the longest time he remained silent. Then he exhaled. 'What happened to Celeste was my fault,' he confessed, in a voice devoid of any emotion.

'How?'

'She'd been suffering from migraines in the months before our wedding. Doctors had recommended tests but she'd pleaded with me to take her on a business trip. I was reluctant, but she talked me into it and I went against her doctors' advice. The headaches got worse when we were away. She suffered an aneurysm mid-flight on her way back home. If she'd stayed at home, or even returned a day earlier, the doctors might've saved her.'

'How can you blame yourself for that? You couldn't have known what would happen. And would she really want you to live in never-ending hell because she died?'

'What's the point of going through hell if you don't learn from it?' he bit out tersely.

'Learning from it is one thing. Shutting yourself off from experiencing anything else is another.'

'*Dio mio.* I'm trying to protect you, Maddie.' His voice was harsh. Ragged.

Her heart wanted to soften, to give in, but what would she be giving in to? A half-dead platonic marriage when she'd had a taste of how things could be if only he opened his heart?

'You can't control the future, Remi. No one can. You think you're protecting me, but what you're doing is insulating yourself from living a full life. I… I don't want that.'

His eyes narrowed. 'What does that mean?'

'It means you can't keep me in a cage, no matter how much you think you're justified in doing so.'

'You are a princess now. In a matter of weeks you'll be my queen. Like it or not, your new position means that in some ways you're constrained by your station. You can't do whatever you want, give in to frivolous dreams.'

'But I don't have to live in misery either, locked away in your Amber Palace. I won't play the out-of-sight-out-of-mind game with you.'

He dragged a hand through his hair, upsetting the neat strands. '*Dio*, none of this is a game. You could be pregnant.'

Her insides shook at the words, at the soul-shaking possibility, but she stood her ground. 'Even if I am, the last I heard pregnancy wasn't a prison sentence.'

'But it carries risks.'

'Walking down the street carries risks. I have first-hand knowledge of that, but I'm still here. Still alive. What if I'm *not* pregnant?'

His lips compressed. 'No protection is risk-free. And since I've proved conclusively that my control is…lacking where you're concerned, it's best if we—'

'Don't you dare say it!' she blurted, distress shaking her voice.

His face closed completely. 'You will remember who you're addressing, Maddie. It's pointless to argue. My mind is made up. This is still only a marriage of convenience, which required consummation to make it lawful. Now we've done our duty there'll be no further intimacy between us.'

And just like that the loud clang of dungeon gates echoed, consigning the marriage she'd dared to hope she could have to a dark and lonely death.

She lifted her chin and looked him in the eyes. 'Very well, *Your Highness*. Since you don't need my permission to leave, I guess if I don't see you around I can assume you're gone.'

'Maddie—'

'If there's nothing else, I think I'll go and get acquainted with my new residence. I'm assuming, again, that your offer of a tour now falls to someone else?'

He gave a brisk nod. 'I have work to do.'

'Then don't let me keep you,' she replied stiffly.

He stayed exactly where he was, staring at her for a full minute before delivering one of his imperious nods. 'Your doctor will be in touch soon. We need to know one way or the other.'

With that, he turned on his heel and left the library.

Maddie sank onto the sofa, the breath knocked out of her lungs. And when she heard a helicopter land and then take off again half an hour later, she couldn't stop the sob that ripped from her throat or the torrent of tears that followed.

She didn't see Remi again for three long weeks, and although every other night she would hear him arrive in his helicopter, he would be gone by morning.

Of course, she mused bitterly. In all things he had to keep up appearances.

Maddie attempted to shrug off insidious despair in favour of getting to know her new home. After exploring every inch of the Amber Palace she spent hours in the elaborate maze, then discovered stables filled with thoroughbreds, stallions and two mares. With her pregnancy unconfirmed, Maddie could only admire them from afar as stable hands tended them.

Keeping herself busy prevented her from doing too much of the one thing that fed her despair—scouring social media for glimpses of Remi. With wedding fever abating, people were now turning their attention to the coronation. And from the looks of it, Remi was fully immersed in preparations—including touring the major cities of his kingdom.

His enigmatic responses when asked about the whereabouts of his wife had begun to fuel speculation of a possible royal baby on the way. She was therefore not surprised when he arrived with her doctor in tow on the twenty-second day.

Maddie was on the back terrace, overlooking the first of several tiered lawns as his helicopter settled on the helipad. Unable to help herself, she searched his face for signs that he'd missed her as much as she'd yearned for him, and deluded herself into thinking that she'd caught a single sizzling, ravenous look in his eyes before his expression gelled into regal neutrality.

'Madeleine,' he murmured stiffly as he brushed a kiss on her cheek.

Her heart quaked at that small contact, but she hardened her resolve. 'Your Highness,' she muttered back, and felt

him stiffen. 'You should've called to tell me you were bringing the doctor. I would've told you not to bother.'

He tensed. 'Excuse me?'

She looked past him to the physician hovering at a respectful distance and pinned her smile in place. 'I'm not
taking the test. We'll know one way or the other in a week
or two anyway.'

'Madeleine—'

'I'm already being treated like fragile glass by the staff.
I'd quite like to live in blissful ignorance for a little longer
before I'm wrapped in cotton wool by the whole kingdom.
So send the doctor away, Remi. Or I will. And while we're
at it you should know my bags are packed. I'm returning to
Playagova with or without your approval. I'm sure everyone's worked out that this honeymoon is over.'

He stared at her as if she'd grown two heads but she
stood her ground.

'If that's what you wish—'

'It is. Thank you.'

The doctor was dispatched in a SUV and Maddie and
Remi returned to the helicopter. During the thirty-five-min-
ute flight Remi conducted phone call after phone call, including a particularly terse one.

'Whatever this is, you need to sort it out, Zak,' he said
in English, before sliding back into Montegovan.

When he hung up his jaw was tense.

'Is everything all right with Zak?' she asked before she
could stop herself.

'It'd better be. I have too much on my plate to deal with
his issues.'

She shrugged. 'I only met him for a short time, but he
seems capable of handling himself more than adequately.'

For the first time since boarding the helicopter, Remi
flicked his gaze to her. It stayed and blazed. Her heart
flipped over and her throat clogged with harrowing yearning, only for her to see the blaze cool seconds later.

'Since you seem to think you're up to handling your new role, we've been invited to my godmother's residence tomorrow evening. She's throwing a pre-coronation dinner in my honour.'

Nerves made her breath catch, but she swallowed them down. 'I... Of course.'

He nodded briskly as the helicopter landed. He alighted first, then turned to help her down the shallow steps. Again her breath caught, and this time when his gaze locked on hers she witnessed a reel of emotion in his eyes. Savage lust. Bleakness. Censure. Regret. All before the brick wall slammed down, shutting her out.

Numbness descended on Maddie, keeping her mercifully insulated as they entered the palace and were greeted by the exuberant staff. She forced herself to smile her way through accepting several bouquets of flowers from their children.

Even Queen Isadora approached as Maddie turned to head to her suite. 'Welcome home, *ma petite*. You're just in time to wish me well on my travels.'

Maddie's eyes widened. 'You're leaving?'

Queen Isadora nodded enthusiastically, her eyes shining with almost child-like glee. 'First stop New Zealand. I've always wanted to visit Hobbiton.'

Maddie smiled. 'I wish you very safe travels.'

'Thank you,' Queen Isadora replied. Her gaze flicked to where Remi stood, talking to his aide, and her face grew serious. 'Things may look bleak and daunting at present, but I've discovered that dogged perseverance reaps rich rewards.'

'I... I'll bear that in mind.'

The queen nodded, then briskly walked away.

Maddie dropped her head and buried her nose in a bouquet of chrysanthemums and peonies as she mulled over Queen Isadora's words.

She was startled out of her thoughts by the click of a camera. Although she knew she'd been caught unawares by the

palace photographer, she dredged up a smile—which froze
on her face when her eyes clashed with Remi's.

His gaze captured hers before dropping to her flat belly.
For a tense moment he remained immobile, with a fierce
look in his eyes that locked the air in her lungs. A second
later he turned his back on her.

That numbing sensation still shrouded her when they drove
through a set of iron gates manned by security guards the
next evening.

They were barely out of the car when a thin, elegantly
dressed woman Maddie had seen only in glossy magazines
hurried towards them. She inhaled sharply.

'Your godmother is Margot Barringhall, the English
Countess?'

'She's half-Montegovan. She's also my mother's best
friend.' His tone was clipped. Resigned.

'You don't sound very happy about being here.'

'I'm fond of her, but Margot likes to play games.'

'What type of games?' she asked.

'You'll see,' he said cryptically.

'Remi, my dear, it's simply wonderful to see you.'

Arms outstretched, Margot hugged him, her smile widening as Remi kissed her on both cheeks.

'Maman wouldn't have forgiven me if I hadn't made time
to see you before the coronation,' he drawled.

Margot laughed, but when her gaze swung to Maddie a
second later her expression cooled. 'Ah, here's the blushing
bride. Forgive me for leaving straight after your wedding
ceremony. I had a prior engagement I simply couldn't break.'
Her gaze dropped to Maddie's flat stomach. 'Even though
it was all so…rushed I wish I'd been able to enjoy all of it.
Anyway, welcome to the family. May I call you Madeleine?'

Remi was the only one who used her full name, and she
was suddenly loath to grant that privilege to anyone else.
She smiled stiffly. 'Maddie is fine.'

'I hope you're adjusting to your new role? It must be daunting.'

'I'm doing fine, but thank you for your concern,' Maddie replied, her insides tightening at the underlying dig. Margot wasn't talking about being a member of royalty. She meant Maddie's place in Remi's life.

Satisfied that her gibe had been delivered, Margot turned back to Remi. 'Come through—everyone's having drinks in the Blue Room.'

She claimed her godson's arm, and for a moment Maddie thought Remi would leave her behind. But his hand gripped hers, sending a bolt of electricity up her arm when their palms slid together.

She was so caught up in not reacting outwardly to that sizzling touch she barely had the wherewithal to gape at the roll call of celebrities and royals gracing Margot's stately home. But when Margot led them purposefully towards a trio of women who bore a striking resemblance to the beautiful Countess, Maddie felt her skin tighten.

'Remi, you remember Charlotte? She's returned from Sydney to accept a position with the UN. I managed to convince her that two years was long enough for her to be away. Who knows? She might take up a post here in Montegova.'

A telling look passed between mother and daughter.

'Welcome home,' Remi responded easily, but his smile held a cool edge. 'I'm sure my ministers can facilitate the appropriate meetings if required.'

Charlotte's face fell a fraction, but she hid it behind her glass of champagne as Remi turned his attention to the other two women, who were introduced as Sage and Violet, identical twins.

'Violet recently returned from New York too. She finished her internship with your brother. I've been trying to reach Zak for the letter of recommendation he promised, but he's been unavailable,' Margot complained.

Remi tensed, but before he could reply Violet inhaled sharply.

'*You've* been trying to reach Zak? I told you not to. I said I'd take care of it, Mother,' she admonished, her voice thin and shaky as her already pale cheeks blanched further.

A memory teased through Maddie's thoughts, reminding her that Violet was the woman she'd spotted on her way up the aisle. The woman Zak had tensed upon seeing.

Margot brushed her daughter away. 'His letter is important. You were under his guidance for six months and you've been home for two. It's time you took the next step in your career.'

Violet went paler. With an abruptly murmured excuse she rushed away.

Margot turned her blinding smile on Remi. 'Ah, here's the butler, come to announce dinner. Shall we go through?'

She looped both arms around Remi's elbow and pointedly led him away, leaving Maddie to follow. Margot Barringhall couldn't have made it clearer that she considered Maddie an outsider if she'd tried. Or the fact that she believed one of her daughters should have become the next Princess of Montegova.

Watching Charlotte Barringhall smile up at Remi as he pulled out her chair, Maddie felt the numbness surrounding her crack, to let in a sharp arrow that left her breathless with pain.

Her composure wasn't helped when over the next three hours nausea began to roll through her belly as rich course after decadent, rich course was ushered to the table. Suffering at the sight of the rich food, alongside Margot's less than subtle attempts to ostracise her, while indulgently nudging Charlotte and Remi into conversation, drained every last ounce of Maddie's poise.

For his part, Remi was the epitome of diplomacy, seemingly content to let his godmother have her way. But every now and then a jagged expression flitted across his face, driving that arrow deeper into Maddie's heart.

Over and over, she swore she wouldn't glance his way but, like a glutton for punishment, she repeatedly flicked her gaze to where he sat with Charlotte, their heads together, talking in low tones.

She couldn't deny they made a striking couple. Nor could she deny the acidic jealousy and wrenching anguish flaying her. Her gaze shifted, and she caught Sage staring at her. At the thinly veiled pity in the other woman's eyes Maddie tightened her fingers around her water glass.

Mercifully, dinner ended shortly after that. Sensing Remi coming her way, she sucked in a fortifying breath—only for her stomach to deliver an almighty heave.

'I need the ladies' room. Excuse me.' She hurried away, aware that his assessing gaze was firmly latched onto her.

Hunched over the water closet, Maddie knew it wasn't just the state of her marriage that was disturbing her stomach. Willing her body and soul to stop shaking, she staggered to the sink, rinsed her mouth and attempted to breathe around the anguish in her heart.

When the agony failed to ease, she turned on the tap and splashed water over her hands.

If she was pregnant—and a fierce instinct she couldn't suppress insisted she was—then this level of distress wasn't good for her unborn child.

She'd thought she knew what she'd let herself in for with this bargain, but Remi's coldness, Margot's callous dismissal, and the topsy-turvy awe and panic at the thought that she might be carrying the next Montegovan heir...

This was a whole new realm of agony.

Maddie was struggling for composure when the door opened and Violet rushed in. She froze at the sight of Maddie, dropping suspiciously teary eyes.

Maddie frowned in concern. 'Are you okay?'

Violet made a flouncy gesture eerily reminiscent of her mother, then paused, her gaze reconnecting with Maddie's.

'I know this is…' She stopped, cleared her throat. 'Has Remi said anything about Zak's whereabouts?' she blurted.

Maddie stopped herself from saying that she and Remi weren't on extended speaking terms. 'No. I'm sorry.'

'Oh, it's fine. Thanks.' Violet flashed a fake smile and left the bathroom.

About to follow her, Maddie reversed her direction abruptly as her belly dipped alarmingly. With a wretched sob she emptied the remaining contents of her stomach and was about to leave the stall when a pair of voices froze her exit.

'I don't know exactly where he dug her up, but perhaps you should warn him, Margot, before he brings the throne into disgrace. The story of her father is most unseemly. Who knows what he's passed down to her?'

Margot laughed. 'Remi doesn't need any warning. My godson's always been wise beyond his years. He'll wake up to his unfortunate error soon enough. Luckily divorce, even amongst royals, is commonplace these days.'

Maddie bit her fist to suppress her painful gasp.

'Are you sure?'

'Absolutely positive. He's doing this to secure his throne. If he's not single again by this time next year I'll buy you lunch at Claridge's. If he is, you can buy me dinner to celebrate my Charlotte's rightful place as the next queen.'

Both women laughed, and then just like that they went on to talk about something else, their decimation of Maddie's soul already a thing of the past.

Five excruciating minutes passed before she was once again alone, her heart in tatters.

She staggered out of the bathroom, her every sense screaming at the thought of returning to the dinner party. She wasn't ready for another episode of the Charlotte and Remi show. Wasn't ready to look into Remi's eyes and wonder if Margot was right. And, worse, wonder if he'd hate her even more for the secret growing into steady reality in her heart.

Spotting a large archway, she headed towards it. It opened up onto a terrace edged with a thick stone balustrade, beyond which lay an endless sweep of immaculate lawn.

Resting her elbows on the stone, Maddie took a deep breath—which immediately evaporated when the space between her shoulders began to tingle.

Awareness raced down her spine, relentlessly engulfing her whole body. The intensity of it shocked her into immobility, which was perhaps a blessing—because she didn't want to face her husband. The man who would soon gain another label—*the father of her child*.

Nor did she wish to face the undeniable fact that, despite the turbulence of their coming together, her feelings had only deepened unrelentingly, without regard to her anguish. Even more desperately, she didn't want him to take one look at her and *know everything*.

'Are you avoiding me, Maddie, or did you simply take a wrong turn when returning to me?' he rasped tautly.

She stayed facing forward, her frantic gaze fixed on the horizon as he prowled closer.

'I needed a breather from all that cloying fawning and shameless matchmaking. You should've warned me properly that I was going to spend the evening being insulted,' she said, her hands tightening around her clutch bag.

'You insisted you were ready to play at the deep end. I simply gave you the chance.'

His voice was close enough for her to feel his breath on her nape. To draw that fleeting contact into her being.

'Well, thanks for the lesson. I'll be suitably armed next time.'

'Turn around, Maddie. Have the courtesy to look at me when you address me,' he commanded tersely.

Praying that her last ounce of composure held, she swung

around, felt a strand of hair escape its knot and slide against her cheek as she forced herself to meet his incisive gaze.

'Where exactly is Charlotte on your list? She *is* on the list, isn't she? She must be near the top if Margot refuses to acknowledge the wedding ring on my finger. Or do they all know this marriage is a sham?'

His face hardened. 'Keep your voice down.'

Her heart twisted. 'That's all you have to say?'

'No. I have a lot more to say. But this isn't the time or place.'

He closed the gap between them and lifted his hand as if to touch the lock of escaped hair. But at the last moment his fist tightened and dropped.

Gut-wrenching anguish gripped her. 'Will it ever be?' she asked tremulously.

He took another step closer. Her breath strangled in her throat as his hands caged her against the balustrade.

His chest brushed hers. Maddie's nipples tightened. For an unshakeable moment they simply stared at each other, wrapped in a fraught little cocoon.

The tinkle of laughter and conversation from the party faded away. Her vision was filled with only Remi. When his head started to descend she stopped breathing, shameless anticipation holding her in place.

For the briefest moment another emotion shifted the savage hunger on his face. Powerful and visceral enough to make her flinch.

It was the same expression she'd witnessed yesterday, when he'd helped her from the helicopter, and again after her exchange with the Queen. It continued to blaze down at her as he slid one hand around her waist, tugged her into the hard column of his body.

With a will of their own her hands rose to his chest, splayed over hard muscle. Untamed hunger charged through his eyes, and with a groan he swooped and captured her mouth with his.

Deep, thorough and devastating, he explored her mouth with suppressed ferocity. In a rush of surrender she shamelessly parted her lips beneath his, let his tongue sweep over her lower lip in a blatant tasting that drew a moan from deep inside her.

Her belly grew hot and heavy with desire, and she gripped his nape and held on tight.

With a rough sound he slid his tongue into her mouth, his breathing harsh as he adjusted his stance until there was no mistaking his level of arousal.

Maddie's whole body rippled with desire-soaked tremors. As if her reaction triggered his, his kiss deepened, his hand trailing up to boldly cup her heavy breast. With a helpless moan she pushed against him, nipped his bottom lip with her teeth. He exhaled harshly, muttering a charged curse against her lips.

She was so caught up in the kiss, in *him*, that it took a moment to notice that he'd stiffened.

He jerked away from her. *'Dio mio!'* he bit out, his hands falling from her waist.

She dropped her hands, shifted sideways away from him as she gulped in several breaths. The sound of the guests' laughter reminded her where she was.

Remi took another step back, the cloak of diplomacy settling on his face once more. But beneath that look she saw lingering anguished regret. As if he was berating himself for the very thing he'd instigated.

A breeze swept up from the garden, chilling her body. She rubbed at her arms but the cold just intensified.

'If we're done with the lesson, can we leave now?' she asked through stiff lips.

'Of course.' His tone was devoid of inflexion, his demeanour staid as he led her back inside.

Neither of them spoke for the duration of the journey back to the palace and the long minutes it took them to walk back to their adjoining suites. Expecting him to escort her to her bedroom door, Maddie felt her skin grow tight with apprehension when he veered into his living room and strode to the arched windows overlooking the landscaped gardens.

A stone jumped into her throat at the flash of bleakness on his face. His gaze stayed in the middle distance for the longest time before a hard edge replaced the bleakness. When he turned to her, she held her breath, a part of her almost afraid of what he would say.

'What happened on the balcony shouldn't have happened.'

Despite the staccato precision of his revelation his anguish was unmistakable. Her insides shrivelled as she watched him wrestle that telling emotion.

There was only one reason behind this disclosure. *Guilt*.

The sharpest knife pierced her at the thought that he would never stop loving his dead fiancée. Hard on its heels, though, came anger.

'It was just a kiss, Remi. You won't burn in hell for it.'

His jaw clenched. 'Nevertheless, I gave you my word—'

'I didn't ask for your word, so don't you dare beg my forgiveness because you think you're dishonouring your fiancée's memory. Or is it something else? Do you hate the fact that you liked it? That your own wife turns you on?'

Icy fury blasted through his eyes. 'Madeleine—'

She affected a shaky shrug, despite the deep tremors coursing through her body. 'You're an intelligent man, Remi. If this meant nothing to you, you wouldn't be so affected by it. And you wouldn't deign to speak to me, never mind attempt to dissect it.'

Grey eyes pinned her as he exhaled harshly. 'You think you have a handle on what makes me tick?'

She laughed. 'No, I don't. I'm just going on the evidence before me. We made love. You *loved* it. Then immediately retreated. Tonight we kissed. You were *transported*. Now you hate me—and hate yourself for responding to a commoner like me.'

He didn't move a muscle but he seemed to grow before her, every inch of his majestic being bristling with affront. 'To hate you I would have to be invested in you, even a small fraction. I'm not. And in future I'll thank you not to attempt to psychoanalyse me.'

The tears she'd striven to hold back all night threatened to break through as the gnawing, traumatising truth took root inside her.

She couldn't save a marriage that had been doomed from inception. She was better off cutting her losses.

'You won't need to worry about that. Not any more,' she said, a heavy wave of desolation sweeping over her.

She wanted to succumb, wanted to surrender to its oblivion. But she forced herself to stay on her feet as he pinned her with his gaze.

'What's that supposed to mean?'

'It means I won't be attending the charity polo match tomorrow. In fact you won't have to suffer my presence for much longer.'

He stiffened, but she caught the tremor that shook through his body. 'What exactly are you trying to tell me, Madeleine?'

She swallowed, knowing she couldn't bury her head in the sand any longer. She was pregnant with Remi's baby. The heir to the Montegovan throne. Finally accepting it filled her with both trepidation and acute joy. She needed time alone to process the news.

'I'm trying to tell you that I think your worst fears have come true,' she announced.

Remi froze, a wave of colour leaving his face as his eyes grew a turbulent black. His fists tightened at his sides and a harsh breath was ripped from his throat before his gaze lanced over her, pausing for one ragged second on her belly before lifting to clash with hers.

'Yes,' she confirmed the question in his eyes. 'I haven't taken the test yet, but…well, call it female intuition. I'm carrying your child, Remi. Tomorrow we'll know for certain, but at least you'll have tonight to start planning how you can truly separate me from your life.'

Her voice broke shamefully, raggedly, on the last words. Unable to withstand the agony any longer, she hurried into her own suite.

She heard him follow, heard him pause on the threshold of their adjoining rooms. He'd never crossed it—not once since they'd said their vows. She whirled to face him as he stepped through and stopped in front of her.

His hands rose as if to touch her. She jerked away. 'What are you doing?'

His face closed but determination blazed from his eyes. 'We need to talk, discuss—'

'Nothing that can't wait till morning,' she interjected bleakly, shifting her gaze away from the vibrant skin beneath his collarbone, from the towering vitality of this man who would never be hers.

She turned away. The result of fake smiling all evening while dealing with Margot and his coolly detached attitude had triggered a dull headache. She tossed her wrap and clutch on the sofa and massaged her temples with tired fingers.

'What's wrong?' he demanded sharply.

Maddie started, unaware he'd followed her. For a tense moment she stared at him, her brain frozen at his closeness.

'I have a headache. I also have to wake up early to talk to my father. I'd rather not do so with a headache…'

It was the first conversation she'd have with her father since she'd left England and he'd gone to Switzerland. She didn't want to miss it. Right now he felt like her only tether to the real world.

Her words trailed off as he strode past her and headed

for her bathroom. Curious despite her breaking heart, she stayed put.

He returned with a pill bottle, shook out two tablets. 'Take these,' he instructed gruffly, handing her a glass of water.

'I'm fine—'

'Take them, Maddie. It's a low dose. It won't affect you or the—' He stopped, clenched his jaw.

Her heart lurched painfully. 'The *baby*, Remi. Not saying the word won't make it any less real.'

He inhaled sharply. 'You think I want to pretend it doesn't exist?'

The question was a stunned, ragged demand. One that drew a cloak of shame over her for even daring to voice the thought.

Unable to answer, or to stem the flare of hope inside her, she took the pills, her stomach pitching as her fingers brushed his warm palm.

He waited until she'd swallowed them before he returned to the living room. Then he turned on her. 'Why didn't you tell me you weren't feeling well?'

'It's just a headache, Remi.'

'Headaches can be an indicator of other things,' he stressed, his tone deep and gravel-rough as his gaze dropped to her now healed arm.

She stared at him, her heart wrenching for him despite her own agony. 'I'm not being blithe or dismissive, Remi. It's just a tension headache. A good night's sleep will take care of it.'

He didn't reply, and the intense look in his eyes told her he wanted to argue. Eventually he gave a terse nod, then strode to her bed and pulled back the cover. For a long moment he stared at the sheets, seemingly lost in thought. Then he muttered a thick, 'Goodnight,' and walked into his own suite.

An hour later her headache was gone, but her desolation

had grown exponentially when she started at the sound of their adjoining door opening.

Remi stood framed in the doorway, still dressed but minus his dinner jacket. His hair was in disarray, as if he'd spent the last hour running his fingers through it, and his eyes were dark pools of intensity.

Her heart leapt into her throat, as she blinked back the tears in her eyes. 'Remi—?'

'I won't leave this,' he said tersely. 'Not another night. Fate hasn't been good to me when I've let things be, Madeleine. You tell me I'm to be a father. Whatever that entails we tackle this. *Tonight.*'

CHAPTER ELEVEN

SHE REMAINED FROZEN, struck dumb, as he strode determinedly to her bedside. Fervently he searched her features. His fingers flexed at his sides but he didn't reach for her.

'How do you feel?'

Her fingers tightened on the luxurious bedspread as she fought to keep her crazy pulse from leaping out of control at his breath-stealing masculine beauty. He was barred to her, she reminded herself. Completely and conclusively. Somewhere in the last hour she'd accepted that her time with Remi was limited. This was her last chance to hoard memories of him.

She licked nervous lips and forced herself to meet his gaze. 'I'm fine. The headache is gone.'

Those all-seeing eyes lingered, dropped to her mouth, and just like that the atmosphere thickened. But this time it was overlaid with an intensity unlike anything she'd ever known.

'Fate hasn't been good to me...'

'Whatever that entails, we tackle this...'

'What...what exactly do you want to tackle?'

He didn't speak immediately, simply continued to watch her with a spine-jarring ferocity that stole her breath.

Time ticked by. The merest frown creased his eyebrow before his face slowly went slack. It was the kind of expression triggered by dawning realisation. Or emotionless calculation.

Self-preservation screamed at Maddie to turn away, to hide from that look in his eyes. But she couldn't move.

Whatever the future held, it was time for her to face it.

* * *

Remi stared down at his wife, the staggering realisation of the last hour slaying him anew.

The last three weeks without her had been hell, with each day worse than the last, because she was the missing part of him he'd never even known he'd lost. He'd planned to tell her that tomorrow. To lay it all on the line when things weren't so volatile between them. But he hadn't even been able to undress, never mind find any semblance of respite.

The staggering notion that time was slipping through his fingers had been overwhelming. And, really, hadn't he wasted enough time? Hadn't he known from that moment she got into his car that Madeleine Myers possessed the ability to shift his world off its axis in the most profound, life-changing way?

How could he have slept, knowing that tomorrow might be too late? That he might lose the woman who held his heart, held his child within her womb?

He shifted his gaze over her face again, fighting the trepidation in his chest, scrambling for words adequate enough to combat that look in her eyes he knew didn't bode well for him. For weeks he'd pushed her away. What if…?

'Madeleine…'

'What is it, Remi? What did you come to say to me?'

He took a long, ragged breath. 'That I'm a husband who has neglected his wife for far too long. I won't be making that mistake again.'

Her breath shook but she held his gaze. 'If this is about confirming my pregnancy, you can go ahead and call the doctor. Neither of us is going to get any sleep anyway. It's best we find out now. But you should know that after that things will change, Remi.'

His heart dropped into his stomach, ice and heat engulfing him simultaneously. He wanted to prolong the eventuality. Wanted to speak the words tripping on his tongue. But for the first time in his life the right words wouldn't form. So he picked up the phone and summoned his physician.

He arrived within half an hour. Endless minutes during which his words still remained locked in his throat, his fate hanging on a knife-edge.

'Royal protocol dictates that the test result be as accurate as possible. A blood test is the most definitive,' Remi heard the physician tell her.

'Right. Of course. And how long before…?'

Remi's vocal cords finally unfroze. 'A matter of hours, I believe?' he replied, his heart racing frantically.

Maddie's breath caught, her gaze finding his. 'Are you… are you going to stay?'

Remi nodded, walked to her side on legs that felt unsteady. 'If it pleases you, I'd very much like us to find out together.'

Maddie willed her heart to stop racing but that look she'd caught in his eyes a moment ago, that flash of deep yearning, continued to replay in her mind. Of course now he stood by her side the look was gone, his expression stoic as the doctor went to work.

The moment he was done Maddie rose from the bed. It was one thing to experience the distance between them from afar; it was another having him right next to her and still feeling as if nothing could breach the wasteland.

'Are you all right?' he asked.

She gave a bitter laugh. 'Do you care?'

'Of course I care.'

He was moving even closer. She knew it because his scent—the unique ice and earth scent she'd missed so much that it was a constant ache inside her—was wrapping itself around her, seeping into her ravenous senses.

Throat-grating laughter spilled again. 'You came to my room over an hour ago and you're yet to say what you came to say. I'm guessing that whatever it is isn't important to you any more.'

She felt him stop behind her. Beneath her nightslip and the dressing gown she'd thrown on her body strained for his with a shocking hunger.

'It's important, Maddie. Probably the most important thing I'll ever say.'

She whirled to face him, anger and despair and wild, unstoppable craving ripping her apart. 'Really? Then what's stopping you? Are you afraid you'll hurt me more than you already have? Whatever it is, say it and be done with it. Or would you prefer me to bow and scrape and pretend civility? Will that help you keep that control you so sorely lack around me? Or have you mastered that already in the weeks you've refused to touch me?'

His face started to tighten but he shook his head. 'I'm beginning to think that was a mistake.'

'Well, bully for you,' she lashed out.

'Maddie…'

His voice was as shaken as the gaze that dropped to her flat belly. His throat worked but he couldn't seem to form more words. He whirled away from her, then reversed direction. Shaky hands cupped her jaw.

Maddie's heart cracked open, but she swallowed the pain. She needed to do this, get through this. 'Something's going to change,' she said.

He tensed. 'What?'

'My father's out of isolation. After I talk to him in the morning I plan to go and see him as soon as I can. And… and then I'm going home—back to London.'

Anguish darkened his eyes and he grew another shade paler. 'No,' he rasped. 'You can't go. You can't leave me. I won't let you.'

The peculiar note in his voice snagged something hard in her chest. 'You can't keep me, Remi. Not like this. We won't survive as long as Celeste—'

'I haven't thought about Celeste since the first time I kissed you,' he interjected thickly.

She gasped. 'What?'

Firm hands grasped her shoulders as his eyes blazed with a new, terrifyingly intense light. 'You seem to think she dictates my every move. I accept that losing her the way I did affected me…badly…but from the moment you got into my car the only time I've thought about her is when I attempted to use her memory to stop myself from feeling what I feel for you.'

A deep tremble surged from the soles of her feet. 'And what *do* you feel for me?'

The hands that rose from her shoulders to cup her cheeks weren't quite steady. 'More than I wanted to at first. More than I could deal with. And I admit it terrified me how much I craved you,' he growled.

'You closed yourself off from me easily enough.'

His low laugh was gruff and self-deprecating. 'You think it was easy? Leaving you was the hardest thing I've ever done. Staying away was even harder. Why do you think I came back every other day?'

'Because you wanted to keep up appearances?'

He uttered a pithy curse under his breath. 'You should know by now that when it comes to you, appearances matter very little to me. No, I returned because even though I tried to stay away from you I yearned for you with every breath. I had to be near you even if I couldn't be with you. And I didn't walk away because of your strength. I walked away because of my weakness. I'm in love with you, Madeleine. But I put you in an impossible position and coerced you into this marriage…and I've spent every waking moment since then fighting my conscience against letting you go. Slipping up with protection seemed to be another sign that I wasn't doing right by you.'

'So…you intend to set me free?' she whispered raggedly.

'That was my intention the morning after our wedding

night…for all of half a second. But to do that I'd have to rip my own heart out because you're so imbedded in it. I can't live without you, Maddie. I was relieved when you insisted on coming back to the palace. But having you close without having you is torture. So I'm here to plead for a fresh start. To see if there is a way we can start over regardless of what the test results show.' His nostrils flared as he inhaled sharply. 'That means you're not allowed to leave me,' he stated.

A tremulous smile broke free. 'I'm not, am I?'

A mixture of pleading and determination stamped his face. 'I'll do whatever you want. We can return to the Amber Palace or we can live here. The staff tell me you've grown attached to the maze at the Amber Palace.'

'It was a place to lose myself for a few hours when I missed you so badly.'

Silver-grey eyes lit up with a churning of emotions so vivid her breath caught. 'I love you, Maddie. Give me another chance. I vow never to be separated from you again.'

'I'll have you on one condition, Remi.'

He inhaled sharply. 'Name it and it's yours.'

'Kiss me, Remi. Love me. Make me yours again. Please.'

He kissed her with a ferocious hunger that filled the ache in her heart. And when he caught her hand and led her through to his suite Maddie went willingly.

She let him take off her clothes and lay her on his bed. When he undressed and pulled her into his arms, she slid her hand over his jaw.

'Remi?'

'Si, amore dea?'

'I love you, too.'

His eyes blazed bright for endless moments before he blinked. 'Will you stay with me? Be my queen? Reign by my side?'

'On one condition…'

He caught and kissed the palm of her hand. 'Celeste's

belongings were returned to her parents the morning after our wedding. There's no trace of her in our home and the staff are under strict instructions to speak as much or as little about her as you dictate. She was a part of me, but she's in my past now. Your strength, your devotion, your courageous challenges and the way you never back down are what I yearn for in my life. What I hope to be privileged enough to receive every day for as long as we live.'

Tears clogged her throat. 'Oh, Remi.'

'It's my turn to demand a kiss.'

She wrapped willing and loving arms around him and gave herself up to him. Then silence reigned as they gave in to bliss.

Two hours later, freshly showered, they descended the grand staircase hand in hand.

To the news from the doctor that she was indeed carrying the Montegovan heir.

Remi promptly swept her off her feet and carried her back upstairs.

After calling his mother to tell her the news, they called her father. Hearing him happy and healthy brought fresh tears to her eyes. She rang off with a promise to visit with Remi, after which she slid back into her husband's arms.

'Are you ready to be a father?'

Eyes feverish with love consumed her as his hand splayed over her belly. 'With you by my side, I can face anything.'

'God, how can love hurt and make me so happy at the same time?'

'Because it's the most powerful emotion of all. And I'm blessed to have yours.'

'I love you. For ever, Remi.'

'Siempre, mia regina.'

EPILOGUE

MADDIE WATCHED HER husband swim towards where she lay on a lounger next to the pool at the Amber Palace.

At five months pregnant, she knew her belly was rounded enough to make her state visible—a fact demonstrated by her husband when he launched himself out of the pool and immediately crossed to her side, his gaze lingering lovingly on her belly.

'Have I told you how breathtaking you look?'

'Not since this morning, no,' she said with a mock pout.

He dropped to his knees beside her, one hand gliding over her swollen stomach as he leaned down to kiss her. 'I can barely catch my breath from how beautiful you are, *dea mia*,' he said gruffly when he lifted his head after a thorough, soul-shaking kiss.

'You take my breath away too, my noble king.'

King Remirez of Montegova had taken to his new title and role with aplomb, and his people were showering even more adoration upon him now than they had at his coronation three months ago.

But it was when Maddie used his title like this in private moments that he loved it most.

His eyes darkened now, an arrogant smile curving his mouth when a thorough scrutiny showed what his focused attention had done to her body. His gaze lingered on her peaked nipples and racing pulse before coming back to hers.

He started to reach for her again, then groaned when his phone rang.

He answered, his features growing irritated as the conversation continued. Then he hung up abruptly and tossed the phone aside.

She caught his hand, wove her fingers through his. 'Is everything okay?'

His lips compressed. 'It looks like Jules isn't the only brother causing waves. Zak isn't answering his phone... again...and Violet Barringhall seems to have disappeared.'

'What? Is she...? Do you need to inform the authorities?'

He shook his head. 'My security team informs me they're both unharmed, and curiously in the same Caribbean location.' His tone was more irritated than furious.

'You think they're together?'

'Most likely. I can only surmise that they wish to remain incommunicado. But, whatever they're up to, I'm not going to let them ruin this moment.'

'Oh? And what moment is that?'

'The most perfect of moments—which is every second I spend with you, my wife, my heart. And with our son. With this love that fills my heart each day.'

He kissed her again, his hand resting on her belly. And, as if fate itself had decreed it, their child gave his first ever kick.

Maddie gasped, tears of joy filling her eyes. 'Oh, my God—did you feel that?'

Remi's smile was shaky. '*Si*. That was our son, confirming what I already know. That we are blessed beyond words. That each day you hold my heart in your hands is a lifetime I would never wish to be without. I love you, Madeleine.'

'I love you, my king. Always.'

* * * * *

BOUND BY HIS DESERT DIAMOND

ANDIE BROCK

To Roger.

Who has spent far more time discussing manly
emotions and reactions and romance in
general than he ever signed up for!

Thank you, Con. x

CHAPTER ONE

CLASPING THE COLD metal railings, Annalina stared down at the swirling black depths of the River Seine. She shivered violently, her heart thumping beneath the tight-fitting bodice of her evening gown, her designer shoes biting into the soft flesh of her heels. Clearly they had not been designed for a mad sprint down the bustling boulevards and cobbled back streets of Paris.

Oh, God. Anna dragged in a shuddering lung full of cold night air. *What had she just done?*

Somewhere behind her in one of Paris's most grand hotels, a society party was in swing. A glittering, star-studded occasion attended by royalty and heads of state, the great, the good and the glamorous from the world over. It was a party being thrown in her honour. And worse, far worse, a party where a man she had only just met was about to announce that she was to be his bride.

She let out a rasping breath, watching the cloud of condensation disperse into the night. She had no idea where she was or what she was going to do now but she did know that there was no going back. The brutal fact was she couldn't go through with this marriage, no matter what the consequences. Right up until tonight she had genuinely believed she could do it, could commit to this union, to please her father and to save her country from financial ruin.

Even yesterday, when she had met her intended for the first time, she had played along. Watching in a kind of dazed stupor as the ring had been slipped onto her finger, a perfunctory gesture performed by a man who had just wanted to get the deed over with, and witnessed by her father, whose steely-eyed glare had left no room for second thoughts or doubts. As King of the small country of Dorrada he was going to make sure that this union took place. That his daughter would marry King Rashid Zahani, ruler of the recently reformed Kingdom of Nabatean, if it was the last thing she ever did.

Which frankly, right now, looked like a distinct possibility. Anna gazed down at the ring on her finger. The enormous diamond glittered back at her, mocking her with its ostentatious sparkle. Heaven only knew what it was worth—enough to pay the entire annual salaries of the palace staff, no doubt, and with money to spare. She tugged it over her cold knuckles and held it in her palm, feeling the burden of its weight settle like a stone in her heart.

To hell with it.

Closing her fist, she raised herself up on tiptoes, leaning as far over the railings as she could. She was going to do this. She was going to fling this hateful ring into the river. She was going to control her own destiny.

He came from out of nowhere—an avalanche of heat, weight and muscle that landed on top of her, knocking the breath from her lungs, flattening her against the granite wall of his chest. She could see nothing except the darkness of him, feel nothing except the strength of the arms that were locked around her like corded steel. Her body went limp, her bones dissolving with shock. Only her poor heart tried to keep her alive, taking up a wild, thundering beat.

'Oh, no, you don't.'

He growled the words over the top of her head, somewhere in the outside world that, until a couple of moments ago, she had quite taken for granted. Now she panicked she would never see it again.

Don't what?

Anna forced her oxygen-starved brain to work out what he meant. Shouldn't it be her telling this mad man what he shouldn't be doing? Like crushing her so hard against him that she was almost asphyxiated. She tried to move inside his grip but the ring of steel tightened still further, pinning her arms to her sides. Her mouth, she suddenly registered, was pressed against flesh. She could touch him with the tip of her tongue, taste the very masculine mix of spice and sweat. She could feel the coarseness of what had to be chest hair against her lips. Forcing her mouth open, she bared her teeth, then brought them down as hard as she could. *Yes!* Her sharp nip connected with a small but significant ridge of his flesh. She felt him buck, then curse loudly in a foreign tongue.

'Why, you little...' Releasing her just enough to be able to see her face, her captor glared at her with ferociously piercing black eyes. 'What the hell are you? Some sort of animal?'

'Me!' Incredulity spiked through the terror as Anna stared back at him, squinting through the dark shadows to try and work out who the hell he was, what the hell he wanted. He seemed somehow familiar but she couldn't pull back far enough to see. 'You call me an animal when you've just leapt out on me from the shadows like some sort of crazed beast!' The jet-black eyes narrowed, glinting with all the menace of a brandished blade. Perhaps it wasn't such a good idea to goad him. 'Look.' She tried for what she hoped was a conciliatory tone, though her voice was too muffled from being squeezed half to death to be able to tell. 'If it's money you want, I'm afraid I don't have any.'

This much was true. She had fled the party without even thinking to snatch up her clutch bag.

'I don't want your money.'

The rush of fear returned. Oh, God, what did he want, then? Terror closed her throat as she desperately tried to come up with something to distract him. Suddenly she remembered the ring that was still digging into her palm. It was worth a try. 'I do have a ring, though—right here in my hand.' She tried unsuccessfully to free her arm to show it to him. 'If you let me go you can have it.'

This produced a mocking snort from above her.

'No, really, it's worth thousands—millions, for all I know.'

'I know exactly what it's worth.'

He did? Anna gasped with relief. So that was what this brute was after—the wretched ring. Well, he was welcome to it. Good riddance. She just wished she could get out of her engagement as easily. She was struggling to thrust it upon him when he spoke again.

'I should do. I signed the cheque.'

Anna stilled. *What?* This wasn't making any sense. Who on earth was this guy? Twisting in his arms, she felt his grip loosen a fraction, enough to let her straighten her spine, tip her chin and gaze into his face. Her heart thundered at what she saw.

Fearsomely handsome features glowered down at her, all sharp-angled planes of chiselled cheekbones, a blade-straight nose and an uncompromising jut of a granite-hewn jaw, all highlighted by the orange glow of the

Victorian street lights. He exuded strength and power, and his sheer forcefulness shivered its way through Anna's body, settling somewhere deep within her core.

She recognised him now. She remembered having seen him out of the corner of her eye somewhere amid the flurry of guests at the party, amid the endless introductions and polite conversations. A dark yet unmissable figure, he had been looming in the background, taking in everything—taking in her, too, before she had haughtily turned her profile to him. Some sort of bodyguard or minder—that was who he had to be. She remembered now the way he had hovered at the side of Rashid Zahani, her new fiancé, always a step behind him but somehow in charge, controlling him, owning the space, the glittering ballroom and everyone in it.

But a bodyguard who picked out engagement rings?

Somehow she couldn't see this towering force of a man lingering over a tray of jewels. Not that that mattered. What mattered was that he took his brutish hands off her and left her alone to carry on making the hideous mess of her life that she seemed so hell-bent on doing.

'So, if I am not being mugged, perhaps you would be kind enough to tell me exactly why you have leapt out of the dark and scared me half to death. And why you're not letting me go now, this instant. Presumably you know who I am?'

'Indeed I do, *Princess.*'

The word 'princess' hissed through his teeth, curdling something in Anna's stomach. Loosening his arms from around her back, he moved his hands to her shoulders, where they weighed down on her with searing heat.

'And, in reply to your question, I'm stopping you from doing something extremely foolish.'

'Flinging this into the river, you mean?' With a contemptuous toss of her head, Anna opened her hand to reveal the hated ring.

'That and yourself along with it.'

'*Myself?*' She scowled up at him. 'You don't mean…? You didn't think..?'

'That you were about to leap to your death? Yes.'

'And why exactly would I want to do that?'

'You tell me, Princess. You flee from your own engagement party in a state of high anxiety, position yourself on a bridge with a thirty-foot drop into a fast-flowing river and then lean forward in an extremely dangerous way. What was I supposed to think?'

'You weren't supposed to think at all. You were supposed to mind your own business and leave me alone.'

'Ah, but this *is* my business. *You* are my business.'

A wave of heat swept over Anna at the possessiveness of his words.

'Well, fine.' She fought to stand her ground. 'Now you can go back to your boss and tell him that you prevented a suicide that was never going to happen by leaping on an innocent woman—a woman who just happens to be a princess, may I remind you?—and scaring her half to death. I'm sure he will be very pleased with you.'

Piercingly dark eyes held hers, flicking over her like the flames of a newly lit fire, mesmerising with a promise of deadly heat. There was something else there too, an amused arrogance, if Anna wasn't mistaken. If 'amused' could ever be used to describe those forbidding features.

'In fact I may decide to press charges.' Anger hardened her voice. 'If you don't get your hands off me within the next second, I will make sure everyone knows of your behaviour.' She jerked at her shoulders to try and dislodge his leaden hold.

'I'll take my hands off you when I am good and ready.'

His voice was as dark and menacing as the river that flowed beneath them. 'And when I do it will be to personally escort you back to the party. There are a number of very important people there waiting for a big announcement, in case you had forgotten.'

'No, not forgotten.' Anna swallowed. 'But, as it happens, I've changed my mind. I've decided I won't be marrying King Rashid after all. In fact, perhaps you would like to go back and inform him of my decision.'

'Ha!' A cruel laugh escaped his lips. 'I can assure you, you will be doing no such thing. You will accompany me back to the ballroom and you will act as if nothing has happened. The engagement will be announced as planned. The wedding will go ahead as planned.'

'I think you are forgetting yourself.' Anna fired back at him. 'You are in no position to speak to me like that.'

'I'll speak to you any way I want, Princess. And you will do as I say. You can start by putting that ring back on your finger.' His hand moved to Anna's, picking up the ring and sending a jolt of awareness through her. For one crazy moment, she thought he was going to slip it back on her finger himself, like some sort of deranged suitor, but instead he handed it to her and waited as she did as she was told, the sheer force of his presence giving her no choice other than to obey.

With her ring in place, he took hold of her arm with manacle-like force and Anna found herself being turned away from the railings, presumably to be marched back to the party. This was outrageous. How dared he treat her like this? She wanted to spell out in the clearest possible terms that she did not take orders from bodyguards, or ring-choosers, or whoever this arrogant piece of work thought he was. But presumably he was working on the orders of King Rashid...

With her mind racing in all directions, she tried to think what on earth she could do—how she could get herself out of this mess. Physically trying to get away from him was clearly not an option. Even if she managed to escape his iron grip—which was highly unlikely, as the forceful fingers wrapped around her cold skin could testify—she would never be able to run fast enough to get away from him. The image of him chasing and finally capturing her flailing body was strangely erotic, given the circumstances.

She would have to use the only thing she had left in her armoury—her feminine wiles. Drawing herself up to her full height, she let her shoulder blades slide down her back, which had the desired effect of pushing her chest forward, accentuating the fullness of her breasts as they spilled over the tight bodice of her gown. Ah, yes, she had his attention now. She felt her nipples harden beneath his veiled scrutiny, sensing rather than witnessing his eyes delve into the valley of her cleavage. Her breath stalled in her throat, a tingling warmth spreading through her entire body, and she fleetingly found herself wondering who was supposed to be seducing who here.

'I'm sure we can come to some sort of mutual agreement.' Her voice came out as a sort of husky burr, more as a result of the sudden dryness of her throat than an attempt at sexiness. Still, it seemed to be working. Bodyguard man was still staring fixedly at her and, even if his granite expression hadn't softened, there was no doubt she was doing something right.

Raising her arms, Anna went to link them behind his neck. She had no clear thought of what she was doing except that maybe she could persuade him with flattery, or perhaps blackmail him after a kiss—he was certainly getting no more that—so that she could make her escape.

It went against her feminist principles but desperate times called for desperate measures.

But before she had the chance to do anything of the sort this hateful man snatched at her wrists, easily clasping them in one hand and bringing them down to her chest at the same time as swinging his other arm around her waist to pull her snugly against him. Anna gasped, the contact with his body, *that* part of his body, the particular *swell* of that part of his body, ricocheting through her with clenching waves. Granite-faced he may be, but that wasn't the only part of his body she had managed to harden.

And, judging by the look on his face, her captor had been taken by surprise too. He was glaring at her with a mixture of horror and hunger, the hand clasping her wrists shaking very slightly before he tightened its grip. Controlling the tremble of her own body, Anna stared back. If this was a small victory, though small was hardly the right word, she was going to make the most of it. Tipping back her head, she trained her eyes on his, forcing his to meet them, to see the temptations that they held, temptations that burned so brightly, even if she had no intention of honouring them. She could sense the quickening of his heartbeat beneath his white shirt, hear the faint rasp in his exhaled breath. She had got him.

'Princess Anna!'

Suddenly there was a blinding flash of light, illuminating their bodies, freezing them against the backdrop of darkness.

'What the hell?' A low growl rumbled from Anna's captor as he spun around to face the photographer that had crept out of the shadows, the shutter of the camera clicking furiously.

Blinking against the glare, Anna felt her wrists being

released as this warrior man lunged towards the photographer, clearly intent on murder. But when she went to move, to make her escape or save the photographer's life—she didn't know which—he was right back by her side again, pulling her forcefully into his arms.

'Oh, no, you don't. You're not going anywhere.'

'Come on, Anna. Show us a kiss!' Bolder now, the photographer took a step closer, the camera flashing all the time.

Anna had a split second to make a decision. If she wanted to get away from this man, avoid being frog-marched back to her own engagement party and forced to announce her betrothal to a man she could never, ever marry, there was one sure way to do it. Standing on tiptoes, she raised her arms to link them behind her captors head, shoving her fingers through the thick swathe of his hair and pulling against his resistance to bring him closer. If this was what the photographer wanted, this was what he was going to get.

With one final, terrifically brave or wildly foolish breath—Anna had no idea which—she reached up to plant her lips firmly on his.

What the hell?

Shock sucked the air from Zahir Zahani's lungs, numbing his senses, closing his fists. Plump and firm, her lips had swiftly turned from cold to warm as they sealed his own, the pressure increasing as she raked her hands through his hair to pull him closer. Her breath rasped between them, her delicate scent filling his nostrils, temporarily freezing his brain yet heating every other part of his body. Zahir went rigid, and the arms that were supposed to be restraining her were no more than useless weights as Annalina continued her relentless assault on his mouth. With the blood roaring in his ears, he found his lips parting, his body screaming to show her just where this could lead if she carried on this very dangerous game.

'Fantastic! Cheers for that, Anna.'

The camera flashes stopped and Annalina finally released him, letting her arms fall by her side. Meanwhile the photographer was already on his scooter, his camera slung over his shoulder.

'I owe you one!'

Turning the scooter around, he noisily zoomed off into the Paris streets, giving a cheery wave over his shoulder.

Zahir stared after him, suffering a split second of silent horror before his brain finally kicked into action again. Reaching into his jacket pocket, he grabbed his mobile phone. He'd have been able to catch the low life on foot if he didn't have this vixen to deal with. But his security team would pick him up—get him stopped and get the camera tossed into the Seine, the photographer along with it, if he had any say.

'No.' Her cold, trembling fingers closed over the phone in his hand. 'It's too late. It's done.'

'The hell it is.' Shaking off her hand, he started to punch in numbers. 'I can get him stopped. I *will* get him stopped.'

'There's no point.'

He stopped short, the cold determination in her voice halting his hand. 'And what exactly do you mean by that?' A trickle of dread started to seep into his veins.

'I'm sorry.' Dark-blue eyes shone back at him. 'But I had to do it.'

Hell! Realisation smacked him across the head. He'd been had. The whole thing was a set-up. This deceitful, conniving little princess had set a trap and he had walked right in. Fury coursed through him. He had no idea what her motive was but he did know that she would live to regret it. *Nobody* made a fool of Zahir Zahani.

'You will be sorry, believe me.' He kept his voice deliberately low, concentrating on controlling the rage that was pumping adrenaline dangerously fast around his veins. 'You will be more than sorry for what you have done.'

'I had no choice!' Her voice was full of anguish now and she even reached out a trembling hand to touch his arm before demurely lowering her eyes to the ground.

Nice try, Princess. But you don't get to fool me more than once.

. Roughly grasping her chin, Zahir tipped back her head so she couldn't escape his searing gaze. He wanted her to look at him. He wanted her to know exactly who she was dealing with here.

'Oh, you had a choice, all right. You've chosen to bring scandal and disrepute to both our countries. And, trust me, you are going to pay for that, young lady. But first you are going to tell me why.'

He saw her slender body begin to tremble, her bare shoulders hunch against the shiver that ran through her. Bizarrely he itched to touch her, to warm that tantalisingly goose-bumped skin with his hot hands. But he would do no such thing.

'Because I am desperate.' Clear blue eyes implored him.

'Desperate?' He repeated the word with disgust.

'Yes. I can't go back to that party.'

'So that's why you set up this little charade?'

'No, I didn't set it up, not in the way you mean. I just took advantage of the situation.' Her voice lowered.

'You tricked me into following you. You arranged for that photographer to be there.'

'No! I had no idea that either of you had followed me.'

'You're lying. That guy knew you.'

'He didn't know me. He knows who I am. There's a difference. The press have been following me around all my life.'

'So you are telling me this wasn't planned?'

Annalina shook her head.

'Think carefully before you speak, Princess. Because, I have to warn you, to lie to me now would be very foolish indeed.'

'It was a spur-of-the-moment decision. And that is the truth.'

Despite everything, Zahir found himself believing her. He dragged in a breath. 'So that…that little display you just put on…?' He curled his lip against the traitorous memory of the way she had leant into him, the way she had messed with his head. 'What exactly did you hope to achieve? What makes you so desperate that you would bring disgrace upon your family? Fabricate a scandal to rock the foundations of both of our countries?'

'Disgrace I can live with. I'm used to it.' Her voice was suddenly very small. 'And the scandal will die down. But to be forced to marry Rashid Zahani is more than I can bear. That would have been a life sentence.'

'How dare you disrespect the King in this way?' Defensive anger roared in his voice. 'The engagement will still be announced. The marriage will still go ahead.'

'No. You can force me to go back to the party, even force me, with the help of my father, to go ahead with the announcement of the engagement. But, once those photographs go online, I'll be dropped like a stone.'

Zahir stared into the beautiful face of this wilful princess. Her skin was so pale in this ghostly light, so delicate, it was almost translucent. But her lips were ruby-red and her eyes as blue as the evening sky.

He knew with a leaden certainty that she meant what she said. There was no way she was going to go through with this marriage. He could still find that photographer, destroy the photos, but ultimately what good would it do? What was to be gained?

Hell and damnation. After all the planning that had gone into this union, the careful handling, the wretched party… It had taken all his powers of persuasion to get Rashid to agree to marry this European princess at all. Months of negotiations to get to this point. And for what? To have the whole thing thrown back in their faces and Rashid humiliated in the most degrading way. No, he could not let that happen. He *would* not let that happen. He had been a fool to trust this wayward princess, to believe the empty promises of her desperate father. But the situation had gone too far now—he had to try and salvage something from this mess. He had to come up with a clever solution.

Decision made, he took hold of Annalina's arm.

'You will accompany me back to the party and we will seek out the King and tell him what has happened. Then we will announce your engagement.'

'Didn't you understand a word I said?' The fight was back in her eyes. 'The King won't marry me now. That's the reason I just did what I did.'

'We will announce your engagement—not to the King, but to his brother, the Prince.'

'Yeah, great idea! I take it you must be employed more for your brawn than your brains.' Zahir felt every muscle in his body stiffen at her mocking jibe. He was going to enjoy punishing her for her insolence. 'The Prince is hardly going to want to marry me either, is he?'

'As of five minutes ago, the Prince has no choice.'

Narrowing his eyes, Zahir watched defiance turn to confusion turn to a creeping realisation. A strangely perverse sense of pleasure stole over him.

Her trembling hand flew to her mouth then made a fist as she stuffed it between her lips, biting down onto her knuckles to stifle her cry.

'Ah, yes, Princess, I see the truth is dawning.' Zahir threw back his shoulders, almost enjoying himself. 'I am Zahir Zahani, Prince of Nabatean, brother of King Rashid. And, as of five minutes ago, your future husband.'

CHAPTER TWO

ANNA FELT FOR the railings of the bridge behind her, grabbing at the bars to stop herself from sliding to the ground.

'You…you are Prince Zahir?'

One arrogant, scowling dark brow raised fractionally in reply.

No. It wasn't possible. The full horror of what she had done gnawed away at her brain. Being caught in a clinch with a bodyguard to get out of her engagement was one thing, but for the 'bodyguard' to be the fiancé's brother was quite another. This went far beyond the realms of scandal. This could cause an international incident.

'I…I had no idea.'

He shrugged. 'Evidently.'

'We need to do something—quickly.' Panic caught up with her, squeezing her vocal cords, spinning her brain around in her head. 'We must stop that photographer.'

Still Zahir Zahani didn't move. What was wrong with him? Why wasn't he doing anything? Anna felt as if she were in a terrible dream, running and running but getting no further away from the monster.

Finally he spoke. 'To use your phrase, Princess, *it's too late. It's done.*'

'But that was before I knew… There's still time to find him, pay him off, stop him.'

'Possibly. But I have no intention of doing any such thing.'

'Wh…what do you mean?' Confusion and frustration held her in their grip, hysteria not far behind. 'I don't understand.'

'Because, like you, I intend to take advantage of the situation. We will go back to the party and we will announce our engagement. Just as I said.'

Horror now joined the bedlam in her head. He wasn't serious. Surely he didn't mean it? She stared into his cold, forbidding features. *Oh, God.* He did—he really did!

Releasing the railings, she pushed herself upright, immediately dwarfed by this towering figure of a man who was blocking her way, her vision, her ability to think clearly. 'No! We can't. The idea is preposterous.'

'Is it, Princess Annalina? He glowered down at her. 'How will you feel tomorrow when those photographs are published? When you have to face your father, your people and the rest of the world? Are you prepared for the consequences?'

Her face crumpled.

'As I thought.' His mocking voice echoed in the dark around them. 'Not quite so preposterous now, is it? You have no alternative but to do as I say.'

'No. There has to be another way.' *Think, Anna, think.* Why did her poor brain seem to have turned to sludge? 'If the photographs are published I'll simply explain that it was all a misunderstanding—that I didn't know who you were…that it meant nothing.'

'And that would achieve what, exactly? Apart from prove that you are the sort of tramp who goes around seducing total strangers on the eve of your engagement and that your fiancé's own brother was caught in your trap. I would never subject Rashid to such humiliation.'

There was a second of silence.

'But we can't just swap!'

'We can and we will. The arrangements are all in place. A commitment has been made between our two countries—between your father and the Kingdom of Nabatean. He has offered your hand and it has been accepted. Nothing will stand in the way of that.' His shadowed face was as hard as stone. 'The commitment will be honoured.'

'But the commitment was to your brother—not you.'

'Then perhaps you should have thought of that before you ran away and started this whole debacle, betraying the trust my brother had put in you.' Anna lowered her eyes against the force of his biting scorn. 'Fortunately for you, it makes no difference which brother honours the commitment. The same objectives will be achieved either way.'

'And that's it? Honouring the commitment is all that matters to you?' She thrashed about, trying to find a way out. 'How can you be so unemotional? This is a marriage we are talking about, a bond that has to last a lifetime.'

'Don't you think I know that, Princess?' Lowering his head, Zahir hissed into her ear, sending a bolt of electricity through her. 'Don't you think I am fully aware of the sacrifice I am making? But, if it is emotion you are looking for, I must warn you to be careful. To expose my opinion of you would be straying into a dark and dangerous territory indeed.'

Cloaked in menace, his words settled over her like a shroud. Anna bit down hard on her lip to control the shiver. She didn't entirely know what he meant by that chilling statement. She wasn't sure she wanted to.

'And if I refuse?' Still she tried, squirming like a worm on a fish hook.

'All I can say is, to refuse would be extremely stupid.' He paused, weighting his words with care. 'I'm sure I don't have to remind you that you already have one failed engagement behind you. Another might cause considerable speculation.'

A sharp jab of pain went through her. So he knew about that, did he? About her humiliating broken engagement to Prince Henrik. Of course he did. Everyone did.

Tears were starting to build now, blocking her throat, scratching at her eyes. Tears of frustration, self-pity and wretched misery that her life had come to this. That she should be forced to marry a man who clearly despised her. A man who was as terrifying as he was alien—an arrogant, untamed brute of a man the like of which she had never come across before. She hadn't begun to process the extraordinary reaction between them when she'd kissed him, the shockingly carnal way his body had responded. That would have to be for another time. But she did know he would never make her happy—that was a certainty. He would never even try.

'You have brought this upon yourself, Princess Annalina.' Somewhere outside the buzz of her head she heard him relentlessly press home the point. 'You have forced my hand, but I am prepared do my duty. And, ultimately, so must you.'

His damning statement was the final nail in the coffin.

And so it was that Anna found herself being unceremoniously marched back to the hotel to meet her fate. With Zahir's arm around her waist, propelling her forward, she had had no choice but to stumble along beside him, needing two or three stiletto-heeled steps to match his forceful stride as he rapidly navigated them through the Parisian streets. Her heart was thumping wildly, her dry breath scouring her throat as she tried to come to terms with what she was about to do—tie herself to this man for ever. But with the heat of his arm burning through the sheer fabric of her dress she found herself trying to fight that assault, the whole shimmering force of his nearness, his muscled flesh, his masculine scent, leaving her brain no space to cope with anything else.

Finally outside the hotel Zahir turned her around to face him, his gaze raking mercilessly over her pale face. With the light spilling from the hotel, they could see each other more clearly now, but Anna had to tear her eyes away from his cruelly handsome features, afraid of what she might see there. Her gaze slid down the broad column of his neck to the open buttons of his shirt, the grey silk tie tugged to one side. And there, plainly visible against the exposed olive skin, was the livid red mark—the bite, where she had sunk her teeth into him. Instinctively her hand flew to her chest.

Alerted by her stare, Zahir swiftly moved to do up his shirt and straighten his tie, his knowing glare spelling out exactly what he thought of her barbarism.

'We will go in together,' he began coldly. 'You will talk to our guests and behave in the appropriate manner. But say nothing to anyone about the engagement. I will find my brother and tell him of the new arrangement.'

Anna nodded, swallowing down her dread. 'But shouldn't I be there when you speak to your brother? Don't I owe him that?'

'I think it's a little late for the guilt to kick in now, Annalina. We are way past that. *I* will deal with Rashid and then explain the situation to your father. Only then can we announce our engagement.'

Her father. In her frenzied state Anna had almost forgotten the man who had brought about this hideous debacle in the first place. It had been King Gustav who had insisted that his only child should marry King Rashid of Nabatean, leaving her no room to argue. Not after she had already let him down once, let her country down, by failing to secure a successful match between herself and Prince Henrik of Ebsberg—something that still both humiliated and swamped Anna with relief in equal measure.

A cold, heartless man, King Gustav had never recovered from the death of his wife, Annalina's mother, who had suffered a fatal brain aneurysm when Anna had been just seven years old. The shock had been too much for him and it seemed to Anna that a part of her father had died with her mother. The loving, caring part. It seemed that just when she had needed him most he had turned away from her. And had never turned back.

He would be utterly furious to find out that she had messed up again—that she was refusing to marry Rashid Zahani and was chucking away the chance to provide financial stability for Dorrada. At least, he would have been, if she hadn't had an alternative plan to offer him. For the first time Anna felt a tinge of relief about what she was doing. Zahir might be the second son but everything about him suggested power and authority, far more so than his elder brother, in fact. She suspected that her father would have no problem accepting the new arrangement. Somehow she had to find it inside herself to do the same.

She looked down, concentrating on arranging the folds of her dress, all too aware of the fire in Zahir's eyes as they licked over her, missing nothing.

'You are ready?'

She nodded, not trusting herself to speak.

'Very well, then, we will do this.'

The arm snaked around her waist again and together

they ascended the red-carpeted steps, the hotel doorman ushering them in with a polite bow.

The scene inside the ballroom appeared even more daunting than when Anna had fled less than an hour ago. More people had arrived, swelling the numbers into the hundreds, and they were milling around beneath the magnificent domed ceiling of the gilded room, illuminated by dozens of huge chandeliers and watched from above by carved marble statues. The air of anticipation had increased too. Anyone who was anyone was here, the great and the good from a host of European and Middle Eastern countries gathered at the invitation of King Gustav of Dorrada for a celebration that had yet to be disclosed.

Not that it took much working out. Presumably everyone in the room knew what this party was in aid of—or at least thought they did. It was common knowledge that King Gustav had been trying, and failing, to make a good marriage for his only daughter for some time. And the newly formed kingdom of Nabatean desperately needed entrée into the notoriously closed shop of 'old' Europe. The fact that the party was being held here, in one of the oldest and most exclusive hotels in Paris, right at the heart of Europe, bore testament to that and was certainly no coincidence.

Anna looked around her, the heat and the noise thundering inside her head, shredding her nerves, fuelling her panic. Zahir had left her side and gone in search of his brother, which should have been a relief, but bizarrely only made her feel more vulnerable and exposed. She could see her father in the distance and her heart took up a shaky beat at the thought of what he was about to be told. Of what they were about to do.

Grabbing a glass of champagne from a passing waiter, she took a deep gulp, followed by a deep breath, and, pulling on what she hoped was the suitably starry-eyed expression of a fiancée-to-be, set about mingling with her guests.

It was not long before Zahir was by her side again. Taking her arm, he steered her away from the curious stares of the small group of people she had been trying to converse with, guests who were clearly starting to wonder what was going on. Anna didn't know who else had witnessed it, but a few minutes ago she had caught sight of Rashid skirting around the edge of the room. Their eyes had met for a fleeting second before he had lowered his head and hurried from the ballroom.

'The necessary arrangements have been made.' Zahir's voice was steely with determination. 'It's time for the announcement.'

So this was it, then. Part of her thought she might wake up at any moment, that this was some sort of crazy dream—no, correction, nightmare. But as she slipped her arm through his, felt herself being pulled to his side, her whole body lit up to his nearness. Her heart thumped as the smooth fabric of his dinner jacket brushed against her bare arm, pinpricks of awareness skittering across her skin. This was real all right. This was actually happening.

As they moved across the floor of the ballroom the guests parted to let them through, something about the purposefulness of Zahir's stride or maybe the mask-like expression on Annalina's face, halting their conversations as they turned to look at them, curiosity glinting in their eyes.

Silencing the orchestra with a raised hand, Zahir waited a second for complete quiet to descend before he began.

'I would like to thank everyone for coming this evening.' Anna heard his calm words through the roaring of her ears. She could feel hundreds of pairs of eyes trained on her.

'We are here to celebrate the coming together of two great nations—Dorrada and the Kingdom of Nabatean. Our countries are to be joined together by the age-old tradition of matrimony.' He paused, scanning the room, which had gone deathly quiet. 'I would like to formally announce that Princess Annalina and I are to be married.'

There was a collective gasp of surprise, followed by furtive whisperings. Obviously Princess Annalina was not marrying the brother the guests had been expecting. Then a small cheer went up and people started to applaud, calling out their congratulations.

Anna's father appeared by her side and she felt for his hand, the little girl in her suddenly needing his reassurance. The smallest squeeze of encouragement would have done. Anything to show that he was pleased with her. That he loved her. He leant towards her and for one hopeful moment Anna thought he was going to do just that, but all hopes were dashed when he whispered in her ear, 'Don't you dare let me down again, Annalina.' Extricating his hand, he took a glass of champagne from the proffered silver tray and waited for Anna and Zahir to do the same. Then, refusing to meet his daughter's eye, he cleared his throat and proposed a toast, instructing everyone to raise their glasses to the happy couple and the future prosperity of their joined nations.

Anna gripped the stem of her glass as their names were chorused by the guests. Beside her she could sense Zahir, all rigid authority and unyielding control, while the false smile she had plastered across her face was in danger of cracking at any moment. In terms of appearing to be a happy couple, she doubted they were fooling anyone. But that wasn't what this was about, was it? This betrothal was a straightforward business deal. Anna just wished that someone would tell her stupid heart.

The next hour was a torturous round of introductions and small talk as Zahir swept her around the room, making sure she was welded to his side at all times. He moved between the ministers and ambassadors of Nabatean, the diplomats and high-ranking officials of Dorrada. It was blatantly nothing more than a networking exercise, making contact with the people that mattered. Congratulations were swiftly swept aside in favour of discussions about policies and politics, Anna left smiling inanely at the wives of these important men, and forced to display the stunning ring on her finger for them to coo over yet again.

Finally finding themselves at the entrance to the ballroom, Zahir announced in lowered tones that they had done their duty and it would now be acceptable for them to leave.

Anna gave a sigh of relief but, looking up, she was immediately caught in the midnight black of Zahir's hooded gaze. Suddenly she felt awkward, like a teenager on her first date. 'I will say goodnight, then.' She went to turn away, desperate to escape to her hotel room, to be free of her captor, at least for a few hours. More than anything she wanted to be alone, to have time to try to come to terms with what she had done.

'Not so fast.' With lightning speed, Zahir laid a restraining hold on her arm. 'This day has not ended yet.'

Anna's heart skipped a beat. What did he mean by that? Surely he wasn't expecting...? He didn't think...? Heat flared across her cheeks, spreading down her neck to her chest that heaved beneath its tight-fitting bodice. Somewhere deep inside her a curl of lust unfurled.

'I can assure you that it has, Zahir.' She touched

primly at her hair. 'I don't know what you are suggesting, but for your information I intend to go to bed now—
alone.'

'You flatter yourself, young lady.' Scorn leeched from
his voice. 'For your information, I do not intend to make
any claims on your body.' He paused, eyes flashing with
lethal intent. 'Not tonight, at least. But neither will I be
letting you out of my sight. Not yet. Not until I feel I can
trust you.'

'What do you mean?' Desperately trying to claw back
some composure, she folded her arms across her chest.
'You can hardly keep me prisoner until our marriage.'
Even as she said the words the terrible thought struck
her that maybe he could. He was a man of such power,
such authority, it was as if his very being demanded to
be obeyed. The glittering lights of the ballroom had only
accentuated his might, his towering height, the long legs
and the broad, muscled shoulders that refused to be tamed
by the fine material of his dinner jacket. Anna had noticed several women openly staring at him, their refined
good manners deserting them in the face of this ruggedly
handsome man.

'Not a prisoner, Princess. But let's just say I want to
keep you somewhere that I can see you.'

'But that is ridiculous. I have given you my word,
made the promise to my father. We have announced our
engagement to the world. What more do I have to do to
convince you?'

'You have to earn my trust, Annalina.' His eyes
roamed over her, flat and considering. 'And that, as I'm
sure you won't be surprised to hear, may take some time.'

'So what are you saying?' Anna bristled beneath his
harsh scrutiny. 'That until I've earned this so-called trust
you're not going to let me out of your sight? That hardly

seems practical. Not least because we happen to live on different continents.'

Zahir shrugged. 'That is of little consequence. The solution is simple—you will return with me to Nabatean.'

Anna stared back at him. His knowing gaze was doing strange things to her head—making it swim. She must have drunk too much champagne.

'That's right, Princess Annalina.' Cold and authoritative, he confirmed what she feared. 'We leave tonight.'

CHAPTER THREE

ANNA PEERED OUT of the window as the plane started to descend, the sight of the dawn sky making her catch her breath. Below her shimmered Medira, the capital city of Nabatean, glowing in the pinks and golds of a new day. Her first glimpse of the country that would be her new home was certainly a stunning one. But it did nothing to lighten Anna's heart.

The little she knew about Nabatean had been gleaned during the first panicked days after she had been informed that she was to marry King Rashid Zahani. There had been a bloody civil war—that much she did know—when the people of Nabatean had fought bravely to overthrow the oppressive regime of Uristan, eventually winning independence and becoming a country in its own right again after more than fifty years.

There had been mention of Rashid and Zahir's parents, the former King and Queen of Nabatean, who had returned after living in exile, only to be murdered by rebel insurgents on the eve of the country's independence. Details of the horrifically tragic event were few and far between and in part Anna was grateful for that. There was frustratingly little documented about the new country at all and she realised just how ignorant she was about the place that she would somehow have to learn to call home.

Just as she knew so little of the man who was bringing her here, who intended to make her his wife. The man who had taken himself off to the office area of the luxury private jet and had spent the long journey so immersed in work, either glued to his laptop or reading through documents, that he had paid her no attention at all.

But what did she expect? When they had boarded the jet he had suggested that Anna retire to the bedroom, making it quite clear that the space would be her own. But stubbornness, or the fact that she knew she would never be able to sleep, or the hope that they might be able to have some meaningful discussion, had made her decline his offer.

Now she knew just how futile that hope had been and, staring at her own anxious reflection in the glass, found herself wondering how it was that her life had always been so controlled by others. First her father and now this dark, brooding force of nature that was to be her husband. Her destiny had never been her own. And now it never would be.

'We land in ten minutes.' With a start, Anna turned around to see that Zahir was standing right beside her, his hand on the back of her seat. For such a large man he moved surprisingly quietly, stealthily. Even his voice was different—raw and untamed, as if capable of sinful pleasure or brutal destruction. 'The distance from the airport to the palace is not a long one. Your journey is almost over. I trust you haven't found it too arduous?'

'No, I'm fine.' That was a lie. She was totally exhausted. But, having turned down his offer of an in-flight bedroom, she wasn't going to admit that.

'I think you will find the palace is most comfortable. You can rest assured that your every need will be catered for.'

'Thanks.' Anna didn't know what else to say. Who did he think she was? A princess from a fairy tale who would be unable to sleep should a pea be placed under her mattress? Or, worse still, some sort of prima donna who expected her every whim instantly to be obeyed?

If so, he couldn't be more wrong. She might have been raised in a palace but it had been as echoing and draughty as it was ancient, with crumbling walls, peeling paint-work and plumbing that only worked when it felt like it. And, as for expecting her every need to be catered for, well, she had been brought up to have no needs, no special treatment. Since her mother's death a succession of nannies—each one more severe, more cold-hearted than the last—had been at pains to point that out to her. Whether it was because they'd been handpicked by her father for that very reason—King Gustav believed his daughter needed a firm hand—or because the chilly con-ditions of the palace somehow had rubbed off on them, Anna didn't know.

She did know that she had never found anyone who had been able to replicate the warm feeling of her moth-er's arms around her, or the soft cushion of her breast, or the light touch of her fingers as she'd swept Annalina's unruly hair from her eyes. Which was why she held on to those feelings as firmly as her seven-year-old's grip would allow, keeping them alive by remembering every-thing she could about her beloved mother, refusing to let the memories fade.

A fleet of limousines was there to whisk Zahir and Anna, plus Rashid and assorted members of staff who had accompanied them on the plane, on the final leg of their journey to the palace. Once inside the palace, they were greeted by more deferential staff and Anna was shown to her suite of rooms, the bedroom dominated by an enormous gilded bed that was surmounted by a coronet and swathes of luxurious, deep-red silk.

It looked incredibly inviting. Finally giving way to her tiredness, Anna headed for the bathroom for a quick shower, taking in the huge, sunken marble bath with its flashy gold fittings and the veined marble walls. Then, climbing into the bed, she closed her eyes and let herself sink into deep, dream-filled sleep.

She was awoken by a tap on the door. Two dark-haired young women appeared, each bearing a tray laden with fruit, cheese, eggs, hummus, pitta bread and olives. She sat forward as they silently plumped up the pillows behind her, then one started to pour a cup of coffee whilst the other one held a plate and a pair of tongs, presumably waiting for Anna to make her selection.

'Oh, thank you.' Pushing the hair out of her eyes, Anna smiled at them, wondering how on earth she was ever going to do justice to this feast. What time was it anyway? A gilded clock on the wall opposite showed it to be just past one o'clock. So, that would be one in the afternoon? She looked back at the food. She was going to have to choose something. Judging by the earnest look on the young girls' faces, she wouldn't have been surprised if they had offered to feed her themselves. 'I think I'll try the eggs—they look delicious.'

Immediately an omelette was set before her and two pairs of eyes watched as she tentatively dug in her fork.

'Do you speak English?' Anna took a mouthful of omelette followed by a mouthful of coffee. The latter was strong, dark and utterly delicious.

'Yes, Your Highness.'

'Does everyone in Nabatean speak English?'

'Yes, Your Highness, it is our second language. You will find everyone can speak it.'

'It's the second language in my country too, so that's handy.' Anna smiled at these two pretty young women. 'And please, call me Annalina. "Your Highness" sounds far too stuffy.'

The women nodded but something told Anna that they would struggle with such informality. 'Can I ask your names?'

'I am Lena and this is Layla.'

'What pretty names. I'm guessing you are sisters?' She tried another forkful of omelette.

'We are. Layla is my younger sister by two years.'

'Well, it's very nice to meet you. Have you worked here in the palace long?' If she couldn't manage to eat much, at least she could distract them with conversation.

'Yes, for nearly two years. Ever since the palace was built. We are very lucky. After our parents died we were given a home in return for serving the King and Prince Zahir.'

So their parents were dead. Anna suspected there were going to be many tales of death and destruction in this country once ravaged by war. She wanted to ask more but Lena's lowered eyes suggested to pry further would be insensitive. Layla, however, had edged closer to the bed, staring at her as if she had been dropped down from another planet.

'I like your hair.'

'Layla!' Her sister admonished her with a sharp rebuke.

'That's okay.' Anna laughed, looking down at the blonde locks that were tumbling in disarray over her shoulders. 'Thank you for the compliment. It takes a lot of brushing in the morning, though, to get the tangles out.'

'I can do that for you,' Layla replied earnestly.

'Well, that's very kind of you but…'

'We are honoured to be able to serve you, Your Royal Highness,' Lena said. 'Prince Zahir has instructed us to attend to your every need.'

He had? Anna found it hard to believe that he would concern himself with such trivialities as her every need. 'Well, in that case, I will take you up on your kind offer. Prince Zahir...' Anna hesitated. She wanted to ask what sort of an employer he was, what sort of a man they thought he was, but suspected that they wouldn't be at liberty to tell her and it would be unfair to ask. 'Do you see very much of him?'

'No. He is away from the palace a lot. And, even when he is here, his needs are very few.'

'Do you have many visitors, here in the palace?'

'Not so many. Mostly foreign businessmen and politicians.'

'We've never had a visitor as pretty as you before,' Layla offered conversationally. 'Do all the women in your country look like you?'

'Well, the women of Dorrada tend to be fair-skinned and blue-eyed. The men too, come to that. Your dark beauty would be much prized in my country. As I'm sure it is here.'

'So, Prince Zahir...' Layla continued. 'You think him handsome?'

'Layla!'

'I am only asking.' Layla stuck out her bottom lip.

'Obviously she thinks him handsome. She wouldn't be marrying him otherwise.'

Anna suppressed a smile as the two sisters set about one another in their own language, waiting for them to finish before speaking again.

'The answer to your question is yes—I do think him handsome.'

The sisters exchanged an excited glance.

'And it is true that you will be marrying and coming to live here in the palace?' This time Lena asked the question, her curiosity overcoming her sense of decorum.

'Yes, that is true.' Saying it out loud didn't make it seem any the less astonishing.

Lena's and Layla's pretty faces broke out into broad smiles and they even reached to clasp each other's hands.

'That is very good news, Your Royal Highness. Very good news indeed.'

Staring at the screen, Zahir cursed under his breath. He had braced himself for a small photograph of the two of them on the bridge, prepared to suffer the mild humiliation of being caught kissing in public, or rather being kissed, when it was put in the wider context of the engagement party. But this wasn't a small photograph. This was a series of images, blown up to reveal every minor detail. With his finger jabbing on the mouse, Zahir scrolled down and down, his blood pressure rocketing as more and more pictures of him locked in a passionate embrace with Annalina flashed before his eyes. There were even several close-ups of the engagement ring, worn on the slender hand that was threaded through his hair, before finally the official photographs of the party appeared, the ones he wanted the world to see. The ones where he and Annalina were standing solemnly side by side, displaying their commitment to each other and to their countries.

And it wasn't just one newspaper. The whole of Europe appeared to be obsessed with the beautiful Princess Annalina, the press in France, the UK, and of course Dorrada itself taking a particular interest, feasting on the titbits that the photographer had no doubt sold to them for a handsome fee.

A rustle behind him made him turn his head and there stood the object of the press's attention, Annalina. At last—it was over an hour since he had sent servants to her room to find out what she was doing, giving orders that she should meet him here in the stateroom at her earliest convenience. Clearly he was going to have to be more specific. Dressed in a simple navy fitted dress, she looked both young, chic and incredibly sexy at the same time. Her ash-blonde hair was loose, tumbling over her shoulders in soft waves, falling well below the swell of her breasts.

Zahir felt his throat go dry. He hadn't been prepared for such hair, only having seen it secured on top of her head in some way before. He had had no idea it would be so long, so fascinating. He had had no idea that he would be fighting the urge to imagine how it would feel against his bare skin.

'Have you seen this?' Angry with himself, with his reaction and this whole damned situation, his voice rasped harshly. He hadn't been able to concentrate all morning, hadn't got through half the work he'd intended to.

She glanced at the laptop, screwing up her eyes. 'Is it bad?'

'See for yourself.'

A soft cloud of floral scent washed over him as she sat down next to him, tucking her hair behind one small, perfect ear. He almost flinched as she reached across him to touch the mouse, quickly scrolling through the images and scanning the text as she moved from one website to the next.

'Well.' She turned in her seat to look at him, her eyes a startling blue. 'I guess it's no worse than we were expecting.'

'You, maybe. I certainly wasn't expecting such mass coverage.'

'Well, there's nothing we can do about it now.' She exhaled, the light breath whispering across the bare skin of his forearm and raising the hairs, raising his blood pressure. 'Are the photos in the Nabatean newspapers too?'

'Fortunately not. The official photographs from the engagement party are all that they will see. My people would not be interested in such a sordid spectacle.'

He watched as she wrinkled her small nose. Her skin was so pale, so clear, like the finest porcelain.

'What?' He didn't want to ask, he hadn't even meant to ask. But her disrespectful gesture refused to be ignored.

'I'm just wondering how you know that—if they aren't given the chance, I mean. That sounds like censorship to me.'

Temper snaked through him, slowing his heart to a dull thud. He narrowed his eyes, the thick lashes blurring his image of this infuriating woman. 'Let me make something clear right from the start, Princess Annalina. I may, or may not, seek your views on matters to do with European culture and traditions that I am not familiar with. That is your role. However, you do *not* attempt to interfere with the running of my country. Your opinions are neither needed nor wanted.'

'If you say so.'

'I do.'

'All I'm saying is…' she raised finely shaped eyebrows '…you can't have it both ways.' It seemed she was determined to stand up to him. To have the last word. 'If you are marrying me solely because I am a Western princess, because you want entrée into Europe that my family, my country, can give you, then you are going to have to accept this sort of media attention. It comes with the job. It comes with me.'

Zahir scowled. Was this true? If so he was going to have to put a stop to it. He had no intention of becoming part of some celebrity circus. But then twenty-four hours ago he had had no intention of marrying at all.

'I have to say, I am somewhat surprised that you would be happy for the first sighting the people of Nabatean have of their new princess to be a grubby little paparazzi shot of you wantonly pressing your body up against mine.' He wished he hadn't reminded himself of that now. Not when she was so close. Not when he knew he wanted her to do it again.

'It doesn't bother me.' She tossed her head, her hair rippling over her shoulders, deliberately countering his pomposity with a throwaway remark. It felt to Zahir as if she was throwing his weakness for her back in his face too, even though he had gone to great pains to cover it up.

'Well, it should bother you. It is hardly becoming.' The pomposity solidified inside him, holding him ram-rod-straight.

'Look. The paparazzi have been following me all my life. I'm used to it—it's part of the role I was unwittingly born into. There are probably hundreds of images of me being *unbecoming*, as you put it.'

Zahir felt himself pale beneath his olive skin. This was worse than he'd thought. In his haste to arrange a suitable match for his brother it appeared he hadn't been thorough enough in his research. He knew there had been a broken engagement but what was she telling him now? That she had a history of debauched behaviour? This woman who he now had to take as his wife.

'It's okay!' Suddenly she let out a laugh, a light-hearted

chuckle that echoed between them, seeming to surprise
the cavernous room as much as it did him. 'There's no
need to look like that.' Now she was reaching for his
hand, laying her own over the top of it. 'I haven't done
anything really terrible! And, who knows, maybe now
that I'm officially engaged the paparazzi will lose interest in me, find someone else to train their zoom lenses
on. Especially as you are not well known in Europe.'

'Unlike your last fiancé, you mean?'

Annalina withdrew her hand, all traces of humour
gone now, colour touching her cheeks at his mention of
her former partner. If he had wanted to snuff out her sunshine, he had achieved it.

'Well, yes, Prince Henrik was well known to the gossip columnists. When that relationship ended it was inevitable that there was going to be a feeding frenzy.'

There was silence as Zahir refilled his coffee cup before returning his gaze to Annalina's face.

'I expect you want to know what happened.' She
twisted her hands in her lap.

'No.'

'I will tell you if you ask.'

'I have no intention of asking. It's none of my business.' And, more than that, he didn't want to think about
it. She continued to stare at him, a strange sort of expression playing across her face, as if she was trying to decide where to go from here.

'I suggest we concentrate on making plans for the future.' There, he could be sensitive, moving her on from
what was obviously a painful subject.

'Yes, of course.'

'I see no reason for a long engagement.'

'No.' Now she was chewing her lip.

'A month should be ample time to make the arrangements. I'm assuming you'll want some sort of society wedding in Dorrada? If we follow that with a blessing here in Nabatean, that should suffice.'

'Right.'

'So I can leave you to organise it? The wedding, I mean? Or hire people to do it, or however these things work.' At the mention of the wedding she seemed to have gone into some kind of stupor. Wasn't the idea of arranging your wedding day supposed to be appealing to a young woman? Clearly not to Annalina. A thought occurred to him and he leant back in his chair. 'If it's money that is concerning you, let me assure you that is not a problem. No expense is to be spared.'

But instead of lessening her worry his statement only furrowed her brow deeper and was now coupled with a distinct look of distaste in her eyes. Perhaps talking about money was distasteful—he had no idea, and frankly he didn't care. Or perhaps he was the thing that she found distasteful. He didn't want to care about that either. But somehow he did. Abruptly scraping back his chair, he pushed himself to his feet, suddenly needing to end this meeting right now.

'Perhaps you will inform me of the date of the wedding as soon as you know it.'

He looked down on Annalina from the superior position of his height. He heard himself, cold and aloof.

CHAPTER FOUR

'YOUR ROYAL HIGHNESS?'

Anna was wandering around the palace when one of the servants came to find her. She had spent the last hour pacing from one room to the next, still fuming too much over Zahir's abrupt departure from their so-called meeting to pay much attention to her opulent surroundings. The way he had just got up and walked out, ending their discussion with no warning, no manners!

She had thought she would try and distract herself by finding her way around this grand edifice but it was all too huge, too daunting, each room grander than the last, all domed ceilings, brightly coloured marble floors and micro-mosaic decorations. But there was nothing homely about it. In fact it had a new, unlived-in feel to it, as if no laughter had ever echoed through its stately rooms, no children's feet had ever raced along its miles of corridors or young bottoms slid down its sweepingly ornate banisters. Which, no doubt, they hadn't. This was a show home, nothing more. A monument erected as a display of wealth and power, a symbol of national pride for the people of Nabatean.

'Prince Zahir has instructed that you are to meet him at the palace entrance.' The servant bowed respectfully. 'If you would like to follow me?'

So that would be right now, would it? This was how it was to be—Zahir issued his orders and she was expected to obey. Just like any other member of his staff. Instinctively Anna wanted to rebel, to say no, just to prove that she wasn't at his beck and call. But what would that achieve, other than deliberately antagonising him? Something which she strongly suspected would not prove to be a good idea. Besides, she had nothing else to do.

A wall of heat hit her when she stepped out into the searing afternoon sun. Shielding her eyes, she could see Zahir standing by the limousine, waiting for the chauffeur to help her inside before getting in beside her.

'Can I ask where we're going?' She settled in her seat, preparing herself to turn and look at him. It still gave her a jolt every single time her eyes met his, every time she stared into his darkly rugged features. It was like a cattle prod to her nervous system. He had changed into a sharply cut suit, she noticed, so presumably this wasn't a pleasure trip.

'The Assembly House in the town square.' He returned her gaze. 'I have arranged a meeting with some officials, members of the senate and the government. It will be an opportunity to introduce you to them, so they can put a face to the name.'

A face to the name? His cold phrase left her in no doubt as to her role here—she was nothing more than a puppet, to be dangled in front of the people that mattered, jiggled around to perform when necessary and presumably put back in her box when she wasn't required. It was a depressing picture but she had to remember that this was what their union was all about, a mutually reciprocal arrangement for the benefit of both of their countries. Nothing more. She needed to catch her sinking stomach before it fell still further.

Breaking his gaze, Anna turned to look out of the window as the limousine swept them through the streets of Medira. It was a city still under construction, enormous cranes swinging above their heads, towering skyscrapers proudly rocketing heavenwards. The place certainly had a buzz about it. Lowering her head, Annalina peered up in awe.

'I hadn't realised Medira was such a metropolis. Is it really true that this whole city has been built in under two years?'

'It has, in common with several other major cities in Nabatean.'

'That's amazing. You must be very proud.'

'It has been a great responsibility.'

Responsibility. The word might as well be indelibly etched across his forehead. In fact it was, Anna realised as she turned to look at him again. It was there in the frown lines that crossed his brow, lines that furrowed into deep grooves when he was lost in thought or displeased. Which seemed to be most of the time. There was no doubt how heavily responsibility weighed on Zahir Zahani's shoulders, that his duty to his country knew no bounds. He was prepared to marry her, after all. What greater sacrifice was there than that?

'But you have achieved so much.' For some reason she wanted to ease his burden. 'Surely you must allow yourself a small acknowledgement of that?'

'The acknowledgement will come from the people, not me. They are the judge and jury. Everything we are doing here in Nabatean is for them.'

'Of course.' Anna turned to look out of the window again. It was pointless trying to reason with him. Through the shimmering heat she could now make out a mountain range, grey against the startling blue of the sky. She was used to mountains—Dorrada had plenty of them—but these were not like the familiar snow-capped peaks of home…these were stark, forbidding.

'The Jagros Mountains.' Zahir followed her gaze. 'They form the border between us and Uristan. They look deceptively close but there is a vast expanse of desert between us and them.'

Just as well. Annalina had no desire to visit them. She remembered, now that he said the name, that they were the mountains that had been the scene of terrible fighting during the war between Nabatean and Uristan.

'If you look over there…' With a jolt of surprise, Anna realised that Zahir had moved across the leather seat and was now right next to her. She registered the heat of his body, his scent, the sound of his breathing as he stretched one arm across her to point at an oval-shaped structure in the distance. 'You can see the new sports stadium. It's nearing completion now. Soon we will be able to host international sporting events. We intend to make a bid for the Olympics.'

Now the pride had crept into his voice. This might be all about the people but there was no doubt what this country meant to Zahir.

'That's very impressive.' His nearness had caught the breath in her throat and she swallowed noisily. How was it that this man affected her so viscerally, so earthily? In a place deep down that she had never even known existed before?

She was grateful when the limousine finally pulled up outside the Assembly House and she was able to escape from its confines. Escape the pull of Zahir's power.

The meeting was as long as it was boring. Having been introduced to large numbers of dignitaries and advisors,

Anna was then given the option of returning to the palace whilst the men—because it was all men—continued with the business of the day. But stubbornness and a vague hope that she might understand some of what they were discussing, that she would get a small insight into the running of Nabatean, made her say she would like to stay. In point of fact, even though the meeting was conducted in English, the items on the agenda were far too complicated for her to get a grip on, and she ended up staring out of the window or sneaking sidelong glances at Zahir as he controlled the proceedings with masterful authority. There was no sign of his brother at the meeting, or even any mention of him. It appeared that Zahir was the man in charge here. The power behind the throne.

They were standing at the top of a short flight of steps, preparing to leave the building, when Zahir suddenly stopped short, unexpectedly moving his arm around Anna's waist to pull her to his side. Looking outside, Anna could see a small crowd of people had gathered, leaning up against the ornate railings, peering up at the building expectantly.

Pulling out his phone, Zahir barked orders into it and from nowhere several security guards appeared. Dispatching a couple of them into the crowd, he waited impatiently, his grip around her waist tightening with every passing second. Anna could see a vein pulsing in his neck as his eyes darted over the crowd, missing nothing, a sudden stillness setting his features in stone. He reminded her of a dog on a leash, waiting to be set free to chase its quarry.

'What is it? What's the matter?'

'That's what I'd like to find out.'

The security guards returned and there was a brief

conversation, during which she saw Zahir scowl, then look back at her with obvious contempt.

'It would seem that the crowd are here to see you.'

'Oh.' Anna stood a little straighter, smoothing the creases of her dress. 'That's nice.'

'Nice?' He repeated the word as if it was poison in his mouth. 'I fail to see what's nice about it.'

'Well, it's not surprising that people want to meet me. They are bound to be curious about your fiancée. I suggest we go out there, shake some hands and say hello.'

'We will do no such thing.'

'Why ever not?'

'Because there is a time and a place for such things. I have no intention of doing an impromptu meet-and-greet on the steps of the Assembly House.'

'These things don't always have to be formal, Zahir. It doesn't work like that.'

'In Nabatean things work the way I say they will work.'

Anna bit down hard on her lip. There really was no answer to that.

'And, quite apart from anything else, there is the security issue.'

'Well, they don't look dangerous to me.' Staring out at the swelling crowd, Anna stood her ground. 'And besides...' she glanced at the security guards around them '... I'm sure these guys are more than capable of dealing with any potential trouble.'

'There will be no trouble. We walk out of here and get straight into the limousine without speaking to anyone—without even looking at anyone. Do I make myself clear?'

'Crystal clear.' Anna shot him an icy glare. Not that she intended to follow his dictate. If she wanted to smile at the crowd, maybe offer a little wave, she jolly well would. Who did he think he was with his stupid rules?

But before she had the chance to do anything she found herself being bundled down the steps, pressed so closely to Zahir's side that she could barely breathe, let alone acknowledge the crowd. She could just about hear their cheers, hear them calling her name, before Zahir, with his hand on the back of her head, pushed her into the car, following behind her with the weight of his body and instructing the driver to move off before the car door was even shut.

'For heaven's sake.' Anna turned to look at him, eyes flashing. 'What was all that about?'

Adjusting the sleeves of his jacket, Zahir sat back, staring straight ahead.

'Anyone would think you were ashamed of me, bundling me into the car like a criminal.'

'Not ashamed of you, Annalina. It was simply a question of getting you into the car as fast as possible and with the minimum of harassment.'

'The only person harassing me was you. That was a few people—*your* people, I might add—who wanted to greet us. If you want real harassment, you should try having thirty or forty paparazzi swarming around you, baying for your blood.'

Zahir shot her a sharp glance. 'And this has happened to you?'

'Yes.' Anna shifted in her seat, suddenly uncomfortable with this subject, especially as Zahir's eyes were now trained on her face, waiting for an explanation. 'When my engagement to Prince Henrik ended.' She lowered her voice. 'And other times too. Though, that was the worst.'

'Well, you will never have to endure such indignity again. I will make sure of that.'

Anna turned to look out of the window, her hands clasped in her lap. He spoke with such authority, such confidence, she had to admit it was comforting. All her life she'd felt as if she was on her own, fighting her own battles, facing up to the trials and traumas, of which she'd suffered more than her fair share, without anyone there to help her, to be on her side. Now, it seemed, she had a protector.

Suddenly she knew she could put her trust in Zahir, that she would put her life in his hands without a second thought, for that matter. Whether it was the paparazzi, a marauding army or a herd of stampeding elephants, come to that, he would deal with it. Such was his presence, the sheer overwhelming power of him. But the flip side was that he was also an arrogant, cold-blooded control freak. And one, Anna was shocked to realise, who was starting to dominate her every thought.

The rest of the journey back was conducted in silence, apart from the sound of Zahir's fingers jabbing at his mobile phone. Only when they were nearing the palace gates did he look up, letting out a curse under his breath. For there was a crowd here too, gathered around the palace gates, including some photographers who had climbed up onto the railings to get a better view.

'Dear God.' Zahir growled under his breath. 'Is this what I have to expect now, every time I leave the palace, every time I go anywhere with you?'

'I don't see your problem with it.' Anna twitched haughtily. 'You should be pleased that the people of Nabatean are interested in us. That they have gone to the trouble of coming to see us. Don't you want to be popular, for people to like you?'

'I don't care a damn whether people like me or not.'

'Well, maybe it's time you started to care.'

There—that had told him. Even so she averted her gaze, having no wish to witness the thunder she knew she would see there. Sitting up straighter, she arranged her hair over her shoulders. The palace gates had opened now and as the crowd parted to let their car through she turned to look out of the window and smiled brightly at everyone, giving a regal wave, the way she had been taught to do as a child. The crowd cheered in response, waving back and calling her name. Small children were held aloft to get a glimpse of her. Cameras flashed. Everybody loved it.

Well, not exactly everybody. A quick glance at her fiancé revealed a scowl that would make a tiger turn tail and run. But Anna refused to be cowed. She had done nothing wrong. Zahir Zahani was the one who needed to lighten up, respect his people by acknowledging their presence. Maybe even look as if he was a tiny bit proud of her. Though there was precious little chance of that.

Once inside, Zahir started to stride away, presumably intending to abandon her once again. But Anna had had enough of this. Taking several quick steps to catch up with him, she reached out, the touch of her hand on his arm stopping him in his tracks.

'I was just wondering…' She hesitated, pulling away her hand. 'Whether we would be having dinner together tonight.'

Zahir scowled, as if the possibility had hitherto never entered his mind. 'Dinner?'

'Yes.' She was tempted to point out that it was the meal at the end of the day that civilised people tended to share together. Self-preservation made her hold her tongue.

'That's not something I had planned.'

Picking up a length of hair, Anna curled it around her finger, suddenly hesitant. 'When you invite someone to your home, it's generally expected that you make some effort to entertain them. That is the role of a host. It's not much fun being left to rattle around here on my own.'

Deep brown eyes caught hers. 'I can see there are a couple of things I need to remind you of, Princess Annalina.' His sensuous mouth flattened into a grim line. 'Firstly, whilst it is true that you are a guest at the palace, I am most certainly not responsible for entertaining you. And, secondly, you should think yourself grateful that you have the freedom to *rattle around* on your own. The alternative would be to secure you in one room, have you watched over day and night. Something I did consider.'

'Don't be ridiculous.' Anna stared at him in horror.

Zahir gave an infuriating shrug. 'So perhaps you should see your freedom for what it is—a chance to prove yourself trustworthy—rather than complain about being neglected.'

Well, that was her put firmly in her place. Cheeks burning, she turned away, wishing she had never mentioned having wretched dinner with this wretched man.

'However, if it would please you, I can find time for us to dine together tonight. Shall we say in one hour's time?'

Anna swung round to face him again, the words *don't bother* tingling on her lips. But there was something about the narrowed gaze of those hooded eyes that made her stop.

It was surprise, she realised. Zahir was surprised that she wanted to any spend time with him. She was surprised too, come to that. It was like he had some sort of power over her, drawing her to the edge of the cliff when all her instincts were telling her to keep away. That blatant, raw masculinity made her keep coming back for more punishment. Anna had never thought of herself as a masochist. Now she was beginning to wonder.

Nervously licking her lips with the tip of her tongue, she saw his eyes flash in response, tightening the tendrils inside her. 'Very well.' Pushing back her shoulders, she tossed her hair over them. 'I will see you later.'

CHAPTER FIVE

ZAHIR STARED AT the young woman at the far end of the table—the European princess who was soon to be his bride. Something he was still desperately struggling to come to terms with. He had no idea who she was, not really. Earlier, when she'd talked about the press attention she'd received over the years, his blood had run cold in his veins. But fear about her morals had swiftly changed to the urge to protect her, his whole person affronted that she should ever have been subjected to such assaults. Because deep down some instinct told him that Princess Annalina was vulnerable and certainly not a woman who would give away her favours easily. Which was odd, when you thought about the way they had met.

She was certainly regal. From the fine bones of her face to the dainty set of her shoulders and the elegant, refined posture. Her hands, he noticed, were particularly delicate, long, slender fingers and pink nails devoid of nail varnish. They looked as if they had never done a day's work in their life. They probably hadn't.

He looked down at his own hands. A warrior's hands. No longer calloused from combat—he hadn't gripped a dagger or curled his finger around the trigger of a gun for over two years now—they were nevertheless stained with the blood of war and always would be. They had been around the throat of too many of his enemies ever to be washed clean—had been used to pull lifeless bodies out caves that had become subterranean battlegrounds, or recover corpses shrivelling in the scorching heat of the desert with the vultures circling overhead.

His hands had closed the eyelids of far too many young men.

And now… Could such hands ever expect to run over the fair skin of the woman before him? Would that be right? Permissible? They wanted to, that was for certain. They itched, burned even, with longing to feel the softness of her pale flesh beneath their fingertips, to be able to trace the contours of her slender body, to travel over the hollow of her waist, the swell of her breasts. They longed to explore every part of her body.

Feeling his eyes on her, Annalina looked up and smiled at him from her end of the table.

'This is delicious.' She indicated the half-eaten plate of food before her with the fork in her hand. 'Lovely and spicy. What's the meat, do you suppose?'

Zahir glanced down at his plate, already scraped clean, as if seeing it for the first time. Food was just fuel to him, something to be grateful for but to be consumed as fast as possible, before it was covered in flies or snatched away by a hungry hound. It was certainly not a subject he ever discussed, nor wanted to.

'Goat, I believe.' He levelled dark eyes at her.

'Oh.' That perfect pink mouth puckered in surprise then pursed shut, her fork left to rest on her plate.

He stifled a smile. Obviously goat was not something she was accustomed to eating. No doubt Annalina was more used to seeing them grazing prettily in wildflower meadows than having them stewed and presented before her in a bowl of couscous. She knew nothing of the ways of this country, he realised, and the smile was immediately replaced with the more familiar scowl.

Had he been wrong to insist that she marry him, to bring her to this foreign land and expect her to be able to fit in, play the role of his wife? It was a huge undertaking to ask of anyone, let alone someone as fragile-looking as her. And yet he already knew that there was more to Annalina than her flawless beauty might suggest. She was strong-willed and she was brave. It had taken real guts to refuse to marry his brother, to stand on that bridge and do whatever she thought it took to get her out of that marriage. To kiss a total stranger. A kiss that still burned on his lips.

It had all backfired, of course. She had leapt straight from the frying pan into the fire, finding herself shackled to him instead. He was nothing like his brother, it was true. But, in terms of a husband, had Annalina made the right choice? Would she have been better sticking with the relative calm of Rashid, his particular demons regulated by carefully prescribed medication?

Or Zahir, whose demons still swirled inside him, drove him on, made him the man he was. Power, control and the overwhelming desire to do the best for his country was the only therapy he could tolerate.

He didn't know, but either way it was too late now. The choice had been made. They were both going to have to live with it.

'I hope I haven't spoiled your appetite?' The food, he noticed, had now been abandoned, Annalina's slender hand gripping the stem of her glass as she took a sip of wine, then another.

'No, it's not that.' She gave an unconvincing smile. 'It's actually quite filling.'

'Then, if you have finished, perhaps you would like to be served coffee somewhere more comfortable.'

'Um, yes, that sounds a good idea.' She touched a napkin to her lips. 'Where were you thinking of?'

'I will take mine in my quarters, but there are any number of seating areas in the palace that are suitable for relaxation. The courtyards are very pleasant too, though they will be chilly at this time of night.'

'I'm sure.' She fiddled with a tendril of hair that had escaped the swept-up style. 'Actually, I think I will join you.' There was determination in her voice, but vulnerability too, as if she might easily crack or splinter if challenged. 'I would like to see your quarters.'

Zahir stilled, something akin to panic creeping over him. He hadn't intended to invite her to his rooms. Far from it. By suggesting that they took their coffee elsewhere, he had been trying to escape from her. Which begged the question, why? Why would he, a man who would take on a band of armed insurgents with the bravery of a thousand warriors combined, be frightened by the thought of sharing a cup of coffee with this young woman? It was ridiculous.

Because he didn't know how to behave around her, that was why. This relationship had been thrust upon him so suddenly that he hadn't had time to figure out how to make it work, how to control it. And being around Annalina only seemed to make the task more difficult. Rather than clarifying the situation, she seemed to mess with his judgement. He found himself torn two ways—one side warning that he must be on his guard, and watch over this wayward princess like a hawk to make sure she didn't try to abscond, while the other side was instructing him to take her to his bed and make her his, officially.

The latter was a tempting prospect for sure. And the way she was looking at him now, eyes shining brightly as she held his gaze, her hands steepled under her chin, fingertips grazing her lips, it would take all his self-control not to give in to it. But control it he would, because control was something he prided himself on. More than that, something he ruled his life by, using it both to drive himself on and deny himself pleasure. Because pleasure was nothing but an indulgence, a form of weakness, a slippery slope that led down to the bowels of hell. That he had discovered to his cost with the most tragic of results: the murder of his parents.

On the eve of his country's independence he had been in a rowdy bar, watching, if not actually participating, as his brave comrades had celebrated their tremendous victory with flowing alcohol and loose women. He had been relaxed, enjoying himself, accepting the accolades, full of pride for what he had achieved. And all the time, a few hundred miles away, his parents were being murdered, a knife being drawn across their throats. A tragedy that he would never, *ever* begin to forgive himself for.

But that didn't stop the weight of lust in his groin grow heavier by the second, spreading its traitorous warmth through his body as he stared back at Annalina's open, inviting face. He had no idea why she was looking at him in that way. The workings of a woman's mind were a complete mystery to him, and not something he had ever thought he would care to concern himself with. But now he found he longed to know what was going on behind those eyes that were glazed perhaps a little too brightly— found that he would pay good money to find out what was going through that clever, complicated mind of hers.

'I doubt you will find anything remotely interesting about my quarters.'

'You will be in them. That's interesting enough for me.'

There she went again, throwing him a curveball, messing with his head. Was she flirting with him? Was that what this was? Zahir had experienced flirting before. His position of power, not to mention his dark good looks, meant he had had his fair share of female attention over the years. Most, but not all, of which he had totally ignored. He was a red-blooded male, after all. Occasionally he would allow himself to slake his thirst. But that was all it had ever been. No emotion, no attachment and certainly no second-guessing what the object of his attentions might be thinking. The way he found himself puzzling now.

'Very well. If you insist.' Summoning one of the hovering waiting staff with a wave of his hand, he gave his orders then, walking round to the back of Annalina's chair, he waited as she rose to her feet. 'If you would like to follow me.'

Setting off at a rapid pace, he found he had to moderate his step in order for Annalina to keep up. She trotted along beside him, her heels clicking on the marble floors, looking around her as if trying to memorise the route back in case she should need to escape. Zahir found himself regretting his decision to allow her into his rooms more and more with every forceful footstep. No woman, other than the palace staff, had ever been in his chambers. There had been no need for it. There was no need for it now. Why had he ever agreed to let this woman invade his personal space?

By the time they had negotiated the labyrinth of corridors and he was inserting the key into the lock of his door, Zahir's mood had blackened still further.

'You lock your door?' Waiting beside him, Annalina looked up in surprise.

'Of course. Security is of paramount importance.'

'Even in your own palace? There are guards everywhere. Do you not trust them to protect your property?'

'Trust no one and you will not be disappointed.' Zahir pushed hard on the heavy door with the palm of his hand.

'Oh, Zahir, that's such a depressing ideology!' Annalina attempted a throwaway laugh but it fell, uncaught, to the ground.

'Depressing it may be.' He stood back to let her enter. 'But I know it to be true.'

Taking in a deep breath, Anna stepped over the threshold. This was not going well. Maybe it had been a mistake to ask to accompany Zahir to his quarters. It had certainly done nothing to improve his mood. The resolve she had had at the start of the evening, to sit down and talk, try to get to know him a bit, discuss their future, had been severely tested during the course of the torturous meal. Every topic of conversation she had tried to initiate had either been met with cool disregard or monosyllabic answers.

All except one. When she had mentioned his parents, tried to tell him how sorry she was to hear of their tragic death, the look on Zahir's face had been terrifying to behold, startling her with its volcanic ferocity. It was clear that subject was most definitely off-limits.

But, where their future was concerned, she had to persevere. She needed to find out what was expected of her, what her role would be. And, more importantly, she needed to tell Zahir about herself, her shameful secret. Before it was too late. Which was why at the end of the meal she had fought against every instinct to turn tail and run to the safety of her bed and had persuaded him to bring her here. And why she found herself being welcomed into his spartan quarters with the all the enthusiasm that would have been given to a jester at a funeral.

For spartan it certainly was. In stark contrast to the rest of the palace, the room she was ushered into was small and dimly lit, with bare floorboards and a low ceiling. There was very little furniture, just a low wooden table and a makeshift seating area covered with tribal rugs.

'As I said.' Briefly following her gaze, Zahir moved to put the key in the lock on this side. He didn't turn it, Anna noticed with relief. 'There is nothing to see here.'

'Something doesn't have to be all glitz and glamour for it to be interesting, you know.' She purposefully took several steps into the room and, placing her hands on her hips, looked around her, displaying what she hoped was a suitably interested expression. 'How many rooms do you have here?'

'Three. This room, an office and a bedroom. Plus a bathroom, of course. I find that to be perfectly adequate.'

'Is this the bedroom?' Nervous energy saw her stride over to an open door in the corner of the room and peer in. In the near darkness she could just about make out the shape of a small bed, low to the ground, rugs scattered on the bare boards of the floor.

So this was where he slept. Anna pictured him, gloriously naked beneath the simple covers of this bed. He was so vital, so very much alive, that it was hard to imagine him doing anything as normal as sleeping. But she wouldn't allow herself to imagine him doing anything else. At least, not with anyone else.

'You obviously don't go in for luxuries here.'

'I do not. The basics are all I need. I find anything else is just an unwanted distraction.'

As was she, no doubt. Anna tamped down the depressing thought. 'So why build a palace like this, then? What's the point?'

'Medira Palace is for the people, a symbol of the power and wealth of Nabatean, something that they can look upon with pride. I may not choose to indulge in its luxuries, but it's not about me. The palace will be here for many generations after I have gone. And, besides, it's not just my home. My brother lives here too, as of course will you.'

'Yes.' Anna swallowed.

'You have no need to worry.' Zahir gave a harsh laugh. 'I don't expect you to share these chambers. You may have the pick of the rooms of the palace, as many and as grand as you wish.'

'And what about you? Will you be giving up these chambers and coming to live in splendour with me?'

'I will not.' Zahir's reply was as bleak as it was damning. What did that mean—that they would inhabit different parts of the palace? That they would live totally separate lives, be man and wife in name only? A knock on the door meant that Anna had to keep this deeply depressing thought to herself for the time being, as a servant bearing a tray of coffee saved Zahir from further questioning. Bending down, she settled herself as best she could on the low seating area, tucking her legs under her before reaching to accept her cup of coffee from the silent servant. It was impossible to get comfortable in her high-heeled shoes so, with her coffee cup balanced in one hand, she took them off with the other, pairing them neatly on the floor beside her. For some reason they suddenly looked ridiculously out of place, like twin sirens in the stark masculinity of this room.

Raising her eyes, Anna saw that Zahir was staring at them too, as if thinking the same thing. She was relieved when he roughly pulled off his own soft leather shoes and sat down beside her.

'So your brother.' She decided to opt for what she hoped was a slightly safer topic of conversation, but as she felt Zahir stiffen beside her she began to wonder.

'You say he lives here in the palace and yet I haven't seen any sign of him.'

'There is no reason for you to have seen him, as he occupies the east wing. Given the circumstances, I doubt that either of you are going to deliberately seek each other out.'

'Well, no.' Annalina pouted slightly. 'Having said that, I don't believe he wished to marry me any more than I did him.'

She waited, pride almost wishing that Zahir would contradict her, tell her that of course Rashid had wanted to marry her, 'what man wouldn't?'.

Instead there was only a telling silence as Zahir drank the contents of his coffee cup in one gulp then reached for the brass pot to refill it.

'There is some truth in that.' Avoiding her gaze, he eventually spoke.

Being right had never felt less rewarding. Drawing in a breath, Anna decided to ask the question that had been niggling her ever since she had first set eyes on Rashid Zahani. 'Can I ask…about Rashid… Is there some sort of medical problem?'

That spun Zahir's head in her direction, the dark eyes flashing dangerously beneath the thick, untidy eyebrows. So close now, Anna could see the amber flecks that radiated from the black pupils, glowing as if they were just about to burst into flames.

'So what are you saying? That anyone who doesn't want to marry you must have some sort of mental deficiency?' Scorn singed the edges of his words.

'No, I just…'

'Because if so you have a very high, not to say misguided, opinion of yourself.'

'That's not fair!' Colour rushed to flush Anna's cheeks,

heating her core as indignation and embarrassment took hold. 'That's not what I meant and you know it.'

'Well, that's what it sounded like.' He looked away and she was left staring at his harsh profile, at the muscle that twitched ominously beneath the stubble of his cheek. There was silence as she battled to control the mixed emotions rioting inside her, as she waited for her skin to cool down.

'My brother has some personal issues to overcome.' Finally Zahir spoke again, leaning forward to replace his cup on the table. 'He suffers from anxiety due to a trauma he suffered and this can affect his mood. He just needs time, that's all. When the right person is found, he will marry and produce a family. Of that I am certain.'

'Of course.' Anna was not going to make the mistake of questioning that statement, even if secretly she had her doubts. There was something about Rashid that she found very unnerving. On the plane journey here she had looked up to see him staring at her in a very peculiar way, almost as if he was looking right through her. 'But does Rashid not get to choose his own wife? You make it sound as if he has no say in the matter.'

'Like me, you mean?' The eyes swung back, lingering this time, tracing a trail over her sensitised skin, across her cheekbones and down her nose, until they rested on her lips. Anna felt their burn as vividly as if she had been touched by a flame.

'And me too.' She just about managed to croak out the words of defiance, even though her heart had gone off like a grenade inside her.

'Indeed.' Something approaching empathy softened his voice. 'We are all victims of circumstance to a greater or lesser extent.'

Greater—definitely greater in her case. To marry this

man, tie herself for ever to this wild, untamed, warrior, had meant taking the biggest leap of faith in her life. But Anna didn't regret it. In the same way as some inner sense had told her that she could never have married Rashid Zahani, it now filled her with nervous excitement at the thought of marrying his brother. Excitement, exhilaration and terror all rolled into one breathtaking surge of adrenaline. But there was worry too—worry that maybe once Zahir knew all the facts he might no longer want to marry her. She was beginning to realise just how devastating that would be. Because she wanted Zahir. In every sense of the word. Drawing in a shaky breath, she decided she was going to have to just plunge in.

'About our marriage, Zahir.' She watched the play of his muscles across his back as he leant forward to refill his coffee cup again. 'There are things we need to discuss.'

'I've told you. I will leave all the arrangements to you. I have neither the time nor the interest to get involved.'

'I'm not talking about the arrangements.'

'What, then?' He settled back against the cushions, his eyes holding hers with a piercing intensity that made her feel like a specimen butterfly being pinned to a board.

She shifted nervously to make sure she still could. 'We need to talk about what sort of marriage it will be.'

'The usual, I imagine.'

'And what exactly does that mean?' Irritation and helplessness spiked her voice. 'There is nothing usual about this marriage, Zahir. From the fact that I have been swapped from one brother to another, to your disclosure just now that we won't be sharing the same rooms. None of it fits the term *usual*.'

Zahir gave that infuriating shrug, as if none of it was of any consequence to him.

'Will you expect us to have full marital relations, for example?' She blurted out the question before she had time to phrase it properly, using language that sounded far more clinical than she felt. But maybe that was a good thing.

'Of course.' His straightforward answer, delivered in that raw, commanding voice and coupled with the burn of amber in those hooded eyes, had the peculiar effect of melting something inside of Anna, fusing her internal organs until she was aware of nothing but a deep pulse somewhere low down in her abdomen. It was a feeling so extraordinary, so remarkable, that she found she wanted to hold on to it, capture it, before it slipped away for ever.

Zahir intended that they should have sex. That in itself was hardly surprising, considering that they were going to be man and wife. Why had it sent her body into a clenching spasm?

'Nabatean is a young country. It is our duty to procreate, to provide a workforce for the future, to build upon the foundations we have established.' Ah, yes: *duty*. They were back to that again. 'But I don't intend to make constant demands on you.' He paused, thick lashes lowering to partly obscure his eyes. 'If that is what you're worrying about.'

Did she look worried? Anna had no idea what expression her face was pulling—she was too busy trying to control her body. And the thought of him making constant demands on her was only intensifying the peculiar feeling inside her. She needed to get a grip, and fast.

'In that case…there is something that you need to know. Before we get married, I mean.'

'Go on.'

Suddenly her whole body was painfully alive to him, every pore of her skin prickling with agonising awareness. The hairs on her arms, on the back of her neck, stood on end with craving, desire and the tortured anxiety of what she had to tell him.

'I'm not sure.' She reached for the security of a tendril of hair, twisting it round and round her finger. 'But it's quite possible that I am not able to…'

'Not able to what?'

'Not able to actually have sexual intercourse.'

CHAPTER SIX

ZAHIR'S DARK BROWS LOWERED, narrowing his hooded gaze until it was little more than twin slits of glinting stone. He twisted slightly so that his knee now touched hers, moving one arm behind them and placing it palm down on the cushions so that it anchored him in place. Anna could sense it, like a rod of muscled strength, inert yet still exuding power. Even seated he was so much taller than her, so much bigger, that she felt dwarfed by him, shaded, as if weakened by his strength.

'I don't understand.' He stared at her full in the face, with no trace of embarrassment or sensitivity for her predicament. She had presented him with a problem, that much was clear from the brooding intensity of his gaze, but it was a determination to get to the facts that had set his face in stone. 'What do you mean, you can't have sexual intercourse? Do you have some sort of physical abnormality?'

'No!' Anna pulled at the neckline of her dress, hoping it would dislodge the lump in her throat as well as cool herself down. The temperature in the small room seemed to have ramped up enormously. 'At least, it wouldn't appear so.'

'Have you been examined by a physician?'

'Yes, I have, actually.'

'And what were the findings?'

'They could find no physical reason for the...problem.'

'So what, then? What are you trying to tell me?'

'I'm trying to tell you that, when it actually comes to... you know...I can't actually...I fear I'm not able to accommodate a man.' Anna finished the sentence all in a rush, lowering her eyes against the shame that was sweeping over her that she should have to confess such a thing to the most virile, the most sexually charged, man she had ever met. A man who was now no doubt about to break off their short engagement.

There was a brief silence punctuated by Zahir's shallow breathing.

'Can I ask what has led you to this conclusion?'

Oh, God. Anna just wanted to make this hell go away. To make Zahir and the problem and the whole miserable issue of having sex at all just disappear. Why couldn't she just forget men, and getting married, and go and live in spinster isolation with nothing but a couple of undemanding cats for company? But beside her Zahir was waiting, the small amount of space between them shimmering with his impatient quest for information. There was nothing for it. She was going to have to tell him.

'Prince Henrik and I...' She paused, cringing inside. 'We never consummated our betrothal. You might as well know, that was why he broke off our engagement.'

'I wasn't aware that that was a prerequisite of a fiancée.' His eyes scoured her face. 'A wife, yes, but surely before marriage a woman is at liberty to withhold her favours?'

'That's just it, I didn't deliberately withhold them. It turned out that I was completely...unsatisfactory.'

'So let me get this straight.' *Oh, dear Lord*, still Zahir persisted with his questions. Couldn't he let it drop now?

In a minute he would be asking her to draw him a diagram. 'You wanted to have sex with your fiancé but for some reason you weren't able?'

'Yes, well, sort of.' Since he had posed the question so baldly, Anna was forced to accept that she hadn't actually wanted to have sex with Henrik at all. In fact, the thought of his pallid, sweaty hands fumbling around her most intimate areas still made her feel a bit sick. But the point was it had been expected of her. And she had failed.

'It was more Henrik's idea. He said it was important that we consummated our relationship before the wedding. "Try before you buy", I believe was his expression.'

Zahir's lip curled with distaste.

'And, as it turned out, it was just as well he did.'

This produced a low growl, like the rumble of a hungry lion, then a silence that Anna felt compelled to fill.

'I just thought you ought to know. Before we marry, I mean. In case it might prove to be a problem for us.'

'And do you think it will, Annalina?' Leaning forward, Zahir stretched out a hand to tuck a stray lock of hair behind her ear, his touch surprisingly gentle. Then, holding her chin between his finger and thumb, he tilted her face so that she had no alternative but to gaze into those bitter-chocolate eyes. 'Do you think it will be a problem for us?'

With her whole body going into paralysis, including the beat of her heart and pump of her lungs, it was quite possible that staying alive might prove to be a problem. She stared at the sweep of his jawline—the one facial feature that probably defined him more than any other. As if hewn from granite, it was as uncompromising and as harshly beautiful as him. There was an indentation in the squared-off chin, she noted—not a dimple. A man like

Zahir Zahani would never be in possession of a dimple. A strong dusting of stubble shaded its planes.

On the bridge in Paris, when she had so recklessly decided to kiss him, she had been dimly aware that his skin had felt smooth, freshly shaved. But how would it would feel tonight, now, with that tempting shadow of dark beard? Suddenly she longed to find out, to feel it rasp against her cheek like the lick of a cat's tongue. He was so very close…so very difficult to resist.

'I don't know.' Finally finding her voice, Anna blinked against the erotic temptation. That was the truth: she didn't. Right now she didn't know anything at all. Except that she wanted Zahir to kiss her more than anything, more than she cared about her next breath. She found herself unconsciously squirming on the makeshift sofa, the rough weave of the tribal rugs scratching the exposed bare skin of her thigh as her dress rode up.

What was she doing? This had not been her plan at all. When she had summoned up her courage, faced Zahir with her guilty, frankly embarrassing, secret, it had been with the intention of letting him know what he was taking on here. That his fiancée was frigid. Anna still felt the pain of the word, hurled at her by Henrik as he had levered his body off her, before pulling on his clothes and storming off into the night. *Frigid*.

His accusation had torn into her, flaying her skin, leaving her staring up at the ceiling in horrified confusion. Not to be able to perform the most basic, natural function of a woman was devastating. She was inadequate, useless. Not a proper woman at all, in fact. The doctor's diagnosis hadn't helped. Being told there was nothing physically wrong with her, that there was no quick fix—no medical fix at all, in fact—had only added to her lack of self-worth. Neither had time softened the blow, her deficiency seeping into her pride and her confidence, leaving her feeling empty, like a hollow shell.

So what on earth was she doing now? Why was she writhing about like some sort of temptress, trying to get Zahir's attention, setting herself up for what was bound to be a painful and embarrassing fall? Because she wanted him, that was why. She wanted his lips against hers, touching, tasting, crushing her mouth, sucking the breath out of her until she was gasping for air. She wanted him to make her feel. The way no one ever had before. The way she now knew with a dizzying certainty that he could.

Zahir stared into Annalina's flushed face that he still held tilted up towards him. At the eyes that were heavy with a drugging sense of what appeared to be arousal. And once again he found himself wondering what the hell was going on in her head. If she had been flirting with him earlier on, this felt more like full-on seduction. And this after she had just told him she was incapable of sexual intercourse. It didn't make any sense. But neither did the drag of lust that was weighing down his bones, making it impossible to move away from her, or the prickle of heat that had swept through his body, like he'd been plugged into the national grid. He could feel it now, right down to his finger tips that were tingling against the soft skin of her chin.

And there was something else bothering him too. It had been building ever since Annalina had started to talk about this ex-fiancé of hers, Prince Henrik, or whatever his wretched name was. Just the thought of him touching Annalina, *his* Annalina, had sent his blood pressure rocketing. By the time she'd got to the bit about them not being able to consummate their relationship, he had been ready to tear the man limb from limb, happy to chuck the remains of his mutilated body to the vultures without a backward glance. And this aggression for a man he had never met—nor ever would, if he wanted to avoid a life sentence for homicide. He could still feel the hatred seething inside him now: that such a man had dared to try and violate this beautiful creature, then discard her like a piece of trash. It had taken all of his self-control not to let Annalina see his revulsion.

Now Zahir spread his hand possessively under her jaw, his eyes still holding hers, neither of them able to break contact.

'There's one sure way to find out.' He heard his words through the roar of blood in his ears, the throb of it pulsing in his veins. Not that he was in any doubt. He knew he could take this beautiful princess and erase the memory of that spineless creep of a creature, take her to his bed and show her what a real man could do. Just the thought of it made his hands tremble and he pressed the pads of his thumbs against her skin to steady them, rhythmically stroking up and down. He watched her eyelashes flutter against his touch and the roar inside him grew louder.

He might not be able to read Anna's mind, but he could read her body, and that was all the encouragement he needed. The angle of her head, the slight arching of her back that pushed her breasts towards him, the soft rasp of her breath, all told him that she was his for the taking. That she wanted him every bit as much as he wanted her. Well, so be it. But this time the kiss would be on *his* terms.

He lowered his head until their mouths were only a fraction apart. *Now*, a voice inside his head commanded. And Zahir obeyed. Planting his lips firmly on Annalina's upturned pout, he felt its warm softness pucker beneath him and the resulting kick of lust in his gut momentarily halted him right there. He inhaled deeply through his nose. This was not going to be a gentle, persuasive kiss. This was going to be hot and heavy and hardcore. This was about possession, domination, a man's need for a woman. His need for her right now.

He angled his head to be able to plunder more deeply, the soft groan as her lips parted to allow him access only fuelling the fire that was raging through him. His tongue delved into the sensual cavern of her mouth, seeking her own with a brutal feverishness that saw it twist around its target, touching, tasting, taking total control, until Anna reciprocated, the lick of her tongue against his taking him to new fervid heights. Releasing her chin, Zahir moved his fingers to the back of her head, pushing them force-fully up through her hair, feeling the combs and grips that held the tresses in their swept-up style dislodge sat-isfyingly beneath his touch until the thick locks of blonde hair fell free, tumbling down through his fingers and over her shoulders.

Grabbing a handful of this glorious, silken wonder, Zahir used it to anchor her in place, to hold her exactly where he wanted her, so that he could increase the pres-sure on her mouth still further, increase the intensity of the kiss, heighten the pleasure that was riotously cours-ing through him. And, when Anna snaked her hands be-hind his neck, pressing herself against him, her breasts so soft, so feminine against the muscled wall of his chest, it was all he could do to stop himself from taking her right there and then. No questions asked, no thoughts, no deliberation, no cross-examination. Nothing but a blind desire to possess her in the most carnal way possible. To make her his.

Which would be totally wrong. Releasing her lips, Zahir pulled back, the breath heaving in his chest, the tightening in his groin almost unbearably painful. A

kiss was one thing, but to take her virginity—for surely
that was what they were talking about here?—was quite
another. This wasn't the time or the place. And to do
it merely to prove himself more of a man than Henrik
would be morally reprehensible. Somehow, from somewhere, he was going to have to find some control.

The look of dazed desire in Annalina's eyes was almost enough to make him claim her again, blow his new-
found resolve to smithereens. But within a split second
her expression had changed and now he saw a wariness,
a fear almost, and that was enough to bring him forcibly to his senses. Realising that he was still clutching
a handful of her hair, he let it drop and pushed himself
away until he found himself on his feet, staring down at
her from a position of towering authority that he felt far
more comfortable with.

'I apologise.' His voice sounded raw, unfamiliar, as
alien to him as the wild sensations that were coursing
through the rest of his body. Sensations that he realised
would be all too evident if Annalina raised her eyes to
his groin. He shifted his position, adjusting the fit of his
trousers.

But Annalina wasn't looking at him. She was busy
with her hair, combing her fingers through the blonde
tresses, arranging it so that it fell over her shoulders. Then
she leant forward to retrieve the clips that had fallen to
the floor.

'What is there to be sorry for?' Now her eyes met his,
cold, controlled, defiant. 'We are engaged, after all.' She
held the largest clip in her hand, a hinged, tortoiseshell
affair which now squeaked as she opened and closed its
teeth, as if it was ready to take a bite out of him. 'You
are perfectly at liberty to kiss me. To do whatever you

like with me, in fact. At least, that's been the impression you have given me so far.'

There was rebellion in her voice now, matched by the arched posture, the arrogant, feline grace. But her lips, Zahir noticed, were still swollen from the force of their kiss, the delicate skin of her jaw flushed pink where his stubbled chin had scraped against her. And for some reason this gave him a twisted sense of achievement—as if he had marked his territory, claimed her. Especially as, now, everything about Annalina was trying to deny it.

'Perhaps you would do well to remember that this is all your doing, Annalina. You have brought about this situation and you only have yourself to blame. I am merely trying to find a workable solution.'

A solution that should not involve ripping the clothes off her the moment they were alone.

'I know, I know.' Rising to her feet, Annalina planted herself squarely in front of him, sticking out her bottom lip like a sulky teenager. Barefoot, she seemed ridiculously tiny, delicate, her temper making her brittle, as if she would snap in two were he to reach forward and grasp her with his warrior's hands.

'And, whilst we're on the subject of workable solutions, perhaps you would like to tell me how long I am expected to stay in Nabatean. I have duties in my own country, you know, matters that require my attention.'

'I'm sure.' Zahir gritted his jaw against the desire to close the small gap between them and punish her impertinence with another bruising kiss. 'In that case, no doubt you will be relieved to know that you'll be returning to Dorrada the day after tomorrow.'

'Oh, right.' Annalina shifted her weight lightly from one foot to the other, placing her hand provocatively on her hip. 'Well, that's good.'

'I have a number of meetings scheduled for tomorrow but have cleared my diary for the following couple of days.'

He watched, not without some satisfaction, as her frown of incomprehension turned to a scowl of realisation. Her toes, he noticed, were curling against the bare boards.

'You mean…?'

'Yes, Annalina. I will be accompanying you. I very much look forward to visiting your country.'

CHAPTER SEVEN

OPENING THE SHUTTERS, Anna shielded her eyes against the glare of the sun. Not the sun glinting off the towering glass edifices of Medira this time, or shimmering above the distant desert, but bouncing off the freshly fallen snow that blanketed the ground, weighing down the fir trees and covering the roofs of the town of Valduz that nestled in the valley in the distance.

She was back at Valduz Castle, the only home she had ever known. Perched on a craggy outcrop at the foothills of the Pyrenees mountain range, the castle was like something out of a fairy tale, or a Dracula movie, depending on your point of view. Built in the fourteenth century, it was all stone walls, turrets and battlements, fully prepared for any marauding invaders. It was not, however, prepared for the twenty-first century. Cold, damp and in desperate need of repair, its occupants—including Anna, her father and the bare minimum of staff—only inhabited a very small portion of it, living in a kind of squalid grandeur: priceless antique furniture had been pushed aside to make room for buckets to catch the drips, steel joists propping up ceilings decorated with stunning fifteenth-century frescoes.

But all this was about to change. Turning around, Anna surveyed her childhood bedroom in all its forlorn glory. Once she married Zahir, money would no longer be a problem for this impoverished nation. Valduz Castle would be restored, and limitless funds would be pumped into the Dorradian economy to improve its infrastructure, houses, hospitals and schools. Dorrada's problems would soon be over. *And hers would be just beginning.*

But she could feel no sense of achievement for her part in turning around Dorrada's fortunes. Instead there was just a hollow dread where maybe pride should have sat—a deep sense of unease that she had sold her soul to the devil. Or at least as close to a devil as she had ever come across. And that very devil was right here, under the leaking roofs of this ancient castle.

They had arrived in Dorrada the previous evening, her father greeting Zahir like an honoured guest, clearly having no concerns that his daughter was marrying the wrong brother. The two of them had retired immediately to her father's study and that had been the last Anna had seen of them. Presumably the financial talks had been the top priority and had gone on long into the night. Anna was obviously of significantly less importance to either of them. Zahir, professional but detached, appeared to be treating this like just another business trip, all traces of the man who had been on the brink of ravishing her banished behind that formidable, impenetrable facade.

Anna closed her eyes against the memory of that kiss—hot, wild, and so forceful it had felt as if he was branding her with his lips, claiming her in the most carnal way. It still did. The memory refused to leave her, still curling her toes, clenching her stomach and heating her very core.

And Zahir had felt it too, no matter how much his subsequent demeanour might be trying to deny it. His arousal had been all too evident—electrifying, empowering. Trapped in his embrace, she had felt alive, confident, sexy. And ready. More than ready, in fact. Desperate for Zahir to take things further, to throw her to the floor and make love to her there and then, any way he wanted. To possess her, make her feel whole, complete, a real woman.

But what had happened? Nothing, that was what. Having taken her to the point of no return, he had stopped, leaving her a quivering, gasping, flushed-faced mess, unable to do anything other than stare up at him as he bit out between gritted teeth that he was sorry. *Sorry?* Anna didn't want sorry. It had taken every ounce of effort to come back from that, to hide the crushing disappointment and act as if she didn't give a damn.

But today was a new day. She was on her own home turf, the sun was shining and the stunning scenery outside was calling her. Pulling on jeans and a thick rollneck sweater, she released the curtain of hair trapped down her back and quickly fashioned two loose plaits. Grabbing a woolly hat, she was good to go.

The virgin snow crunched beneath her boots as she trudged around the wall of the castle, the white puff of her breath going before her. She didn't know exactly where she was headed, except that she wanted to enjoy this moment alone, commit it to memory. She loved mornings like this, bright and still, unchanged down the centuries. But how many more would she experience? No doubt once she was married she would be expected to spend all her time in Nabatean, to swap the sparkling cold of the mountains for the sweltering heat of the desert, the stark loneliness of her life here for the scary unknown that was her future with Zahir.

It was time to leave the child behind—Anna knew that. Time to grow up and do something meaningful with her life. And being born a princess meant making an advantageous marriage. She should have accepted the idea by now. After all, she'd had twenty-five years to get used to it. But even so, now it was actually happening, the thought of leaving everything she knew and marching off into the desert sun with this dark and mysterious stranger was completely terrifying.

The lingering child in her made her bend down and scoop up a large handful of snow, compacting it into a hard ball and then smoothing it between her icy hands. Her eyes scanned the scene for a target. A robin eyed her nervously before swooping off to the branches of a nearby tree. An urn at the top of the crenulated wall that wound its way down the stone steps had no such escape, though, and, taking aim, Anna held the icy missile aloft and prepared to fire.

'You'll never get any power behind it like that.' A strong, startlingly warm hand gripped her wrist, bringing her arm down by her side. 'Throwing is all about the velocity. You need to stand with your feet apart and then turn at the waist, like this.' The hands now spanned her midriff, twisting her body in readiness for the perfect aim. Anna tensed, staring at the snowball in her hand, frankly surprised to see it still there. The heat coursing through her body felt powerful enough to melt an iceberg. 'Now bring back your arm, like this...' he bent her elbow, holding her arm behind her '...and you are ready to go. Don't forget to follow through.'

The snowball arced above them before disappearing with a soft thud into a deep snowdrift.

'Hmm...' Turning to face her, Zahir quirked a thick brow. 'I can see more practice is needed.'

Anna stared back at him, drinking in the sight. He looked very foreign, exotic, in the bright, snowy whiteness of these surroundings. Wearing a long charcoal cashmere coat, the collar turned up, his skin appeared darker somehow, his close-cropped hair blacker, his broad body too warm—too hot, even—for these sub-zero temperatures. It was almost as if he could defy nature by appearing so unaffected by the cold. That you could remove the man from the desert, but not the desert from the man. Anna adjusted her hat, regretting her choice of headgear as she felt the silly bobble on top do a wobble. 'It's too late for me, I fear. After all, I won't be here for much longer.'

'Will you miss your country?' The question came out of nowhere with its usual directness. But his eyes showed his seriousness as he waited for her answer.

'Yes, of course.' Anna bit down on her lip, determined that the bobble on her hat was the only thing that was going to wobble. She would be strong now. Show Zahir that she was a capable, independent woman. That she would be an asset to him, not a burden. 'But I am looking forward to the challenges of a new life, with you. I am one hundred percent committed to making this union work, for the sake of both of our countries.'

'That's good to hear.' Still his gaze raked across her like a heat-seeking missile. 'And what about on a more personal level, Annalina? You and me. Are you one hundred percent committed to making that union work too?'

'Yes, of course.' Anna fought against the heat of his stare. What was he trying to do to her? She was struggling to put on a convincing performance here. She didn't need him messing with the script. 'I will try to be a good wife to you, to fulfil my duty to the best of my abilities.'

'*Duty*, Annalina. Is that what this is all about?'

'Well, yes. As it is with you.' Dark eyebrows raised and then fell again, taking Anna's stomach with them. 'But that doesn't mean we can't be happy.'

'Then you might want to tell your face.' Raising a hand, he cupped her jaw, his hand so large that it covered her chin and lower cheeks, seductively grazing her bottom lip. Anna trembled, his touch halting her cold breath painfully in her throat. 'What is it that you fear, Annalina? Is it the thought of tying yourself to a man such as myself? A man ignorant of the manners of Western culture, more at home in a desert sandstorm, or riding bareback on an Arab stallion, than making polite conversation in a grand salon or waltzing you around a palace ballroom?'

'No…it's not that.'

'I am not the cultured European prince you were hoping for?' Suddenly bitterness crept into his voice.

'No, it's not that, Zahir. Really.'

'What, then? I need to know.' The searing intensity in his eyes left her in no doubt about that. 'Do you fear that I am such a difficult man to please?' His voice dropped.

Yes. 'Impossible' might be a better word. Anna stared back at him, tracing the map of his face with her eyes: the grooves between eyebrows that were so used to being pulled into a scowl, the lines scored across a forehead that frowned all too easily. Had she ever even seen him smile? She wasn't sure. How did she have any hope of pleasing such a man?

'I fear I may need time to learn the ways to make you happy.' She chose her words carefully, trying to avoid snagging herself on the barbed wire all around her. Trying to conceal the inbuilt dread that she might not be able to satisfy him. Her abortive night of shame with Henrik still haunted her, plagued her with worry and self-doubt. And the way Zahir had dismissed it had done nothing to allay her fears either, merely demonstrated that he no idea of the scale of the problem. That he didn't understand.

'All being well, time is something we have plenty of, my princess.' The very masculine gleam in his eye only made Anna feel a hundred times worse. 'A lifetime together, in fact.'

'Yes, indeed. A lifetime...' Her voice tailed off.

'And learning to please one another need not be such an arduous task.' His thumb stroked over her lower lip.

'No, of course not.' Anna's heart took up a thumping beat. His gentle touch, the depth of his dark stare, spelled out exactly the sort of pleasure he was talking about: intimate, sexual pleasure. It shone in his eyes and it clenched deep down in Anna's belly.

She had spent so long worrying about how to satisfy Zahir that it hadn't even occurred to her that sex was a reciprocal thing. That he might be thinking of ways to pleasure her. Now hot bolts of desire ricocheted through her at the thought of it. Of Zahir's large rough-skinned hands travelling over her naked body, moving between her thighs, pushing them apart, spanning the mound of her sex before exploring within. A shiver of longing rippled through her and she had to squeeze her muscles tight to halt its progress.

'I must go.' Releasing her chin, Zahir let his thumb rest against her lip for a second, gently dragging it down. Then he took a step away. 'Your father has meetings arranged for me all morning. However, I have set aside this afternoon for us to spend some time together.'

'You have?' Anna couldn't keep the surprise from her voice, nor cover up the leap of excitement that coloured her cheeks.

'After your little lecture about the role of a host, I assume you will be willing to show me around Dorrada?'

'Yes, of course.'

'Time is limited—I leave for Nabatean first thing

tomorrow—but I should like to take in some of the sights before I go.'

'You're going back to Nabatean tomorrow?' This was news to her.

'Correct.'

'Alone?'

'I take it that won't be a problem?'

'Not for me, I can assure you.' Anna fiddled with one of her plaits. 'So does this mean you finally trust me or am I to be surrounded by your minders?'

'No minders.' Zahir narrowed his eyes as he contemplated her question. 'But trust is not something I find easy to give. Once you have suffered the sort of betrayal I have, it is hard to ever completely trust anyone again.'

'I'm sure.' Anna lowered her eyes. At first she had thought he was talking about her, what she had done on the bridge in Paris. But the pain in his eyes ran deeper than that, far deeper. She wanted to ask more but Zahir was already pulling down the shutters, aware that he had said too much.

'However, I'm prepared to give you the freedom to prove yourself.' He levelled dark eyes at her. 'Just make sure you don't let me down.'

'I suppose we should be getting back to the castle.' Night was starting to close in, the first stars appearing in the sky, and reluctantly Anna felt in her pocket for the car keys. Their whistle-stop tour of Dorrada was nearly over, something that disappointed Anna more than she would ever have imagined.

Zahir hadn't bothered to hide his surprise when she had pulled up in front of the castle in the battered old four-by-four vehicle and gestured to him to get in beside her. Warily easing himself into the passenger seat, he had shot her one of his now familiar hooded stares, leaving her in no doubt that this was a situation he did *not* feel comfortable with—whether that was being driven by a woman, or her in particular, she didn't know. And didn't care. She was a good driver, she knew the roads around here like the back of her hand, and the challenging conditions of this wintry climate posed no problems for her. And even if he'd looked as though he was coming perilously close to grabbing the wheel off her a couple of times—especially on some of the spectacular hairpin bends that snaked up through the mountains—he had just about managed to restrain himself, travelling every inch of the road with his eyes instead.

Deciding where to take her guest had been difficult. Dorrada was only a small country but the scenery was spectacular and there were so many places Anna would have liked to show him. But time was short so she had limited herself to a trip up into the mountains, with several stops to admire the views, including the place where an ancient cable car still vertiginously cranked tourists down to the valley below. Then she had given him a rapid tour of the town of Valduz, unable to stop because she'd known they would attract too much attention. People turned to stare at them as they passed anyway, rapidly pulling out their phones to take a photo, or just waving excitedly as their princess and her exotic fiancé drove by.

The last stop on Anna's tour had brought them to this mountain lakeside, one of her favourite places. Originally she hadn't intended to bring Zahir here but somehow it had happened and now she was glad of that. Because as they had crunched their way along the shoreline, stopped to take in the stunning sunset rippling across the crystal-clear water, she knew that Zahir was feeling the beauty of the place every bit as much as her. Not that he said so. Zahir was a man of few words, using communication as a mere necessity to have his wishes understood or his orders obeyed. But there had been a stillness as he'd gazed across the water to the snow-capped mountains beyond, an alertness in the way he'd held his body, that had told Anna how much he was feeling the magic of this place. They hadn't needed any words.

'There's no rush, is there?' Zahir turned to look at her, his face all sharp-angled lines and shadows in the dim light.

'Well, no, but it's getting dark. There's not much point in me taking you sightseeing if you can't see the sights.'

'I like the dark.' Zahir laid the statement baldly before her, as if it was all that was needed to be said. Anna didn't doubt it. She already thought of him a man of the night, a shadowed, stealthy predator that would stalk his prey— would curl his hands around the throat of an enemy before they even knew of his existence. 'Is that some sort of cabin over there between those trees?'

Anna followed his finger, which was pointing to the other side of the lake. 'Yes, it's an old hunter's cabin.'

'Shall we take a look?'

Anna hesitated. She didn't need to take a look, she was all too familiar with the modest cabin. She should be. She'd been escaping here for years, to her own little bolthole, whenever the bleak reality of her life in the castle got too much for her.

It was to here that she had fled all those years ago, on being told that her mother had died. That she would never see her again. Here, too, much more recently, she'd sat staring at the rustic walls, trying to come to terms with the fact that a marriage had been arranged for her. That she was to be shipped off to a place called Nabatean to marry the newly crowned king. And look how that had turned out.

The cabin was her secret place. Taking Zahir there would feel strange. But somehow exciting too.

'Sure, if you like.' Affecting a casual tone, she started walking. 'D'you want to follow me?'

They set off, Anna leading the way around the lake and into the fringes of the forest of pine trees. It was too dark to see much but she knew the way by heart. Zahir was right behind her every step, so close that they moved as almost one being, their feet crunching on snow that had crystallised to ice. She could sense the heat from his body, feel the power of it all around her. It made her feel both safe and jumpy at the same time, butterflies leaping about in her tummy.

Finally they came to a small clearing and there was the log cabin before them, looking like a life-size gingerbread house. The door was wedged shut by a drift of snow but with a few swift kicks Zahir had cleared it and soon they were both standing inside.

'There should be some matches here somewhere.' Running her hands over the table next to her, Anna opened the drawer, relieved to feel the box beneath her fingertips. 'I'll just light the paraffin lamp.'

'Here, let me.' Taking the matches from her Zahir reached up and, removing the glass funnel from the lamp, touched a flame to the wick. 'Hmm…' With a grunt of approval, he looked around him in the flickering light. 'Basic but perfectly functional. You say it was a hunter's cabin?'

'Yes, hence the trophies.' Anna pointed to the mounted deer heads that gazed down on them with glassy-eyed stares. 'But it hasn't been used for years. Valduz Castle used to host hunting parties in the past, but, thankfully for the local wildlife, those days have gone.'

'But you come here?'

'Well, yes, now and again.' Was it that obvious? His directness immediately put her on the defensive. 'I used to like it here as a kid. Other children had play houses and I had my own log cabin!' She attempted a light-hearted laugh but as the light played over Zahir's harsh features they showed no softening. He merely waited for her to elaborate. 'And now I sometimes come here when I want to think, you know? Get away from it all.'

'I understand.' The deep rumble of his voice, coupled with the hint of compassion in his dark eyes threatened to unravel something deep inside her.

'Shall we light a fire?' Hideously chirpy—she'd be asking him if he wanted to play mummies and daddies in a minute—Anna moved over to the open hearth. 'There should be plenty of logs.'

Immediately Zahir took charge, deftly getting the fire going with the efficiency of a man well used to such a task. Anna watched as he sat forward on his haunches, blowing onto the scraps of bark until the smoke turned to flames and the flames took hold. There was something primal about his movements. Hypnotic. Mission accomplished, he sat back on his heels.

'I think there's some brandy here somewhere if you'd like some?' Needing to break the spell, Anna moved over to a cupboard and pulled out a dusty bottle and a couple of tumblers.

'I never drink alcohol.'

'Oh.' Now she thought about it, she realised she had never seen him drink. 'Is that because of your religion or for some other reason?' She poured a modest amount into one glass.

'I don't believe in deliberately altering the state of my mind with toxic substances.'

Right. Anna glanced at the drink in her hand, sheer contrariness making her add another good measure before turning back to look around her. There was only one chair in the cabin, a rickety old wooden rocker, but the bare floor was scattered with animal skins and she moved to seat herself beside Zahir in front of the fire.

Zahir cast her a sideways glance, as if unsure how to deal with this situation, before finally settling his large frame beside her, sitting cross-legged and staring into the flames. For a moment there was silence, just the crackling of the logs. Anna took a gulp of brandy, screwing up her eyes against its burn.

'So.' She'd been tempted to remain quiet, to see how long it would be before Zahir instigated some sort of conversation, but she suspected that would be the wrong side of never. 'What do you think of Dorrada?'

'Its economy has been very badly handled. I fail to see how a country with such potential, such a noble history, can have got itself in such a mess.'

Anna pouted. If she'd been expecting a comment on the beauty of the scenery or the quality of the air, she should have known better. 'Well, we don't all have the benefit of gallons of crude oil gushing out of the ground. I'm sure it's easy to be a wealthy country when you have that as a natural resource.'

Spinning round, his jaw held rigid, Zahir's looked ready to take a bite out of her. 'If you think there has been anything remotely *easy* about reforming a nation like Nabatean then I would urge you to hastily reconsider. Nabatean has not been built on oil but on the spilt blood of its young men. Not on the value of its exports of but on the courage and strength of its people. You would do well to remember that.'

'I'm sorry.' Suitably chastened, Anna took another sip

of brandy. Perhaps that had been a stupid thing to say. He had turned back towards the fire now, his whole body radiating his disapproval. 'I didn't mean any disrespect. I still know so little of the ways of your country.'

'You will have ample opportunity to learn our ways, our language and our ethos once you are living there. And may I remind you that Nabatean will shortly be *your* country too?'

'Yes, I know that.' Anna swallowed. 'And I will do my best to embrace the culture and learn all I can. But it would help me if you told me more about it now.'

Zahir shrugged broad shoulders.

'You say the war that brought about the independence of Nabatean cost many lives?'

'Indeed.' He shifted his weight beside her.

'And you yourself were in the army, fighting along-side your fellow countrymen?'

'Yes. As the second son, I always knew that the army would be my calling. It was an honour to serve my country.'

'But you must have seen some terrible atrocities.'

'War is one long atrocity. But sometimes it is the only answer.'

'And your parents…' Anna knew she was straying into dangerous territory here. 'I understand that they…died?'

'They were murdered, Annalina, as I am sure you well know. Their throats cut as they slept.' He stared into the flames as if transfixed. 'Less than twenty-four hours after Uristan had capitulated and the end of the war declared, they were dead. I was celebrating our victory with the people of Nabatean when a rebel insurgent took advantage of the lapse in security and crept into my parents' bedchamber to slaughter them as a final act of barbarity.'

'Oh, Zahir.' Anna's hands fluttered to her throat. 'How terrible. I'm so sorry.'

'It is I who should be sorry. It was my job to protect them and I failed. I will carry that responsibility with me to my grave.'

'But you can't torture yourself with that for ever, Zahir. You can't carry all that burden on your shoulders.'

'Oh, but I can. And I will.' His jaw tightened. 'It was supposed to have been a safe house. I had only moved them out of exile a week before, along with my brother. I was convinced no one knew of their whereabouts. But I was betrayed by a guard I thought I could trust.'

'And your brother, Rashid? He obviously escaped the assassin?'

'He awoke to hear my mother screaming his name. Even with a knife at her throat, seconds from death and with her husband already slaughtered beside her, my mother managed to find enough strength to warn her son. To save him. But, had I been there, I could have saved them all. I *would* have saved them all.'

Anna didn't doubt it for one moment. There wasn't an armed assassin in the world that would stand a chance against someone like Zahir.

'Your mother sounds like an amazing woman.'

'She was.'

'And I'm sure she and your father would be very proud of what you have achieved. You and Rashid.'

'Rashid, as I am sure you are aware, has not yet fully recovered from his ordeal.' His held his profile steady, stark and uncompromising.

Anna hesitated, choosing her words with care. She had no desire to get her head bitten off again. 'And that's the reason you're governing the kingdom, rather than him?'

'My brother is happy to let me run the country as I see

fit. His role is more that of a figurehead. He is temporarily unsuited to the rigours of leadership.'

So it was just as she thought. Zahir Zahani was the power and brains behind the success of Nabatean. She sat up a little straighter. 'I hope that you will allow me to assist you?' Determined that he should see some worth in her, she almost implored him. 'I'm a hard worker and a quick learner. I'm sure I have skills that you can utilise.'

'I'm sure you have.' Zahir turned towards her, his eyelids heavy, thick, dark lashes lowered. 'And I look forward to utilising them.'

The rasp of his words sent a tremor of anticipation through her. With the flames licking the shadows of his face, shining blue-black on his hair and gleaming in his eyes, she felt her heart pound, her body melt with the power of his raw sexual energy. There had been no mistaking the meaning behind his words. It pulsed from him, throbbed in the air between them, weakening her limbs with its promise.

Impulse made her reach for his cheek and gently run the back of her hand against it, feel the scratch of his stubble, the burn of the heat from the fire. Immediately he grasped her wrist, twisting her hand so that her fingers brushed his mouth and then, taking her index finger between his lips, holding it between his teeth, clenching down so that it was trapped, warm and damp from his breath, his bite hard but controlled. It was an action so unexpected, so intimate, and so deeply sexy that for a moment Anna could do nothing but stare at him, her whole body going into heart-stopping free fall.

She wanted more. She knew that with a certainty that thundered in her head, roared the blood in her ears and pulsed down low in her abdomen. She wanted him the way she had never wanted any other man in her life. She had no idea what would happen when it came to it, to the point where she had failed so pitifully before, but she knew she wanted to try. Right now.

CHAPTER EIGHT

THEIR GAZES CLASHED and Anna watched, spellbound, as the firelight danced across the surface of Zahir's black eyes. Slowly, seductively, his tongue licked the tip of her finger, sending a wave of pure lust crashing over her. She waited, desperate for him to suck it into his mouth, and when he released his teeth and did just that she closed her eyes and moaned with pleasure, revelling in the rasp of his tongue, the powerful suck of his mouth, the graze of his teeth against her knuckles.

She craved more, the thought of the suck of that mouth against other parts of her body…against her nipples, her inner thighs, her most intimate place…building inside her like a fleeting promise that she had to grab on to before it was taken away from her, before it vanished into thin air. Opening her eyes, she saw him staring at her, solemn and unsmiling, but exuding enough sexual chemistry to decimate an entire country.

'You leave tomorrow, Zahir.' Leaning towards him, she placed her hands on his shoulders, running them over the rough wool of the thick army jumper he was wearing. She loved the feel of him, the strength of the muscles, the way the thick column of his corded neck carried the pulse of his veins. 'I won't see you again before the wedding.'

'No.' His voice rumbled, deep and low, between them.

'If you wanted to make love to me...' she hesitated, trying very hard to control herself '...beforehand—now, even, I mean—I wouldn't object.'

'Of course you wouldn't.

Anna gasped at his chauvinistic attitude. But challenging it was going to be difficult when her body was still leaning in to him, inviting him, betraying her in the most obvious way.

'Are you so sure of yourself that you think you can have any woman of your choosing?'

'We are not talking about any woman. We are talking about my fiancée. You.' He lowered his mouth, his breath fanning across her face.

Anna swallowed. 'And that makes your conceit acceptable, does it?'

'Acceptable, inevitable, call it whatever you like.' His hand strayed to her neck, pushing aside the curtain of hair. 'And as for having no say in the matter...' Now his mouth was on her skin, the drag of his lips following the graceful sweep of her neck down to the hollow between her collarbone, muffling his words. 'You and I both know that you're desperate for me to make love to you.'

'That is very...' With her head thrown back to allow him more access to her throat, to make sure he had no excuse to stop lavishing this glorious attention on her neck, words were surprisingly hard to formulate. 'Ungallant.'

This produced a harsh laugh. 'I have never claimed to be gallant. Nor would you expect me to be. And, right now, I suspect gallantry is the last thing on your mind.' He raised his head his eyes drilling into her soul. 'Tell me, Annalina, which would you rather—a polite request to allow me access to your breasts, or an order that you remove your jumper?'

Anna gasped, the thrill of his audacious demand immediately shrivelling her nipples, producing a heavy ache in her breasts that rapidly spread throughout her body. It was outrageous, preposterous, that he should order her to strip.

'I thought as much.' Her second of silence was met with a growl of approval. 'Do it now, Annalina. Take off your jumper.'

She stared back at him, dumbfounded by the way this had suddenly turned around. How her tentative attempt to initiate lovemaking had resulted in an order to obey.

But still her fingers strayed to the bottom of her woollen jumper and she found herself pulling it up over her head, taking the tee-shirt underneath with it, until she was stripped down to her bra, her naked skin gleaming in the firelight.

'Very good.' Zahir's eyes travelled over her, his eyelids heavy, dark lashes flickering. Anna heard him swallow. 'Now, stay still.'

Raising both hands, he held them in front of her, their span so large, their skin so dark, as they hovered over the lacy white material of her bra. They were shaking, Anna realised. She was making the hands of this warrior man shake. Slowly they closed over her breasts, the heat of them searing into her, roaring through every part of her, right down to her fingertips that prickled by her side. And when his fingers traced where the swell of one of her breasts met the lacy fabric, dipping into the hollow of her cleavage before moving to explore the other, she thought she would combust with the agony and the ecstasy of it.

'Remove your bra.'

Reaching behind her, Anna did as she was told, any pretence of denying him or regaining control vanishing on the tidal wave of lust. As the bra fell to the floor, she kept her eyes fixed on Zahir's face, determined that she should see, as well as feel, his every reaction. He let out a guttural growl that arched her back, pushing her breasts towards him, inviting him to take her.

And take her he did. Cupping her naked breasts, one in each hand, he touched her hardened nipples with the pads of his thumbs, starting a rhythmic circular movement that had her writhing in front of him. Then, lowering his head, he took one nipple in his mouth, his breath scorching against her as he slathered her with hot, wet saliva before moving to the puckered peak, teasing his tongue against it with a slow, drugging forcefulness.

Anna groaned, her body on fire, dampness pooling between her legs, her skinny jeans suddenly unbearably tight, horribly uncomfortable. She wanted to take them off—bizarrely she wanted Zahir to tell her to take them off. But first she needed him to attend to her other breast before she died of longing.

A ragged sigh escaped her when he did just that, his attention to her second breast no more hurried, no less glorious. Anna plunged her fingers into his hair, pulling him closer to increase the pressure, to hold herself steady. She stared down, her eyes glazed, trance-like, as she watched his head rock against her, his mouth still working its incredible magic. And when he stopped, pulling away, ordering her to remove her jeans, she had no hesitation, falling over herself to stand up, undo the buttons and tug them down, cursing as they clung to her ankles and standing, first on one wobbly leg and then the other, as she pulled them inside out to get them off, ending up all but falling into Zahir's lap.

Strong arms encircled her, adjusting her position so that he held her, straddled across him, taking a second simply to look at her, his eyes raking over her like hot coals. She was acutely aware that she was virtually naked, whereas he was still fully dressed in rugged outdoor clothes, but for some reason this only increased her rabid desire. The scratch of his rough woollen jumper against her bare skin, the graze of the zips on the pockets of his cargo pants beneath her thighs, was something else, something so thrillingly erotic, that Anna couldn't hold back a squeak of surprise.

Zahir's erection, the enormous, rock-hard length of it, was like a rod of steel positioned between her buttocks, pulsing against her from behind. She tried to turn, to lift herself off so that she could find the zipper of his fly, her trembling fingers longing to yank it down, to release him so that she could see for herself, *feel* for herself, this extraordinary phenomenon. But Zahir held her firm, his hands around her waist gripping her so tightly that she could only move where he positioned her, which was squarely down on his lap again. She squirmed provocatively against him, the only small movement she could make. But even that was not allowed, as with a low growl Zahir lifted her up, the small space between them suddenly feeling like a yawning cavern of rejection, before he adjusted his position and sat her back down on him.

'Do not move.' The words roared softly into her ear from behind and Anna could only nod her acceptance as she felt one hand release her waist and move round to her front, where it trailed down over her clenching stomach muscles and slipped silently under the front of her skimpy lace knickers. The shock halted her breath, setting up a tremble that she couldn't tell whether was from inside her, or out, or both. She found herself desperately hoping that this didn't count as moving because she couldn't bear to disobey him now—not if it meant he was going to stop what he was doing. Gingerly tipping back her head, she rested it against the ridge of his collarbone, relieved when he seemed happy with this.

'That's right.'

His fingers brushed over her until they met the damp, throbbing centre of her core. Anna waited, poised on the brink of delirium, as one finger parted her sensitive folds, then slid into her with a slow but a deliberately controlled movement that shook her whole body from top to toe.

'Open your legs.'

The voice behind her commanded and Anna obeyed, parting her thighs, amazed that she had any control over any part of herself.

'Now, stop. Stay like that.'

It was like asking a jelly to stop wobbling, but Anna did the best she could, and with her head pressed hard back against his shoulder she screwed her eyes shut. Drawing in a breath, she waited, ready to give herself over to him completely, to do with her whatever he saw fit.

It was the most glorious, astonishing, explosion of mind-altering sensations. As his finger moved inside her, it rubbed against the swollen nub of her clitoris until he was just there, in that one spot, stroking it again and again with a pressure that could never be too much and never be enough. With the agonisingly pleasurable sensation swelling and swelling inside her, it felt as if her whole world had distilled into this moment, this momentous feeling. She would trade her entire life for the concentrated pleasure of this building ecstasy.

But trying to stay still was an impossibility. Even with the weight of Zahir's arm diagonally across her body she couldn't help writhing and bucking.

With his breath hot in her ear, the rock-hard swell of him beneath her buttocks, there was no way she could stop her legs from parting further, her back from arching against him, her bottom from pressing down into him. And as he continued his glorious attentions the pressure built more and more until what had seemed just tantalisingly out of reach was suddenly there upon her, crashing over her, carrying her with it. And, as that wave subsided and Zahir continued to touch her, another one followed, just as intense, then another and another, until Anna thought the moment might never end and that she had left the real world for ever.

But finally his hand stilled and slowly, slowly the feelings started to subside, sending sharp twitches through her body as reminders of what she had just experienced. Anna opened her eyes to see him staring down at her.

She looked so beautiful. Never had Zahir witnessed such beauty, such wild abandonment. Removing his arm, he released her body, moving her off his lap so that he could stand up, rip off his clothes and devour her in the way that he had been so desperate to do for the past hour…for the past twenty-four hours…ever since he had first clapped eyes on her. He had told himself that he would wait until after they were married, that that would be the right thing to do. But now waiting was an impossibility. Now the right thing, the *only* thing, he could think of was to claim this beautiful young woman for his own. To take her now, for himself, to satisfy his immense carnal need in the only way possible. By having her beneath him and making love to her in a way that neither of them would ever, ever forget.

With his breath coming in harsh pants, his chest heaving beneath the sweater that he tugged over his head, he was down to his boxer shorts in seconds, his powerful erection straining against the black cotton fabric, swollen and painful with need. He knew Anna was watching his every move from the floor, and that only increased his fervour, fuelled the frantic craving that was coursing through him.

'Lie down.' He barked the order without knowing why he felt the need to be so domineering.

Primal lust roared in his ears as he watched Annalina do as she was told, stretching out on the animal-skin rug, her body so pale in the flickering light of the fire, so delicate, so desirable. Bending down beside her, he pulled the scrap of fabric that was her panties down and over her legs, screwing them into a ball in his hand. Then he removed his boxers with a forceful tug and straddled her body with his own, holding his weight above her with locked elbows on either side of her head. She seemed so fragile compared to him, so impossibly perfect, that for a moment he could only gaze down at her, the corded muscles in his arms rigidly holding him in place, defying the tremor that was rippling through the rest of his body.

'You want this, Annalina?' He ground out the words, suddenly needing to hear her consent before he allowed himself to take her, this most precious creature.

'Yes.' It was the smallest word, spoken in little more than a whisper, but it was enough. And when her hand snaked between them, tentatively feeling for his member, he closed his eyes against the ecstasy, lowering his elbows enough to reach her lips and seal their coupling with a searing kiss.

Lifting himself off her, he unscrewed his eyes to look down at her again. Her hand was circling his shaft and it was taking all of his control not to position himself and plunge right into her. His need was so great, unlike anything he had ever felt before, that his body was screaming at him just to do it, to take her as fast and furiously as he liked, anything to satisfy this infernal craving. But he knew he had to find some restraint. If Annalina was a virgin, which it seemed she was, he had to try to take it slowly, make sure she was ready, control the barbarian in him. Though if she carried on the way she was right now, her fingers exploring the length of him, caressing the swollen tip, his body was going to have severe trouble obeying his commands.

'Is this right?' Slowly her hand moved up and down.

Zahir let out a moan of assent. Frankly she could have done it any damned way she liked, could have done anything she wanted. He was past the point of being able to judge.

'I don't want to disappoint you.'

Disappoint him? That was not going to happen. He was sure about that. He moved one arm to cover her hand with his own, to position himself over her, to the place he so desperately needed to be able to enter her. His fingers strayed to find her, to part her in readiness, but then something made him hesitate. The catch in her voice, the slight tremor, suddenly permeated the lust-ridden fog of his mind and now he rapidly scanned her face for clues.

'What is it? You have changed your mind?' It killed him to ask but he had to be sure.

'No, it's not that.'

'What, then?' So he had been right—there was something.

'Nothing, really.' She removed her hand, bringing her arms around his back. But, as they skittered over the play of his muscles, their touch was as unconvincing as her words.

'Tell me, Annalina.'

'Well, it's just…I'm a bit nervous.' Her throat moved beneath the pale skin of her throat. 'I hadn't realised that you would be so…large.'

'And that's a problem?'

'I don't know. I suppose it could be. I mean, there was a problem with me and Henrik, and he wasn't anything like as big...'

Henrik. The mention of his name on her lips had the effect of pouring an icy waterfall over Zahir, at the same time as stirring a roaring tiger in his chest. Henrik. He knew what he'd like to do if he ever got his hands on that slimy creep of an individual. He couldn't bear to think of him touching Annalina at any time, ever. But he particularly couldn't bear to think of him now.

'But I think we should try.' Still she was talking, seemingly oblivious to the cold rage sweeping through him, her voice nervous but determined in the now suffocating air of the cabin. 'Now—before we marry, I mean—to see if we can. I'm worried because of what happened with Henrik...'

'Henrik!' Zahir roared his name, making Annalina jump beneath him. 'Do you really think I want to hear about Henrik?' He moved his body off her, leaping to his feet, cursing the damned erection that refused to die, mocking him with its disobedient show of power. 'Do you really think I want to be compared to your failed lover?'

'Well, no, but...I just meant...' Annalina sat up, covering her chest with her arms, her blue eyes staring up at him, wide, frightened and beseeching.

'I know what you meant. You meant that I'm not the man that you were meant to marry, the man you wanted to marry. You meant that having sex with me was a chore that you were prepared to endure. Or maybe not.' Another thought tore through his tortured mind. 'Maybe you thought that if we weren't able to have sex, if you could prove that, you wouldn't have to marry me at all.'

'No, Zahir, you're wrong. You've got it all wrong.'

'Because, if so, you are going to be sorely disappointed. We will marry, as planned, and we will consummate our marriage on our wedding night. And believe me, Annalina, when we do, I will drive all thoughts of Henrik from your mind. Banish all thoughts of not being able, or not being ready, or whatever other pathetic excuses you seem to be toying with. For when we do make love, when it finally happens, you'll be thinking of nothing but me. Nothing but the way *I* am making you feel. And that, Annalina, is a promise.

CHAPTER NINE

FROM INSIDE THE chapel the organ music paused and Princess Annalina's grip on her bouquet tightened. As the strains of Wagner's *Wedding March* began she felt for her father's arm, slipping her own through the crook of it. This was it, then. There was no going back now.

Not that she had any choice. Beside her King Gustav stood rigidly to attention, his gaze fixed straight ahead. If he had any misgivings about handing over his only daughter to this warrior prince, then he wasn't letting it show. As far as he was concerned this wedding was a business deal, a means to an end, and his job was to deliver his daughter to her fate. And to make sure that this time nothing went wrong.

Sitting side by side in the vintage car taking them the short journey from the castle to the chapel on the Valduz estate, Anna had thought maybe this would be the moment her father would say something encouraging, comforting—she didn't really know what. Instead he had simply checked his watch a dozen times, tugged on the sleeves of his morning coat and looked distractedly out of the window at the cheering crowds that lined the route as they passed. And when her hand had reached for his he had looked at it in surprise before awkwardly patting it a couple of times and handing it back.

More than anything in the world right now, Anna wished that her mother could be here to give her a hug, to make everything better. But sadly wishes didn't come true, even for princesses, so instead she ended up blinking back the tears as she stared out of the window, forcing herself to smile and wave at the crowds brandishing their paper flags. But inside she had never felt more lost. More alone.

The chapel doors opened to reveal the stage set for the ceremony. And it was beautiful. This was the first wedding the chapel had seen since her parents' nuptials and no expense had been spared, though it didn't take a genius to work out where the money had come from. With a green-and-white theme, the ancient pews were festooned with alpine flowers, their scent mingling with the incense in the air. Huge arrangements of ivy and ferns were positioned at the top of the aisle and behind the altar at the end—somewhere that Anna couldn't look at just yet. Because that was where Zahir would be standing. Waiting. That was where, in just a few short minutes from now, the ceremony would begin that would see her signing away her life, at least the only life she had ever known. Where she would hand herself over to this man, become his wife, move to his country, to all intents and purposes become his property to do with as he saw fit.

And Anna had been left in no doubt as to what that would entail, at least as far as the bedroom was concerned. It had been four weeks since that fateful evening in the log cabin, but the brutal memory of it would stay with her for ever—the way Zahir had taken her from wild ecstasy to the pit of misery before the aftershocks of delirium had even left her body. His rage when she had mentioned Henrik had been palpable, terrifying, a dark force that had shocked her with its vehemence, leaving her no chance to try and explain why she had said it, to justify herself. Instead she had hurried to pull on her clothes and followed him out into the night, the snow falling as he had unerringly led them back to where their vehicle was parked and sat beside her in stony silence as she had driven them back to the castle.

Zahir had returned to Nabatean the next morning and they hadn't seen each other since, any contact between them limited to perfunctory emails or the occasional phone call. But his parting words still clamoured in her head. *We will consummate our marriage on our wedding night.* It had sounded more like a threat than a promise, but that didn't stop it sending a thrill of tumult through Anna whenever she recalled it. Like now, for example. Because tonight was the night that Zahir would fulfil his prophecy.

But first she had a job to do. Glancing behind her, she forced a smile at her attendants, four little bridesmaids and two pageboys. The daughters and sons of foreign royalty she didn't even know, they were nevertheless taking their duties very seriously, meticulously arranging the train of Anna's beautiful lace wedding dress, the girls bossing the boys around, straightening their emerald-green sashes for them before clasping their posies to their chests, ready to begin.

The procession started, slowly making its way down the red carpet, the congregation turning to catch their first glimpse of the blushing bride, gasping at what they saw. Because Annalina looked stunning, every inch the fairy-tale princess about to marry her Prince Charming. She wore a white lace gown, the wide V neck leaving her collarbone bare to show off the diamond necklace that had belonged to her mother. With sheer lace sleeves and a nipped-in waist, it cascaded to the floor with metres of lace and tulle that rustled with every step. Every step that took her closer and closer to the towering, dark figure that stood with his back to her—rigid, unmoving, impossible to read.

Zahir Zahani. The man she knew so little of, but who was about to become her husband. The man whose hooded gaze burnt into her soul, whose harshly sculpted face haunted her very being. The man who somehow, terrifyingly, she seemed to have become totally obsessed with. Even during the weeks when they had been apart it had felt as if her every waking moment had been filled with the overpowering sense of him. And not just her waking moments. The force of his magnetism had invaded her dreams too, seeing her writhing around in her sleep, waking up gasping for air, her heart thumping in her chest as the erotic images slowly faded into the reality of the day.

Now she took her position beside Zahir, beside this immovable mountain of a man who still stared fixedly ahead. His immaculate tailored suit only accentuated the width of his back, the length of his legs, and when Anna risked a sideways glance she saw how stiffly he held his neck against the starched white collar of his dress shirt, how rigidly his jaw was clenched beneath the smooth, olive skin.

Next to him stood Rashid, who was to serve as best man. In contrast to Zahir's complete stillness he fidgeted, shifting his weight from foot to foot, smoothing his hands over the trousers of his suit. He shot Anna a cold glance and again she registered that same peculiar sense of unease.

And so the long ceremony began. The sonorous voice of the priest echoed around the vaulted ceiling of the chapel—a chapel full of honoured guests from around the world. But Anna was only aware of one man, so acutely aware that she thought she must shimmer with it, radiate an aura that was plain for all to see.

Somehow she managed to get through the service, the daze of hymns, prayers, readings and blessings, only seriously faltering once, when Zahir slipped the platinum wedding ring onto her finger. The sight of it there, looking so real, so *final*, sent her eyes flying to his face, searching for a crumb of comfort, some sort of affirmation that they were doing the right thing. But all she saw was the same closed, dark expression that refused to give anything away.

Finally the organ struck up for the last time and the bride and groom made their way back up the aisle as man and wife. As they stepped outside, they were met with a loud roar from the crowd and a barrage of flashing cameras. It seemed thousands of people had gathered to be a part of this special day, braving hours of standing in the cold to catch a glimpse of their princess and her new husband. A short distance away, the car was waiting to take them back to the castle for the wedding breakfast, but first Anna was going to spend a few minutes chatting to the crowd. They deserved that, at least. Walking over to the barrier, she bent down to accept a posy of flowers from a young child, smiling at the sight of his chubby little cheeks red from the cold. The crowd roared louder and suddenly arms were reaching out everywhere, bunches of flowers thrust at them, cameras and phones held out to capture the moment.

'We need to get into the car, Annalina.' Zahir was right behind her, whispering harshly into her ear.

'All in good time.' She politely accepted another bunch of flowers. 'First we need to acknowledge the kindness of these people who have been hanging around for hours waiting to congratulate us.' She could feel Zahir's displeasure radiating from him in waves but she didn't care. They weren't in Nabatean now. This was her country and she was going to set the rules. She continued to smile into the crowd, accepting armfuls of flowers that she then passed to a couple of burly men who had appeared behind them. She noticed they shot a startled glance at Zahir. 'Why don't you go and talk to the people over there?' She gestured to the barrier on the other side.

'Because this is not on the schedule, that's why.'

'So what? Life doesn't always have to run to a schedule.' She passed more flowers back to the minders, enjoying herself now, especially the sight of these burly men wreathed in blooms. 'You need to loosen up a bit, accept that this is the way things are done here.'

But Zahir showed no signs of loosening up. Instead he continued to move her forward by the sheer wall of his presence, so close behind her that his barely repressed ire bound them together. Anna turned her head, hissing the words past her smile: 'You might at least try and look as if you're happy.'

'This isn't about being happy.' No, of course it wasn't. How foolish of Anna to forget for a moment. 'Schedules are there for a reason. And impromptu *walkabouts* provide the ideal chance for a terrorist to strike.'

'This is Dorrada, Zahir.' Still she persisted. 'We don't have any terrorists.'

They had reached the car now, Zahir having to duck his head to get in to this ancient vehicle that had once been her father's pride and joy. He seemed far too big for it, caged in by it, as the doors closed behind them, muffling the cheers of the crowd.

'May I remind you that you are now married to me,

Annalina? To Prince Zahir of Nabatean?' He turned to
face her, his eyes as black as stone. 'And *we* do. From now
on, you will treat security with the respect it deserves.
Otherwise, you may not live to regret it.'

Zahir's eyes strayed across the crowded ballroom yet
again, searching out Annalina. She wasn't difficult to
find. Still wearing her wedding dress, she was by far the
most beautiful woman in the room without exception,
moving amongst the guests with practised ease, charming them with her grace and beauty, occasionally taking
to the floor to be whisked around by some daring young
buck or crusty old dignitary.

Zahir didn't dance. Never had he seen the need. But
tonight he found himself wishing that he did, that he
could have parted the crowd on the dance floor, firmly
tapped on the shoulder whichever interloper it was at
the time and removed Annalina from his clutches. Other
men touching his bride did not sit well with him. More
than that, it spread a hot tide of possessiveness through
him, the like of which he had never known before. It was
something he knew he had to keep in check.

At least until tonight, when he would have Annalina
in his bed. Then she would be all his, in every sense of
the word. It was that thought that had got him through
today: the long-drawn-out ceremony, the tedious wedding breakfast and now this irksome ball that it appeared
would never come to an end. His tolerance and patience
had been severely tested, neither being qualities that he
had in abundance. But the day was finally drawing to
a close, the waiting nearly over. And as the time approached when at last they would be together, alone, so
the thrum of awareness increased, spreading through

him, until it was no longer a thrum but a thudding, pounding urge that held his body taut, rang in his ears.

From across the other side of the room Annalina looked up, meeting his gaze, a gaze which he knew he had held for too long, that was in danger of betraying him with its intensity. She angled her head, something approaching a smile playing across her lips, her eyes deliberately holding his, refusing to look away.

God, she was beautiful. A fresh wave of lust washed over him, tightening the fit of his tailored trousers. She might be all demure decorum now but tonight he would have those restrained lips screaming his name in pleasure, those searching eyes screwed shut against the delirium of his touch, his heated thrust. Bringing her to orgasm that night in the log cabin had been the single most erotic experience of his life. But the experience had ended badly—seeing him consumed with rage, fighting to maintain his composure, dangerously close to losing it. This was what Annalina did to him. She stirred up emotions that were totally uncalled for. Awoke the warrior in him when the situation called for restraint and respect—not pumping testosterone and raging hormones.

As the supreme leader of the army of Nabatean, Zahir had seen some terrible things, had done some terrible things, that still had the power to haunt him when he closed his eyes against the night. But that was war, the most brutal savagery imaginable, man turning on his fellow man. It had been a hideous, necessary evil but he was vindicated by the fact that Nabatean was now a successful, independent country, free from the oppression and tyranny of its war-mongering neighbour. Many would say that Zahir should be extremely proud of his achievements. That he had accomplished what no man had ever thought possible. But, despite his pride in his country, Zahir would never be able to accept praise for his victory, let alone celebrate it. Not when his parents had paid for his success with their lives.

He had learned his lesson in the most painful way possible. Never again would he allow himself the luxury of such gratification, no matter for how brief a period of time. Self-indulgent pleasure was to be avoided at all costs. He just needed to remember that when he was around Annalina.

Not that his feelings for her were all about pleasure, far from it. Annalina stirred up extremes of emotions that were as threatening as they were mystifying.

For a slightly built young woman, weighing, he would estimate, little more than eight stone, this was extremely perplexing. Even if she'd been a trained assassin, armed to the teeth, he knew he would have no trouble overpowering her, throwing her to the ground, dispatching her if necessary. But she wasn't a trained assassin and she wasn't armed, at least, not with a recognisable weapon. She was no threat. So why did his body insist that she was, firing the blood through his veins as if he had stepped into an ambush, had a blade at his throat?

Because Annalina's weapons were of a different kind. Ice-blue eyes that flashed with a mystery all of their own. Plump lips, pert breasts, hair that tumbled over her shoulders...curves that begged to be stroked. These were her weapons. And Zahir was beginning to realise that they were more lethal than any he had come across before. They consumed his mind, invaded his consciousness, provoking feelings of anger, lust and a desperate need that had only increased in the weeks they had been apart. And there was another emotion, one he had never experienced before. *Jealousy.* The thought of Annalina with another man, past or present, innocent or not, gripped

him hard enough to paralyse his whole body. It frightened him with its force, weakened him with its power.

Forcing himself to relax, he leant against a pillar festooned with winter foliage, flexing his fingers, half-
closing his eyes. Eyes that still followed Annalina as she
started talking to another guest—that narrowed further
when he saw the man taking her hand in his, raising it
to his lips, holding it there longer than was strictly necessary. He sucked in a breath. *Control yourself, Zahir.
And find enough patience for another hour.* When they
finally did come together, it would be all the sweeter
for the wait.

He was glad now that they hadn't had sex that night
in the cabin. At the time it had only been blind rage that
had stopped him. But now he knew the timing hadn't
been right. He had wanted her—God how he had wanted
her! But deep down had he felt uneasy about despoiling
such an exquisite creature? Felt unworthy, even? Now
Annalina was his bride, his wife. Now he could legitimately claim her. And any unusually sensitive worries
he might have had, any hesitancy about his rights or his
responsibilities, had long since vanished in a sea of carnal craving.

Shouldering himself away from the pillar, he decided
to go outside in search of some fresh air. He needed to
cool himself down.

It was a beautiful night, crisp and clear, with a full
moon shining on the virgin snow. Zahir paused to take
in the view, the town of Valduz spread out in the valley below twinkling prettily, the mountains all around
them soaring into the night sky. He set off around the
side of the castle, his footprints sinking deep into the
crunchy snow, breathing in deeply to relish the cold air
that scoured his lungs. But then he stopped, his senses

on high alert. Someone else was out here. He could hear the huff of their breath, a sort of shuffling noise, a mumbled voice.

Zahir moved stealthily forward, tracking the sound like the trained killer that he was. Now he could make out the shape of man leaning against the wall of the castle, see the glow of a cigarette burn more brightly as he took a deep drag before flicking it away into the snow. He watched as the figure raised a bottle to his lips—whisky, if Zahir had to guess—glugging from it greedily then wiping the back of his hand across his mouth before staggering a couple of steps sideways, then back again. The mumbling was him talking to himself. There was no one else was around. He was clearly very drunk.

Zahir stepped out of the shadows.

'I think you've had enough of this.' Removing the bottle from the man's grasp, Zahir flung it behind him.

'Hey!' Lunging forward, the man peered at him with glassy-eyed aggression. 'What the hell do you think you're doing?'

Zahir silently positioned himself in front of this creature, squaring his chest, towering over him. He wasn't looking for a fight, but neither was he going to let this guy drink himself into oblivion. Not here, at his wedding party.

'You have no right to…' Squinting up at Zahir, the man suddenly stopped. 'Well, look who it is. The mighty desert Prince.' A sneer twisted his thin lips. 'What brings you out here? Trying to escape already?'

Zahir's fists balled by his sides. This individual was seriously asking for a punch.

'You don't know who I am, do you?' Pushing himself unsteadily off the wall, he straightened up, holding Zahir's gaze, emboldened by the alcohol or stupidity, or both. 'Allow me to introduce myself. Prince Henrik of Ebsberg.' He extended a limp arm. 'Delighted to meet you.'

Blood roared in Zahir's ears, raging through his body, turning his muscles to stone. So this was the revolting individual who had once been engaged to Annalina. His fists by his sides flexed, then balled again, his nails digging into his palms.

'Ha.' With a dismissive laugh, Henrik withdrew his hand, folding his arms over his chest. 'So my name's familiar to you, then.' He put his head on one side, the sneer still curving his lips. 'You may not want to shake my hand, old chap, but perhaps you will accept my heartfelt commiserations instead. You have my deepest sympathies.'

A growl erupted from somewhere deep inside Zahir as he adjusted his stance, planting his feet further apart. 'And just what do you mean by that?'

'Oh, dear.' With a giggle, Henrik moved his hand to his mouth. 'Don't tell me you don't know. This is *so* much worse than I thought.'

'Don't know what?' Zahir ground out the question, more as a diversionary tactic to stop his hands from travelling to this man's throat rather than because he wanted an answer.

'About your new bride. I'm sorry to be the bearer of bad news, but Princess Annalina is not only as pure as the driven snow, she's as frozen as it.' Misinterpreting Zahir's thunderous silence, Henrik warmed to his theme. 'Yes, it's true. Beneath that pretty exterior there lies nothing but a block of ice.'

'Hold your tongue.' Zahir bent down, his face just inches away from his prey. 'You will not speak of my wife in such a way. Not if you know what's good for you.'

'Why not?' Henrik blithely carried on. 'I'm only tell-ing you the truth. Annalina is the original ice maiden. You will get no satisfaction from her. Take it from me. I should know. I've been there.'

Unbidden, Zahir's hands flew to Henrik's throat, grasping a handful of shirt and lifting his feet clean off the ground. The fury that engulfed him was so strong he could taste it, feel it rising up his throat, burning behind his eyes. The thought that this man had even touched Annalina was enough for Zahir to wish upon him the most slow and painful death. But to brag about it. To speak of her in that hideously insulting manner... Death would be too good for him.

He looked down at Henrik, now squirming in his grasp. Then, taking a deep breath, he let him go, watch-ing as he fell to his knees before scrabbling to stand up-right again.

'Tut, tut.' Brushing the snow from his hands, Henrik staggered a couple of steps away. 'It's not my fault that you've married a dud, Zahani. You should have taken a leaf out of my book and had the sense to try her out first. I had a lucky escape. But you, my friend, have been duped.'

'Why, you little...' Raging fury had all but closed Za-hir's throat, grinding his words to a low snarl. 'Get out of my sight while you can still walk.'

'Very well. But it won't change anything. The fact is, pretty Annalina is frigid. If it's any consolation, I had no idea either—not until she was in my bed, until she was under me, until it came to the actual point of—'

Crack. Zahir's fist connected with Henrik's nose, making a noise like the fall of a branch in the forest. With this vilest of creatures now splayed at his feet, his first thought was of satisfaction, that he had finally silenced his revolting words. But rampant fury was still pumping through his body, the temptation to finish what he had started holding him taut, tensing his muscles, grinding his jaw. He looked down at Henrik, who was whimpering pathetically, blood pouring from his nose.

'Get up.' He realised he wasn't done with him yet. He wanted him on his feet again, wanted him to fight back, to give him the opportunity to have another swipe at him. But Henrik only moaned. 'I said, get up.' Bending down, Zahir lifted him by the scruff of the neck again, holding him before him like a rag doll. 'Now put your fists up. Fight like a man.'

'Please, no.' Henrik raised a hand, but only to touch his damaged nose, recoiling in horror when it came away covered in blood. 'Let me go. I don't want to fight.'

'I bet you don't.' Zahir set him down again, watching Henrik's knees buckle in the struggle to keep him upright. 'Call yourself a man, *Prince Henrik of Ebsberg*?' He spat out the name with utter revulsion. 'You are nothing more than a pathetic piece of scum, a vile and despicable low life. And if I ever hear you so much as utter Princess Annalina's name, let alone defile her character as you have just done, you will not live to tell the tale. Is that understood?'

Henrik nodded and Zahir turned away, taking several steps, inhaling deeply as he did so, trying to purge himself of this man. He was ten or twelve feet away when Henrik called after him.

'So it's true what they say about you.'

Zahir froze, then slowly turned around.

'You really *are* an animal. The Beast of Nabatean.' His words slurred into one another. 'You do know that's what they call you, don't you?' He started to giggle idiotically. 'Despite your marriage, Europe will never accept you. So you see, you and Annalina, it's all been for nothing. Beauty and the Beast—you deserve each other.'

The space between them was closed in an instant, even though Henrik was backing away as fast as his collapsing legs would let him.

Zahir's fist connected with Henrik's face again—this time it was his jaw. And, when he fell to the snow again, this time there was no getting up.

CHAPTER TEN

CLOSING THE DOOR, Anna leant back against it and looked around. The room was empty. She was the first to arrive. Swallowing down the jittery disappointment, she drew in a deep breath. It was fine. She would have time to prepare herself before Zahir came to her. And when he did she would be ready. They would make love and everything would be wonderful. This was the night that finally, please God, she would lose not only her virginity but the terrible stigma that had haunted her for so long.

The room assigned to the newlyweds had been dressed for the occasion. Rugs were scattered over the polished wooden floor, heavy curtains pulled against the freezing night, an enormous tapestry adorning one stone wall. A fire roared in the grate and that, along with the guttering candles in the iron chandelier overhead, provided the only light.

Anna moved over to the bed. Centuries old, the oak construction was raised off the floor by a stepped platform, with four columns to support the heavy square-panelled canopy. Drapes were tied back to reveal the sumptuous bedding, piles of pillows and embroidered silk throws. She sat on the edge, sinking down into the soft mattress, then ran her fingers over the coverlet, her eyes immediately drawn to the wedding ring on her finger. So it was true—she really had married her dashing Arabian prince. There was her evidence.

Being reunited with Zahir today, seeing him again in all his gorgeously taut, olive-skinned flesh, had been both wonderful and agonising. Because it had confirmed what she already knew in her heart. That Zahir was like a drug to her, a dangerous addiction that had invaded her cells to the point where she found she craved him, ached for him. But, just like an addiction, she knew she had to face up to it in order to be able to control it.

Because giving in to her weakness, letting it take over, control her, would be her undoing. Over the years she had learnt how protect herself, to hide her emotional vulnerability. She had had to. Because there had been precious little love in her life since her mother had died. She didn't blame her father for his coldness. It wasn't his fault that he couldn't love her the way she wanted him to. It was hers. And when she'd tried to please him—agreeing to marry Henrik, for example—she'd ended up just making things worse. The broken engagement, the dreadful shame, the *crippling humiliation* only served to compound her feelings of lack of self-worth. She feared she wasn't capable of being loved, in any sense of the word. And for that reason she had to protect her own heart. She had to be very, very careful.

She thought back over the day she and Zahir had just shared, their wedding day. She had been so aware of his presence—every second of every hour—that it had felt almost like a physical pain. Standing rigidly beside her during the ceremony, silently consuming his meal next to her at the wedding breakfast or scowling across at her during the ball, her skin had prickled from the sense of him, the hairs on the back of her neck standing on end, her nerve endings tingling.

But then towards the end of the evening something had happened, something telling—thrilling. Their eyes had met across the ballroom and they had shared a look, an understanding. Zahir's gaze had scorched a path between them, his hooded, mesmerising eyes spelling out exactly what was on his mind. *Hunger and desire.* It had been a look of such unconscious seduction, such inevitability, that it had weakened her knees, caught the breath in her throat. Zahir wanted her. She was sure of that. And she wanted him too, more than she could ever have imagined wanting any man, *ever.* That didn't mean she could let down her guard—in fact now she would need to protect herself more than ever. But it did mean that the time was right. They were both ready.

So when Zahir had turned and left the ballroom Anna had prepared to leave too. Heart thumping, she had made her excuses to her guests, hurrying her goodbyes in her rush to follow him, to be with him. Because tonight was the night that Zahir would make love to her. And this time she was determined that everything would be all right.

Now she smoothed her hands over the folds of her wedding dress. All day long she had had visions of Zahir undressing her, his fingers impatiently tugging at the fiddly buttons, pulling the fine lace over her shoulders, watching the dress fall to the ground.

Well, maybe she would save him the bother. Standing up, she twisted behind her and undid the top buttons as best she could then wriggled out of the dress and placed it carefully over the back of a chair. Next she pulled out the clips that held up her hair, undoing the braids and threading her fingers through to release them until her hair tumbled over her shoulders. She looked down at herself. At the white lace bra and panties, the white silk stockings that revealed several inches of bare skin at the top of her thighs. Goosebumps skittered over her. Away from the fire, the room felt cold. But inside Anna already burned for Zahir's touch, her body clenching at the thought of it. She wanted him so badly.

On impulse she pulled back the covers and got into bed, squirming into the sheets. Would it please Zahir to come across her like this—still in her underwear? She had no idea. She had no sexual experiences to draw on. All she knew was that, lying here semi-naked like this, she felt as sexy as hell, and that had to be a good place to start. Her hand strayed to her panties, to the soft mound of hair beneath. Tentatively her fingers slipped under the skimpy fabric, finding their way to her intimate folds. She was damp, already very aroused. Slowly, slowly, she started to gently rub herself, prepare herself for Zahir, for what was to come. Letting out a sigh, she rested her head back against the pillow and closed her eyes.

A sudden noise snapped them open again—the wail of an ambulance siren. Pushing herself up to sitting, Anna rubbed her eyes. She hoped a guest hadn't been taken ill. What time was it? And where was Zahir? She noticed that the fire was burning low in the grate—she must have fallen asleep. Checking her watch, she realised that nearly an hour had passed since she had come to the bridal suite. More than enough time for Zahir to have joined her.

A terrible fear gripped her heart. Pulling back the covers, she tugged a throw off the bed and wrapped it around her, her body already starting to shake. She moved over to the fireplace, bending to pick up a log and throw it onto the glowing embers, watching the shower of sparks. Then, settling into a low chair, she drew up her knees and pulled the throw around her, her mind racing in all directions.

Maybe he had been waylaid. Perhaps one of the guests,

one of the many foreign dignitaries that he had been conversing with all day, had suggested they talked business before he retired to bed.

Maybe he hadn't been able to find the right room. Maybe he was wandering around the castle right now, opening doors, calling her name. Although it was pushing it to think that a man who could navigate the vastness of the desert by the stars alone would have trouble finding his way to the marital bed.

Or maybe he had been taken ill. The ambulance she had heard just now might be coming to whisk him to hospital because he'd been struck down with some mystery ailment. But that seemed equally unlikely. It was impossible to believe that Zahir Zahani had ever had a day's sickness in his life.

Which only left one more possibility—the most painful one of all. *He wasn't coming.* She must have misinterpreted the look he had given her in the ballroom—or, worse, she had imagined it completely. Like a starving dog, she had gobbled up the scrap being thrown to her, convinced that it was the start of a feast, that her hunger would finally be satisfied. But she had been wrong. And now, like a useless cur, she had been abandoned.

As she stared into the flames that were starting to leap into life, she felt the tears blocking her throat. Now the real reason Zahir wasn't here was all too obvious.

He didn't want her. Now he knew the truth, that she was frigid, incapable of ever being able to satisfy him, he had no use for her. *Somehow this time, without even having got Zahir to her bed, she had managed to fail yet again.*

Zahir stared at the man sprawled at his feet. Anger was still coursing through him, clenching his fists and his teeth, holding every muscle rigid in his body.

Bending down, he grabbed hold of Henrik's shoulder and roughly turned him over, hearing him moan as he did so. Blood stained the snow where his face had been, seeping into the icy imprint. His face was a mess with blood flowing from his nose and mouth, his lip split and swelling. Judging from the angle of his jaw, it was definitely dislocated.

Zahir let out a long, slow breath, releasing the last of his rage into the darkness of the night. *The Beast of Nabatean.* So that was how he was known in the West. And now he had just lived up to his name.

Well, so be it. He didn't give a damn. If European society wanted to look over their monocles, hide behind their simpering manners and call him a beast, then he would accept the title. Accept it with pride, in fact. For it was his strength, his fearlessness—and, yes, at times the brutality of his decisions—that had won his country their independence. He would value that over their delicate Western sensibilities a thousand times.

But Annalina…that was a different matter. Was that how she thought of him? Like some sort of beast or barbarian that fate had cruelly delivered to her door? To her bed? The thought struck him like a savage blow. Certainly he had done nothing to dispel the myth. He had never shown her the slightest care or consideration. Because he didn't know how. He was a military man, comfortable only with logic and detachment, proud of his nerves of steel. He could cope with any situation, no matter how horrific. Hadn't he demonstrated that with the way he had handled the slaughter of his parents? A situation that would have tested the strongest man. That had ripped his brother apart, both mentally and physically. But he had taken charge, dealt with the carnage the only way he knew how. By banishing his emotions, refusing to give in to any weakness and concentrating on finding the perpetrators. Then trying to minimise the repercussions for all concerned. He had never even let himself grieve. He couldn't afford to.

But the war was over now, and the military training that had held him in such good stead no longer applied. Now he found he didn't know how to behave. Now he was left wondering who the hell he was.

He looked down at his battered victim again. Beneath the anger he could feel another emotion pushing through—disgust. And not just for the man at his feet, although that was a palpable force. But disgust at himself too. Raising his hand, he saw the blood that stained his knuckles, knuckles that were swelling from the force of his punch.

He could have walked away. He *should* have walked away. But he couldn't do it, could he? He couldn't control himself. He was deserving of his title. A beast.

What he didn't deserve was the beautiful young woman he had married today. Who was expecting him in her bed tonight. Who no doubt was bracing herself, preparing to accept the fate that he had spelt out that night in the cabin. Not because she wanted to, but because she had no alternative other than to do as she was told. Zahir wanted her so badly, he had tried to justify his arrogant, dictatorial behaviour by telling himself it was her duty, not least because she was now his wife. But this wasn't about duty, no matter how much he tried to dress it up. It was about his carnal cravings. And there was no way he would allow himself to indulge them tonight. He had another man's blood on his hands. How could he even consider using these same hands to touch Annalina, to claim her for himself? He couldn't. It would be an insult to her beauty and to her innocence. Denying himself that pleasure would be his penance.

Henrik groaned again. He needed medical attention— that much was obvious. Pulling his mobile phone out of his pocket, Zahir called for an ambulance, ending the conversation before the operator could ask him any more questions. They knew enough to come and patch him up, restore his pretty-boy good looks.

Throwing his victim one last look of revulsion, he turned away. Then, jamming his hands down into his pockets, he hunched his shoulders against the cold and began to walk. He didn't know where to and he didn't know how far. All he did know was that he had to get away from here, from this creature, from the castle, and from the desperate temptation to slide into bed next to the luscious body of his new bride.

CHAPTER ELEVEN

A SMALL RECEPTION party had lined up to welcome Prince Zahir and his new wife when they arrived back at Medira Palace. As Zahir swept them through the massive doors, Anna forced herself to smile at everyone, especially when she saw Lana and Layla, standing on tiptoes trying to get a better look at them. They looked so excited it made her want to cry.

Little more than twenty-four hours had passed since their marriage ceremony, since they had stood side by side in the chapel in Dorrada and made their vows. But it had been long enough to spell out just what sort of a marriage it would be. Hollow and empty and desperately lonely. Long enough to firmly dash any hopes she might have foolishly fostered that they could ever be a real couple, come together as husband and wife, as lovers.

It was also a marriage where she was going to have to be constantly on her guard, hide her true feelings from Zahir. Because to show him even a glimmer of what was in her heart would be emotional suicide. She could hardly bring herself to examine the insanity of her own feelings, let alone expose them to the cold and cruel claws of her husband.

Her wedding night had been miserably sad, plagued by fitful dreams and long periods of wakefulness in a bed that had seemed increasingly empty as the hours of darkness had dragged by. Forcing herself to go down to breakfast this morning had taken all the will power she possessed but she'd known she had to face Zahir sometime. Somehow she had to cover up her broken heart. But as it turned out she'd been met, not by her husband, but with a note presented on a silver salver and written in Zahir's bold hand, stating that she was to meet him at the airport in two hours' time. That they would be flying back to Nabatean without delay. And that was it. No explanation as to where he had been all night, where he was now. No apology or excuses of any kind.

Because, as far as Zahir was concerned, she didn't deserve any explanations. She was now his property—by dint of their marriage, he had effectively bought her, no matter how it had been dressed up with fancy ceremonies and profuse congratulations. Now she belonged to him, in the same way as a herd of camel or an Arabian stallion. Except she was of considerably less use. If she couldn't satisfy him in bed, couldn't give him an heir, then, other than the connection with Europe that came with her position, what purpose did she actually serve?

No doubt Zahir was wondering the same thing. No doubt that was the reason he hadn't come to her bed last night and the reason he had totally ignored her on the flight to Nabatean, preferring the company of his laptop instead. The reason why his mood was as black as thunder as he briskly moved past the reception party and headed straight down the maze of corridors that lead to his private quarters.

Anna stood in the echoing reception chamber and looked around her, breathing in the foreign air of this gilded cage. Here she was in her new role, her new life. And she had no idea what she was supposed to do with it.

Declining the offer of refreshments, she allowed herself to be shown to the suite of rooms that had been assigned to her and Zahir. The grand marital bedroom had a raised bed centre-stage, like some sort of mocking altar, and the only slightly less grand bedroom, which she was solemnly informed was her personal room, just served to increase her sense of isolation, filled her with misery. What sort of marriage needed separate bedrooms right from the off? Sadly, she already knew the answer to that.

Wandering downstairs again, she found herself in one of the many empty salons and sat down on a window seat that overlooked a verdant courtyard. Darkness had fallen, the night having arrived with indecent haste in this part of the world, and the courtyard was flood-lit, the palm trees and the fountain illuminated with a ghostly orange glow.

Anna felt for her phone in her handbag. She needed a distraction to stop herself from bursting into tears or running screaming into the wilderness of the desert, or both. Clicking on the site of a national newspaper in Dorrada, she scrolled through the headlines until she found what she was looking for. Just as she had expected, there was extensive coverage of the wedding of Princess Annalina to Prince Zahir of Nabatean, gushing descriptions of the beautiful ceremony, the sumptuous banquet and the glittering ball that had followed. Other European papers hadn't stinted either, all showing the official photographs accompanied by the obligatory text describing the couple's happy day.

Anna studied the images. She and Zahir, standing side by side, her arm linked through his. She could see the tension in her face, that the smile was in danger of cracking. And Zahir, tall, commanding, looking impossibly handsome with his shoulders back and his head held high. But his expression was masked, closed, impossible to fathom, no matter how much Anna stared at it. She was left wondering just who this man was that she had married.

She was about to put her phone away when a headline on one of the sidebars caught her eye. The shot of a battered face, captured by a zoom lens, by the look of it, was accompanied by the headline: *Prince Henrik arrives at hospital with facial injuries.*

A cold dread swept over her. With a shaky hand, she clicked on the link.

Prince Henrik of Ebsberg was seen arriving at a Valduz hospital on the night of his ex-fiancée's wedding, sporting what appeared to be significant facial injuries. One can only speculate as to how he acquired them.

Prince Henrik is known to have attended the grand ball thrown to celebrate the marriage of Princess Annalina of Dorrada to Prince Zahir of Nabatean. Could it be that the two men came to blows over the beautiful blonde princess? If so, it would appear that Prince Zahir's reputation as a formidable opponent is fully justified. Neither Prince Henrik nor Prince Zahir was available for comment.

No! Anna's heart plummeted inside her. Had Zahir done this to Henrik? She didn't want to believe it but her gut was telling her it had to be him. Head spinning, she desperately tried to think up some other explanation, figure out what could possibly have happened.

As European royals, the King and Queen of Ebsberg had been present at the wedding but Anna had been thankful, at that point, to see that their son, Henrik, hadn't joined them. She had completely forgotten about him until much later at the ball when out of the corner of her eye she had seen him arrive, looking unsteady on his feet, as if he had already been drinking. Having absolutely no desire to speak to him, she had deliberately kept out of his way, relieved that the relatively late hour meant she could legitimately slip away before he could corner her. But had Zahir spoken to him? Deliberately sought him out? Had it always been his intention to beat up her ex-fiancé?

The barbaric thought made Anna feel physically sick. But there was only one way to find out if it was true.

Leaping to her feet, she set off to find Zahir, pausing only briefly to try and get her bearings, to remember the way to his private quarters. With her pace quickening along with her temper, she flew along the echoing corridors, finally arriving at his door breathless and panting with anger. Rapping loudly on the panelling, she hurtled in without waiting for a reply.

'What is the meaning of this?' She advanced towards him, brandishing her phone before her like a weapon.

Rising from where he had been seated at a computer, Zahir met her head-on, towering before her. 'I could ask the same of you.' Deep-set eyes flashed dangerously black. 'I don't take kindly to being ambushed in my own study.'

'And I don't suppose Prince Henrik takes kindly to being beaten up by some vicious thug.' Trembling with animosity, Anna thrust the phone in his face. Taking it from her, Zahir gave it a cursory glance before tossing it back. Anna fumbled to catch it. 'Well? What do you have to say?' She could feel the hysteria rising in the face of his silence and the mounting realisation that she was right—Zahir had assaulted Henrik. 'Do you know about this? Did you *do* this?'

'I fail to see that this is any of your concern.'

'Not my concern?' Her voice screeched with incredulity. 'How can you say that? It's obvious that you attacked Henrik because of his association with me!'

'Trust me, there are any number of reasons I could have hit that creature.'

'So you admit it, then? You did assault Henrik?'

Zahir shrugged and his dismissive gesture only served to pour more fuel onto Anna's fury.

'And that's it? That's all you have to say on the matter?' She threw back her head so he couldn't escape her livid gaze. 'Aren't you at least going to offer some explanation, show some concern for what you've done?'

'I think you're showing enough concern for both of us.'

The air crackled between them, stirring the shadows of this cave-like room.

'What do you mean by that?'

'Some might say that you are unduly concerned about someone you should no longer have any attachment to.'

'Don't be ridiculous.'

'That you are displaying the behaviour of someone who still has feelings for this man.'

'No…'

'Are you regretting the past? Is that what it is? Do you wish you were married to him instead of me?'

'No, no, it's not that at all.'

'Isn't it, Annalina? Are you sure? You've told me yourself that it was Henrik who broke off your engagement. You still want him, don't you? That's the reason you are displaying such irrational behaviour.'

Irrational behaviour? Anna's eyes glittered back at him like shards of glass. She knew what he was doing:

he was trying to make out that she was overreacting—
that, even though he was the one who had committed
the crime, she was the one who should be examining her
motives. Well, she wasn't having it. Positioning herself
squarely in front of him, she clenched her teeth, ready
to fire at him with both barrels.

'Has it ever occurred to you, Zahir...' she swallowed
audibly '...that I may be displaying the behaviour of someone who's worried that they have married a monster?'

A terrible silence fell between them. For a moment
neither of them moved, their eyes locked in a lethal clash
that Anna couldn't break but that tore into her soul. She
could hear the roar of blood in her ears, feel the heavy
thud of her heartbeat, but she was paralysed, Zahir's painfully piercing black stare holding her captive as surely
as if she'd been nailed to the ground.

'And that's what you think, is it?' His voice was lethally low, barely more than a murmur. But it carried
the weight of the loudest scream. 'You think that I am
a monster?'

'I didn't actually say that.'

'Well, you are not alone. The Beast of Nabatean—isn't
that what they call me?'

'No, I mean...'

'Don't bother to try and deny it. I know full well how
the European bourgeoisie perceive me.'

'But not me, Zahir. I would never call you such a
thing.' Anna had heard the insulting title—of course she
had—but a loathing of prejudice and bigotry, and maybe
a smattering of fear, had made her dismiss it. Until now.
'This isn't about what other people call you. And it's
nothing to do with how I feel about Henrik. It's about
you going around beating people up.'

'And you think that's what I do?'

'Well, what am I supposed to think?'

'I'd like you to leave now.' He turned away and she was suddenly presented with the impenetrable wall of his back.

'What? No!' Horrified, she reached forward, her fingers clawing at the fabric of his shirt. 'I'm not going until we have discussed this, until you have heard me out.'

'I *said* I want you to leave.'

'And if I refuse?'

'Who knows what might happen, Annalina? How I might react.' Swinging round, he closed the space between them with a single step, then towered over her, his fixed gaze as black as a raven's wing. 'Are you prepared to take that risk? Are you prepared to incur the wrath of such a monster as me?' His words were clearly designed to intimidate her and it was working, at least to start with, Anna's throat drying, her hands shaking from the sheer force of his might.

But as she continued to stare at him a different reaction started to seep in. Suddenly her breasts felt heavy, her nipples contracting, her belly clenching with a fierceness that rippled down to her core, holding it tight in its grip. Suddenly her whole body was alive to him. And it was nothing to do with fear.

She watched as his pupils dilated, her own doing the same in response. So he felt it too. Anger still pulsed between them but now it was laced with hunger, a carnal craving that was growing more powerful with each suspenseful second.

She forced herself to swallow. How could she want this man so badly? It didn't make any sense. How could she have given her heart to a man capable of such savagery? Capable of hurting her so badly? The wounds inflicted on their wedding night, still raw and bleeding, were a painful testament to that. But a monster? No. Arrogant, insufferable, formidable… Anna could reel off a list of his shortcomings. But loyal too and fiercely protective. She had seen the way he was with his brother, glimpsed the burden of pain and suffering caused by his parents' tragic deaths before he had pulled down the shutters and pushed her away. She had heard the pride in his voice whenever he spoke of his country. No, Zahir was no monster.

'Well?' He bit out the word but there was an edge to his voice that betrayed him, angered him. He extended his arm, roughly clasping the back of her head, threading his fingers through her hair to bring her closer to him. 'I'm still waiting for your answer.'

His breath was hot on her face and Anna's tongue darted to wet her lips. 'I'm still here, aren't I?'

'So it would seem.' He moved fractionally closer until their bodies were touching. Heat roared between them, the unmistakable stirring beneath Zahir's trousers making Anna tremble violently. 'But what does that tell me? That you don't think that I'm a monster? Or that right now you don't care?'

'I'm not frightened of you, Zahir, if that's what you mean.'

'Hmm. And yet you are shaking. Why is that, Annalina?'

'I d-don't know.'

'Maybe it's that you crave the beast in me.' He moved closer still, pressing the length of his body against her, all heat and flexed muscle, hard bones beneath tautly drawn flesh. And raw, potent, sexual energy.

'And if I do?'

'Then perhaps it is my duty to satisfy that craving.'

Finally his lips came down to claim hers with a punishing kiss that sucked the air from her lungs, pumped the blood wildly around her body. He plundered her mouth, his tongue seeking and taking, his breath feverishly hot as he panted into her. It was a kiss that left Anna reeling from its force, melting beneath its pressure. She gasped as he finally pulled away, feeling her lips engorging with blood before he was kissing her again, moving his hands to span the small of her back, pressing her firmly against his erection. Complete abandonment washed over her as the most gloriously erotic feeling took over, obliterating all thought. Other than that Zahir *had* to make love to her. *Now.*

When their lips finally pulled apart she worked her hands around his waist to the strip of bare skin between his shirt and the low-slung pants, feeling him buck satisfyingly beneath her touch. Easily sliding her hands beneath the waistband, she slipped them lower, letting out a guttural gasp of longing when she realised he was naked underneath. Her fingertips skittered over the bare skin of his buttocks, leaving a trail of goosebumps behind them, the muscles clenching tightly beneath her touch. He felt so good, so gloriously hard, tight and male that Anna realised she was panting with excitement, her breath coming in short gasps.

Sliding her hands down further, she traced the underside of his buttocks and when she firmly cupped both cheeks in her hands, squeezing them tightly with a strength born of pure need, she was rewarded with a sharp hiss of breath and a bucking movement that thrust the shape of his mighty erection against her stomach.

Anna let out a low moan. Reaching up on tiptoe, she tried to make herself as tall as possible so she could feel his erection where she so desperately wanted it—against her groin. But Zahir went one better, lifting her off her feet as if she were weightless, one ankle boot dropping to the ground with a thud. Wrapping her legs around his waist, the glorious feel of him was now pressing against her sex and she closed her eyes against the thrill as she clung dizzily to him, her arms around his neck, feeling him turn and move towards his bedroom.

She opened them again as he set her down, wobbling unsteadily on her feet as she watched him tear his shirt over his head, his breathing heavy with need. It was dark in this cave-like room, the shutters closed against the night, the bed no more than a low shape on the floor. Stripped to the waist, Zahir brought Anna towards him again, sweeping her hair over one shoulder, nuzzling her neck with his lips as his hands slid the zipper of her dress down her back.

'You want this, Anna?'

It was the same question he had asked her in the log cabin before it had all gone horribly wrong. But she wasn't going to mess it up this time. Want was too small a word to describe the fervour she felt for Zahir right now. It was an overpowering, all-consuming madness. Something she couldn't bring herself to examine. For now, a simple yes would have to suffice.

She groaned the word hotly against his shoulder as he tugged at her dress and it fell to the ground. Now he was undoing the clasp of her bra, releasing her breasts until they were caught, heavy and aching with need, by his caressing palms, his thumb stroking over nipples that had shrivelled into hard peaks. Anna's hands strayed down to his loose-fitting trousers again, tugging at them until they were low over his hips, finally falling to the ground. He was naked, the force of his erection escaping at last, throbbing between them.

'Say it again, Annalina.' He ground out the words,

one hand reaching for her panties, pulling them down her legs, taking the remaining boot with them.

'I want you.'

With a guttural growl he swept her off her feet again, laying her down on the bed and positioning himself over her, his eyes shining like jet in the darkness as they raked over her face. With his jaw held fast, the sharp angles of his cheeks hollowed and shadowed, he looked magnificent. And he looked like a man on the edge.

'You're going to have to control me, Annalina.' He lowered his body until it was held fractionally above her by the flexed columns of his arms, his mouth just a centimetre from her own. 'Take me at the speed you are comfortable with.'

Anna gulped. She had totally lost control of herself—what hope did she have of controlling him? And 'comfortable' was not a word she was interested in. She wanted mind-blowing, all-consuming sex. Speech had all but deserted her but she did manage to drag up something that she suddenly knew to be true.

'I trust you, Zahir.'

This produced a stab of surprise that had his eyes widen then narrow again. Zahir hesitated, as if about to say something, then he changed his mind, moving his hand between her legs instead, pushing her thighs apart so that he could slide his fingers inside her.

Anna shuddered with pleasure at his touch, his fingers working to intensify her arousal, increase the wetness that slicked her core. As her whole body began to shake, she reached behind his back to steady herself, to stop him from moving away, her hands desperately gripping on to him. Her legs splayed wider, her back arching into his touch.

'God, Annalina. You have no idea what you do to

me.' He growled deeply before he took her mouth again, his tongue licking and tasting at the same speed as his finger stroked and rubbed. 'You need to say now if you want this to stop.'

'Don't stop, Zahir. Do it—make love to me.'

'Uh-uh.' With another thickly uttered growl, Zahir withdrew his hand and, reaching for Anna's, guided it to his member, curling her fist around the silky, heated girth of him. 'You are in control, Anna. Remember that. Whatever happens now is down to you.'

Oh, dear Lord. Anna wasn't prepared for this. She had fantasised about this moment for so long, yearned, craved and ached for it almost since the first moment she had clapped eyes on Zahir. But she had stressed about it too, agonised over what might happen, the dreadful accusation that had been implanted in her mind by Henrik refusing to be totally banished. But in every imagined scenario it had been Zahir taking command, taking her any way he wanted to, dominating her the way he had when they'd been in the cabin. Not that that hadn't been indescribably, erotically mind-blowing. But it had held an element of fear too.

This was different. As she started to slide her hand up and down the thick length of him, felt him shudder beneath her touch, any traces of fear subsided. He was big, so astonishingly, eye-wateringly enormous, but she wasn't scared. Just mindlessly high with exhilaration, as if he was a drug she could never get enough of.

And she knew she was ready for him, ready in mind and body.

Shifting her bottom, she spread her legs wider, positioning the head of his shaft exactly where she wanted it. Zahir froze, not moving, not even breathing, his whole body rigid with unspoken, unleashed power. She started to make small, circling movements with him, pressing him against her most sensitive spot, small mews escaping her lips. She was so wet now, so aroused. She paused, seeking his eyes, eyes that were black with desire, as drugged and drowning as her own.

'Now, Zahir.' She whispered the command hoarsely.

He didn't need telling twice. With his arms braced on either side of her head, he lowered his hips, plunging the head of his member into Anna's wet, tight, sensitised core. Anna gasped, her muscles clenching around him, holding him firm as her legs drew up, her hands clawing at his back.

'Annalina?'

'More, Zahir. I want more.'

'Oh, God.' With a primal groan, Zahir obeyed, pushing more of his length into her with a slick, hot, juddering force. He paused again as Anna's legs clamped around him, her nails digging into his flesh.

'All of it, Zahir. I want to feel all of you.' She had no idea who this dominatrix was—who had taken over her body—just knew that the control was intoxicating, banishing her fears. To have a man like Zahir obeying her commands was wildly exhilarating. Mind-blowing. And the feel of him inside her was indescribably, gloriously wonderful.

With one final, punishing thrust he was there, fully inside her, firmly gripped by muscles that pulsed and contracted with ripples of ecstasy. With a whimper of abandonment, Anna lifted her head and flung her arms around his neck, pulling his mouth down to meet hers, plunging her fingers into the thick mass of his hair to keep him there. With their breath and saliva mingled, their bodies sealed with sweat and joined in the most carnal of ways, Zahir began to move. Slowly at first, easing his length out of her, almost to the tip, before thrusting in again. But, as Anna urged him on with rasped, pleading words of need, he took over, the control now firmly his, pumping harder and faster, his breathing heavy and harsh, as again and again he plundered her body, each thrust bringing her further and further towards the oblivion of orgasm.

'Zahir!' She gasped his name as the tremendous sensation built and built until she could take no more, until she was at the very brink, hanging on with an agonising ecstasy that couldn't last any longer. 'Please…please…'

'Say it, Anna. What do you want?'

'You, Zahir.' Anna let out a whimper that ended in a strangled scream. 'I want you to come, now, with me.'

Her body started to shudder, trembling violently as she surrendered to the tremendous surge of sensation that flooded her from head to toe. She heard Zahir's breathing grow hoarse, felt his muscles flex and jerk as he pounded into her with the final delirious thrusts, his beautiful face contorted with the concentration and effort. For a split second he stopped, holding himself rigid, and then he was there, his orgasm intensifying hers, taking them both to unknown realms of euphoria. Anna cried out, totally lost in the moment.

But it was Zahir's primal roar that echoed round the room.

CHAPTER TWELVE

ANNA AWOKE WITH a start. The room was pitch-black and for a moment she had no idea where she was. Then in a rush she remembered: she was in Zahir's bedroom, in his bed. They had had sex—more than that, they had made love. And it had been the single most wonderful experience of her life.

She let the memory flood over her, reliving the wonder of it, the incredible coupling they had shared. The intensity of feelings she had experienced had gone far beyond just sex, or losing her virginity, or proving that there wasn't actually anything wrong with her, that she was a proper woman after all. In fact, it had gone far beyond anything she ever could have possibly imagined. Something momentous had happened between them, something very special. The floodgates had opened without permission from either of them, washing away all the anger and pride, the fears, resentment and battle for control that had been so painfully consuming them up until now. All gone on a tidal wave of unadulterated passion.

But something else had been washed away too. *The pretence.* The notion that what she felt for Zahir was simply infatuation or a wild obsession or a silly crush that she could somehow control. Because now she knew the indisputable truth. She was in love with Zahir Zahani. Deeply, desperately, dangerously in love.

Anna closed her eyes against the sheer force of the truth, powerless to do anything except accept it. She thought back to lying in Zahir's arms, sated and exhausted, to the pure pleasure of being held by him, listening to him breathing, her euphoria keeping her awake long after he had surrendered to sleep. She couldn't worry about the consequences of her love for him—at least not now, not tonight. She refused to let anything spoil this one, remarkable night.

Except maybe it was already spoiled. Stretching an arm across the crumpled sheets, she already knew that Zahir had gone. The fact that bed was still warm beside her was no consolation.

Anna held herself very still, listening. There it was again, the noise that had woken her up, a series of dull thuds coming from somewhere far away in the palace. Sitting up in bed, she pulled the covers around her shoulders. What was it? It sounded almost like a wrecking ball, a tremendous weight hitting something solid over and over again. She could hear voices now, muffled shouting, as if the whole of the palace had woken up. And then she heard the most frightening sound of all. A howl, like a wild animal, echoing through the night, and again, louder and more desperate. But what made it all the more terrifying, what made Anna cower back into the mattress, was the fact that the sound definitely came from a human.

Cautiously she got up off the bed. Now her eyes had acclimatised to the gloom, she could make out their discarded clothes scattered on the floor. She found her knickers, hastily pulled them on and was holding Zahir's shirt in her hand when another howl cut through the air. It seemed even louder this time. Suddenly finding the right clothes didn't matter. Getting out of here definitely did.

Hastily tugging Zahir's shirt over her head, she stepped out into the unlit corridor. The sounds were coming from somewhere above, harsh voices, a thumping noise like furniture being turned over, and still that horrendous howling. She knew she had to find her way back to her suite of rooms which were somewhere on the first floor but fear made her hesitate. What on earth was going on? What sort of a mad house had she come to?

Out of the corner of her eye she noticed a flight of stairs leading off the corridor to her left. They were narrow and dark but right now they seemed a better alternative to wandering into the main atrium of the palace and exposing herself to whatever hell was happening out there.

Stealthily climbing the stairs, she lifted the latch of the heavy wooden door at the top and it creaked open. She was in another corridor, wider this time, and dimly lit by wall lights. Hurriedly following what seemed like miles of passageway, her bare feet soundless on the wooden floor, Anna tried to figure out where she was, how she could find her way back to somewhere she recognised. When the corridor ended with another, grander door, she hesitated, listening for sounds on the other side. Nothing.

The howling had stopped now, along with the crashing and banging. All seemed quiet. Spookily so. She noticed that there was a key in the lock on this side of the door but the door opened easily on her turning the handle. She stepped into the room just as a strangled scream pierced the air. It took a moment to realise it had come from her.

She was standing in her own bedroom. And it had been totally trashed. The furniture had been reduced to firewood, an enormous gilt-framed mirror smashed to smithereens, glass all over the floor. The bed was in ruins, the stuffing pulled out of the mattress, the pictures on the walls punched through or hanging crazily from their hooks. Anna gazed around in speechless horror. The wardrobe was lying on its back, all her clothes wrenched from it and violently ripped to pieces, shredded by some maniacal hand. Dresses had been slashed and hurled to the ground. Tops, trousers, even her underwear, hadn't escaped the vicious attack, bras and panties torn to bits and scattered in amongst the piles of debris. It was a terrifying scene.

And in the middle of it were the two brothers—Zahir and Rashid. Rashid was crouched down, his head in his hands, silently rocking. Zahir was standing over him, wearing nothing but the same loose trousers Anna had lowered from his body a short while ago. But, as he turned to look at her, Anna heard herself scream again. His chest was smeared with blood, deep, vertical lacerations that looked as if they'd been made by some sort of animal. There were scratches all over his arms too, on the hands that he held up to ward her off.

'Get out of here, Annalina!'

But Anna couldn't move, frozen by the horror of the sight, her brain unsure if this was real or if she'd stepped into some terrible nightmare.

'I said *go.*'

No, this was real, all right. Zahir was advancing towards her now, bearing down on her with the look of a man who would not be disobeyed. Anna felt herself back away until she could feel the wall behind her.

'Wh…what has happened?' She tried to peer around Zahir's advancing body to look at Rashid, who had wrapped his arms around his knees and was still rocking back and forth.

'I'm dealing with this, Annalina.'

Zahir was right in front of her now, trying to control her with eyes that shone wild and black. She could see the thick corded veins throbbing in his neck, smell the sweat on him, sense the fight in him that he was struggling to control.

'And I am telling you to go.' Grabbing hold of her upper arms, his forceful grip biting into her soft flesh, he started to turn her in the direction she had come from. 'You are to go back to my chambers and wait for me.' When she finally nodded, he let out a breath. 'And lock the door behind you.'

She nodded again, her knees starting to shake now as Zahir herded her towards the door. Looking over her shoulder, she took in the scene of devastation once more, the thought of the demons that must be possessing Rashid to bring about such violence, to cause such destruction, striking fear into her heart. Because Rashid had done this. She had no doubt about that.

Suddenly Rashid threw back his head. Their eyes met and there was that stare again, only this time it was far more chilling, far more deranged. She watched as he stealthily rose to his feet, hunching his shoulders and clenching his fists by his sides. Now he was starting to step silently towards them but, intent on getting Anna out of the room, Zahir hadn't seen him. With her brain refusing to process what she was seeing, it was a second before Anna let out the cry that spun him around. A second too late. Because Rashid had leapt between them, knocking her to the ground and clasping his hands around her throat. She caught the bulging madness in his eyes as the pressure increased, heard Zahir's roar echo round the room, and then the weight of a tangle of bodies on top of her followed by silence. And then nothing but darkness.

Zahir stared down at Anna's sleeping face, so pale in the glow of light from the single bedside lamp. Her hair was spread across the pillow like spun gold, like the stuff of fairy tales. *Beauty and the Beast.* Suddenly he remembered how that creature Henrik had referred to them and now he wondered if he had been right. Because Zahir had never felt more of a beast than he did now.

Seeing Rashid attack Anna had all but crucified him, the shock of it still firing through his veins. That he had let it happen, failed to protect someone dear to him *yet again*, filled him with such self-loathing that he thought he might vomit from the strength of it. And the fact that this terrible attack had made him face up to his feelings only added to his torment. Because Annalina was dear to him. Dangerously, alarmingly dear. And that meant he had to take drastic action.

Somehow he had managed to control the surge of violence towards Rashid. It had been strong enough to slay him on the spot, or at the very least punch him to the ground, the way he had with Henrik. Because that was his answer to everything, wasn't it? Violence. The only language he understood. But with Annalina still in danger he had driven that thought from his mind. Prising his brother's fingers from around her neck, he had shoved him to one side, taking the punishment of his increasingly feeble blows to his back and his head as he'd bent over Annalina, gathering her against his chest and shielding her with his body as he'd crossed the debris-strewn room and locked the door behind him. Leaving Rashid and his terrible madness inside.

Out in the corridor a doctor was already hurrying

towards them. Zahir had called him earlier to attend to Rashid, before foolishly trying to go and reason with him himself. But right now Rashid would have to wait. Right now nothing mattered except Annalina. Ordering the doctor to follow him, he pounded along the corridors with Annalina in his arms, bursting into the nearest bedroom and laying her down on the bed like the most precious thing in the world. Because suddenly he realised that she was.

Her eyes were already fluttering open when the doctor bent to examine her—his verdict that the marks on her neck were only superficial, that she had most probably fainted from the shock, a massive relief before it had given way to the feelings of utter disgust towards himself.

With the doctor insisting that the only treatment Annalina needed was rest, Zahir had reluctantly left her in the care of the servants to be put to bed for what was left of the night. Annalina was already insisting that she was fine, that she was sorry for having been such a drama queen, that he should go to Rashid to see how he was.

But Zahir returned to his chambers, having no desire to see any more of his brother tonight. He didn't trust himself—his emotions were still running far too high. And, besides, the doctor would have sedated Rashid by now. He would be blissfully unconscious. Zahir could only yearn for the same oblivion. There was no way he would sleep tonight.

So instead he took a shower, feeling a masochistic pleasure in the sting of the water as it pounded over the cuts and scratches inflicted by his brother, towelling himself dry with excessive roughness over the clawed wounds on his chest, staring at the blood on the towel, as if looking for absolution, before tossing it to the ground.

Because there was no absolution to be had. Quite the reverse.

The thought that Annalina could so easily have ended up married to Rashid tore at his soul. Because the betrothal had been all his idea, his appalling lack of judgement. He had convinced himself that marriage and a family would be beneficial for Rashid, then had bullied him into agreeing to his plan.

He had told himself that his brother was getting better, that his problems would soon be solved with a bit more time and the right medication. Not because it was the truth—dear God, this evening had shown how desperately far from the truth it was—but because that was what he had wanted to believe. And not even for Rashid's sake, but for his own. To ease the weight of guilt. If it hadn't been for Annalina's courage, her bravery that night on the bridge in Paris, she would have found herself married to a dangerously unstable man. A man who clearly meant to do her harm. And that was something else Zahir could add to the growing list of things he would never forgive himself for.

The confines of his rooms felt increasingly claustrophobic as he paced around, the silence he had thought he craved so badly resonating like a death knell in his ears. And coming across Annalina's dress lying on his bedroom floor only intensified his suffering. Picking it up, he laid it across the bed, the sight of the crumpled sheets sending a bolt of twisted torment through him.

For sex with Annalina had been unlike any sexual experience Zahir had ever had before—so powerful in its intensity that it had obliterated all reason, all doubts. And, even more astonishing, afterwards he had fallen asleep, drugged by a curious contentment totally unknown to him. For Zahir had never, *ever* slept in a woman's arms.

The only sex he had ever known had been perfunctory, used solely as a means of release, leaving him feeling vaguely soiled, as if debased by his own physical needs. In short, once the deed had been done, he had been out of there. But with Annalina it had been different. He had felt stronger for having made love to her, calmer, more complete. Somehow made whole. But then with Anna everything was different.

But his euphoric peace had been short-lived, shattered first by howls and then sounds of destruction that he instantly knew had to be his brother. In his haste to go to him he had abandoned Annalina, not thinking that she would follow him, that she was the one who was in danger. That she would end up being attacked.

A surge of impotent energy saw him retracing his steps back up to the bedroom where she was sleeping, startling the young servant, Lana, who for some reason had taken it upon herself to keep a bedside vigil. Curtly dismissing her, he had taken her place, the realisation of what he had to do growing with every minute that passed as he gazed down at Anna's peaceful face. He had been wrong to marry her, to bring her here. No good would ever come of it. If he wanted to protect her, he knew what he had to do. He had to set her free.

Anna opened her eyes, at first startled, then feeling her heart leap when she saw that Zahir was at her bedside, staring at her with silent intensity.

'What time is it?' She started to push herself up against the pillows. What day was it, come to that? Crossing time zones, the glorious wonder of sex with Zahir, the terror of Rashid's assault meant she had totally lost all sense of date and time. Her hand went to her throat as the dreadful memory came back. It felt slightly tender, nothing more.

'About four a.m.' Zahir shifted in his seat but his eyes never left her face.

Anna sat up further, brushing the hair away from her face. 'What are you doing here?' Something about Zahir's still demeanour, the dispassionate way he was observing her, was starting to alarm her. She moved her hand across the coverlet to find his but, instead of taking it, he folded his arms across his chest, sitting ramrod-straight in his chair. 'Is it Rashid? Has something happened to him?'

'Rashid has been sedated. He will give us no further trouble tonight.'

'Well, that's good, I suppose.'

'You should go back to sleep. The doctor said you must rest.' Zahir rose to his feet. For a moment Anna thought he was going to leave but instead he moved round to the end of the bed where he stood watching her like a dark angel. A couple of seconds of silence ticked by before he spoke again. 'Your neck.' His voice was gruff, as if he had been the one with the hands around his throat. 'Does it hurt?'

'No.' His obvious anguish made Anna want to lessen his burden. 'Honestly, I'm fine. But what about you? The marks on your chest, Zahir, they looked bad.'

'They are nothing.' He immediately closed her down. They were obviously to be covered up by more than the loose white shirt that now clad his chest.

'I'm sorry that I made the situation worse by swooning like a Victorian heroine.' She pulled an apologetic face. 'I don't know what came over me. I think it must have been the shock.'

'You have nothing to apologise for.' His hands gripped the end of the bed. 'It is I who should be sorry.'

'What happened, Zahir?' She lowered her voice. 'Why did Rashid go berserk like that?'

Zahir looked away into the darkness of the room. 'Apparently he failed to take his medication when he was in Dorrada.'

'And that…that fury was the result?' She bit down on her lip. 'But why did he target me, Zahir? Rip up *my* clothes, try to attack me? What does he have against me?'

'He had no idea what he was doing. He attacked me too, his own brother.'

'But only because you were trying to stop him from trashing my room.' She hadn't been sure until that moment, but now she saw that she was right.

'It seems he regards you as some sort of threat.' Zahir still couldn't meet her eye. 'In his deranged state, he's somehow confusing you with the person who killed our parents.'

'Oh, how awful.' Anna's heart lurched with compassion and maybe a tinge of fear. 'Poor Rashid. Maybe if I tried to speak to him—when he's calmed down, I mean.'

'No.' Now his black gaze bored into her.

'Well, is he having any other treatment, apart from medication? Counselling, for example? I'm sure there will be a doctor in Europe who could help him. I could make enquiries?' She looked earnestly across at his shadowed form.

'That won't be necessary. Rashid is my problem and I will deal with him.'

'Actually, I think he is my problem too, in view of what you've just told me… In view of what happened tonight.' Hurt at the way Zahir curtly dismissed her offer of help hardened her voice.

'That will never happen again.'

'How can you be so sure when we're both living under the same roof?'

'Because you won't be for much longer.'

'What do you mean? Are you going to send him away?'

'No, Annalina.'

The seed of a terrible truth started to germinate. She stared at him in frozen horror.

'You're not saying…?' She swallowed past her closing throat. 'You are not intending to send *me* away?'

'I've come to the conclusion that bringing you here was a mistake.'

'A mistake?' The dead look in Zahir's eyes sent panic to her heart. 'What do you mean, a mistake?'

'I've decided that you should return to Dorrada.'

'But how can I go back to Dorrada when you are here in Nabatean?' She spoke quickly, trying to drown out the scream in her head. 'I am your wife. I should be by your side.'

'That was a mistake too.' A terrible chill cloaked the room. 'The marriage will be annulled.'

'No!' She heard the word echo around them.

'I have made up my mind, Annalina.'

This wasn't possible…it couldn't be happening. Pulling back the covers, Anna scrambled across the bed until she landed in front of Zahir with a small thump. He took a step back but the desperation in her eyes halted his retreat. He didn't mean it. He couldn't be ending their marriage, casting her aside just like that. *Could he?* But one look at the determined set of his jaw, the terrible blackness of his eyes, told her that he could. And he was.

Anna clasped her hands on either side of her head as if to stop it exploding. Had she failed again so spectacularly that Zahir was prepared to end their marriage without even giving it a chance? And to do it now—when she had only just accepted how deeply she had fallen in love with him—felt like the cruellest, most heart-breaking twist of all. Seconds passed before one small question found its way through the choking fog.

'But what about last night?' She despised herself for the pitiful bleat in her voice as she searched his face for a flicker of compassion. 'Did that not mean anything to you?'

His jaw clenched in response, the shadowed planes of his handsome face hardening still further in the dim light. A twitching muscle in his cheek was the only sign of insubordination.

'Legally it will make the marriage more difficult to annul, that's true.' He raised his hand to his jaw, pressing his thumb against the rebellious muscle. 'But I'm sure it can be arranged for a price.'

Was she hearing right? Had the single most wonderful experience of her life meant nothing to Zahir? Or, worse still, had she got it so wrong, somehow been such a failure without realising it, that he would pay any price to be rid of her?

'I don't understand.' She tried again, her voice cracking as she reached forward, placing the palm on her hand on his chest, as if trying to find the heart in him, make it change Zahir's mind for her. *Make him love her.* But instead all she found was unyielding bone and taut muscle concealed beneath the cotton shirt. 'Why are you doing this?'

'I've told you. Our marriage should never have taken place. It was an error of judgement on my part. I accept full responsibility for that and am now taking steps to rectify the situation.'

'And what about me?' Her voice was little more than a whisper. 'Do I have no say in the matter?'

'No, Annalina. You do not.'

Anna turned away in a daze of unshed tears. So this was it, then. Once more she was at the mercy of a man's decisions. Once more she was being rejected, pushed away for being inadequate. Not by her father this time, with his frozen heart, or Henrik, with his selfish needs. But Zahir. Her Zahir. Her only love.

The pain ripping through her was so fierce that she thought she might fold from the strength of it. But seconds passed and she found she was still standing, still breathing. She forced herself to think.

Clearly Zahir wasn't going to change his mind. The whole mountain of his body was drawn taut with resolve, grim determination holding him stock-still in the gloom of the room. She could beg. The idea certainly crossed her mind, desperation all too ready to push aside any dignity, pride or self-respect. But ultimately she knew it would be pointless. Zahir would not be moved, emotionally or practically. She could see that the decision had already taken root in the bedrock of his resolve. So that left only one course of action. She would leave. And she would leave right now.

Turning away, she ran into the middle of the room, but then stopped short, suddenly realising she had no clothes to wear. Her entire wardrobe had been ripped to shreds, along with her heart and soul. She looked down at the nightdress she was wearing. Lana had found it for her. She remembered her tenderly removing Zahir's shirt, remembered seeing the blood smeared across it from where he had held her to his chest, before Lana had slipped this plain cotton gown over her shaking body and helped her into bed.

But she could hardly go out dressed like this. Covering her face with her hands, she tried to decide what to do. The clothes that she had travelled in what seemed like several centuries ago now were scattered somewhere in Zahir's chambers. Much as she dreaded going back there, she had no alternative.

Turning on her heel, she set off, fighting back the tears as she hurtled down the corridors, down the stairs, Zahir following right behind her.

'What do you think you're doing?'

Anna quickened her pace, grateful that for once her sense of direction wasn't letting her down. She recognised this corridor. She knew where she was.

'I'm going to collect my clothes from your rooms and then I'm leaving.'

'Not tonight, you're not.' He was right by her shoulder, effortlessly keeping pace with her.

'Yes, tonight.' She had reached his door now, flinging it open, relieved to find it wasn't locked. She marched into his bedroom, switching on the light, hardly able to bring herself to look at the room that such a short space of time ago had been the scene of such joy. There was her dress, laid out on the bed like a shed skin, a previous incarnation. She rushed over to it, struggling to pull the nightgown over her head, not caring that apart from a pair of panties she was naked—that Zahir, who was standing silently in the doorway, was watching her every move, branding her bare skin with his eyes.

What did it matter? What did any of it matter now?

Stepping into the dress, she tugged up the back zipper as far as she could then cast around looking for her boots. Finding one, she clutched it to her chest and headed for the door, desperate to get out of this hateful den of misery while she still had the strength and the breath to do it.

But Zahir stood in the doorway, blocking her way.

'There is no need for this, Annalina.' Anna felt the searing heat of his hand wrap around her upper arm.

'On the contrary, there is every need.' She jerked her arm but it only made his grip tighten still further. 'Do you seriously think I would stay here a moment longer? Now I know that I am nothing more than a *mistake*, an *error of judgement*?' The words fell from her mouth like shards of glass.

'You will stay here until the morning.' He looked down at her, eyes wild and black, his heavy breath, like that of an angry bull, fanning the top of her head. 'I am not letting you leave while you're in this hysterical state.'

Hysterical state? The sheer injustice of his words misted her eyes red. Didn't she have every right to be hysterical? Didn't she have the right to scream and rant and rave—join Rashid in his madness, in fact—after the way Zahir had treated her tonight?

Yanking herself free from his clutch, she ducked under his arm and into the outer room, seizing her other boot and hopping from foot to foot as she pulled them on.

'I'll tell you what's hysterical, Zahir.' She spoke over her back, refusing to look at him. 'Me thinking that we could ever make a go of this marriage.' She straightened up, flinging her hair over her shoulders as her eyes darted around, searching for her bag and her phone. 'That we could be a proper couple, partners, lovers. That I could be a good wife to you. That what we did last night…a few hours ago…whenever the hell it was…' she choked on a rising sob '…was actually something very special.'

She stopped, making herself drag in a ragged breath before she passed out completely, shaking with misery, rage and the miserable injustice of it all.

But suddenly, there in the darkest moment, she saw

the gleam of truth. Suddenly she realised she had nothing to lose any more. The barriers between them had all come down, were flattened, destroyed. There was no reason to keep the very worst agony to herself any longer.

'And do you want to know the most hysterical thing of all?' She spun around now, pinning him to the spot with the truth of her stare, letting the rush of abandonment take control of her.

'I'm in love with you, Zahir.' A harsh laugh caught in her throat, coming out as a strangled scream. 'How totally *hysterical* is that?'

CHAPTER THIRTEEN

ZAHIR FELT THE words drive through him like a knife in his guts. *She was in love with him?* How was that even possible?

He stared back in numbed silence at the flushed cheeks, the glazed eyes, the tousled blonde hair that fell down over her heaving breasts.

He longed to go to her, to break the spell, to pin her down, literally there on the floor where she stood blinking up at him. He wanted to make her say the words again, to feel them against his lips as he devoured her, made love to her again. But instead he hardened his heart. If it was true that she loved him, then that was all the more reason for him to do the right thing, the only thing, and set her free. Before he dragged her down, weakened her, destroyed her, the way he did anyone who was unfortunate enough to care for him. He simply couldn't bear that to happen to Anna.

'Well?' Finally she spoke, her voice sounding hollow, empty. 'Do you have nothing to say?'

Zahir wrestled with his conscience, with his heart, with every damned part of his body that yearned to go to her.

'It makes no difference to my decision, if that's what you mean.' His damning words were delivered with a cruel coldness born of bitter, desperate frustration. He watched as Annalina's lovely face twitched, then crumpled, her lip trembling, her eyes glittering with the sheen of tears. He deliberately made himself watch the torture, because that was what it was. He had to feel the punishment in order to keep strong.

'So...' She pushed her hair away from her face with a shaky hand. 'This is it, then?' She spoke quietly, almost as if she was asking the question of herself. But her eyes held his, the pupils dilated, like twin portals to her soul.

Zahir looked away. He couldn't witness this, not even in the name of punishment.

He sensed Annalina hesitate for a second, then heard a rustle and turned to see her slinging her bag over her shoulder and marching towards the door. A roar of frustration rang in his ears and he closed his eyes, digging his nails into the palms of his clenched fists. He would allow himself the indulgence of a couple of minutes of the agony before setting off after her.

She was at the main entrance when he caught up with her, tugging furiously at the handle of the door that was securely locked, becoming ever more desperate as she heard him approach.

'You are not leaving like this, Annalina.' He stood behind her, solid, implacable.

'No? Just try and stop me.'

'And where exactly do you think you're going, and how are you going to get there?'

'I don't know and I don't care.' She was banging her fists against the panelled door now. 'And don't pretend you care either. This is what you want, isn't it? To be rid of me as soon as possible? I'll find someone to take me to the airport and then you need never see me again.'

Reaching over her shoulder, Zahir covered her flailing fists with one hand, but Annalina pulled them away from under him.

'I mean it, Zahir. I can't stay here a minute longer. I'm leaving now.'

'Very well.' Pulling his phone from his pocket, he made a call, punching in the code of the wall safe to retrieve the keys to both the front door and his SUV as he waited for the reply. He opened a wall cupboard, taking out a coat and passing it to Anna without meeting her eye.

She was right. This was what he had told her he wanted: her gone, out of his life. The fact that it was tearing him apart only proved his point. Proved what a lethally dangerous combination they were. 'I will drive you to the airport myself.'

Anna listened as he ordered the jet to be put on standby, silently taking the coat from him before he unlocked the door and ushered her out into the cold night air. So it was really happening. She was to be banished. Cast aside like the worthless acquisition that he obviously thought she was.

Once inside the powerful SUV, she was grateful for the feeling of paralysis that had come over her, as if her body was protecting her the best it could by rendering her almost comatose. She couldn't look at Zahir, in the same way that he couldn't look at her. Instead he focussed with leaden concentration on manoeuvring the vehicle out of the electric gates that swung open for them.

They drove in total silence, Anna fighting to hold on to the merciful state of the numbness, frightened it could so easily thaw into a tidal wave of grief if she let it. She felt weighted down by the sense of him all around her, the invisible pressure bearing down on her shoulders, ringing in her ears. She stared through the windscreen, at the world that was still there, seemingly impervious to her heartbreak. Dawn was starting to break, a thread of orange lining the horizon in front of them.

The car sped silently towards it, the orange glow spreading rapidly as the peep of the sun appeared, tingeing the wispy clouds pink against the baby-blue of the sky, blackening the desert below it.

The headlights picked up the sign for the airport as they flashed past. Soon they would be there. Soon she would be leaving this country, presumably never to return. For some reason, that realisation felt like another body blow, as if someone had kicked her in the guts when she was already writhing on the ground.

She bit down on her lip, twisted her hands in her lap and fought madly to stop the tears from falling as she stared fixedly ahead at the unfolding drama of the dawn. Sunrise over the desert—one of nature's most spectacular displays.

Suddenly Anna wanted to experience it, to be a part of it. Not from here, from the agonising confines of the car, but out in the open with the cold air against her skin and the freedom to breathe it in, to be able look all around her, lean back and let the majesty unfold above her head. She needed to prove to herself that there was wonder and beauty to be had in this world, no matter how it might feel right now. If she was leaving this remarkable land for ever, she wanted one lasting memory that wasn't all about sorrow and heartbreak.

She turned her head, steeling herself to break the brittle silence, the sight of Zahir's harsh profile spawning a fresh onslaught of pain. His Adam's apple moved as he swallowed, the only visible sign that he was aware of her gaze.

'Stop the car.'

Zahir's hands tightened on the steering wheel as he shot her a wild-eyed glance.

'What?'

'I want you to stop the car. Please.'

'Why?' Alarm sounded in his voice as his eyes flashed from the road to her face and back again. 'Are you ill?'

'No, not ill.' Anna shifted in her seat. 'I want to watch the sunrise.' She tipped her chin, fighting to hold it steady, swallowing down the catch in her voice. 'Before I leave Nabatean for good, I would like to see the sunrise over the desert.'

She saw Zahir's flicker of surprise before the brows drew together, lowering to a scowl. There was a second's silence as the car continued to speed onward.

'Very well.' His jaw tightened. 'But not here. I will find a more advantageous view.'

Anna sat back, releasing a breath she didn't even know she'd been holding in. She had no doubt that Zahir would know exactly where to take them. It seemed to her that he knew every grain of sand of this desert, that it was a part of him, of who he was, wild and bleak.

Sure enough, a short while later he swung the vehicle off the main road, bumping it over the rough terrain, and almost immediately they appeared to have left civilisation completely and become part of the barren wilderness of the desert. Zahir pushed the SUV hard, bouncing it over the hard ridges of compacted sand at great speed, navigating along a dried-up riverbed before swinging off to the right and powering up the side of a dune the size of a small mountain.

Beside him Anna clung to her seat, grateful for the mad recklessness of the journey that temporarily obliterated all other thoughts. Finally they skidded to a halt with a spray of sand and she peered through the speckled windscreen, seeing nothing but the grey shadowed desert. Abruptly getting out of the car, Zahir came round and opened her door for her.

'We will need to do the last bit on foot.' He held out his hand but Anna ignored it, jumping down unaided and focussing on nothing but this one goal as she followed Zahir up the towering peak of the dune, her thighs aching as she tried to keep up with him, her boots sinking into the shifting sand. Ahead of her Zahir had stopped to hold out his hand again and this time Anna took it, feeling herself being pulled up onto the very top of the dune. And into another world.

If it was wondrous beauty that she wanted, here it was, spread out before her. The sky was on fire with oranges, reds and yellows, the horizon a vivid slash of violet, the colours so amazingly vibrant that they looked to have been splashed from a children's paint box. Before them the dunes rolled like waves of the sea, washed pink by the fast-rising sun that highlighted the thousands of rippled ridges with finely detailed shadows.

Anna dropped to her knees and just stared and stared, intent on blocking everything else out, storing this image so that it would be there for ever. She didn't even notice the tears that were starting to fall.

Zahir cast his eyes down to where Annalina knelt beside him, her profile glowing amber in the light of the sun. The sight of the tears rolling unchecked down her cheeks threatened to undo him so completely that he had to look away. Whatever had he been thinking, bringing her here? What madness had made him want to prolong the torture? He scowled, channelling his agony into determination. He had to be cruel to be kind.

Minutes passed with no sound except the occasional cry of a bird, the rustle of the wind as it danced across the sand, the beat of his pulse in his ears. He had never known Annalina to be so silent, so still. The soft breeze that lifted her hair went unnoticed. It almost felt as if she had left him already. He pushed the sharp pain of that thought away and, staring out at the barren landscape, sought to find some words to end this agony.

'This is for your own good, Annalina.' He forced the words past the jagged blades in his throat. 'After what happened with Rashid, it is clear that you can no longer stay here.'

He saw her twitch inside the coat that she had pulled tight around her body. But she remained infuriatingly silent.

'And besides.' Her refusal to agree with him only made him more coldly determined, crueller. 'This is no place for you. You don't belong here and you never will.'

'Is that so?' She spoke quietly into the cold, new day, still refusing to look at him.

'Yes. It is.'

'And now I will never be given the chance to prove otherwise.' She hunched her shoulders, still staring straight ahead. 'By banishing me, you're simply confirming your assumptions. You're shoring up your own prejudices.'

'I am doing no such thing.' He heard himself roar his reply. Raising a hand, he covered his eyes, squeezing his temples to take away the anger and the pain. Why did she persist in arguing like this, goading him? Or had he provoked the reaction—in which case, why? He was certainly regretting it now. 'That is not true.'

'No? Are you sure, Zahir?' He could hear her fighting to control the tremor in her voice. 'Because that's what it feels like to me. There is no reason for me to leave Nabatean. We could find some help for Rashid—intensive psychiatric counselling. We could focus on making our relationship work, on building a future together.' She turned to give him a look full of scorn but beneath the scorn was hurt, that terrible hurt. 'But, what you really mean is, you don't want me here.'

Zahir forced himself to watch as she turned back, roughly brushing away the tears and biting down on her lip to steady it. He wanted her to stay more than he had ever wanted anything in his life. But he could not let her see that. He could not let his lack of judgement jeopardise her safety any more than it had already. Let his own desires compromise her well-being. More than that, he could not let his *selfishness* crush the life out of this precious creature. Because that was what would happen if she put her happiness in his hands.

'Very well.' He hardened his heart until it felt like lump of stone inside him. 'Since you put it that way, you are right. I don't want you here.' It crucified him to say the words, but say them he had to. 'The sooner you leave, the better for all concerned.'

She flinched as if he had struck her, and Zahir experienced the same horror, as if he had done just that.

'Well, thank you for the truth.' Finally she spoke, her words floating softly into the air before the dreadful silence wrapped itself around them again.

Zahir looked over his shoulder. He couldn't take any more of this. 'We need to get going.' He paced several steps across the top of the dune, glancing back to where Annalina hadn't moved. 'The crew will have the jet ready for take-off.'

He didn't give a damn about the jet or the crew. He just knew he had get away from here, deliver Annalina to the airport and put an end to this agony.

'In a minute.' She spoke with icy clarity. 'First I would like a little time alone. You go back to the car.'

Curbing the desire to tell her that he was the one who gave the orders around here, and that furthermore he expected her to obey them, Zahir drew in a steadying breath. Certainly there was no way he was going to leave her up here on her own. 'Five minutes, then.' He looked around them, pointing his finger. 'I will wait for you over there.'

Anna watched as he strode away, the breeze billowing the loose fabric of his trousers as he climbed up onto the next dune and stood there with his hands on his hips, tall and dark against the skyline.

The shock of his rejection had hardened now, the misery solidifying inside her until it felt less like a bad dream and more like leaden reality. The way Zahir had so callously dismissed her declaration of love still threatened to flay her skin but now she saw that it had been inevitable. A man such as Zahir would never be able to graciously accept such a sentiment. He didn't know how. His own heart was too neglected. It was buried too deep.

She was staring into the crimson wash of the sky when a sudden thought came to her, dawning like the new day. It trickled slowly at first, but soon started to warm her, to heat her from within, until she began to throb with the idea of it—whether through hope, desperation or fear she didn't know. If Zahir's heart was so buried, so unreachable, perhaps it was up to her to try and change that.

Perhaps it was her duty to try and find it.

Zahir watched as Annalina got to her feet, expecting to see her start the descent back to the car. But instead she was heading towards him, scrambling over the sand that was shifting beneath her feet in her hurry to reach him. He saw her stumble and instinctively started to go to her but she was up on her feet again, using her hands now to propel herself forward until she had reached the top of the dune and pulled herself up beside him.

'I know you don't want to hear it but I'm going to say it again anyway.' Her words came out all of a rush as her breath rasped in her throat, her chest heaving beneath the padded coat. 'I love you, Zahir.' She gulped painfully. 'And nothing you can say or do will ever alter that.'

She was staring at him now, her hair blowing around her flushed cheeks, those beautiful blue eyes searching his face, beseeching him. Why? For what reason? He didn't even know.

'Love has no place here.' He struggled wildly to release himself from her gaze, from the grip of her declaration. But when that bleak statement didn't work, when she still refused to look away, he tried again, desperately searching for some sort of logic to make her see sense.

'Besides, I suspect it is no more than an aberration.' He tried to soften his voice, to sound reasonable, even though he had never felt less reasonable, more cut loose from sanity, in his life. 'When you return to your country, you will see that.'

'This is no aberration, Zahir.' Stubbornly she refused to back down. 'I will do as you say. I will get on that plane and fly back to Dorrada. But I guarantee it will change nothing, no matter how much you want it to. Neither time nor distance nor death itself will change how I feel. I love you, Zahir. And I always will.'

Zahir closed his eyes against the astonishingly punishing power of her words. He couldn't accept them. He refused to accept them. A beautiful creature such as Annalina could never truly love a brute like him. He struggled to try and find the words to explain that to her, cursing when they refused to come to him, as if his vocabulary was deliberately defying him.

'And what's more…' She held the moment in her hand, poised for the final thrust. 'I think that you love me too.'

CHAPTER FOURTEEN

ANNA SAW HIM FLINCH, felt the twist of it inside her. She had no idea if it was true. It was as deranged a notion as it was incredible. The tortured look on Zahir's face told her nothing either, except that her rash words had affected him deeply. But it was worth a try. What did she have to lose? Certainly not her pride—there was precious little of that left to worry about. And self-respect? If that was hanging by a thread too maybe it was time to stand up for herself, to challenge Zahir's decision. All her life she had been the victim of other people's schemes and machinations. Well enough. This time she was going to fight for what *she* wanted. She was going to fight for the man she loved.

'Zahir?' Gathering her courage around her, she broke the silence softly, like popping a bubble in the air. 'Do you have nothing to say?' She stretched out a hand to his face, turning him towards her. 'Look at me, Zahir. Tell me what you're feeling.'

'I see no purpose in that.' He turned against her hand, his stubbled jaw rough against her fingers as he presented her with his most harsh profile.

'Tell me why you flinch when I talk about love.' Still Anna persisted. 'What is it about the idea that frightens you so much?'

This spun his head back round, made her drop her hands from his cheeks. The notion of Zahir being frightened of anything was totally ridiculous and yet, as she searched his furious gaze, she could see that it was true.

'I have no idea what love is,' he fired back. 'It is beyond my reasoning.'

'No, Zahir. I don't believe you. I could hear the love in your voice when you spoke to me of your mother. I can see it in the patience you show to Rashid. You are capable of love, no matter how much you want to deny it.'

'And look what happened to them, to my parents, to Rashid.' He let out a cry that echoed around them. 'Look what happens to the people that you claim I love. They are either murdered or left mentally deranged. Is that what you want for yourself, Annalina?

'Stop this, Zahir!' She matched his cry. 'You can't go on blaming yourself for what happened for ever.'

'I can and I will.'

'Then so be it.' She knew there would be no changing his mind when it came to that terrible night. The guilt was too deep-rooted, too all-encompassing. 'But you have no right to punish me for it as well.'

'You!' His eyes flashed with fire. 'Can't you see I'm trying to protect you, not punish you? I'm trying to save you from the hideous consequences of falling in love with me.'

'It's too late for that. And, even if it weren't, I would be prepared to take the risk if there was any possibility that you might return my love.'

'Really? Then you are a fool. Because misery is the only reward you will get from such a return.'

'No, I am not a fool, Zahir. I love you.' She countered his temper with calm assertion, pressing down on the tightly coiled spring inside her to stop it from wreaking unimaginable havoc. 'I think I have always loved you, from the very first moment we met. It is an emotion out of my control. There is absolutely nothing I can do about it.'

She paused, her eyes trained on his, refusing even to blink. 'Up until the time we made love, only a few short hours ago, I would never have dared to think that you might love me too. But I felt the heat of your body as you touched me, heard your cry of release when you came, listened to the beat of your heart as you fell asleep with me in your arms. And that has given me hope.

'So, if there is any chance that you might love me too, then I'm going to drag it out of you. It doesn't have to make any difference to our relationship. I will still leave for Dorrada, if that's what you want. I will agree to the annulment of the marriage, sever all contact with you for ever, if you truly believe that's how it has to be. But, if you feel any love for me, I believe I have the right to be told.'

Zahir felt Anna's impassioned speech rock the very foundation of his being, dislodging the corner stone that kept him upright, made him the man he was. He could feel himself wobble, threatening to tumble like a pile of building blocks at her feet.

All his life he had been so sure of his focus. His beloved country had been what mattered. That was at the heart of everything he did, including the reason he had married Annalina and brought her here. But his judgement had been flawed, and not for the first time. Now she was challenging his decision to release her, pushing and pushing, messing with his head until he no longer knew right from wrong any more. Her declaration of love, delivered with such composure, had ripped him wide open. And now she seemed determined to make him stare into the very depths of his own heart.

He looked down at her beautiful, open face, so moved by her words that he couldn't think straight. He wanted to be able to formulate some sort of reply but nothing would come, his throat choked with something that felt alarmingly like tears. Turning his head away, he swallowed madly.

'Zahir?' She reached for him again, taking his face in her hands and holding it firmly in her cold grip, her gaze raking mercilessly over every tortured inch of it. Zahir tried to blink, to look away, but it was too late. She had already seen the sheen in his eyes. 'Oh, Zahir!'

Raising herself up, she touched his lips with her own, nudging them with the gentlest feather-light pressure. 'Say it. Say it to me now.'

'No!' Her breath was a soft whisper on his skin but still he fought off its assault. Anger was beginning to surge through him now at the way she was clawing at his masculinity, delving into his soul. That he, Zahir Zahani, the warrior prince, had been almost reduced to tears by this young woman was unthinkable. He would not stand for it. 'I will not say it. I cannot.'

'Why, Zahir? Because it isn't true? Or because you refuse to accept it?'

'Either, both, I don't know.' Screwing up his eyes, he wrenched her hands from his face and took a step back. 'This subject is now closed. We are going back to the car.'

'No, not yet.' Still she persisted, her feet firmly planted in front of him. 'I'm not going anywhere until I have seen you let yourself open up to the possibility of the truth.'

Zahir scowled at her through the slits of his eyes. 'And what the hell does that mean?'

'It means that I want you to promise that you will sit and let yourself feel. Just this once. Just for me. I want you to banish the pride, the fear or whatever else it is that's holding you back and let the truth come through. Set it free. Whatever that truth is, I will accept it and I will never ask you to speak it again. But you owe me this one thing, Zahir.'

Zahir hesitated. If this hippy nonsense meant that she would finally release him, end this terrible inquisition, then maybe he would do it. 'Very well.' He watched as Annalina moved away to give him some space, sitting herself down and hugging her knees, her focus straight ahead. Suddenly it was just him and the sparkling clarity of the new day. There was nowhere to hide.

He let his eyelids drop. Presumably this was what she expected of him so he would play along. He breathed in and out, letting his shoulders drop, the arms that were folded so tightly across his chest loosen. He felt himself relax.

Annalina. The spirit of her came out of nowhere, filling his head, his heart, his whole body. He tried to fight against it, against the witchcraft, black magic or whatever spell it was that she had cast over him, but it was hopeless. Suddenly he was exposed, laid bare, everything he had been denying, blocking out, pushing away, presented before him with bruising clarity. And, more than that, as if a tap was being turned on inside him he could feel the empty vessel that he had once been filling, gushing and gushing until he was almost drowning from the flood of it, gasping for air. And then it was too late, he had no control any more, and the wave crashed over him. And suddenly he recognised the phenomenon for what it was: the acceptance of love.

Beside her Anna felt Zahir move, closing the gap between them until he was in front of her, standing so tall that he blotted out the rising sun. She forced her eyes slowly to travel up the length of his body but they halted at his chest, the terrible fear of what she might see refusing to let them go to his face. She was wrong. He didn't love her. It was a crazy, stupid idea, born of desperation and the blindness of her own feelings.

'Anna?' He stretched out his hands to her and she took hold of them, letting herself be pulled to standing. It was the first time she had heard him shorten her name. 'Please forgive me.' She felt her heart stutter with panic as his eyes sought hers, the near-black intensity impossible to read.

'Just now I called you a fool, but now I see that I am the fool.' He spoke softly but with grim determination. 'Now I see that what I took for strength and responsibility was actually bullying and intimidation. Never once did I allow myself to stop and look at you for who you really are because that would have exposed my own weakness.' He looked down at their joined hands then back to her face.

'For not only are you beautiful, Annalina—the most remarkable, extraordinary woman that I have ever met—but you are also brave. So much braver than me. Somehow you found the courage to declare your feelings for me, even in the face of my callous hostility. Whereas I...' He paused, the effort of overthrowing a lifetime of crippling detachment evident from the glitter in the depths of his eyes. 'I was too scared to examine how I felt for fear of what I would find there. A man who was unworthy of you in every way, who could never hope to earn your affection, let alone your love. I thought your love was far beyond anything I could ever deserve and that is why I dismissed it so cruelly. And the reason why I beg your forgiveness.'

'There is nothing to forgive, really.' Suddenly Anna didn't want to hear any more. If this was Zahir letting her down gently it was even more unbearably painful than his cold-blooded disregard. 'You don't have to explain any further.'

'Oh, but I do.' He brought her hands to his chest, clasping them against his heart. 'I have been callous and I have been cruel. By sending you away I thought I was protecting you from my brother but in reality I was only protecting myself, my own heart. But your courage has stripped away that defence and made me see what was there all along. And that is this.' He paused, raking in a breath that came from deep, deep within his soul. 'I love you, Annalina. I think I always have and I know I always will.'

For a second Anna let the words sink in, feeling them spread through her body with a ripple of pleasure that grew and grew until she thought she might explode with the joy of it. Then, throwing herself forward, she fell against him, revelling in the glorious strength of his arms as they wrapped around her, holding her so tightly against him. For several precious heartbeats they stayed locked in this embrace until Zahir loosened his hold and pulled back so that he could take her face in his hands.

'My most precious Annalina. You have shone light into my darkness, filled a void that I didn't know was there, stirred a heart that didn't know how to beat. And you have even made me find the words to tell you that.' He smiled now, the most wonderful, tender smile, and Anna felt the warmth of it flood over her, filling her to the brim with love. 'If you will have me, I am yours for ever more.'

'Oh, yes, I will have you.' With his features blurred by tears, Anna let her fingers trace the familiar contours of his face. 'And what's more, Zahir, I will never, ever let you go.'

Zahir gave a primal groan, lowering his head until he found her lips and immediately the arousal leapt between them, just as it always did. Just as it had that very first time when Anna had forced him to kiss her on the bridge in Paris. As the kiss deepened their bodies melted, moulding into one another, becoming one.

And all around them the new day burst into life.

'I have something for you.' Coming up behind her, Zahir spoke softly into the ear exposed by the swept-up tresses of Anna's intricate hairstyle.

Anna turned to look up at him, catching her breath at the stunning sight of her husband in Eastern clothes. He was wearing a long cream *shirwani* with a stand-up collar and a single row of buttons down the front and loose dark-red trousers beneath. He looked more impossibly handsome than any man had a right to be. Because he was.

Lana and Layla, who had been tweaking the folds of Anna's splendid red-and-gold gown, respectfully stepped back into the shadows of the dressing room.

'I don't think you should be here.' Anna smiled into his serious eyes, her mild rebuke melting like a wafer on her tongue. 'Isn't it supposed to be unlucky to see me before the ceremony?'

'We make our own luck, *aziziti*. Besides, this is blessing, not a wedding. I don't believe the same rules apply.'

'And even if they did I doubt very much whether you would obey them.'

'It is true that I would never obey a rule that kept me away from you.' His solemn words, accompanied by the furrowed brow, threatened to turn Anna's bones to jelly once again. That would teach her for trying to be flippant.

These past few weeks had been the most wonderful, magical time imaginable. With Zahir permitting himself some rare free time, they had scarcely left each other's sides, travelling around Nabatean so that he could show off his country, finding secret hideaways that only he knew about—a shaded oasis in the desert or ancient caves with prehistoric paintings on the walls, where he would show off something rather more private, and definitely more thrilling.

She had watched him as he worked too, patiently explaining the procedures he was involved with or taking her to meetings where he made sure that her views were respected, his obvious respect for her opinions filling her with pride. But it was the nights that had been the most special. Exploring each other's bodies in the dark, finding new ways to bring each other to soaring heights of ecstasy, before finally falling asleep in a tangle of sweat-sealed limbs. Anna marvelled at how they could never seem to get enough of one another, rejoicing in the fact that they would never have to. Because this was just the start of their lifetime together.

'So what is it, then—this something you have for me?' Tamping down the curl of longing, she smiled up at him.

'Um…it's just this.'

She watched as he felt in his pocket, producing a blue velvet ring box. He was nervous, she realised, definitely out of his very masculine comfort zone. And that made her love him all the more. He opened the lid of the box and offered it to her, almost shyly.

'Zahir!' Anna gasped at the sight of the sapphire ring, the stunning stone set in platinum and surrounded by a circle of diamonds. 'It is absolutely beautiful. Thank you!'

'I'm glad you like it. I thought the colour would match your eyes.' He gave a small cough, clearly ill at ease. 'Consider it a late engagement ring. I've noticed that you never wear the other one.'

'No.' Now it was Anna's turn to feel uncomfortable. 'I'm sorry, but…'

'You don't need to apologise, or explain.' Zahir interrupted her, taking her hand and slipping the ring onto her finger where it sat so perfectly, felt so right, that Anna could only stare at it, brimming with happiness. 'The other ring was never meant for us. By rights it should be somewhere in the mud at the bottom of the Seine. In fact…' He flashed her a mischievous grin. 'If you like, I will take you back to Paris and you can finish what you started and chuck the thing in.'

'No!' Anna raised her eyes from admiring her ring and placed her hands gently on his shoulders. 'I've got a much better idea. We will keep it safe for Rashid until he finds someone to love, someone who will make him the perfect wife.'

'Do you think that will ever happen?'

'Of course. He has only being undergoing treatment with Dr Meyer for a week but I understand that he's already making tremendous progress.'

'And I have you to thank for that, *aziziti*. For forcing me to swallow my pride and accept proper help for him. For using your contacts in Europe to find the very best doctor for him. Thank you so much.'

'Think nothing of it. Seeing Rashid return from Germany having banished his demons is the only thanks I want. And it will happen. I am sure of it.'

'You know what? I'm sure of it too.' Zahir took her hands and pressed them to his lips. 'You are the most wonderful, remarkable woman, Princess Annalina Zahani. Have I ever told you that?'

'Once or twice, I think.' Anna put her head on one

side thoughtfully. 'But a girl can never receive too many compliments.'

'Hmm… Well, maybe I'll save them until after the ceremony. We don't want your head getting too big for that tiara thing, now, do we?'

He glanced across to where Lana was still patiently waiting with the jewelled headdress in her hands.

'I guess not.' Leaning forward, Anna kissed him on the lips then, turning her head, whispered in his ear. 'And I will save something for you until after the ceremony too.'

Pulling away, their eyes met, Anna's wicked twinkle dancing across Zahir's heated gaze. 'In that case, my princess, I suggest we start the ceremony without further ado. Suddenly I find I am rather impatient.'

'Suddenly I find that I agree with you.'

Sitting down just long enough for Lana to secure the headdress, Anna rose majestically to her feet and, linking her arm through Zahir's, the couple prepared to leave for the throne room.

'I love you, Annalina Zahani.' They started walking, perfectly in step, towards their future together.

'I love you too, Zahir Zahani.'

Somewhere behind them Lana and Layla sighed with delight.

* * * * *

CONVENIENTLY WED TO THE PRINCE

NINA MILNE

This book is for my lovely parents, who made my childhood a happy place.

Thank you!

PROLOGUE

Eighteen months ago, Il Boschetto di Sole—a lemon grove situated in the mountains of Lycander

HOLLY ROMANO STARED at her reflection. The dress was ivory perfection, a bridal confection of froth and lace, beauty and elegance, and she loved it. Happiness bubbled inside her—this was the fairy tale she'd dreamed of, the happy-ever-after she'd vowed would be hers. She and Graham were about to embark on a marriage as unlike her parents' as possible—a partnership of mutual love.

Not for Holly the bitterness and constant recrimination—a union based on the drear of duty on her father's part and the daily misery of unrequited love on her mother's. Their marriage had eventually shattered, and in the final confetti shards of acrimony her mother had walked away and never come back. Leaving eight-year-old Holly behind without so much as a backward glance.

Holly pushed the images from her mind—she only wanted happy thoughts today, so she reminded herself of her father's love. A love she valued with all her heart because, although he never spoke of it, she knew of his disappointment that Holly had not been the longed-for son. And yet he had never shown her anything but love. Unlike her mother, who had never got over the bitter let-down of her daughter's gender and had never shown Holly even an iota of affection, let alone love.

Enough. Happy thoughts, remember?

Such as her additional joy that her father wholeheartedly approved of his soon-to-be son-in-law. Graham Salani was the perfect addition to the Romano family—a man who worked the land and would be an asset to Il Boschetto di Sole, the lemon grove the Romano family had worked on for generations. For over a century the job of overseer had passed from father to son, until Holly had broken the chain. But now Graham would be the son her father had always wanted.

It was all perfect.

Holly smiled at her reflection and half turned as the door opened and her best friend Rosa came in. It took her a second to register that Rosa wasn't in her bridesmaid dress—which didn't make sense as the horse-drawn carriage was at the door, ready to convey them to the chapel.

'Rosa...?'

'Holly, I'm sorry. I can't go through with this. You need to know.' Rosa's face held compassion as she stepped forward.

'I don't understand.'

She didn't want to understand as impending knowledge threatened to make her implode. Suddenly the dress felt weighted, each pearl bead filled with lead, and the smile on her face froze into a rictus.

'What do I need to know?'

'Graham is having an affair.' Rosa stepped towards her, hand outstretched. 'He has been for the past year.'

'That's not true.'

It couldn't be. But why would Rosa lie? She was Graham's sister—Holly's best friend.

'Ask your father.'

The door opened and Thomas Romano entered. Holly forced herself to meet her father's eyes, saw the truth there and felt pain lance her.

'Holly, it is true. I am sorry.'

'Are you sure?'

'Yes. I have spoken with Graham myself. He claims it meant nothing, that he still loves you, still wants you to marry him.'

Holly tried to think, tried to cling to the crumbling, fading fairy tale.

'I can't do that.'

How could she possibly marry a man who had cheated on her? When she had spent years watching the ruins of a marriage brought down by infidelity? In thought and intent if not in deed. Holly closed her eyes. She had been such a fool—she hadn't had an inkling, not a clue. Humiliation flushed her skin, seeped into her very soul.

Her father stepped towards her, placed an arm around her. 'I am so sorry.'

She could hear the pain in his voice, the guilt.

'I had no idea.'

'I know you didn't.'

Graham didn't love her. The bleak thought spread through her system and she closed her eyes, braced herself. An image of the chapel, the carefully chosen flowers, the rows of people, family and friends happy in anticipation, flashed across her mind.

'We need to cancel the wedding.'

CHAPTER ONE

Present day, Notting Hill, London

STEFAN PETRELLI, EXILED Prince of Lycander, pushed his half-eaten breakfast across the cherrywood table in an abrupt movement.

It was a lesson to him not to open his post whilst eating—though, to be fair, he could hardly have anticipated *this* letter. Sprinkled with legalese, it summoned him to a meeting at the London law offices of Simpson, Wright and Gallagher for the reading of a will.

The will of Roberto Bianchi, Count of Lycander.

Lycander—the place of Stefan's birth, the backdrop of a childhood he'd rather forget. The place he'd consigned to oblivion when he'd left aged eighteen, with his father's curses echoing in his ears.

'If you leave Lycander you will not be coming back. I will take all your lands, your assets and privileges, and you will be an outcast.'

Just the mention of Lycander was sufficient to chase away his appetite and bring a scowl to his face—a grimace that deepened as he stared down at the document. The temptation to crumple it up and lob it into the recycling bin was childish at best, and at twenty-six he had thankfully long since left the horror of childhood behind

What on earth could Roberto Bianchi have left him? And why? The Count had been his mother Eloise's godfather and guardian—the man who had allowed his ward to marry Stefan's father, Alphonse, for the status and privileges the marriage would bring.

What a disaster *that* had been. The union had been beyond miserable, and the ensuing divorce a medley of bitterness and humiliation with Stefan a hapless pawn. Alphonse might have been ruler of Lycander, but he had also been a first class, bona fide bastard, who had ground Eloise into the dust.

Enough. The memories of his childhood—the pain and misery of his father's *Toughen Stefan up and Make him a Prince* Regime, the enduring ache of missing his mother, whom he had only been allowed to see on infrequent occasions, his guilt at the growing realisation that his mother's plight was due to her love for *him* and the culminating pain of his mother's exile—could not be changed.

Alphonse was dead—had been for three years—and Eloise had died long before that, in dismal poverty. Stefan would never forgive himself for her death, and now Stefan's half-brother, Crown Prince Frederick, ruled Lycander.

Frederick. For a moment he dwelled on his older sibling. Alphonse had delighted in pitting his sons against each other, and as result there was little love lost between the brothers.

True, since he'd come to the throne Frederick had reached out to him—even offered to reinstate the lands, assets and rights Alphonse had stripped from him—but Stefan had refused. *Forget it. No way.* Stefan would never be beholden to a ruler of Lycander again and he would not return on his brother's sufferance.

He'd built his own life—left Lycander with an utter determination to succeed, to show his father, show Lycander, show the *world* what Stefan Petrelli was made of. Now he was worth millions. He had built up a global property and construction firm. Technically, he could afford to buy up most of Lycander. In reality, though, he couldn't purchase so much as an acre—his father had passed a decree that banned Stefan from buying land or property there.

Stefan shook his head to dislodge the bitter memories—that way lay nothing but misery. His life was good, and he'd long ago accepted that Lycander was closed to him, so there was no reason to get worked up over this letter. He'd go and see what bequest had been left to him and he'd donate it to his charitable foundation. *End of.*

Yet foreboding persisted in prickling his nerve-endings as instinct told him that it wouldn't be that easy.

Holly Romano tucked a tendril of blonde hair behind her ear and stared at the impressive exterior of the offices that housed Simpson, Wright and Gallagher, a firm of lawyers renowned for their circumspection, discretion and the size of the fees they charged their often celebrity clientele.

Last chance to bottle it, and her feet threatened to swivel her around and head her straight back to the tube station.

No. There was nothing to be afraid of. Roberto Bianchi had owned Il Boschetto di Sole. The Romano family had been employed by the Bianchis for generations and therefore Roberto had decided to leave Holly something. Hence the letter that had summoned her here to be told details of the bequest.

But it didn't make sense. Roberto Bianchi had been only a shadowy figure in Holly's life. In childhood he had seemed all-powerful as the owner of the place her family lived in and loved—a man known to be old-fashioned in his values, strict but fair, and a great believer in tradition. Owner of many vast lands and estates in Lycander, he had

had a soft spot for Il Boschetto di Sole—the crown jewel of his possessions.

As an employer he had been hands-off,. He had trusted her father completely. And although he'd shown a polite interest in Holly he had never singled her out in any way. Plus she'd had no contact with him in the past eighteen months, since her decision to leave Lycander for a while.

The aftermath of her wedding fiasco had been too much—the humiliation, the looks of either pity or censure, and the nagging knowledge that her father was disappointed. Not because he questioned her decision to cancel the wedding, but because it was his dream to see her happily married, to have the prospect of grandsons and the knowledge Romano traditions and legacies were secured.

There had also been her need to escape Graham. At first he had been contrite, in pursuit of reconciliation, but when she had declined to marry him his justifications had become cruel. Because he had never loved her. And eventually, at their last meeting, he had admitted it.

'I wooed you because I wanted promotion—wanted an in on the Romanos' wealth and position. I never loved you. You are so young, so inexperienced. And Bianca... she is all-woman.'

That had been the cruellest cut of all. Because somehow, especially when she had seen Bianca, a tiny bit of Holly hadn't blamed him. Bianca was not just beautiful, she seemed to radiate desirability, and seeing her had made Holly look back on her nights with Graham and cringe.

Even now, eighteen months later, standing on a London street with the autumn breeze blowing her hair any which way, a flush of humiliation threatened as she recalled what a fool she had made of herself with her expressions of love and devotion, her inept fumbling. And the whole time Graham would have been comparing her to Bianca, laughing his cotton socks off.

Come on, Holly. Focus on the here and now.

And right now she needed to walk through the revolving glass door.

Three minutes later she followed the receptionist into the office of Mr James Simpson. It was akin to stepping into the past. The atmosphere was nigh on Victorian. Heavy tomes lined three of the panelled walls, and a portrait hung above the huge mahogany desk of a jowly, bearded, whiskered man from a bygone era. And yet she noticed that atop the desk there was a sleek state-of-the-art computer that indicated the law firm had at least one foot firmly in the current century.

A pinstripe-suited man rose to greet her: thin, balding, with bright blue eyes that shone with innate shrewd intelligence.

Holly moved forward with a smile, and as she did so her attention snagged on the other occupant of the room—a man who stood by the window, fingers drumming his thigh in a staccato burst that exuded an edge of impatience.

He was not conventionally handsome, in the drop-dead gorgeous sense, although there was certainly nothing wrong with his looks. A shade under six feet tall, he had dark unruly hair with a hint of curl, a lean face, a nose that jutted with intent and intense dark grey eyes under strong brows that pulled together in a frown.

Unlike Holly, he hadn't deemed the occasion worthy of formal wear and was dressed in faded jeans and a thick blue and green checked shirt over a white T-shirt. His build was lean and lithe, and whilst he wasn't built like a power house he emitted strength, and an impression that he propelled his way through life fuelled by sheer force of personality.

The man behind the desk cleared his throat and heat tinged her cheeks as she realised she had stopped dead in her tracks to gawp. She further realised that the object of her gawping looked somewhat exasperated. An expression that morphed into something else as he returned her gaze, studied her face with a dawning of... Of what? Awareness? Arrest? Whatever it was, it sent a funny little fizz through her veins. Then his scowl deepened further, and quickly she turned away and resumed her progress towards the desk.

'Mr Simpson? I'm Holly Romano. Apologies for being a little late.' No need to explain the reason had been a sheer blue funk.

The lawyer looked at his watch, a courteous smile on his thin lips. 'Not a problem. I'm sure His Highness will agree.'

His Highness?

As her brain joined the dots and his identity dawned on her 'His Highness'—contrary to all probability—managed to look even grumpier as he pushed away from the wall.

'I don't use the title. Stefan is fine—or if you prefer to maintain formality go with Mr Petrelli.' A definitive edge tinged his tone and indicated that Stefan Petrelli felt strongly on the matter.

Stefan Petrelli. A wave of sheer animosity surprised her with its intensity as she surveyed the son of Eloise, one-time Crown Princess of Lycander. The very same Eloise whom her father had once loved, with a love that had infused her parents' marriage with bitterness and doomed it to joylessness.

As a child Holly had heard the name Eloise flung at her father in hatred time after time, until Eloise had haunted her dreams as the wicked witch of the Romano household, her shadowy ghostly presence a third person in her parents' marriage.

Of course she knew that this was not the fault of Stefan Petrelli, and furthermore Eloise was no longer a threat. The former Princess had died years before. Yet as she looked at him an instinctive visceral hostility still sparked. Her mother's words, screamed at her father, were still fresh in her head as they echoed down the tunnel of memories.

'Your precious Eloise with her son—something else she could have given you that I can't. That is what you want more than anything—a Stefan of your own.'

Those words had imbued her three-year-old self with an irrational jealousy of a boy she'd never met. Holly had wanted to be a boy so much she had ached with it. She had known how much both her parents had prayed for a boy, how bitterly disappointed they had been with a girl.

Her mother had never got over it, never forgiven her for her gender, and that knowledge was a bleak one that right now, rationally or not, added to the linger of a stupid jealousy of this man. It prompted her to duck down in a curtsey that she hoped conveyed irony. 'Your Highness,' she said, with deliberate emphasis.

His eyebrows rose and his eyes narrowed. 'Ms Romano,' he returned.

His deep voice ran over her skin, and before she could prevent it his hand had clasped hers to pull her up.

'You must have missed what I told Mr Simpson. I prefer not to use my title.'

Holly would have loved to have thought of a witty retort, but unfortunately her brain seemed unable to put together even a single syllable. Because her central nervous system seemed to have short-circuited as a result of his touch. Which was, of course, insane. Even with Graham this hadn't happened, so until now she would have pooh-

poohed the idea of sparks and electric shocks as ridiculous figments of an overwrought imagination.

And yet the best her vocal cords could eventually manage was, 'Okey-dokey.'

Okey-dokey? For real, Holly?

With an immense effort she tugged her hand free and hauled herself together. 'Right. Um… Now introductions are over perhaps we could…?'

'Get down to business,' James Simpson interpolated. 'Of course. Please have a seat, both of you.'

In truth it was a relief to sink onto the surprisingly comfortable straight-backed chair. *Focus.*

James Simpson cleared his throat. 'Thank you for coming. Count Roberto wrote his will with both of you in mind. As you may or may not know, the bulk of his vast estate has gone to a distant Bianchi cousin, who will also inherit the title. However, I wish to speak to you about Count Bianchi's wishes with regards to Il Boschetto di Sole—the lemon grove he loved so much and where he spent a lot of the later years of his life. Holly's family, the Romanos, have lived on the grove for many generations, working the land. And Crown Princess Eloise spent many happy times there before her marriage.'

Next to her Holly felt Stefan's body tense, almost as if that fact was news to him. She leant forward, her mind racing with curiosity.

James steepled his fingers together. 'In a nutshell, the terms of Roberto's will state that Il Boschetto di Sole will go to either one of you, dependent on which of you marries first and remains married for a year.'

Say what?

Holly blinked as her brain attempted to decode the words. Even as blind primitive instinct kicked in an image of the beauty of the land, the touch of the soil, the scent of lemons pervaded her brain. The Romanos had given heart and soul, blood and sweat to the land for generations. Stefan Petrelli had turned his back on Lycander. And yet if he married the grove would go to *him*, to Eloise's son. *No*.

Before she could speak, the dry voice of the lawyer continued.

'If neither of you has succeeded in meeting the criteria of the will in three years from this date Il Boschetto di Sole will go to the Crown—to Crown Prince Frederick of Lycander or whoever is then ruler.'

There was a silence, broken eventually by Stefan Petrelli. 'That is a somewhat unusual provision.'

Was that all he could say? '"Unusual"?' Holly echoed. 'It's *ridiculous*!'

The lawyer looked unmoved by her comment. 'The Count has left you each a letter, wherein I assume he explains his decision. Can I suggest a short break? Mr Petrelli, if you'd care to read your letter in the annexe room to your left. Ms Romano, you can remain here.'

Reaching into his desk drawer, he pulled out two envelopes sealed with the Bianchi crest.

Stefan accepted his document and strode towards the door indicated by the lawyer. James Simpson then handed Holly hers and she waited until he left the room before she tugged it open with impatient fingers.

Dear Holly

You are no doubt wondering if I have lost my mind. Rest assured I have not. Il Boschetto di Sole is dear to my old-fashioned heart, and I want it to continue as it has for generations as an independent business.

The Bianchi heir is not a man I approve of, but I have little choice but to leave a vast amount of my estates to him. However, the grove is unentailed, and as he has made it clear to me that he would sell it to a corporation I feel no compunction in leaving Il Boschetto di Sole elsewhere.

But where? I have no children of my own and it is time to find a new family. I wish for Il Boschetto di Sole to pass from father and mother to son or daughter, for tradition to continue. So of course my mind goes to the Romanos, who have given so much to the land over the years.

You may be wondering why I have not simply left the grove to your father. Why I have involved Prince Stefan. To be blunt, your father is getting on, and his good health is in question. Once he is no longer on this earth Il Boschetto di Sole would go to you, and I do not know if that is what you wish for.

You have chosen to live in London and make a life there. Now I need you to look into your heart. If you decide that you wish for ownership of Il Boschetto di Sole then I need some indication that this wish is real—that you are willing to settle down. If you have no wish for this I would not burden you.

Whatever you decide, I wish you well in life.

Yours with affection,

Roberto Bianchi

The letter was so typical of Count Roberto that Holly could almost hear his baritone voice speaking the words. He wanted the land he loved to go to someone who held his own values and shared his vision. He knew her father did, but he didn't know if Holly did or not. In truth, she wasn't sure herself. But she also knew that in this case it didn't matter. Her father loved Il Boschetto di Sole—it was the land of his heart—and to own it would give him pure, sheer joy. She loved her father, and therefore she would fight for Il Boschetto di Sole with all her might.

Simple.

Holly clenched her hands into fists and stared at the door to await the return of the exiled Prince of Lycander.

CHAPTER TWO

STEFAN SEATED HIMSELF in the small annexe room and glared down at the letter, distaste already curdling inside him. The whole thing was reminiscent of the manipulative ploys and stratagems his father had favoured. Alphonse had delighted in the pulling of strings and the resultant antics of those whom he controlled.

During the custody battle he had stripped Eloise of everything—material possessions and every last vestige of dignity—and relished her humiliation. He had smeared her name, branded her a harlot and a tramp, an unfit mother and a gold-digger. All because he had held the trump card at every negotiation. He'd had physical possession of Stefan, and under Lycandrian law, as ruler, he had the final say in court. So, under threat of never seeing her son again, Eloise had accepted whatever terms Alphonse offered, all through her love for Stefan.

She had given up everything, allowed herself to be vilified simply in order to be granted an occasional visit with her son at Alphonse's whim.

In the end even those had been taken from her. Alphonse had decided that the visits 'weakened' his son, and that his attachment to his mother was 'bad' for him. That he could never be tough enough, princely enough, whilst he still saw his mother. So he had rescinded her visitation rights and cast Eloise from Lycander.

Once in London Eloise had suffered a breakdown, followed by a mercifully short but terminal illness.

Guilt twisted his insides anew—he had failed her.

Enough. He would not walk that bleak memory-lined road now. Because the past could not be changed. Right now he needed to read this letter and figure out what to do about this unexpected curveball.

Distasteful and manipulative it might be, but it was an opportunity to win possession of some important land in Lycander in his own right. The idea brought him a surge of satisfaction—his father had not prohibited him from *inheriting* land. So this would allow him to return to Lycander on his terms. But it was more than that... The idea of owning a place his mother had loved touched him with a warmth he couldn't fully understand. Perhaps on Il Boschetto di Sole he could feel close to her again.

So all he needed to do was beat Holly Romano.

Holly Romano... Curiosity surfaced. The look she had cast him when she'd learned his identity had held more than a hint of animosity, and that had been before they'd heard the terms of the will. Perhaps she had simply suspected that they were destined to be cast as adversaries, but instinct told him it was more than that. There had been something personal in that look of deep dislike, and yet he was positive they had never met.

No way would he have forgotten. Her beauty was unquestionable—corn-blonde hair cascaded halfway down her back, eyes of cerulean blue shone under strong brows, and she had a retroussé nose, a generous mouth...and a body that Stefan suspected would haunt his dreams. *Whoa.* No need to go over the top. After all, he was no stranger to beautiful women—the combination of his royal status and his wealth made him a constant target for women on the catch, sure they could ensnare him into marriage.

Stefan had little or no compunction in disillusioning them.

Enough. Open the damn letter, Petrelli.

The handwriting was curved and loopy, but strong, Roberto Bianchi might have been ill but he had been firm of purpose.

Dear Stefan

I am sure you are surprised by the terms of my will. Let me explain.

Your mother was like a daughter to me. I was her godfather, and after her parents' death I became her guardian. As she grew up she spent a lot of her time at Il Boschetto di Sole and I believe she was happy there, on that beautiful, fragrant land.

It was a happiness that ceased very soon after her marriage to your father—a marriage I deeply regret I encouraged her to go through with.

In my—poor—defence I was dazzled by the idea of a royal alliance, and Alphonse could be charming when he chose. I believed he would care for your mother and that she would be able to do good as ruler of Lycander.

I also did not wish to encourage her relationship with Thomas Romano—a man of indifferent social status who was already engaged.

Stefan stopped reading as his mind assimilated that information. His mother and Thomas Romano had been an item. A pang of sorrow hit him. There was so much he didn't know about Eloise—so much he wished he could have had time to find out.

As you know, your parents' marriage was destined for disaster, and by the time I realised my mistake there was nothing I could do.

Your father forbade Eloise from seeing me, and not even my influence could change that. In the end he made it a part of the custody agreement that if Eloise saw me she would be denied even the very few visits she was allowed with you.

Stefan stopped reading as white-hot anger burned inside him. There had been no end to Alphonse's vindictiveness. Familiar guilt intensified within him. Eloise had given up so very much for him, and had had no redress in a court in a land where the ruler's word was law.

When Eloise left Lycander I was unable to find her—I promise you, I tried. I wish with all my heart she had contacted me—I believe and I hope she would have if illness hadn't overcome her.

If Eloise were alive I would leave Il Boschetto di Sole to her. Instead I have decided to give you, her son, a chance to own it. In this way I hope I can make up to you the wrong I did your mother. I want to give you the opportunity to return to Lycander as I believe your mother would have wished.

Eloise was happy at Il Boschetto di Sole, and I truly believe that if she is looking down it will give her peace to see you settled on the land she loved. Land you could pass on to your children, allowing the grove to continue as it has for generations—as an independent business that passes from father and mother to son or daughter.

If you wish this, then I wish you luck.

Yours sincerely,

Roberto Bianchi

Stefan let the letter fall onto his knees as he considered its contents. He hadn't set foot in Lycander for eight years. The idea of a return to his birthplace was an impossibility unless he accepted his brother's charity. But now he had an opportunity to return under his own steam, to own land in his own right, defy his father's edict and win the place his mother had loved—a place she would have wanted him to have.

He closed his eyes and could almost see her, her delicate face framed with dark hair, her gentle smile.

But what about the Romano claim?

Not his concern—*he* hadn't made this will. Roberto Bianchi had decided that the grove should go either to Holly Romano or himself. So be it. This was his way back to Lycander and he would take it. But he was damned if he'd jump to Roberto Bianchi's tune.

Holly watched as Stefan re-entered the room, his stride full of purpose as he faced the lawyer.

'I'll need a copy of the will to be sent to my lawyers asap.'

James Simpson rose from behind his desk. 'Not a problem. Can I ask why?'

'Because I plan to overturn the terms of the will.'

The lawyer shook his head and a small smile touched his thin lips. 'With all due respect, you can try but you will not succeed. Roberto Bianchi was no fool and neither am I. You will not be able to do it.'

'That remains to be seen,' Stefan said, a stubborn tilt to the square of his jaw. 'But in the meantime perhaps it would be better for you to tell us any other provisions the Count saw fit to insert.'

'No matter what the outcome, Thomas Romano retains the right to live in the house he currently occupies until his death, and an amount of three times his current annual salary will be paid to him every year, regardless of his job status.'

Holly frowned. 'So in other words the new owner can sack him but he will still have to pay him and he can keep his house?'

She could see that sounded fair enough, but she knew that her father would dwindle away if his job was taken from him—if he had to watch someone else manage Il Boschetto di Sole. Especially Stefan Petrelli—the son of the woman he had once loved, the woman who had rejected him and broken his heart.

'Correct.' James Simpson inclined his head. 'There are no other provisions.'

Stefan leant forward. 'In that case I would appreciate a chance to speak with Ms Romano in private.'

Suspicion sparked—perhaps Stefan Petrelli thought he could buy her off? But alongside her wariness was a flicker of anticipation at the idea of being alone with him. How stupid was *that*? Hard to believe her hormones hadn't caught up with the message—this man was the enemy. Although perhaps it didn't have to be like that. Perhaps she could persuade him to cede his claim. After all, he hadn't set foot in Lycander in years—why on earth did he even *want* Il Boschetto di Sole?

'Agreed.'

The lawyer inclined his head. 'There is a meeting room down the hall.'

Minutes later they were in a room full of gleaming chrome and glass, where modern art splashed bright white walls and vast windows overlooked the City and proclaimed that Simpson, Wright and Gallagher were undoubtedly prime players in the world of law.

'So,' Stefan said. 'This isn't what I was expecting when I woke up this morning.'

'That's an understatement.'

His gaze assessed her. 'Surely this can't be a surprise to you? You knew Roberto Bianchi, and it sounds like the Romanos have been an integral part of Il Boschetto di Sole for centuries.'

'Roberto Bianchi was a man who believed in duty above all else. I thought he would leave his estate intact. Turns out he couldn't bear the thought of the grove being sucked up by a corporation.'

'Why?'

Holly stared at him. He looked genuinely bemused. 'Because to Count Roberto Il Boschetto di Sole truly was a place of sunshine—he loved it, heart and soul. As my father does.' She gave a heartbeat of hesitation. 'As I do.'

Something flashed across his eyes—something she couldn't fathom. But whatever it was it hardened his expression.

'Yet you live and work in London?'

'How do you know where I work or live? Did you check me out?'

'I checked out your public profiles. That is the point of them—they are *public*.'

'Yes. But…' Though really there were no 'buts'—he was correct, and yet irrationally she was still outraged.

'I did a basic social media search—you work for Lamberts Marketing, as part of their admin team. That doesn't sound like someone whose heart and soul are linked to a lemon grove in Lycander.'

'It's temporary. I thought working for a marketing company for a short time would give me some useful insights and skills which will be transferrable to Il Boschetto di Sole. My plan is to return in six months.'

Yes, she loved London, but she had always known it was a short-term stay. Her father would be devastated if she decided not to return to Lycander, to her life on Il Boschetto di Sole. She was a Romano, and that was where she belonged. Of course he wouldn't force her return—but he needed her.

Ever since her mother had left Holly had vowed she would look after him—especially since he'd been diagnosed with a long-term heart condition. There was no immediate danger, and provided he looked after himself he should be fine. But that wasn't his forte. He was a workaholic and the extent of his cooking ability was to dial for a take away.

Guilt panged anew—she shouldn't have left in the first place. The least she could have done for the man who had brought her up singlehandedly from the age of eight was not abandon him. But she visited regularly, checked up nearly daily, and she would be home soon.

Stefan stepped a little closer to her—not into her space, but close enough that for a stupid moment she caught a whiff of his scent, a citrus woodsy smell that sent her absurdly dizzy.

For a second his body tensed, and she would have sworn he caught his breath, and then he frowned—as though he'd lost track of the conversational thread just as she had.

Focus.

'I'd like to discuss a deal,' he said eventually, as the frown deepened into what she was coming to think of as his trademark scowl. 'What will it take for you to walk away from this? I understand that you are worried about your father—but I would guarantee that his job is safe, that nothing will change for him. If anything, he would have more autonomy to do as he wishes with the grove. And you can name your price—what do you want?'

Holly's eyes narrowed. 'I don't want anything.'

'You don't even want to think about it?' Disbelief tinged each syllable.

'Nope.'

'Why not?' The question was genuine, but lined with an edge—this was a man used to getting his own way.

'Because the Romanos have toiled on that land for generations—now we have a chance to own the land in our own right. Nothing is worth more than that. *Nothing.* Surely you see that?'

'No, I don't. It is just soil and fruit and land—the same as any other on Lycander. Take the money and buy another lemon grove—a new one that can belong to the Romanos from the start.'

His tone implied that he genuinely believed this to be a viable solution. 'It doesn't work like that. We have a history with Il Boschetto di Sole—a connection, a bond. *You* don't.'

His frown deepened but he remained silent; it was impossible to tell his thoughts.

'So why don't you take your own advice? You have more than enough money to buy a score of lemon groves. Why do you want *this* one?'

'That's my business,' he said. 'The point is I am willing to pay you well over the market price. I suggest you think carefully about my offer. Because I am also willing to fight it out, and if I win then you will have nothing. No money and no guarantee that your father will keep his job.'

For a second her blood chilled and anger soared. 'So if you win you would take his job from him?'

'Perhaps. If I win the grove it will be mine to do with as I wish.'

For a second a small doubt trickled through her—what if she lost and was left with nothing? But this wasn't about money; this was about the land of her father's heart. This was her opportunity to give her father something infinitely precious, and she had no intention of rolling over and conceding.

'No deal. If you want a fight, bring it on. This meeting is over.'

Before she could head around the immense table he moved to intercept her. 'Where are you going? To marry the first man you find?'

'Perhaps I am. Or perhaps I already have a boyfriend ready and eager to walk me to the altar.'

As if. Post-Graham she had decided to eschew boyfriends and to run away screaming from any altar in sight.

'Equally, I'm sure there will be women queuing round the block to marry *you*.'

He gusted out a sigh, looking less than enamoured at the thought. 'For a start, I'm pretty sure it's not that easy to just get married—there will be plenty of red tape and bureaucracy to get through. Secondly, I have a better idea than instant matrimony, even if it were possible. Let's call a truce on the race to the altar whilst my lawyers look at the will and see if this whole marriage stipulation can be overturned. There has to be a better way to settle this.'

'No argument here—that makes sense.' Caution kicked in. 'In theory…' Because it could be a trick—why should she believe anything Stefan Petrelli said? 'But what's to stop you from marrying someone during our 'truce' as a back-up plan?'

Call her cynical, but she had little doubt that a millionaire prince could find a way to obliterate all red tape and bureaucracy.

'The fact that even the thought of marriage makes me come out in hives.'

'Hives may be a worthwhile price to pay for Il Boschetto di Sole.'

'Point taken. In truth there is nothing to stop either of us reneging on a truce—and it would be foolish for either of us to trust the other.' Rubbing the back of his neck, he looked at her. 'The lawyers will work fast—that's what I pay them for. We're probably only talking twenty-four hours—two days, tops. We'll need to stick together until they get back to us.'

Stick together. The words resonated in the echoey confines of the meeting room, pinged into the sudden silence, bounced off the chrome and glass and writhed into images that brought heat to her cheeks.

Something sparked in his grey eyes, calling to her to close the gap between them and plaster herself to his chest.

'No way.' The words fell from her lips with vehemence, though whether it was directed at herself or him she wasn't sure.

In truth, he looked a little poleaxed himself, and in that instant Holly wondered if this attraction could be mutual.

Then, as if with an effort, he shrugged. 'What's the alternative? Seems to me it's a good idea to spend one weekend together in the hope that we can avoid a year of marriage.'

Deep breath, Holly. His words held reason, and no way would she actually succumb to this insane attraction— she'd steered clear of the opposite sex for eighteen months now, without regret. Yet the whole idea of sticking to Stefan Petrelli caused her lungs to constrict. *Go figure.*

'How would it work?'

'I suggest a hotel. Neutral ground. We can get a suite. Two bedrooms and a living area.'

Had there been undue emphasis on the word 'two'? A glance at his expression showed tension in his jaw— clearly he wasn't overly keen on the logistics of them sticking together either. But she couldn't come up with an alternative—couldn't risk him heading to the altar, and definitely couldn't trust him. And this was doable. A suite. Separate bedrooms.

So… 'That could work.'

'What are your plans for the weekend? We can do our best to incorporate them.'

'Nothing I can't reschedule.'

In fact her plans had been to work, chill out and continue her exploration of London—maybe meet up with a colleague for a quick drink or to catch a film. But such a programme made her sound like a complete Billy-no-mates. In truth she had kept herself to herself in London, because she'd figured there was no point getting too settled in a life she knew to be strictly temporary.

'I do have some work to do, but I can do that anywhere with internet. What about you?'

'I've got some meetings, but like you I should be able to reschedule. Though I do have one site visit I can't postpone. I suggest we go there first, then find a hotel and swing by our respective houses for some clothes.'

'Works for me.'

It would all be fine.

One weekend—how hard could it be?

CHAPTER THREE

STEFAN FIDGETED IN the incredibly comfortable Tudor-style seat that blended into the discreetly lavish décor of the Knightsbridge hotel. Gold fabrics adorned the lounge furniture, contrasting with the deep red of the thick curtains, and the walls were hung with paintings that depicted the Tudor era—Henry VIII in all his glory, surrounded by miniatures of all his wives.

The irony was not lost on Stefan—his own father was reminiscent of that monarch of centuries ago. Cruel, greedy, and with a propensity to get through wives. Alphonse's tally had been four.

Stefan tugged his gaze from the jewelled pomp of Henry, fidgeted again, drummed his fingers on the ornamental desk, then realised he was doing so and gritted his teeth. What was *wrong* with him?

Don't kid yourself.

He'd already identified the problem—he was distracted by the sheer proximity of Holly Romano. Had been all day. To be fair, it wasn't her fault. Earlier, at his suggestion, she'd remained in the car whilst he conducted the site visit; now they were in the hotel and for the most part she was absorbed in her work. Her focus on the computer screen nearly absolute.

Nearly.

But every so often her gaze flickered to him and he'd hear a small intake of breath, glimpse the crossing and uncrossing of long, slender jean-clad legs and he'd know that Holly was every bit as aware of him as he was of her.

Dammit!

Attraction—mutual or otherwise—had no place here. Misplaced allure could *not* muddy the waters. He wanted Il Boschetto di Sole.

An afternoon of fact-finding had elicited the news that the lemon grove wasn't just lucrative—a fact that meant nothing to him—but was also strategically important. Its produce was renowned. It generated a significant amount of employment and a large chunk of tax revenue for the crown.

Ownership of Il Boschetto di Sole would bring him influence in Lycander—give him back something that his father had taken from him and that his brother would grant only as a favour. For it to come from a place his mother had loved would add a poignancy that mattered more than he wanted to acknowledge. Perhaps there he could feel closer to her—less guilty, less tormented by the memory of his betrayal.

He could even move her urn of ashes from the anonymous London cemetery where her funeral service had taken place. For years he had done his best, made regular pilgrimage, laid flowers. He had had an expensive plaque made, donated money for a remembrance garden. But if he owned the grove he would be able to scatter her ashes in a place she had loved, a place where she could be at peace.

His gaze drifted to Holly Romano again. He wanted to come to a fair deal with her, despite her vehement repudiation of the idea. His father had never cared about fairness, simply about winning, crushing his opponent—Stefan had vowed never to be like that. Any deal he made would be a fair one. Yes, he'd win, but he'd do it fair and square and where possible he'd treat his adversary with respect.

He pushed thoughts of Alphonse from his mind, allowed himself instead to study Holly's face. There was a small wrinkle to her brow as she surveyed the screen in front of her, her blonde head tilted to one side, the glorious curtain of golden hair piled over one shoulder. Every so often she'd raise her hand to push a tendril behind her ear, only for it to fall loose once more. There came that insidious tug of desire again—one he needed to dampen down.

As if sensing his scrutiny, she looked up.

Good one, Petrelli. Caught staring like an adolescent. 'Just wondering what you're working on. Admin isn't usually so absorbing.'

There was a hesitation, and then she spun the screen round to show him. 'It's no big deal. One of the managers at work has offered to mentor me and she's given me an assignment.' She gave a hitch of her slender shoulders. 'It's just some research—no big deal.'

Only clearly it was—the repetition, her failed attempt to appear casual indicated that.

'Maybe you should consider asking to move out of admin and into a marketing role.'

'No point. I'm going back home in a few months.'

Then why bother to be mentored? he wondered.

As if in answer to his unspoken question she turned to face him, her arms folded. 'I want to learn as much as I can whilst I'm here, to maximise how I can help when I get back.'

It made sense, and yet he intuited it was more than that. Perhaps he should file it away as potentially useful information. Perhaps he should make a push to find something he could bring to the negotiating table.

'Fair enough.' A glance outside showed the autumn

dusk had settled in, which meant… 'I'm ready for dinner—what about you?'

'Um… I didn't realise it was so late. I'm quite happy to grab a sandwich in my room. I bet Room Service is pretty spectacular here.'

'I'm sure it is, but I've heard the restaurant is incredible.'

Blue eyes surveyed him for a moment. 'So you're suggesting we go and have dinner together in the restaurant?'

'Sure. Why not? The reviews are fantastic.'

'And you're still hoping to convince me to cut a deal and cede my claim.'

'Yes.'

'It won't work.' There was steel in her voice.

'That doesn't mean I shouldn't try. Hell, don't you want to convince me to do the same?'

'Well, yes, but…'

'Then we may as well pitch over a Michelin-starred meal, don't you think?'

She chewed her bottom lip, blue eyes bright with suspicion, and then her tummy gave a less than discreet growl. She rolled her eyes, but her lips turned up in a sudden smile.

'See? Your stomach is voting with me.'

'Guess my brain is outvoted, then,' she muttered, and she rose from the chair. 'I'll be five minutes.'

True to her word she emerged just a few moments later. She'd changed back into the charcoal skirt she'd worn earlier, topped now by a crimson blouse. Her hair was swept up in an artlessly elegant arrangement, with tendrils free to frame her face.

In that moment he wished with a strangely fierce yearn that this was a date—a casual, easy, get-to-know-you dinner with the possibility of their attraction progressing.

But it wasn't and it couldn't be. This was a fact-finding mission.

Suddenly his father's words echoed in his ears with a discordant buzz.

'*Information is power, Stefan. Once you know what makes someone tick you can work out how to turn that tick to a tock.*'

That was what he needed to focus on—gaining information. Not to penalise her but so that he could work out a fair deal.

Resolutely turning his gaze away from her, he made for the door. But as they headed down plush carpeted corridors and polished wooden stairs it was difficult to remain resolute. Somehow the glimpse of her hand as it slid down the gleaming oak banister, the elusive drift of her scent, the way she smoothed down her skirt all combined to add to the desire that tugged in his gut.

She paused on the threshold of the buzzing restaurant, a look of slight dismay on her face. 'I don't think I'm exactly dressed for this.'

'You look…' *Beautiful. Gorgeous.* Way better than any of the women sitting in white cushioned chairs braided with gold, around circular tables illuminated by candles atop them and chandeliers above. 'Fine,' he settled on.

Smooth, Petrelli, very smooth.

But oddly enough it seemed to do the trick. She looked up at him and a small smile tugged her lips upwards. 'Thank you. I know clothes shouldn't matter, but I am feeling a little inadequate in the designer department.'

'I'm hardly up to standard either,' he pointed out. 'I'm channelling the lumberjack look—the whole jeans and checked shirt image.'

The maître d' approached, a slightly pained expression on his face until he realised who Stefan was and his expression morphed to ingratiating. 'Mr Petrelli. This way, please.'

'People are wondering why we've been allowed in,' Holly whispered. 'They're all looking at us.'

'Let them look. In a minute George here will have discreetly spread the word as to who I am and that should do it. Royal entrepreneurial millionaire status transcends dress code. Especially when accompanied by a mystery guest.'

'Dressed from the High Street.' Her tone sounded panicked. 'Oh, God. They won't call the press or anything, will they?'

'Not if they know what's good for them.'

She glanced over the menu at him. 'You don't like publicity, do you?'

In fact he loathed it—because no matter what he did, how many millions he'd made, whatever point he tried to get across, the press all wanted to talk about Lycander and he didn't. *Period.*

'Nope. So I think we're safe. Let's choose.'

After a moment of careful perusal he leant back.

'Hmm... What do you think? The duck sounds amazing—especially with the crushed pink peppercorns—but I'm not sure about adding cilantro in as well. But it could work. The starters look good too—though, again, I'm still not sure about fusion recipes.'

A small gurgle of laughter interrupted him and he glanced across at her.

'What?'

'I didn't have you down as a food buff. The lumberjack look didn't make me think gourmet.'

'I'm a man of many surprises.'

In truth, food was important to him—a result of his childhood. Alphonse's toughening up regime had meant rationed food, and the clichéd bread and water diet had been a regular feature. His stomach panged in sudden memory of the gnaw of hunger, the doughy texture of the bread on his tongue as he tried to savour each nibble. He'd summoned up imaginary feasts, used his mind to conjure a cacophony of tastes and smells and textures. Vowed that one day he'd make those banquets real.

Whoa. Time to turn the memory tap off. Clearly his repressed memory banks had sprung a leak—one he intended to dam up right now.

The arrival of the waiter was a welcome distraction, and once they'd both ordered he focused on Holly. Her cerulean eyes were fringed by impossibly long dark lashes that contrasted with the corn-gold of her hair.

'And do you cook? Or just appreciate others' cooking?' she asked.

'I can cook, but I'm not an expert. When I have time I enjoy it. What about you?'

Holly grimaced. 'I can cook too, but I'm not inspired at all. I am a strict by-the-recipe girl. I wish I enjoyed it more, but I've always found it quite stressful.' Discomfort creased her forehead for a second, as if she regretted the words, and she looked down. 'Anyway, today I don't need to cook.'

For a stupid moment he wanted to probe, wanted to question the reason for that sudden flitting of sadness across her face.

Focus on the goal here, Petrelli.

He leant forward. 'If you accept my offer of a deal you could eat out every day. You need never touch a saucepan again.'

'Nice try, but no thanks. I'll soldier on. Truly, Stefan, nothing you offer me can top the idea of presenting Il Boschetto di Sole to my father.'

'That's the plan?'

'Yup.'

'You'll sign it over lock, stock and barrel?'

'Yup.'

'But that's nuts. Why hand over control?' The very idea gave him a sense of queasiness.

'Because it's the right thing to do.'

'If Roberto Bianchi had wanted your father to have the grove he'd have left it to him.'

Something that looked remarkably like guilt crossed her face as she shook her head. 'My father has given his life to Il Boschetto di Sole—I could never ask him to work for me. I respect him too much. If the Romanos are to own the grove then it will be done properly. Traditionally.'

'Pah!' The noise he'd emitted hopefully conveyed his feelings. 'Tradition? You will hand over control because of *tradition*?'

'What is so wrong with that? Just because you have decided to turn your back on tradition it doesn't mean that's the right thing to do.'

His turn to hide the physical impact he felt at her words—at the knowledge that Holly, like the rest of Lycander, had judged him and found him wanting.

No doubt she believed the propaganda and lies Alphonse had spread and Stefan hadn't refuted. Because in truth he'd welcomed it all. To him it had put him in the same camp as his mother, had made the guilt at his failure a little less.

'So you believe that just because something is traditional it is right?'

'I didn't say that. But I believe history and tradition are important.'

'History is a great thing to learn from, but it doesn't have to be repeated. It is progress that is important—and if you don't change you can't progress. What if the inventor of the wheel had decided not to bother because *traditionally* people travelled by foot or on horseback? What about appalling traditions like slavery?'

'So do you believe monarchy is an appalling or outdated tradition? Do you believe Lycander should be a democracy?'

'I believe that is a debatable point. I do not believe that just because there has been a monarch for centuries there needs to be one for the next century. My point is that if the crown headed my way I would refuse it. Not on democratic principles but for personal reasons. I don't want to rule and I wouldn't change my whole life for the sake of tradition. Or duty.'

'So if Frederick had decided not to take the throne you would have refused it?'

'Yup.'

Stefan had no doubt of that. In truth he'd been surprised that Frederick had agreed. Their older half-brother Axel, Lycander's 'Golden Prince', had been destined to rule, and from all accounts would have made a great ruler.

As a child Stefan hadn't known Axel well—he had been at boarding school, a distant figure, though he had always shown Stefan kindness when he'd seen him. Enough so that when Axel had died in a tragic car accident Stefan had felt grief and would have attended the funeral if his father had let him. But Alphonse had refused to allow Stefan to set foot on Lycandrian soil.

Axel's death had left Frederick next in line and his brother had stepped up. *More fool him.*

'My younger brothers would be welcome to it.'

'You'd have handed over the Lycandrian crown to one of the "Truly Terrible Twins"?'

An image of his half-brothers splashed on the front page of the tabloids crossed his mind. Emerson and Barrett rarely set foot in Lycander, but their exploits sold any number of scurrilous rags.

'Yes,' he stated—though even he could hear that his voice lacked total conviction.

Holly surveyed him through narrowed eyes. 'Forget tradition. What about duty? Wouldn't you have felt a *duty* to rule? A duty to your country?'

'Nope. I think Frederick's a first-class nutcase to take it on. I have one life, Holly, and I intend to live it for myself.' Exactly as he so wished his mother had done. 'I don't see anything wrong with that as long as I don't hurt anyone.'

She leaned across the table and her blue eyes sparkled, her face animated by the discourse. 'You could argue that by not taking the throne Frederick would have been hurting a whole country.'

Stefan surveyed her across the table and she nodded for emphasis, her lips parted in a small 'hah' of triumph at the point she'd made, and his gaze snagged on her mouth. Hard to remember the last time a date had sparked this level of discussion, had been happy to flat-out contradict him. Not that Holly *was* a date…

As the silence stretched a fraction too long her lips tipped in a small smirk. 'No answer to that?'

'Actually, I do. I just got distracted.'

For a moment confusion replaced the smirk. 'By wh—?' And then she realised, and a small flush climbed her cheekbones.

Now the silence shimmered. Her eyes dropped, skimmed over his chest, and then she rallied.

'Good excuse, Mr Petrelli, but I'm not buying it. You have no answer.'

For a moment he couldn't even remember the question. *Think. They had been talking about Frederick.* What might have happened if he had refused the throne…

'I have an answer. It could be that Emerson or Barrett would turn into a great ruler. Or Lycander would become a successful democracy.'

'And you would be fine with that?'

'Sure. It doesn't mean I don't care about Lycander—I'm just not willing to give up my whole life for it, for the sake of tradition or because I "should". One life. One chance.'

His mother's life had been so short, so tragic, because of the decisions she'd made—decisions triggered by duty and love.

'Don't you agree?'

'No. Sometimes you have to do what you "should" do because it is the *right* thing to do. And that is more important than what you *want* to do.'

Stefan frowned, suspecting that she was speaking in specific terms rather than general. 'So what are your dreams? Your plans for life. Let's say you win Il Boschetto di Sole and give it to your father—what then?'

'Then I will help him—work the land, have kids...' Her voice was even; the animation had vanished.

'And if you don't win?'

'I *will* win.'

He raised an eyebrow. 'Humour me. It's a hypothetical question.'

'I don't know... I would have to see what my father wished to do—whether he wanted to stay on at Il Boschetto di Sole, what your plans for the grove would be.'

'OK. So let's say your father decides to retire, live out the rest of his life peacefully in his home or elsewhere in Lycander.' A memory of her utter focus on her work earlier came to him. 'What about marketing? Would you like to give that a go? Build a career?'

There was a flash in her blue eyes; he blinked and it was gone.

'My career is on Il Boschetto di Sole.'

'What is your job there?'

'I've helped out with most things, but I was working in admin before…before I came to London.'

'Tell me about what you were working on earlier today. In the suite.'

A hesitation and then a shrug. A pause as the waiter arrived with their starters. She thanked him, speared a king prawn and then started to speak.

'Lamberts have a pretty major client in the publishing field and they're looking to rebrand their crime line. I've been working on that.'

Her voice started out matter-of-fact, but as she talked her features lit up and her gestures were expressive of the sheer enthusiasm the project had ignited in her.

'I've helped put a survey together—you know, a sort of list of twenty questions about what makes a reader choose a new book or author, what sort of cover would inspire them to give something a try… Blood and gore versus a good-looking protagonist. Also, do people prefer series or stand-alones? We'll need to analyse all the data and come up with some options and then get reader opinion across a broad spectrum. Because we also want to attract readers who don't usually read that genre. Then we need some social media, some—'

She broke off.

'Oh, God. How long have I been talking for? You should have stopped me before you went comatose with boredom.'

'Impossible.'

'To stop me?'

Her stricken look made him smile. 'No! I meant it would have been impossible for me to have been bored. When you speak of this project you light up with sheer passion.'

The word caused him to pause, conjuring up other types

of passion, and he wondered if her thoughts had gone the same way.

Unable to stop himself, he reached out, gently stroked her cheek. 'You are flushed with enthusiasm…your eyes are alight, your whole body is engaged.'

Stop right there. Move your hand away.

Yet that was nigh on impossible. The softness of her skin, her small gasp, the way her teeth had caught her under lip as her eyes widened… All he wanted to do was kiss her.

Cool it, Petrelli.

Failing finding a handy waiter with an ice bucket, he was going to have to find some inner ice.

Leaning back, he forced his voice into objective mode. 'Sounds to me as though what you want to do is pursue a career in marketing. Not take up a job on Il Boschetto di Sole.'

She blinked, as if his words had broken a spell, and her lips pressed together and her eyes narrowed as she shook her head. Shook it hard enough that tendrils of hair fell loose from her strategically messy bun.

'That is not for me. I couldn't do what you did. Walk away from my duty to pursue a career.'

Her words served as effectively as an ice bucket could have and he couldn't hold back an instinctive sound of denial. 'That's not exactly how it went down.'

'So how *did* it go down? As I remember it, you decided to renounce Lycander and your royal duties to live your own life—away from a country you felt you had no allegiance to. But you were happy to accept a severance hand-out from Alphonse to help set you up in the property business.'

Gall twisted his insides that she should believe that.

'Alphonse gave me nothing.'

And Stefan wouldn't have taken it if he had tried.

'I ended up in property because it was the only job I could find.'

He could still taste the bitter tang of grief, fear and desperation. He'd arrived in London buoyed up by a sense of freedom and relief that he'd finally escaped his father, determined to find out what had happened to his mother. His discoveries had caused a cold anger to burn inside him alongside a raging inferno of guilt.

His mother had suffered a serious mental breakdown. The staff at the hostel that had taken her in had had no idea of her identity, but to Stefan's eternal gratitude they had looked after her. Though Eloise had never really recovered, relapsing and lurching from periods of depression to episodes of relative calm until illness had overtaken her.

In his anger and grief he had started his search for a job under an assumed name, changed his surname by deed poll and got himself new documentation, determined to prove himself without any reference to his royal status.

It hadn't been easy. And he would be grateful for ever to the small independent estate agent who'd taken pity on him. His need for commission had honed his hitherto non-existent sales skills and negotiating had come naturally to him.

'Luckily I was a natural and it piqued my interest.'

Holly tipped her head to one side. 'But how did you go from that job to a multibillion-pound business?'

Was that suspicion in her voice? The idea that she still believed Alphonse had funded him shouldn't matter but it did.

'I worked hard and I saved hard. I worked multiple jobs, I persuaded a bank to take a chance on me, I studied the market and invested in properties until I had a diverse portfolio. Some properties I bought, did up and sold, others I rented out. Once my portfolio became big enough I set up a company. It all spiralled from there.'

And when it had he had resumed his own identity, wanting the world to know what he had made of himself.

'You make it sound easy.'

'It wasn't. Point is, though, I did it on my own.'

Holly was silent for a moment, almost absentmindedly forking up some Udon noodles. 'So what about today? That site we visited? It looked like it was in a pretty poor area.'

'It is. We're building social housing. Projects like that are taken on by a separate arm of my business. The problem with the housing market is the huge differential in regional properties, and overall houses are becoming unaffordable—which is wrong. Equally, there is insufficient social housing and the system can backfire, or people are expected to live in unsafe, horrible conditions and not have a lot of redress. I work to try and prevent that. I plough a proportion of the company's profits back into building more houses, better houses. More affordable houses. Both for young people to buy and people who can't afford to buy to rent at reasonable prices. And for those who haven't the money to afford the most basic of rent. The amount of homelessness in rich countries is criminal and—'

He broke off.

'Sorry. It's a bit of a pet peeve I have. No need to bore you with it.' But it was a subject that he felt strongly about. His mother had spent periods of time homeless, too ill after her breakdown to figure out the benefits system.

'I'm not bored either,' Holly said softly. 'I think your commitment to put money into the system, to help people, is fantastic. Your enthusiasm lights up your face.'

She lifted her hand in a mirror gesture of his earlier one and touched his cheek, and his heart pounded his ribcage.

'I admire that. As well as your phenomenal success. I feel bad that I believed Alphonse funded it.'

'It's OK.' He knew the whole of Lycander believed the

same; his father's propaganda machine had churned out fictional anti-Stefan stories with scurrilous precision.

'But why don't you set the record straight?'

Her hand dropped to cover his; she stroked her thumb across the back and his body stilled as desire pooled in his gut.

'There is no point. For a start, who would believe me? Plus, at the end of the day I did walk away from Lycander.'

'Then why do you want Il Boschetto di Sole? You own properties throughout Europe. Why do you want one Lycandrian lemon grove if you have no love for Lycander at all?'

An image of his birthplace suddenly hit him—the roll of verdant fields, the swoop and soar and dip of the hills, the spires and turrets of the architecture of the city, the scent of lemon and blossom and spices borne on a breeze…

Whoa. It was a beautiful place but he owed it nothing. Rather it was the other way round. His father had taken away what was rightfully his and this was a way to redress the balance. A way to take his mother's ashes to their final resting place. *That* was what was important. This visceral reaction to Holly needed to be doused, and this emotional conversation with its undertones of attraction needed to cease.

'I'm a businessman, Holly. Why would I pass up the chance to add this to my portfolio?'

Her hand flew from his as if burnt, and he realised the words had come out with a harshness he hadn't intended. But it didn't matter. He and Holly Romano were adversaries, not potential bed-mates.

Her eyes hardened, as if she had caught the same thought. 'Good question. And now, seeing as the point of this dinner is to pitch to each other, do you mind if I go first?'

Stefan nodded. 'Go ahead.'

CHAPTER FOUR

HOLLY WAITED AS their main courses arrived, smiling up at the waiter, relieved at the time-out as her mind and body struggled to come to terms with the conversation. Her cheek still tingled from his touch and her fingers still held the roughness of his five o'clock shadow, the strength and breadth of his hand under hers.

This whole dinner had been a mistake, but somehow she had to try and salvage it. Though she suspected it was a doomed pitch, because she had nothing to offer. The only thing she could sell was the moral high ground, launching an appeal to his better, altruistic self. And whilst he clearly *had* one she didn't think it would come to the table on this issue.

So here went nothing.

'I understand you don't believe in tradition, but I hope you believe in fairness. I believe the Romano claim is stronger than yours. We have a true connection with Il Boschetto di Sole and we already fulfil one of Roberto Bianchi's wishes. For the grove to be a family affair, handed on from generation to generation.'

A pause showed her that he looked unmoved, his expression neutral as he listened.

'Also, you have no real financial incentive to pursue this—if you truly wish for land in Lycander you can afford to buy it. I know your father passed a law that made that difficult but surely your brother would rescind that decree?'

His dark eyebrows jerked upwards. 'And what do you base *that* opinion on? I didn't realise you had an inside track to the Crown Prince.'

A flush touched her cheek as she realised he was right; she had no idea of the relationship between the brothers but it obviously wasn't a close one.

'Are you saying he won't?'

'No. I am saying I don't wish to ask him.' His face was shuttered now, his lips set in a grim line, his eyes shadowed. 'This is my opportunity to own land in Lycander. Lucrative, strategic land—the equivalent to what I lost. You can't change my mind on this, I accept you have a case, but I'll fight you all the way.'

'Even if your lawyers can't find a loophole and you have to get married?' Perhaps she was clutching at straws, but she had to try. 'You said the thought of marriage makes you break out in hives. Imagine what actually going through with it would do to you? Surely you'd rather ask Frederick to grant you a land licence?'

Forget shutters. This time the metaphorical equivalent of a metal grille slammed down on his expression.

'Nope. If I have to get married for a year I'll suck it up.'

'But it's more complicated than that.'

'How so?'

'What about children?'

'What *about* them?'

Holly sighed. 'As I've already mentioned, Roberto Bianchi wanted Il Boschetto di Sole to pass from generation to generation—from father to son, or mother to daughter. That means that technically you'd need a son or daughter to pass it on to.'

He placed his fork down with a clatter. 'Without disrespect, Holly, Count Roberto is dead, and he certainly cannot dictate whether or not I choose to have children.'

'No, but surely you want to respect his wishes?'

'Why? I think the whole will is nuts—that's why I am trying to overturn it.'

'And I agree with that. But I don't think we can ignore what he wanted long-term. He truly *loved* Il Boschetto di Sole.'

'And I hope it brought him happiness in his lifetime. Now he is gone, and I will not alter my entire life to accommodate him. I certainly won't bring children into this world solely to be heir to a lemon grove. That would hardly be fair to them *or* me.'

She couldn't help but flinch, and hastily reached out for her wine glass in an attempt to cover it up. After all that was exactly why her parents had wanted a child so desperately—only they hadn't just wanted a child. They'd wanted a son.

His forehead creased in curiosity as he leaned over to top up her wine glass. 'Would you do it?'

'No. Not only for that!'

And yet she found her gaze skittering away from his. Her whole life her father had impressed upon her the importance of marriage and children, the need for a Romano heir to carry on tradition.

'Yes, I wanted to get married and have a family, but not only for the sake of Il Boschetto di Sole. I wanted it for *me*.'

The whole package: to love and be loved, to experience family life as it should be. With two loving parents offering unconditional love, untinged by disappointment.

One of those detestable eyebrows rose. '*Wanted?* Past tense?'

Holly speared a lightly roasted cherry tomato with un-necessary force. '*Want*. That is what I want.'

'So what happens if your children don't want to run a lemon grove? If they have other dreams or ambitions? What if they want to become a pilot or a doctor or a surfer?'

'Then of course they can.' And if he raised that bloody eyebrow again, so help her, she'd figure out a way to shave it off.

'But what about tradition and duty then? Surely if it's right for *you* to follow the path of duty it is right for them too?'

'I *want* to follow that path. I hope my children will want to as well, but if they don't I won't force them to.' Could she sound *any* lamer? Time to change tack. 'Anyway, at least I'll have a shot at fulfilling Roberto's wishes. Are you saying you have *no* plans to have children?'

'Got it in one. I have no intention of getting married if I can avoid it, or entering into any form of long-term re-lationship, and I won't risk my child being torn between two parents. It is as simple as that.'

His tone was flat, but for a second Holly had a glimpse of the younger Stefan, who had been torn between two parents. The custody battle, whilst one-sided, had been long and drawn-out, though the outcome had never been in doubt. An outcome that Alphonse had, of course, claimed to be better for Stefan—after all, Eloise had been con-demned as an unfit mother, an unfaithful wife who had only married Alphonse for his money.

Holly had believed every word—after all, Eloise had already ruined her parents' marriage.

But… 'Some parents manage to negotiate a fair agree-ment.'

'That's not a risk I'm willing to take. I will not bring a

child into this world unless I can guarantee a happy child-hood. As I can't, I won't.'

'You could opt for single parenthood. Adopt?'

He shook his head. 'Not for me. There are plenty of cou-ples out there who want to adopt and can offer way more than I can. So, no. If the lawyers can't get us out of this I'll get married for a year. I'll do what it takes to win. Or my offer still stands. I'll buy you out here and now. You can start afresh—start a whole new Romano tradition if that's what floats your boat. That way you have a guaranteed win. Or you fight it out and risk ending up with nothing.'

The waiter returned, removed their empty plates and placed the dessert menu in front of them with discreet fluid movements, giving her a moment to let his deep chocolate tones run over her skin. Doubts swirled. Stefan Petrelli wanted Il Boschetto di Sole and she knew one way or an-other he would go all-out to get it.

She could end up with nothing. And yet... 'My father loves Il Boschetto di Sole—for him it would be unthink-able to give up the opportunity to own it.'

'What about you?'

Stefan held her gaze and she resisted the urge to wrig-gle on her seat.

'Is it unthinkable for you?'

Don't look away.

'Absolutely,' she stated.

There was no way she could let her father down over this—no way she could hand it over to Stefan. That was unthinkable.

So... 'No deal, Stefan. I too will fight and I will go all-out to win.'

'Then here's to a fair fight.'

The clink of glass against glass felt momentous, and then their mutual challenge seemed to swirl and change, morph into something else—an awareness and a mad, stupid urge to move around the table and kiss him.

Without meaning to she moistened her lips, and his grey eyes darkened with a veritable storm of desire.

Get a grip.

Yet she couldn't seem to break the spell. Any minute now she was going to do something inexplicably stupid.

Pushing her chair back with as much dignity as she could muster, she forced herself to smile. 'Just need the loo,' she said and, resisting the urge to run, she forced her feet to walk towards the door.

Stefan breathed out a deep breath he hadn't even been aware he'd been holding and tried to ignore the fact that his pulse-rate seemed to have upped a notch or three. This reaction to Holly was nuts. All he could hope was that his lawyers came through soon and this enforced proximity would come to a close.

Goodness only knew what it was about her… Yes, she was stunning, but it was more than that. There was something vulnerable about her, and that was exactly why he should be extra-wary. Thanks to the will Holly was on the opposite side of enemy lines, so any knight in shining armour urge needed to be tamped down. In truth, vulnerability did not usually appeal to him; he was no knight and well he knew it.

He took a few surreptitious deep breaths and kept his expression neutral as she walked back to the table, sat down and took up her knife and fork almost as if they were weaponry.

'So,' she said. 'Now the plan is to fight it out what happens next?'

'The truce holds until my lawyers call and then, depending on what they say, all bets are off. No loophole and we race to the nearest altar with whoever will marry us. If there *is* a loophole we fight it out in the courts.'

His mind whirred, looking for another option, because in truth neither of those appealed.

'Hard to know what to wish for.'

'The no marriage option has my vote.'

'But if it ends up in the courts it will come down to who has a better case. And how on earth can any judge decide that? It could drag on for years, and if it does Il Boschetto di Sole will end up with Crown Prince Frederick by default.'

Stefan's mouth hardened; there was no way on this earth he would let that happen.

He looked at her. 'So you'd prefer to duel it out through marriage?'

'I wouldn't call it a preference, exactly.' Her expression was suddenly unreadable. 'But maybe it would be easier?'

Stefan shook his head. 'It would be an equally big mess. For starters, let's say I find a bride before you find a groom. That still doesn't mean I win. I have to stay married for a year. What do I do if six months in she decides to divorce me, or threatens to divorce me?'

Not happening. He would not put himself in anyone's power. Ever again. As a child he'd been in his father's control. As an adult he controlled his own life, and the best way to maintain that control was not to cede it to anyone else. Physically or emotionally.

'Hmm…' She took a contemplative sip of wine, rubbed the tip of her nose in consideration. 'Or I could marry someone and stay married. Then I win and *then* he divorces me and demands half of Il Boschetto di Sole.'

Stefan watched her brooding expression and had a funny feeling she wasn't talking about a mythical person here.

'Or, even worse,' he offered, 'what if I marry someone and at the end of the year she wants to stay married and refuses to divorce me?'

Holly considered that for a moment and narrowed her eyes. 'What if it happens the other way round? She wants a divorce and you want to stay married?'

'Not happening.' Not on any planet, in any universe.

'Arrogant, much?'

'It's not arrogance. Most women in my experience are keen on the starry-eyed, happy-ever-after scenario. They must be overwhelmed by my good looks and rugged charm. Or could it be my bank balance and royal status?'

'Cynical, much?'

'Realistic, plenty.' Not one of the women he'd been with in the past years had been unaffected by his status.

'And that doesn't bother you?' Curiosity tinged her voice. 'That women want to be with you because of your assets—?' She broke off, a tinge of pink climbing her cheekbones as he raised his brows. 'Your *material* assets is what I meant. It *must* bother you.'

'Why? It makes it easier; we both make our terms clear at the outset. I always explain there will be no wedding bells ringing, that any relationship has no long-term future but I am happy to be generous in the interim and hopefully we'll have fun.'

'So, to sum you up: Stefan Petrelli—excellent taste but short shelf-life and no long-term nourishment.'

'I can see why you're in marketing.' A sudden need to defend his position overcame him. 'I've had no complaints so far. I'm upfront, and I'm excellent boyfriend material. In fact next time I'm in the market for a girlfriend I'll give you a call to represent me.'

'No can do. I'm not sure I approve of the product.'

'Ha-ha!' Though he was pretty sure she wasn't joking

She tipped her head to one side. 'So at the beginning of a relationship you tell a woman there can be no future in it but they all date you anyway?' Her tone indicated pure bafflement.

'Not all. Some women decline to take it beyond the first date, and I'm good with that. Others are happy with what's on offer.'

'So for you every relationship is a deal?'

'Yes. That makes sense to me.' And he wasn't about to apologise for it. 'There's no point starting a relationship if you both want completely different things. That's a sure-fire path to hurt and angst.'

A shadow crossed her face. 'Maybe you're right.' A quick shake of her head and she pushed her plate away, rested her elbows on the table and propped her chin in her hands. She watched him with evident fascination. 'So then what happens? You both set out your terms and then what?'

Aware of a slight sense of defensiveness, he continued. 'We go on another date and take things from there...'

'Take things *where*? If you both know there's no future, there is no destination.'

'That doesn't mean we can't enjoy the journey. Because it's not the future that is important. It's the here and now.'

Stefan had spent all his childhood focused on the future because his present had sucked. It had then turned out that the future he'd pictured hadn't panned out either. So now he figured it was all about optimising the present.

'If you spend all your time homing in on the future you never actually enjoy the here and now.'

'So if the two of you keep on enjoying the "here and now", why curtail that enjoyment? You may as well keep going on into the future.'

'Never happened. I guess I like variety.' Even *he* cringed as he said it, but better to see the distaste that glinted in her eyes than pretend anything different. 'And so do the women I spend time with. I do my best to get involved with women with the same outlook as me. For the record, sometimes *she* ends it first—she opts to move on. Maybe to someone who has an interest in being seen, making headlines. Someone who wants to take extended holidays in the latest celeb hotspot.'

'So essentially you use each other and then trade in for a different model?'

'It works for me.'

He would never risk the idea that a woman's expectations might change, so it was always better to end it early so no one got hurt.

'On your terms?'

'On *agreed* terms. All we want is a good physical connection and some conversational sparkle over the dinner table every so often.'

'Define "every so often".'

'Once a week…once a fortnight. Depends on work commitments—hers and mine.'

There was a moment of silence—an instant during which Holly's eyes widened and looked almost dreamy, as if she were contemplating the whole idea. His heartrate quickened and once again a wish that this *was* a date, that this conversation wasn't theoretical, pulsed through him. The urge to reach out, to take her hand, pull her up from the table and take her upstairs nearly overwhelmed him, and as her gaze met his he could feel his legs tense to propel him off his seat.

Whoa. Easy, Petrelli.

He didn't even know what her relationship criteria were. Whilst he'd been leaking information like a sieve he had no idea of *her* status.

'So what about you?'

'What *about* me?'

'What's your relationship slogan?'

'Holly Romano: uninterested, unavailable and un… something else. I'm on a relationship break.'

'Why?'

'Complicated break-up.'

He had the feeling she'd used that line before, perhaps to deflect unwanted attention, and the shadows in her eyes showed the truth of her words. Bleak shadows, like storm clouds on a summer's day. And there was a slump to her shoulders that betokened weariness. Only for an instant, though, and then her body straightened and she met his gaze.

'But if your lawyers don't find a loophole I'll get over it. *Fast*. Because, like it or not, we'll both have to contemplate matrimony. With or without romance.'

Picking up the bottle of wine, he topped up their glasses. 'Yes, we will.'

A germ of an idea niggled at the back of his brain, but before he could grasp it his phone buzzed. A glance down showed his lawyer's name. He looked around the still crowded restaurant and picked up.

'John. I'll call you back in five.'

Holly's eyes looked a question.

'Lawyer.' He rose to his feet. 'Guess we'll have to skip dessert. I'd rather talk to him in private, so let's head upstairs.'

CHAPTER FIVE

Once in the lounge area of their suite, Holly perched on the edge of a brocaded chair and watched as Stefan pulled his phone out of his pocket and pushed a button. Nerves sashayed through her as he paced the room with lithe strides. But her edginess wasn't only down to trepidation about his lawyer's verdict; her whole body was in a tizz.

There had been a moment—hell, way too many moments—over dinner, when she'd wanted nothing more than to be like one of the women he'd described. A woman happy to pursue the here and now and take advantage of the promise of a physical connection with him.

Ridiculous. And of all the men for her hormones to zone in on Stefan Petrelli was the most unsuitable—on a plethora of levels. She focused on the conversation.

'It's Stefan.'

He listened for a moment and his expression clouded, lips set in a line.

'You're sure?'

Another moment and he hung up, dropped the phone in his pocket and turned to face her.

Holly leant forward. 'There's no loophole, is there?'

'Not even a pinhead-sized one. James Simpson did a sterling job.'

'So we'll have to get married. Undertake that race to the altar.'

Holly clenched her hands as realisation washed over her. What an idiot she'd been. Instead of dining with Stefan Petrelli, getting her knickers in a knot over a Michelin-starred meal, she should have been shut up her room formulating a back-up plan. A marriage plan.

Chill.

It wasn't as if Stefan had been out there searching for a bride. That was the whole point of them staying together this weekend.

'Yes.'

The tightness of the syllable, the drumming of his fingers on his thigh, the increased speed of his stride all conveyed his dissatisfaction with the idea.

Holly got to her feet. 'Right. I'd better get going, then. The truce is over. The stick-together phase is finished.'

Yet her feet seemed reluctant to move—or rather, for reasons she couldn't fathom, they wanted to move towards Stefan rather than away. *Get a grip.* Talk about getting it wrong. Stefan was now officially the enemy.

'So I guess this is it.'

There was no guesswork involved. This was over. Next time she saw Stefan it would be in a court of law, once one of them had succeeded in marrying. So this was their last few minutes together.

Get a grip faster, Holly.

She'd only met the man this morning. What did she want? A greeting card moment?

Damn it. She knew exactly what she wanted and this was her only chance to get it.

Without allowing common sense to intervene, she let her hormones propel her forward. She was so close to him now that the merest sliver of air separated them. His scent assailed her, her whole body tingled, and her tummy felt weighted with a pool of heat. The scowl had vanished from his expression and his grey eyes gleamed in the moonlight. Molten desire sparked in their depths as he closed the tiny gap between them.

'I know this is mad,' she whispered. 'But as we won't be seeing each other again would you mind…kissing me?'

'Not a problem,' he growled instantly.

Sweet Lord—she couldn't have imagined a kiss such as this. His lips were firm, and she could taste a tang of wine, a hint of lemon… And then nothing mattered except the vortex of sheer sensation that flooded her every sense.

Desire mounted, and her calf muscles stretched as she went on tiptoe and twined her arms around his neck to pull him closer, pressed her body against his in a delicious wriggle of pleasure. She heard his groan, felt the heat of his large hands against the small of her back.

It was a kiss that might have gone on for ever, but eventually he gently pulled away. For a moment she stood, swayed, the only sound the mingle of their ragged breathing. Slowly reality intruded—the red and gold décor, the darkness outside illuminated by the London streetlights and the brightness of the moon.

Think. Speak. Move.

The directions seemed to be blocked. Her synapses were clearly misfiring…all signals from her brain were fuzzed by the aftershock of the kiss.

Do something.

Finally the order made its way through and she took a shaky step backwards, regained control of her vocal cords. 'Right. I'll be on my way, then.'

'No. Wait.'

To her irritation he had pulled himself together way

faster than she had and now stood there eyeing her with a gleam of something she couldn't interpret.

'There is no need for me to wait.' To her relief, annoyance had served to dispel the effect of their lip-lock. 'I *need* to go and locate a groom.'

'Do you have anyone in mind?'

There was an edge to his voice. His grey eyes held a speculative nuance and she wondered if he was trying to probe her for information in the hope of using it against her.

'I have options,' she said, and kept her voice noncommittal even as she reviewed said options.

Her father had suggested he speak with one of the Il Boschetto di Sole employees, but the idea left Holly cold. Graham still worked on the grove—and the thought of marrying *another* Il Boschetto di Sole employee, even in name only, felt foolhardy. An employee might well hold out hopes of becoming a co-owner, of remaining married to her. Come to that, *anyone* she married might think the same.

She ran her London colleagues through her mind— whittled them down to three possibilities. But she could hardly call them up and propose. Plus, she barely knew them—how could she trust any of them to stick to an agreement? Il Boschetto di Sole was a huge asset—an immensely lucrative business.

'But no one specific?' he persisted.

'I'm not a fool. I wouldn't tell you if I had. Do *you* have a bride lined up?'

Now his lips quirked up in a smile that left her both baffled and suspicious. 'I'm not sure. Let's just say I have an idea.'

Which put him ahead of the game—seeing as his tone

indicated that *his* idea was a good one and hers sucked. 'Bully for you. Now, I really need to go.'

'Give me five minutes. I need to make a phone call to my lawyers. I may have a way out of this. Promise me you won't go until I've talked to them.'

Holly hesitated. 'A way out that your hotshot lawyers haven't already thought of?'

'They don't call me The Negotiator for nothing.'

'I didn't know they called you The Negotiator at all.'

'I'll be five minutes. Tops.'

'OK. I'll pack slowly.'

In fact he was marginally longer than the allotted time, and she had her suitcase packed and was at the door before he emerged from his bedroom. To her irritation her tummy did a little flip-flop—he looked gorgeous, and his smile held a vestige of triumph as he walked towards her and gestured to the sofa.

'You may want to sit.'

'I'm good here. Right by the door.'

Warning bells began to peal in her head; his smile was too self-assured for her liking. *Dammit.* Maybe he'd discovered a legal way to grant him victory.

'Just say it, Stefan.'

'Marry me.'

Holly stared at him as her brain scrambled to comprehend the words, tried to work out the trick, the punchline. Because there had to be one.

'Is this your idea of a joke? It's either that or you've gone loop-the-loop bananas.'

'No joke. I'm not entirely sure on the bananas front, but it makes sense.'

'On planet bananas, maybe.'

'Hear me out. If we marry each other we effectively

cancel out the competitive element of the will because we *both* fulfil the marriage criteria.'

The thought arrested her and she moved further into the room, studied his face more closely. 'But we'd have to stay married for a year.'

'Correct.'

'What would happen at the end of the year?'

'We would co-own Il Boschetto di Sole. Yesterday neither of us thought we'd own even an acre, so why not settle for fifty-fifty?'

'Split it?'

'Yes. Why not? This way guarantees us half each—I realise we'd need to figure out a fair way to actually divide the land, but I would be happy to do that up-front.'

Suspicion tugged at her as she searched for an ulterior motive. Was this some way to trick her out of everything? But instinct told her Stefan Petrelli didn't work like that.

Get real, Holly.

Had she learnt nothing? Her instinct when it came to men and their motives was hardly stellar.

'I don't get it. Why are you happy to do this?'

'A guaranteed fifty percent works for me. This way it also means I don't end up with a wife who will try to manipulate me. We would both be equally invested in the marriage and the subsequent divorce. This works. For *both* of us. If we have to marry, it makes sense to marry each other.'

Logic dictated that he was correct. Her brain computed the facts. She knew that her father would be more than content with ownership of any percentage of Il Boschetto di Sole. Plus she had to marry *someone*—way better to marry someone who wouldn't have power over her. But as she looked at him her tummy clenched at the mere thought of marrying him. She would be signing up to a year under the same roof as a man her hormones had targeted as the equivalent of the Holy Grail.

Grow up and suck it up.

This made sense—guaranteed her father ownership of the land he loved.

'This could work.' Deep breath. 'But we'd need to work out the rules. The practicalities.' Another deep breath. 'This would be a marriage of convenience.'

To her annoyance, she could hear the hint of a question in her tone.

Clearly so could he.

His eyebrow rose. 'Unless you have something else in mind?'

'No!' Though a small voice piped up asking *Why not?* This man was sex on legs, and they were attracted to each other. They would be sharing a roof for a year—didn't it make sense to take advantage?

Yet every instinct warned her that it was a bad idea. Stefan had freely admitted his only commitment was to a relationship carousel and she had no wish to climb aboard. What would happen when his need for variety came into play? If…*when*…she wasn't woman enough? She could almost taste the humiliation.

'This would be a strictly business arrangement.'

'Agreed. I make it a general rule not to mix business and pleasure. So, subject to working out the details, do we have a deal?'

'We have a deal.'

Without thought Holly held out her hand, and with only a fractional hesitation he stepped forward and took it.

Mistake. As she stared down at their clasped hands sensation shot through her and her body rewound to their kiss, imagined the heat of his hand on her back.

Quickly she tugged her hand free. 'I'm headed to bed.

I'll see you in the morning and we can iron out the details.'
With that, she grabbed her suitcase and forced herself to
walk rather than sprint for her bedroom.

Stefan stared at the closed door for a long moment. Was
this marriage idea lunacy or genius? Best to go with the latter. This gained him land in Lycander and a place to scatter
his mother's ashes. It also gave him control of the situation.
The only issue was the thorny one of attraction—one that
needed to be uprooted.

Holly did not fulfil his relationship criteria. She wanted
a family, a relationship that held more than just the physical, and he couldn't offer that. If he couldn't pay he
shouldn't play—and he shouldn't even have considered
the idea that their marriage might be anything other than
strictly business. He'd still been under the spell of that
kiss. From now on in he'd make sure to keep his distance,
and he was pretty damn sure Holly would do the same.

His phone buzzed and surprise shot through him as he
saw the caller's identity. Take the call or decline the call?
In the end curiosity won out.

He sank into the armchair and put the phone to his ear.
'Hi, Marcus. What can I do for you?'

Marcus Alriksson was Chief Advisor and one of the
most influential men in Lycander—a man who was close
to Prince Frederick, and a man who worked behind the
scenes to help shape Lycander's future.

'Stefan. We need to talk. Any chance of setting up a
video call?'

Hell, why not? It would be a relief to have his thoughts
distracted from Holly.

'Sure.'

Minutes later Stefan faced Marcus, keeping his body
deliberately relaxed as he studied the dark-haired man on

the screen. The Chief Advisor gave nothing away, but his dark blue eyes studied Stefan with equal interest.

'So, Marcus, what can I do for you?'

'I want to discuss the situation with Il Boschetto di Sole. Will you be pursuing your claim?'

'Yes.'

'Good.'

Stefan raised his eyebrows. 'I'm flattered, Marcus. I didn't know you cared.'

'I *do* care. More to the point, Frederick cares. You and he could be friends. You choose not to be.'

That was not an avenue he wanted to go down. He didn't want to be friends with his half-brother—didn't want to be anything. He wanted to maintain a simple indifference.

Liar.

Deep down he still craved an older brother who'd fight his corner. Once Frederick had done that. Then he'd withdrawn. Stefan knew why—because Frederick had blamed his younger brother for Eloise's departure. Worst of all, Frederick had been right to condemn him.

All too aware of the other man's scrutiny, he dispelled the memories. Now was not the time.

'Is that what this is about? A call to friendship?'

'I want to discuss a deal.'

'What sort of deal?'

'I'll get to that, but first some background. Have you heard of an organisation called DFL?'

Stefan frowned in thought. 'It stands for Democracy for Lycander, right?'

'Correct. It is growing in prominence and support.' Marcus's expression matched his grim tone, and his dark eyebrows slashed in a frown. 'But I *will* take it down.'

Stefan emitted a snort. 'People are entitled to their opinions. *Everyone* can't agree with the idea of a monarchy.

Months ago you told me Frederick wanted to allow freedom of opinion, planned to be less tyrannical than our father. Yet you want to "take it down"?'

'People *are* entitled to their opinions. But I have a personal dislike for those people who choose to express said opinions through violence and racism.'

Marcus pressed a button on his screen and turned it round for Stefan to see.

Stefan perused the site, quickly assimilating sufficient information to realise that Democracy for Lycander was an organisation of the type that turned his stomach: a group that incited racism and violence under the guise of freedom and democracy.

'OK. I take your point and I hope you nail them. But I'm not sure what this has to do with *me*.'

'Times have been hard recently. Frederick is doing his best to reverse the injustices perpetrated by your father but he needs time. Under Alphonse, housing, hospitals, education—every system—was allowed to fall into disrepair and the people are restless. The storm last year caused further damage to property, land and livelihoods. Frederick is still not trusted by everyone—is still judged as the Playboy Prince, despite the fact he is now married with a son.'

Stefan shrugged, tried to block off the unwanted pang of emotion. He'd meant what he said to Holly over dinner—this was not his problem. He owed Frederick nothing… owed Lycander even less.

'I'm still not sure where I come in.'

'If you plan to pursue your claim to Il Boschetto di Sole then I assume you're getting married?'

No surprise that Marcus Alriksson knew the terms of the Bianchi will—perhaps the only shocker was how long it had taken him to make contact.

'Yup.'

'Good. Then I have a deal to offer you.'

Not interested. Stefan bit the words back. Marcus wasn't a fool. He wouldn't have come to the table unless he was sure he had something concrete to offer.

'I'm listening.'

'Your marriage could be an opportunity for you and Frederick to mend fences.'

Stefan snorted. 'Don't play me for a fool. You don't give a damn about a touching Petrelli reunion—this is *politics*.'

'Partly. As I explained, Frederick could do with some support and the people could do with some positivity. You could provide both. The return of the exiled Prince… If you come back to support your brother it would show solidarity, and your acceptance and approval would boost Frederick's popularity. Especially if you gild that return with a wedding.'

'I'm not even sure I *do* accept and approve of Frederick and his policies.'

'Then come and see for yourself. Frederick and Sunita are in India at the moment. Come to Lycander—have a look. Then make a judgement call.'

'And if I approve? What do I get from this deal?'

'I want to use your marriage to bring you back into the family. Whether we like it or not there will be media coverage of your marriage, and there will be a lot of speculation about the will.' Marcus's face suddenly relaxed into a smile that seemed to transform it. 'My wife April…' Now his voice glowed with pride. 'She is a reporter and she assures me this is celebrity news gold. It will be played out as brother versus brother. Your story will be latched on to and revisited and I'm guessing you won't like that.'

'No, I won't. But I don't think there's a damn thing you can do about it.'

'I can provide you with a suitable bride and I can help orchestrate the publicity around your wedding.'

'I can do that myself. Hell, I could have a private ceremony on a secluded island and hide out there for a year. I get that you want to big up the marriage—make it a public spectacle for Lycander—and that you want the whole reunion and brotherly support. What do I get in return?'

'In return Frederick will restore your lands and titles, *and...*' He paused as if for an imaginary drum roll '...we'll give your mother recognition. Set the record straight once and for all—set up a foundation in her name. Whatever you want.'

Stefan's heart pounded in his ribcage.

Don't show emotion. Maintain a poker face.

But there was little point in faking either. He knew that many people believed the worst of his mother—thought her departure from Lycander had been an abandonment of her son and saw her through the tainted veil of rigged history—and he loathed it. This was a chance to vindicate her memory and he'd take it.

'Deal. But only if Frederick is on the level.' If his brother was simply a 'mini-me' of Alphonse, there was no way Stefan would play nice. 'I'll need to judge that.'

'Understood. The bride I have in mind is Lady Mary Fairweather. The licence is sorted and the helicopter is ready to go. You can be in Lycander in two hours.'

Stefan rose. 'Not so fast. I've already got a fiancée. I'm marrying Holly Romano.'

It gave him some satisfaction to see the surprise on Marcus's face.

Before he could react, Stefan finished, 'We'll talk again tomorrow.'

CHAPTER SIX

STEFAN RUBBED A hand over his face and tried to tell himself that two hours' sleep was sufficient. He pushed open the door to the living area of the hotel suite and came to a halt on the threshold. Holly stood by the window, her blonde hair tousled and shower damp, clad simply in jeans and a thick cable knit navy jumper, bare feet peeping out.

Desire tugged in his gut even as he recognised the supreme irony of the situation. This was his fiancée and she was completely off-limits. There could be no repeat of that kiss, no more allowing their attraction to haze and shimmer the air between them. For a start Holly did not share his relationship values, and secondly they now had a deal—one in which the stakes were now even higher.

For him it wasn't only Il Boschetto di Sole to be won. He could have all that Alphonse had taken from him in a deal that did not leave him beholden. And, even more importantly, he could win public recognition for his mother; set the rumours and falsehoods to rest once and for all.

But to do that he and Holly would have to play their marriage out in the public eye—something he needed to know she was on board with. It also meant they could not risk any complications, and giving in to their attraction would rate way up there on the 'complicated' scoreboard.

'Good morning.'

She turned from the window, her eyes full of caution. 'Good morning.' She gestured outside. 'Look at all those people out there...going about their normal business whilst *my* world has been upended.'

He moved closer, tried to block out the tantalising scent of freshly washed hair, the tang of citrus and an underlying scent that urged him to pull her into his arms and to hell with the consequences. But life didn't work like that. Actions had consequences, and once you'd acted you couldn't take that act back. Lord knew, *he* knew that.

So instead he stood beside her, careful not to touch, and looked outside at the scurrying figures. 'You'll find that a lot of those people will be experiencing their own upheavals and worries. But I agree—yesterday was a humdinger of a life-changer. But it is only temporary. One year and then you can have your life back. And half of Il Boschetto di Sole.'

One year. Three hundred and sixty-five days. Fifty-two weeks. God knew how many hours.

'And life doesn't have to change *that* much,' she added hopefully. 'I've thought about it. I know we have to live under the same roof, but if we can find a big enough roof we don't have to actually *see* each other much. We could even get somewhere with separate kitchens, or work out a rota or...'

'I get it—and I appreciate the amount of thought you've put into it.' Obscurely, a frisson of hurt touched him, even though he knew he should applaud her plan. It wasn't as if he wanted to act out happy coupledom. 'That sounds good, but before we settle down to wedded bliss there's the actual wedding to think about.'

'Yes. But that's not so complicated, is it? We'll give twenty-eight days' notice and then we can do a quick register office ceremony. Simple.'

'It's a little more complex than that.'

Go easy here. Clearly Holly's ideas for the wedding were a long way from the public spectacle now on the cards.

Suspicion narrowed her eyes. 'Complex *how*?'

'How about we discuss this over breakfast? And coffee?'

Coward.

'Fine.' Her forehead creased. 'Though I have the distinct impression that you hope food and drink will soften me up.'

'Busted.'

She sighed. 'Dinner does feel like a lifetime ago, and I *am* hungry. But do you mind if we go someplace else? Perhaps we could grab a takeaway coffee and walk for a while? I'd appreciate a chance to clear my head.'

'Works for me.' A chance to move, to expend some energy—perhaps the fresh air would blow away the cobwebs of intrigue. 'Any preference as to where?'

'I thought we could go to the Chelsea Physic Garden,' she suggested. 'It's not far from here. Every Sunday since I've got here I've explored somewhere in London. To begin with I did all the usual tourist places—you know, Big Ben and St Paul's Cathedral, which is awe-inspiring. I went to watch the Changing of the Guards too.'

Her smile was bright and contagious, and for an instant he could picture her, eyes wide, intent on watching the traditional ceremony.

She shook her head. 'Sorry—I must sound so gauche. It's my first time away from Lycander and I decided to...'

'Make the most of it?'

'Explore as much as I could. But I've also discovered lots of amazing quirky places, and the Physic Garden is one of them.'

So five minutes later they headed across the marble lobby, through the sleek glass revolving doors and out onto the cold but sunny autumn street. Russet leaves fluttered past in the breeze and the sun shone down from a cloudless sky.

They walked briskly. Holly made no attempt to make conversation and yet the silence felt comfortable rather than awkward. For him it was a much-needed buffer until they sat down to negotiate exactly how their marriage would work.

Fifteen minutes and a café stop brought them to the gardens, with bacon and avocado sandwiches and takeaway coffees in hand. As they wended their way through he looked around, feeling a sense of tranquillity and awe at the number of different plants on show and their medicinal properties.

'We'll walk through the rock garden, if you like?' Holly offered. 'It's the oldest rock garden in the world, partly made with stones from the Tower of London and also Icelandic lava that was brought over here in 1772.'

Her face was animated as she spoke, and for an instant he wished that they could simply wander around and explore this place she clearly loved. That there was no agenda.

'Once we get through here, and then go round a bit, there is a secluded part where we can sit.'

Different scents wafted through the air, and soon they arrived at a pretty walled area and settled onto a bench.

Once seated, he unwrapped his sandwich and turned to face her. He waited until she'd taken her first appreciative bite and figured it was as good a time as any.

'So the wedding—there's been a change of plan. I've decided to go public with our engagement.'

She stilled, her sandwich halfway to her mouth.

'This is a good time for the exiled Prince to return to Lycander—I want to use our wedding as a publicity stunt to smooth that return.'

Lowering the sandwich, she opted for a gulp of coffee. 'When exactly did you decide that? You didn't mention any return over dinner. Or when you "proposed".' She tilted her head to one side, her blonde hair rippling in the breeze as she studied his expression, her blue eyes now wary, as if in search of a trap.

'I spoke with Marcus Alriksson last night. Lycander's—'

'Chief Advisor. I know who Marcus Alriksson is.'

'And we agreed that this is an optimum moment for my return.'

'Because Crown Prince Frederick could do with some family support,' Holly agreed, and suddenly there was that smile again. 'I *knew* you couldn't be as indifferent about Lycander as you made out yesterday.'

For a daft second Stefan wished he deserved the approval that radiated from her—but he didn't, and he wouldn't let her cast him in family-man mode, nor as a knight in shining armour.

'That is not my motivation. Marcus and I have made a deal. If he can convince me that Frederick is genuine about reform in Lycander then, yes, I will offer my support—in return for the lands my father took from me. No land, no support, no return.'

Careful here. He had no intention of sharing *all* the details of the deal he'd made, and he didn't want to bring up Eloise.

He forced himself to hold Holly's gaze, saw the flash of disappointment and steeled himself not to give a damn. He owed Frederick nothing. The whole point of severing family ties was the fact that they no longer existed—couldn't be used to push or pull.

'But my motivation is beside the point. The point is that it does change the parameters of our marriage. The wedding will now be a grand spectacle, acted out on the global stage, and our marriage will be under public scrutiny. In order to be able to offer Frederick support I need the Lycandrian public to accept me—and you would be a key player in that. I would want you to be in charge of "branding" us as well, of course, as being part of that brand. I will pay you a generous salary for that.'

That was the bunch of carrots. Now for the stick...

'However, if this is too much for you take on board, I understand. We can abandon our marriage plan and go back to the marriage race. But I think it's fair to tell you that Marcus has a bride lined up for me.'

There was silence as she thought, her hands cupped tightly around her coffee cup. He realised he was holding his breath, his whole body tense as he awaited her decision. *Relax*. Worst-case scenario: he'd marry Marcus's choice of bride. Not his preferred option, but not the end of the world either.

Turning, she looked at him. 'I accept your offer—but I have an additional condition.'

'What?'

'If you don't have children I would like you to leave your share of Il Boschetto di Sole to me or my children. That way one day the land will be reunited. It seems fair to me. You are asking for my help to win more land for yourself—this way my family will gain something in the future. Something important.' Her gaze didn't leave his. 'Of course you can refuse. Marry whoever Marcus has chosen. But I think you have a better chance of pulling off a "branding" exercise with me. Otherwise, I guarantee all the publicity will be about the "marriage race".'

Annoyance warred with admiration. It turned out Holly

had a talent for negotiation too. Her request was unusual, but reasonable.

'Agreed.' No point prolonging negotiations. 'So we have a new deal?'

'Yes.'

This time she nodded her head, kept her hands firmly around her cup. 'But I'll be up-front. I *do* think you have a better chance with me, but this wedding won't be an easy sell. People will realise we are getting married through legal necessity. We certainly can't pretend it's a love match. Especially when we plan to start divorce proceedings in a year.'

'You'll need to find some positive spin.'

'Ha-ha! I'm not sure an army of washing machines could provide enough spin.'

Placing the coffee down, she tugged a serviette from her bag, a pen from her pocket and began to scribble.

'The terms of the will are bound to be published, so any story we come up with needs to acknowledge the legal necessity of our marriage. But we need to incorporate some sort of "feel-good" factor into it.'

For a few minutes she stared into space and he watched her, seeing the intense concentration on her face, the faint crease on her brow, hearing the click-click of the pen as she fiddled with it. Her blonde hair gleamed in the autumn sunlight, gold flecks seemed to shimmer in the light breeze. His gaze snagged on her lips and a sudden rush of memory hit him. The taste of her lips, the warmth of her response...

'Stefan! Earth to Stefan!'

'Sorry.'

Get with it, Petrelli.

'How about this? When I came to London a year ago I was intrigued by you—the exiled Prince of my country— so I called you up and asked to meet you. We hit it off and started a relationship. A low-key relationship, because that suited both of us. Perhaps Roberto Bianchi found out—we'll never know. Anyway, when we came to know the terms of the will we really did not want to fight—we even wondered if he'd been hoping we'd marry each other and that's what we decided to do. It could be that it won't work, and we both know that, but in that case we will each own half the grove.'

Stefan looked at her appreciatively. 'I like it. That has a definite ring of authenticity and, whilst we *are* fibbing, it isn't so great a fib as all that. Hell, it could even have happened like that.'

For a second his imagination ran with the idea. Their meeting, the tug of attraction... Only in this version it was an attraction that had no barriers, an attraction that could be fulfilled...

Whoa. Rein it in.

The silence twanged. Her cheeks flushed and then she let out a sigh. 'I think we need to role-play it.'

'Huh?' Given where his imagination had been heading, he couldn't hold back the note of shock.

'No!' Her flush deepened; pink climbed the angles of her cheekbones. 'I don't mean every detail. *Obviously.* I mean we're going to be questioned closely on this. How did we meet? Where was it? What were we wearing? How did we feel? I assume part of this gig will involve press interviews and appearances on TV. So I think we need to have a practice run. I know it feels stupid, but I think it's important.'

Stefan shrugged. 'OK. Here and now?'

'Sure. Why not?' Holly looked around, checked there was no one to see them, no one close enough to overhear them. 'So... I've written to you, asking to meet with you. Why do you agree, given that you are known to have little interest in Lycander?'

'You sent a photo?'

'No!'

'Joking! I'm *joking.*'

'Well, I'm not laughing.'

But he wasn't fooled. There was smile in her eyes—he could see it. 'Inside you are. But, OK, fair enough. I can see why this is a good idea. But let's back up a step. What did you say in your letter?'

'Hmm… Let's work backwards—what would have persuaded you to meet me? How about if I'd asked for help? For Lycander? Extolled Frederick's virtues?'

'I'd have told you to take a hike. Preferably a long way away.'

'All right. Let's say that's what you did and I took umbrage and demanded an apology. I turned up at your offices, sweet-talked my way past the front desk and…'

'You'd never have got past my PA.'

She glared at him. 'OK. I lingered behind a potted plant until she left to make a cup of coffee—or maybe she was on holiday, so it was a temp and…'

'You got into my office and I was so intrigued by your initiative I agreed to listen.'

'Perfect. We got talking and decided to continue the conversation over dinner.'

'Italian. I think we had spaghetti marinara and fettucine Alfredo.'

Dammit, he could almost taste the tangy tomato sauce, smell the oregano, picture her forking up the spaghetti with a twirl, her laugh when she ended up with a spot of sauce on the tip of her nose.

'And then a tiramisu to share, with coffee and a liqueur.'

There was a silence, and he was suddenly intensely aware of how close Holly was. Somehow during their conversation they had moved closer to each other, caught up in the replay. Now the animation had slipped from her face left her wide-eyed, lips slightly parted. One hand rose to tuck a tendril of hair behind her ear.

She looked exactly as she would have looked on that mythical first date.

'And then this…' he said and, moving across he turned to face her, cupped her face in his hand and kissed her.

Imagination and reality fused. The surrounding scents of the garden combined with the idea that this was really a date. The kiss was sweet, and yet underlain with a passion that heated up as she gave a small moan against his mouth. In response he deepened the kiss, felt the pull of desire, the caress of her fingers on the nape of his neck.

He had no idea how long they kissed until the real world intruded in the shape of a terrier. The small dog bounded up to them and started barking, leaping up, desperate for the remains of Holly's abandoned bacon sandwich.

They pulled apart. His expression was no doubt as dazed as hers, and her lips were swollen, her hair dishevelled. The dog, uncaring, continued to target the bacon, and within minutes its owner had hurried up, hand in hand with a toddler.

The little girl beamed at them. 'Hello!'

Stefan pulled himself together. 'Hello. Is this your dog?'

'Yes. He's called Teddy.'

'What a lovely name.' Holly leaned down and patted the dog, which promptly rolled over and presented his tummy.

'He likes you.'

'I like him too.'

'Come on, Lily. Come on, Teddy.' The woman grinned at them. 'Sorry for the interruption!'

'No problem,' Holly managed.

Once the trio had receded into the depths of the gardens she put her head in her hands. 'I am *beyond* embarrassed.'

'The exiled Prince of Lycander and his fiancée—caught necking like a couple of teenagers.'

'On a bench over a bacon and avocado butty!'

Suddenly Holly began to giggle and, unable to help himself, Stefan chuckled. Within minutes they both couldn't stop laughing. As soon as his laughter nearly subsided he would catch her eye and he'd be off again. In truth, he couldn't remember the last time he'd laughed so freely.

Eventually they leant back, breathless, and Holly shook her head. 'I'm exhausted!'

Stefan glanced at his watch. 'And we've still got loads to do if we're going to catch a plane tomorrow morning.'

'Tomorrow morning?'

'Yup. We're headed to Lycander first thing.'

The words were a reminder of what this was all about. The reason for their role-play was to create an illusion, to enable him to keep his deal with Marcus.

'There's no point hanging about—especially as I want to pre-empt any publicity about the will.'

The private jet was already booked. Marcus had offered the use of a royal helicopter, but Stefan had been resolute in his refusal. Until he sussed out whether Frederick was on the level he would accept nothing from the monarchy.

'I can't just pack up and go at such short notice. I have a job and...'

'I am sure Lamberts will understand—especially given the publicity potential. If they kick up a fuss negotiate. Say you'll use them to help with the wedding.'

All trace of laughter had disappeared from her eyes now. 'Is *everything* a deal to you?'

He rose to his feet. 'Everything in life is a deal. You'd do well to remember that.'

CHAPTER SEVEN

THE FOLLOWING MORNING Holly unclicked her seat belt as the jet cleaved its way through the clouds. The whole idea that she was aboard a private jet seemed surreal; in fact the whole situation seemed to personify the idea of a waking dream.

The past day they had been caught up in a whirl of arrangements—conference calls with Marcus Alriksson, packing, planning, plotting… Oddly, the most real event had been their time in the Physic Garden. Great—how messed up was her head when that role play felt real?

A glance at Stefan and her breath caught in her throat. Damn the man for the way he affected her hormones. Their kiss was still seared on her brain—just the thought of it was enough to tingle her lips, send a shimmer of desire over her skin. But it was a dead-end desire and she knew it—it was imperative that she focus on reality. Actual cold, hard facts.

This marriage was to be undertaken for legal reasons and the wedding itself was to be a publicity stunt—a means for the exiled Prince to stage a return.

A sudden sense of empathy surfaced in her. If this was surreal to *her*…

Tucking a tendril of hair behind her ear, she looked

away from the window and towards him. 'How are you feeling?'

'Fine.'

'Hang on…' Reaching out, she prodded his chest and a fizz jolted through her, demonstrating that their attraction was still alive and kick-boxing.

'What are you doing?'

'A check to see if you're made of granite or some strange alien substance. Because, assuming you are flesh and blood, you *must* be feeling something other than "fine". You haven't been to Lycander in eight years…you're about to be reunited with your brother…you—'

'I'm *fine*. It's just a place like any other.'

But his gaze couldn't quite hold hers, and for a tell-tale second his eyes scooted to the window, as if to gauge their direction, estimate the time that remained until they got there.

She shook her head. 'I don't believe you can be fine.'

'You can believe what you want.' He ran a hand over his face. 'Sorry. I didn't mean to snap, but how about we change the subject? Go through the plan of action?'

'Distraction therapy?'

'Whatever.' But his tone belied the word, held a hint of a smile. 'Let's just do it.'

'OK.' Holly ticked the points off on her fingers. 'First up, a meet-and-greet and a joint press interview with general questions.'

Stefan nodded. 'Marcus will be there, and his wife April. She'll take us off to coach us for the television interview.'

'What about Frederick?'

'He and Sunita are on a trip to India—they have an educational charitable foundation out there. I told Marcus I'd rather postpone the touching reunion scene until I've had a chance to look around…see if I want to support him.'

Holly glanced at him, caught the note of bitterness. 'You must be nervous about seeing him again?'

'Nope. He's just a person.'

'It doesn't work like that. Lycander isn't "just a place". It's the place where you were born, part of your royal heritage, and so it's part of you. Frederick is your *brother*. You grew up with him.'

Wistfulness touched her. If only *she* had had a brother her whole life would have been different. Her whole family's life would have been different. Perhaps her parents' marriage would have blossomed instead of withering; perhaps her mother would have loved her…bonded with her.

'That has to mean something.'

'Not necessarily anything good.'

His tone was flat, dismissive, and yet she sensed an underlying hurt. 'I don't buy the whole flesh-and-blood bond.'

'It's not about that. You spent time together—you shared a family life. That bonds you…gives you something to build on.'

Or it should. Sadness touched her that it hadn't worked that way for her—that her mother had been unable to find it in her to love her. Had been able to walk away and leave her behind without a backward glance in the quest for a life of her own.

Perhaps Stefan would agree that her mother had done the right thing? One life. One chance. Every man or woman for themselves. But at least he had specified that the mantra only worked as long as no one got hurt. Holly *had* been hurt, with a searing pain that had banded her chest daily in the immediate aftermath, with the realisation that she would never win her mother's love. Even now sometimes she would catch herself studying her reflection, wondering what it was about her that was so damn unlovable.

Stop, Holly. This wasn't about her.

'I just think that you should give Frederick a chance.'

'That is exactly what I *am* doing,' he said evenly. 'Marcus has arranged various visits and meetings with government officials. I'll be doing some of my own spot-visits as well. If Frederick is on the level I will uphold my end of the deal.'

In theory he was right. But she could sense his resistance to the idea that this could be more than a deal—sensed too that it was time to leave the subject.

'Right. I'm going to go and change.'

'You look fine to me.'

Holly glanced down at her outfit. 'I'm in jeans and a T-shirt,' she pointed out. 'I don't want Lycander's first impression of me as their exiled Prince's fiancée to be that I couldn't be bothered to dress up a bit.' She eyed him. 'And neither do you.'

It was his turn to look down. 'What's wrong with it? I'm still channelling the lumberjack look.' His smile was still drop-dead gorgeous, but his chin jutted with stubbornness. 'I am not going to play the *part* of a prince. I *am* one—whether the people like it or not.'

'So you're going for the accept-me-as-you-see-me approach?'

'Yes. I asked you to sell my brand—this is it. Jeans, T-shirt and shirt.'

Holly studied his expression, knew there was some undercurrent there that she didn't understand. 'Actually you asked me to *create* our brand.'

'Tom-ay-to, tom-ah-to.' He waved a hand in dismissal.

Royal dismissal, no doubt, that brooked no argument. Well, *tough*.

'You are asking me to help you win the support of the Lycandrian people. You must know that feelings are mixed about you in Lycander?'

'The people who hate me will hate me whatever I do or say.'

Why was he being so stubborn about this? He wasn't an idiot. What was his problem with playing the part of a prince? After all he had *chosen* to make this return from exile.

'What you wear is your choice. I can't strip you down and dress you in—'

Oh, hell. Had she really just said that?

'You could try,' he offered, and his voice was like molten chocolate.

'I'll pass, thank you.' Her attempt to keep her voice ice-cold was marred by a slight tremble she couldn't mask. 'The point is…'

What *was* the point? Oh, yes…

Narrowing her eyes, she erased the vision of a naked Stefan and snapped her fingers in an *aha* movement. 'When you went for that estate agent interview all those years ago, what did you wear?'

'A suit.'

'Why?'

'Because I needed to show respect. I needed to project the right image because I was the seeker, the supplicant.'

'Well, like it or not, that's what you are now. Not with the people who will hate you regardless, but the people who are willing to give you a chance. Show them that you care what they think—give them a good first impression. Once they get to know you then you can go lumberjack whenever you want. This isn't about proving you're a prince—it's about showing them what sort of prince you *are*.'

His jaw clenched and she sensed her words had hit home, though she didn't know why.

Then he shook his head. 'Point taken. But I didn't pack a suit.'

'Lucky for you, I did. Or rather I got Marcus to sort one out. It's in the back.'

There was a pause and she braced herself, then he huffed out a sigh. 'You're *good*. I'll be back in five.'

'Me too.' No point in Stefan looking the part if she didn't too.

Holly grabbed her case and headed towards the bathroom. Half an hour later she surveyed herself with satisfaction. She loved the outfit she'd chosen for her debut appearance as the exiled Prince's fiancée. Not too over the top, she'd blended designer with High Street. A pretty floral dress, with a matching cardigan over the top.

Right. Time to rock and roll.

As she re-entered the seating area her feet ground to a halt. The man was gorgeous in his uniform of checked shirt and jeans, but *this*…this was something else. The grey of the suit echoed his eyes, seeming to enhance their intensity, and the snowy shirt was unbuttoned to reveal the strong column of his throat. All she could think about was the encased power of his body, the shape of his hands, the unruly black curl on the curve of his neck…

Oh, God.

She swallowed the whimper that threatened to emerge. 'I approve.' Wholeheartedly.

The pilot's voice came over the intercom, announcing their imminent landing, and she hauled in a breath. For a moment their gazes held and she saw the sudden skitter of vulnerability in his.

No matter what he said, his nerves must be making their presence felt. Soon enough he'd set foot on Lycandrian soil for the first time in nigh on a decade. What had happened between him and Alphonse? Why hadn't he returned for his father's funeral or his brother's wedding? How was he feeling?

No doubt if she asked he'd say 'fine'. So there was no point.

Instead she stepped forward, placed her hands on the wall of his chest, feeling the pounding of his heart through the silky shirt material. She stood on tiptoe and gently brushed her lips against his. Stepped back and smiled.

He tipped her face up gently, the touch of his fingers against her chin soft and sensuous, and then he lowered his lips to hers, gently brushed them with his own. The sensation was so sweet, so tender, that she closed her eyes.

The plane jolted onto the runway, lurching enough to bring her to her senses even as his arms steadied her, ensuring she had her balance before he released her.

Then he held out his hand. 'Let's do this.'

CHAPTER EIGHT

As THEY DESCENDED onto the tarmac the smell hit Stefan with an intensity he hadn't expected. Lemons and citrus blossoms mingled with the tang of fuel, floating towards him on a breeze that had a lightness found nowhere else in the world. Familiarity hit him, and his head whirled with a miasma of repressed memories.

For an instant he froze—couldn't move, couldn't breathe—his gut lurched and he set his defence barriers at maximum in an attempt to quell the tumble of emotions that swirled inside him.

Images of his younger self—the iniquities and bleakness of his formative years, the anger and the pain and the dull ache of grief. The determination that the moment he could escape his father's control he would turn his back on being a prince.

And now he was back. Perhaps this had been a mistake.

A pressure on his hand tugged him back to reality. Holly's warm clasp offered comfort and gave him the impetus to move forward. Hell—he'd be damned if he'd show weakness. The exiled Prince would return in style.

A glance down at Holly strengthened that resolve, caused the fake rictus on his lips to morph into a genuine smile. He was back for a reason—to regain his rights, and most of all to vindicate his mother, set the record straight.

He'd walked away from Lycander with nothing—he sure as hell could walk back in now. Stand tall in his mother's memory.

Scanning the crowd, he spotted Marcus at the back of a line of press, a vibrant redhead by his side, and then questions flooded the air.

'Stefan, how does it feel to be back?'

'When are you meeting Frederick?'

'Holly, how did the two of you meet?'

'When is the wedding? What about the will?'

'Why have you come back?'

The barrage pumped his adrenaline as he worded his answers, strove for balance, aware that each answer needed to be closed against misinterpretation and twist.

'Overwhelming…in a good way… As soon as possible, but I'd like our first meeting to be in private…'

Holly's turn, and she didn't even flinch.

'I moved to London for a couple of years and curiosity overcame me—I wanted to know more about the exiled Prince, and once I got to know him better I wanted to bring him home.'

Holly again.

'I'm sure you've all heard rumours about Count Roberto's will and its connection with us—we will explain it, but in an official interview.'

Marcus stepped forward. 'Time to break it up now, guys. I promise you'll have a chance to ask more questions in the next few days. Contact my office for the official schedule, if you haven't already.'

'Hold on,' Stefan interrupted. 'I think there was one more question. Someone asked why I've come back, and I'd like to answer that. I've come back because Lycander is part of my heritage. It's the place where I was born and where I grew up—it is the place that helped make me who I am today.'

With that, and with Holly's hand still firmly clasped in his, he followed Marcus and April towards a dark chauffeured car.

Once inside the spacious interior, Marcus leant forward. 'Did you mean that last answer?'

'Does it matter?'

'No. I was just curious.' The Chief Advisor sat back. Turning, he looked at his wife and smiled, his whole face transformed with warmth. 'April will take you to your hotel now.'

'Yup. Ostensibly I'm doing an interview for my old magazine,' April explained. 'But I'll also be coaching you, checking you can pull this off.'

Stefan glanced at Holly, relieved that she had gone through their story in such detail. 'Sounds like a plan.'

Within minutes the car pulled up and Marcus nodded. 'This is my stop. I'll see you both tomorrow, for the first round of official visits.'

Soon the car pulled up again, outside a charming hotel-front, and Stefan inwardly applauded Marcus's choice— expensive without being in-your-face luxurious, just the right backdrop for a younger brother who didn't wish to upstage Lycander's ruler. The hotel had an olde-worlde charm—it was a converted chateau, complete with ancient stone walls, a paved courtyard and iron balconies.

They all climbed out, and there loomed the might of the palace in the middle distance. More memories crowded in—flash images of times he would rather forget. The enforced physical regime, the pain as he forced his trembling muscles into yet another push-up, another hoist of weights. Knowing if he missed his target by even a single rep there would be no food. And, worse, that it would be even longer until he saw his mother again.

His father's voice.

'You'll thank me for this one day, Stefan. You'll be a tougher man than me, a better prince. Tough enough so you won't fall prey to the stupidity of love. It never lasts. It never lives up to what you expect it to be. And it makes you weak. Look at your mother. Her life is miserable because she won't give you up. I would have given her wealth, prestige, but she wouldn't take it. Look at you—you show your weakness by your refusal to give her up. Your love for each other gives me the power, gives me the control.'

His father's words seemed to float towards him on the breeze, echoing in his ears, and he realised that April was staring at him. But before the red-haired woman could say anything Holly had launched into a series of questions about the forthcoming interviews and photographs, about whether April would be covering the wedding.

They were questions that politeness forced April to respond to, giving him time to recover. This had to stop; he would *not* let his father control him from the grave.

'OK. Follow me,' April said. 'Franco will bring in your luggage. I've booked a room where we can chat in private and set it up to look like your television interview will.'

Minutes later they were ensconced in a meeting room. April sat herself on a comfortable leather chair and gestured for them to sit on a small sofa.

Stefan glanced at the seat—it didn't look as if there was any choice but for them to sit up close and personal. Trying for nonchalance, he lowered himself onto the red velvet fabric and waited whilst Holly manoeuvred herself next to him. Under April's expectant gaze Holly shifted closer to him, the warmth of her thigh pressed against his, and he willed his body not to tense.

'Right,' April said briskly. 'I know the truth, but I'd like you both to act as though I don't. As if you are on camera.' Green eyes studied them critically. 'You need to look more relaxed at being so close.'

Easier said than done.

'Show you're comfortable together and that you get re-assurance from each other. Like you did when you arrived.'

Stefan blinked as an alarm bell rang in his head; he *hadn't* been acting when he'd descended from that plane into Lycander's heat-laden breeze. *No biggie.* He'd have clutched anyone's hand for reassurance when he'd been so stupidly stricken by memories.

'Let's get started,' he suggested.

April ran them through their first meeting and nodded her approval at the end. 'Good. Now, the next complicated question you'll need to field is: what happens in a year? Is this wedding just a legal necessity?'

Holly leant forward. 'We wouldn't have got married now if it weren't for the will, because it's so early in our relationship.'

'But you went to London a year ago—many would say that is a long time.'

Stefan shook his head. 'Marriage is way too important to rush into until you're sure. My father had four wives and he married each of them within weeks of meeting them. I'd like to think I've learnt from his mistakes.'

'Fair enough.' April nodded. 'But that still hasn't an-swered the question. What happens in a year?'

Holly intervened. 'Neither of us can predict the future; all we can do is wait and see and assess our relationship then. But...'

'Obviously we want a happy ending,' Stefan finished for her.

'That works,' April said. 'But you need to look at each

other when you say that. Look as if the happy ending you're picturing is riding off into the sunset together—not waving farewell in the divorce court.'

Holly exhaled a small sigh and Stefan felt a pang of guilt that he had asked her to do this—go on air and fake a relationship. Without thought he reached out and covered her hand with his.

'Good idea,' April said with approval.

He tried to look as though it was all part of the role-play, reminding himself that Holly stood to gain from this too. Guilt did not have to come into play.

'So, next big question,' April continued. 'Are you in love? Holly, you go first.'

The silence went on too long. 'We're…um…certainly headed that way…'

'No, no, *no*!' April said. 'That is not going to work. You try, Stefan. Are you in love?'

Stefan met the green eyes. 'Absolutely,' he stated, but even he could hear the false bonhomie.

The green eyes closed. 'OK. That is going to fool no one. To be blunt, it's pants, and you are going to have to practise. Given the circumstances, you *will* be asked that question or a variant.'

'Fine, we'll work on it.' Stefan shifted on the chair. 'Now, can we please move on to some easier questions?'

April met his gaze. 'I'm not sure there *are* many easy questions. For example, you will be asked why you left Lysander. About your relationship with your father.'

Stefan could feel moisture sheen his neck. 'Then I'll decline to answer. I'll confirm what everyone knows: we parted on bad terms.'

No way would he bare his soul or the memories of his childhood for the media to grab hold of. He didn't even like sharing memories with himself—had locked them away deep inside. And that was where they would stay.

'And your mother?'

'I'll tell the truth about her. That she was a good, loving woman who didn't deserve the type of divorce that was meted out to her. But I won't be drawn into a big discussion.'

Next to him he sensed Holly's withdrawal, a movement of discomfort as if she were about to say something.

April frowned, glanced across at both of them. 'Is there a problem with that?'

'Of course not.' Holly's voice sounded sure, but he could still sense her tension.

'Good.' April closed her notebook with a snap and smiled. 'You need to work on being more lovey-dovey and then I reckon you can pull it off. As a reporter, I don't usually condone lies, but I have learnt that sometimes there are shades of grey and I think what you are trying to do here is a good thing for Lycander. But it *is* risky. So please be careful. People will be watching you; they will be looking for evidence of a break-up or a fake-up. There will be a huge amount of interest in you both and you will be subject to intense and invasive scrutiny. People will do *anything* to get information, because information is valuable. So stay in character.' April rose. 'I'll be in touch for another practice session before the television interview.'

'We'll look forward to it.' He made no attempt to hide the irony but April took no umbrage, merely smiled at him

'I'll let Marcus know how it went.'

Stefan nodded. 'I'll see you out.'

Holly watched as Stefan and April exited the meeting room and exhaled a long breath. She felt as if she'd run a marathon. Her whole body ached from the conflicting signal she'd sent it for the past two hours. Pretending to be attracted to a man she was desperately attracted to but didn't want to be at all attracted to—the conundrum was testing her hormones to the limit.

She looked up as he re-entered the room. 'I've asked the kitchens to rustle us up a picnic supper and bring it to our room,' he said.

To her surprise her stomach gave a small gurgle, and it occurred to her that she was hungry. 'That sounds brilliant.' She looked at him. 'You are very good at providing meals.'

The idea was a novelty. Ever since her mother had left Holly had taken on the role of cook, desperately wanting to look after her father, and the correct meals had become even more important when her father's heart condition had been diagnosed.

'Food is way too important to miss,' Stefan said.

'No arguments here.'

They made their way up the stairs to their suite, and Holly halted on the threshold. The suite was an exquisite mixture of contemporary comfort and historic detail. The stone walls of the lounge boasted a medieval fireplace, ornate gilded mirrors and beautifully woven tapestries. Latticed windows showed a view of the mountains in the distance and the hustle and bustle of the city below. The furniture was the last word in simple luxury—warm wood, and a sofa and armchairs that beckoned you to sink into their comfort.

So she kicked off her heels and did exactly that, just as someone knocked on the door.

Stefan let a waiter in and the young man pushed in a trolley laden with sandwiches, mini-pastries, slices of quiche, miniature pies and bowls of salad in a kaleido-scope of greens and reds.

Once the repast was arranged the waiter withdrew. Stefan seated himself opposite her and they both served themselves.

'This place is utterly incredible,' Holly said. 'Just the sort of place I imagined princesses living in when I was a little girl.'

'Is that what you wanted to be when you grew up?'

'It was one of many scenarios. I also wanted to be an award-winning actress, a famous pop star, a ballerina, an astronaut and a prize-winning scientist. The key elements in all these scenarios was that I'd win prizes… Oh, and for some reason I also always imagined myself arriving to pick up my prize in a pink limo!'

Perhaps that had been her own personal assertion that she was a girl and everyone would just have to lump it.

'What about you? What did you imagine yourself being when you grew up? I mean, you were already a prince.'

Stefan's face tightened and a shadow crossed his eyes. She knew her words had twanged a memory, and not a good one. But then he shrugged,

'I was never a real prince; that's why I left my kingdom as soon as I could. But I'm back now, and if we're going to pull this off we have some more work to do.'

Her tummy plummeted as she wondered if he was going to suggest they practise being 'lovey-dovey.' Not a good plan—not here and now, with her body already seesawing after the forced proximity of their interview.

'I think we need to get to know more about each other,' she said. 'The kind of facts you learn over time. So how about we do twenty questions? I'll go first. Favourite colour: pink.'

One eyebrow rose and his lips quirked with a small hint of amusement. She had little doubt that he knew exactly why she was rushing into a fact-finding mission.

'Dark blue. Favourite film genre: Action.'

'I'll watch anything. Ditto with books.'

'Anything sci-fi.'

Forty minutes later he stretched. 'That was a good session—and now I'm ready to hit the sack. Unless, of course, you want to practise anything else?'

'Nope.' As far as she was concerned the whole lovey-dovey issue could wait. 'I'm ready for bed too.'

In one synchronised movement they both looked around.

In one synchronised syllable they both cursed. 'Damn.'

There was only one interconnecting door.

Stefan walked over to it and pushed it open to reveal one bedroom. *Well, duh.* Of *course* they only had one bedroom. They were meant to be in a relationship.

'Um… I'm happy to take the sofa and you can have the bedroom.' Even as she made the offer she knew it was foolish—knew what he'd say, knew he would be right.

On cue: 'Too risky. Given what April said, I'm sure the hotel staff will practically have a forensics team in here tomorrow. The last thing we need is a story on how we didn't share a bed.'

'So what are we going to do?' Her voice emerged as a panic-engendered squeak.

Stefan frowned. 'You're completely safe, Holly. I won't try anything on.'

That was the least of her worries—she was more concerned with what *she* might do. 'I know that.'

'So what's the problem?'

Yet for all his nonchalance a tiny bead of perspiration dotted his temple and she could see that his jaw was clenched. Maybe he was as spooked as she was.

'The problem is…' *I'm scared I'll jump you in my sleep.* 'I don't want us to get carried away by mistake.'

'We won't.' Now his voice was firm, all sign of strain gone. 'We both agreed this is a business arrangement, a marriage of convenience. That is the point of it—convenience. So adding any form of intimacy into the mix would be foolish, and I'm not a fool. We're both adults. Let's act like that. We are hardly going to succumb to pangs of lust like adolescents. The bed is huge—plenty of room for both of us to sleep in.'

Stefan seemed totally capable of letting his brain rule his pants and she should be pleased about that. His words all made perfect sense and yet hurt pinged inside her, each syllable a pin-prick of irrational pain. If he were truly attracted to her wouldn't it be hard for him to be so logical, so rational and in control?

Graham's words still echoed in her brain: *'Not woman enough...' 'Inexperienced...'* Maybe she wasn't woman enough for Stefan either—maybe he thought she was behaving like an adolescent. Maybe she'd got those kisses all wrong. Maybe what had been dynamite for her had been a damp squib for him.

'You're right.' No, no, *no*! That sounded colourless and flat, as if she didn't really believe he was right. 'It would be stupid to muddy the water when the whole point of this is to make it clean and fair. Entering into a physical relationship with each other would be messy—and I'm not a big believer in your type of sex anyway.'

'*My* type of sex? What the hell is that supposed to mean?'

His anger flashed now, but Holly didn't care. If he could sit there so calm and unbothered by the idea of spending a whole night next to each other then she might as well throw diplomacy out of the window.

'The kind that has no emotional context. It's negotiated physical sex. That's too clinical for me.' A part of Holly reeled at the sheer idiocy of this statement. But the principle was sound.

'I've had no complaints.' There was an edge of frost in his voice now.

'That's because you go for the sort of woman who is on the same page as you. I'm not.'

That at least was true. Stefan Petrelli liked variety—swapped his women out at regular intervals. That was not for her.

'In which case sharing a bed with me shouldn't pose a problem.' The frost had dropped a few degrees to ice now. 'I'm turning in. Would you like to use the bathroom first?'

'Yes, please.'

Perhaps a cold shower would help. She felt hot and bothered, mixed up, deflated, angry, relieved... Every emotion in the lexicon swirled inside her. Hell—they weren't even married yet.

Fifteen minutes later she was safely under the duvet on her side of the king-sized four-poster bed, flanked by a barricade of pillows, clad in flannel pyjamas buttoned to the top, eyes tightly shut as she simulated sleep.

The bathroom door opened and closed, then a few minutes later opened again. A scent of sandalwood, a burst of steam and she sensed him by the bed. Then there was a shift of the duvet, a depression of the bed.

Holly wriggled closer to the edge of the bed and waited for dawn.

CHAPTER NINE

HOLLY OPENED HER EYES, her synapses slowly firing into life. Warm. Safe. Comfortable. *Mmm...* Her cheek seemed to be pillowed on soft cotton underlain by a hard wall of muscle. Her leg was looped over—

Her synapses quickened and her brain began putting sums together...

Oh, hell!

So much for the barricade—somehow she had cleared that in a sleep-ridden assault and she was now plastered all over Stefan. Stefan, who—thank God—was dressed in boxers and a T-shirt. Probably because he didn't own any pyjamas...which meant he usually slept naked.

Suppressing the urge to leap up with a scream, she tried very, very slowly to disentangle herself.

Too late.

His arm tightened around her and then his body stilled. Clearly he went from asleep to awake far more quickly than she did, and his eyes opened to meet hers, his expression a mix of ruefulness and question.

Panic lent her speed and now she *did* move, rolling away in a scramble devoid of dignity and hampered by the row of stupid, *useless* pillows.

'Sorry. No idea how that happened. Sorry. I'm going to have a shower.'

A shower went some way to restoring her equilibrium—perhaps one day in about a hundred years she would even be able to laugh at the whole incident.

Poking her head round the bathroom door, she felt relief wash over her that Stefan was nowhere to be seen. *Chill.* It was imperative that she focused on the day and their trip to Il Boschetto di Sole. The thought brought a semblance of calm, a reminder that all this was worth it because it would enable her to give her father his dream.

She took a deep breath and went into the living area, just as the door opened and Stefan entered.

Goodbye, equilibrium. His hair was shower-damp, its curl more pronounced. He was dressed in a tracksuit and T-shirt and her gaze snagged on his forearms, their muscular definition, the smattering of hair.

'I went to the hotel gym—showered there.'

'Good plan.'

Silence resumed, and then he grinned. 'About earlier…'

'I'd rather not talk about it.' After all her protestations of being uninterested in his type of sex she'd made an utter idiot of herself.

'Don't worry about it. It's no biggie.'

'That's not how it felt to me.' Oh, God, had she *said* that? The innuendo was not what she had meant at all. The blush threatened to burn her up. 'I mean…'

Now his grin widened. 'It's OK. I know what you mean, but I'll take the compliment anyway.'

'Please could we just agree to forget the entire incident?'

But despite herself she could feel her lips twitch; somehow the sheer mortification had receded before the force of his smile.

'Deal.' There was a knock at the door and he moved towards it. 'I've ordered a room service breakfast—smoked salmon, scrambled eggs and pancakes—so we can talk in private. Hope that's OK?'

'Sounds good.'

Five minutes later she forked up a fluffy mouthful of egg and gave a small sound of appreciation.

'What do you want to talk about?'

'Well, we've talked about a whole lot of things, but we haven't talked about how we handle our actual presence on Il Boschetto di Sole.'

He studied her expression for a moment and she focused on maintaining neutrality.

'How does your father feel about it all? About our deal?'

'My father is honoured that the Romanos will own part of Il Boschetto di Sole.'

Holly remembered his face, and the awe that had touched it when she'd video-called him with the news. Once again a conflict of emotion swirled inside her—a happiness that she could give this to him, repay her father for the years of love, the years of bringing her up single-handedly. And a selfish underlying of sadness that any hope of a career away from Il Boschetto di Sole had receded further into the realm of impossibility.

'I will need you now more than ever before, Holly. Roberto Bianchi has given the Romanos a chance to create a dynasty of our own, entrusted us with the place he loved most. To pass on for generations to come.'

'Holly?'

Stefan's voice pulled her back to the present and she pushed away any thoughts of negativity. Until eighteen months ago she had been genuinely content to live her life on Il Boschetto di Sole, to live the fairy tale happy-ever-after with Graham, have children, fulfil her father's expectations. Once she returned to her home that same contentment would return.

And if it didn't she'd fake it—because she had no intention of letting her father down. Full stop.

Focus.

Stefan continued to look at her. 'Why do I get the feeling there's something you're not telling me? If I'm right you need to 'fess up. Because I do not want any surprises.'

Stefan was right. 'It's all a bit…complicated. My father is thrilled…*honoured* to be in line for part ownership. He believes the split is fair and that this marriage is an equitable solution. But I'm not sure how he feels about *you*.'

Her father had withdrawn behind an emotionless mask when she'd explained the marriage deal, that she and Stefan would come to visit him, that he would need to welcome Stefan as his son-in-law. He had agreed to play his part, but Holly had no idea how he felt about the idea of meeting Eloise's son.

'Why? Because he disapproves of me? Half of Lycander disapproves of me, so I can understand that.'

For a moment she was tempted to let him believe that, allow that to be her explanation as to why she was worried about this visit. But there was a bitter flavour to his words that she wanted to diffuse.

'It's more personal than that. It's because of Eloise.'

'My mother? Why?'

Now his voice was a growl, and she knew that this was a touchy subject. Hell, she could relate to that—her own mother was not a topic she wished to discuss. Come to that, she wasn't over-keen on talking about *his*.

'Our parents—my father and your mother—they were…involved.'

'Roberto mentioned that in my letter, but it was the first I'd heard of it.'

'Well, they were an item. My father loved her and she threw him over in favour of royalty.' Try as she might, she couldn't keep the anger from her voice. 'Broke his heart.' Thus doomed his marriage to her mother from the outset. 'In return for the crown jewels.'

Now anger zig-zagged in his grey eyes; his hands were clenched and she could see the effort it took him to unfurl his fingers. 'My mother was *not* a gold-digger.'

'Then why did she marry Alphonse?'

'According to Roberto Bianchi because Roberto persuaded her into it—he saw it as a grand alliance, believed she would make a great princess, and he wanted to scotch the romance between her and your father. Partly because of their social disparity, partly because your father was already engaged.'

'She didn't have to agree.'

'No, she didn't. But she didn't agree for the money or the prestige. She wasn't like that.'

His tone brooked no argument and his eyes were shaded with so much emotion that she stilled in her chair even as her own emotions were in tumult inside her.

Part of her wanted to howl, *How do you know that?* But she bit the words back. Stefan had the right to hold a rose-coloured vision of his mother, but Holly had no wish to share it. Her childhood had been blighted by Eloise; *she* had been the reason for acrimony, slammed doors and misery. So Holly had no wish to hear any defence of the woman who had doomed her parents' marriage. The only thing that might have salvaged it was a son. When that hadn't happened the bitterness had continued for eight years of Holly's life. Until Eloise had left Lycander; soon after that her mother had walked out.

'I know what you want to do, Thomas. You want to follow her. You never got over a woman who rejected you, treated you like the dirt beneath her designer shoes.'

Her mother's voice had been full of weary venom and

Holly had put her hands over her ears in a familiar futile attempt to block it out.

'Go if you wish. But I will not be here when you come back, rejected again. I have had enough. We could have been happy if you could have returned my love.'

'I always told you, Angela, that our marriage would not be one of love; it would be one of duty.'

'And it could have been happy if you had been able to let go of her, given us a chance.'

'I could say the same to you.'

That had been her father's weary voice.

'Would you have loved me if I'd given you a son?'

'Perhaps I would have cared for you more if you could have shown love to our daughter.'

'What does she have that I don't? Why do you love her when you can't love me?'

'She is my daughter—my flesh and blood. How can I not love her? Her gender isn't her fault.'

Holly had pulled the blanket over her head then—variations of that conversation had been played out so many times. But that time there had been a different end: the next day her mother had packed her bags and gone. All because of Eloise.

Holly tore off a minute piece of croissant, glanced down at it, rolled it between her fingers and told herself that none of that was Stefan's fault. Or his business.

'Perhaps we need to focus on the here and now. I believe my father has complicated feelings about this marriage because of who you are, but he understands the role he needs to play and he has explained the will to the staff and workers and told them the same story we're telling the world. All we need to do today is reassure everyone that nothing will change—that their jobs are safe.'

Stefan studied her for a moment, then nodded tersely. 'Understood. Let's get this show on the road.'

The journey to Il Boschetto di Sole was achieved in silence—a silence that contained a spikiness that neither of them broached or breached. The memories evoked by mention of Eloise swirled in Holly's mind in an unsettling whirlwind, and worry surfaced about her father's state of mind and whether all this would impact his physical health.

The car slowed as they approached their destination. Further memories floated into its interior as she rolled the tinted window down so the fragrance of lemon could waft in. The familiarity of the scent soothed her, calling up images of the beauty of the lemon grove, reminding her of times tagging along at her father's heels, racing through the fields of trees, watching in fascination as the lemons were harvested, loving the tart hit of the juice.

But there had been other, less salubrious times. Despair at her mother's treatment of her counterbalanced by gratitude for her father's kindness. The fairy tale of falling in love with Graham and the pain of the betrayal that had followed. Somehow now only the pain felt real, because the happy times with Graham had been nothing but an illusion.

A glance at Stefan and she saw his look of concentration, the way his eyes were scanning the surroundings as though in search of something. Perhaps it was an attempt to picture his mother, the girl she'd once been, the young woman who had apparently spent happy times here. *Eloise* His mother. Her nemesis.

Sudden guilt ran over her—she hadn't even given him a chance to talk about Eloise. Eloise had left Lycande when Stefan had been a child—whatever her shortcomings, that must have hit him hard. Lord knew she could sympathise with that.

Almost without meaning to she moved a little close

to him. 'There are people here who will remember your mother,' she said softly. 'I'll make sure I introduce you. If you want.'

There was a pause. His grey eyes seemed to look into the distance, perhaps into the past, and then he nodded. 'Thank you. I'd like that. And Holly...?'

'Yes.'

Reaching out, he took her hand in his. 'About earlier. Whatever happened between your father and my mother all those years ago it sounds like your father ended up hurt, and I'm sorry for that. I truly believe my mother acted as she thought best, but I accept I can't know how it all went down.'

Neither could she. The realisation was ridiculously shocking. In truth, all she had was her own interpretation of her parents' viewpoints. Eloise could never put her side forward now.

The car arrived on the gravelled driveway and Holly saw that the entire staff had congregated to greet them. Embarrassment tinted her cheeks. 'Sorry... I wasn't expecting this.'

'No worries. It's good practice. In a few weeks we'll be on show for the world en route to the altar.'

'That makes me feel heaps better.'

'You'll be fine.' Stefan smiled, and all of a sudden, against all logic, she did feel better.

Franco opened the door and she climbed out, saw her father at the head of the group and ran forward.

'Papa.' Anxiety touched her—Thomas looked older than when she'd seen him a couple of months before. 'Are you taking your medicine?' She made sure she kept her voice low and the smile on her face.

'Of course. You must not worry. The past days have been very emotional, that is all. That the Romanos will

own part of this… That you are marrying Prince Stefan…
It is a lot to take in.'

'The marriage is for one year only, Papa. You do understand that?'

Worry began to seep in along with her sense of guilt.
Thomas looked thinner, even his face was gaunter than a
year before. She shouldn't have run to London. Since her
mother had left she had looked after her father—made
sure he ate, took the medication he needed to manage his
heart condition. Provided he followed all advice the doctors were confident he could go on for many years. But
had he been following the advice?

'Of course I do. Now, let us move on. Introduce me.'

Stefan moved forward, his hand held out, and the older
man took it. 'Welcome, Your Highness,' he said, his voice
full of dignity.

'Please call me Stefan. It is good to meet you, sir.'

'You too, Stefan.'

For a long moment grey eyes met blue, and Holly felt a
jolt of something akin to her jealousy of years before. Was
her father looking at Stefan and thinking of what might
have been? That this was the son he might have had with
Eloise? Was he wishing Holly away?

Stop. That way led madness.

'I thought you might like a tour.'

'Very much so.'

Thomas stepped back and smiled, though Holly could
see the strain in his eyes. 'I think it would be fitting if
Holly shows you round. Soon this land will belong to the
two of you.'

'I told you, Papa. It will belong to *you*.'

'It will belong to our family.' He turned to Stefan
'When you are done come and join me for a drink and

will answer any questions you may have. And of course feel free to ask anyone whatever you wish.'

With that he turned and headed towards the house. Holly submerged her anxiety, tried to quell the worries, suspecting that her father was overcome with emotion because the sight of Stefan had triggered memories of the past, of wandering round Il Boschetto di Sole with Eloise.

Later. She would speak with him later. Now it was all about Stefan and the creation of a good impression. Soon some of these employees would work for Stefan—men and women Holly had grown up with, people who had looked out for her and after her. Others she knew less well…a couple were new faces completely. But to a degree she held the responsibility for their well-being, and the idea was both scary and challenging.

She started the round of introductions, then stood back to allow the staff to assess Stefan, watching with mixed emotions as their wariness and in some cases suspicions thawed as they spoke with him. Stefan was courteous without being fawning, and best of all he seemed genuine.

When he spoke to each individual he listened and focused his attention on that person, which allowed Holly to observe *him*. The way he tipped his head very slightly to the left as he concentrated, the glint of the autumn sun on his dark hair, the strong curve of his jaw, the intensity of his gaze, the firm line of his mouth, the contained power of his body.

'I have a lot to learn,' he said, once he had spoken with everyone. 'But I'll do my best to be a willing pupil. I want to get to know Il Boschetto di Sole, to understand how it works.'

Once the employees had dispersed Holly looked at him in query. 'Did you mean that?'

'If I am going to own it then I accept the responsibilities that go with it. Now, how about that tour?'

Five minutes later Stefan followed Holly through a mosaic paved courtyard and up a steep flight of drystone stairs cut into the mountainside. He came to a standstill as he gazed out at the panorama of terraced areas that positively burst with lemon trees, the fruit so bright, the fragrance so intense that he felt dizzy.

'This is…incredible.'

For a strange instant the whole moment transcended time and he could almost picture his mother here, walking amongst the trees, inhaling the scent, lost in dreams of a happy future.

Next to him Holly too had stilled, perhaps reliving memories of her own childhood. Then she grinned up at him, as if pleased that he shared her appreciation of the vista.

'It's pretty cool, yes? This is the last couple of months of harvest; some people say the lemons are at their best earlier, but I reckon these are damned good. Come and try one.'

She wended her way through the trees, surveyed each and every one, finally decided on the lemon she wanted, reached up and plucked it. His eyes didn't waver from her, absorbed in the lithe grace with which she moved, the way her floral skirt caught the breeze, her unconscious poise and elegance as she turned and handed him the fruit.

'Just peel it and taste!'

The fruit was surprisingly easy to peel, the burst of scent tart and refreshing, and as he divided it into segments and popped one into his mouth he raised his brows in surprise. 'I thought it would be more bitter.'

Holly shook her head. 'It's what makes our lemons stand apart; their taste is unique—tart with a layer of sweetness.'

He handed over a segment to her, felt a sudden jolt as his fingers, sticky with juice, touched hers. He watched as she raised it to her mouth and rubbed it over her lips.

'And the texture is pretty amazing too; they stay firm for longer. That's why—'

His gaze snagged on the luscious softness of her parted lips and suddenly all his senses were heightened. The taste of the lemon lingered on his taste buds with exquisite sharpness, the trees took on an even more intense hue; the noise of a circling bird was preternaturally loud. Holly had broken off, her blue eyes had widened, and he forced himself to snap out of it. Before he did something foolish…like kiss her.

'Why what?'

'It doesn't matter.'

'Yes, it does.' Shaking away the tendrils of desire, he realised it *did* matter. 'Come on. I'm really interested.'

She shrugged, continued to walk through the tree-lined area. 'That's why I believe we should focus on a different aspect of the business.'

'Such as?'

'Well, at the moment we stock the majority of Lycandrian supermarkets and we have a pretty successful export market. All of which is great. But—'

Again she broke off and he came to a halt. 'Go on.'

'I want to make it more…*personal*. I'd like to install a factory. Make products with the lemons ourselves. We could make lemonade, cakes… There are Romano recipes going back generations. My grandmother made the best lemon cake in Europe! And there are other dishes as well—really amazing ones. Lemon chutneys and jams… And I'd like to do tours, have a museum. Honestly, the history of this place is amazing and the history of the lemons themselves is… It's really interesting. Did you know this lemon has taken hundreds of years to get like this? Originally it was a fraction of this size and inedible, bitter. Farmers were intrigued, though, and they crossed it with local oranges and eventually we ended up with this.'

'So why not do it? Take these ideas and run with them?' The enthusiasm in her voice lit her face.

Holly shook her head. 'The cost would be phenomenal; my father won't do it. I'm not sure he would want tourists here, or to be involved in making and selling products. To him all that matters is the production of the best lemons in Lycander.'

Stefan frowned. 'And he is to be commended for that. But in today's day and age you are right—other markets should be considered. You are the future of Il Boschetto di Sole and these ideas are good.'

'Maybe. But they need experience I don't have, even if I *could* persuade my father to implement them. You said it yourself—you didn't build your business overnight.'

'No, but I was starting from scratch. You already have a means of raising money. But I agree—you do need more experience first. So why not pursue the marketing idea? That would give you excellent additional experience on top of what you have already learnt. Why not ask Lamberts if they would train you?'

Holly shook her head. 'Because I don't think it would work. They've already offered me a trainee position for next year.'

'That's brilliant.' There was a silence and he frowned. 'Isn't it?'

'It's kind of them, but I refused.'

'Why?'

'For a start they're only offering it because of my new

elevated status as soon-to-be princess. For a second thing there's no point. My future is on Il Boschetto di Sole. My half of it.'

'If you believe you can do the job it doesn't matter *why* they're offering it. Plus, this job would help with your future plans for Il Boschetto di Sole.'

'I really don't think my father will buy the idea. Plus, I'd need more than a year's experience. Plus, I don't want to be based in London after our year.'

'OK. Then you could transfer to a PR company here. Even better.'

Holly sighed. 'Maybe I *will* do that one day. But not yet. My father wants me here...learning the ropes.'

There was something else. 'I'm missing something, aren't I?' he asked. 'I don't get why you can't do both. Have a job you love in marketing *and* learn the ropes. There's no rush. Why not have it all?'

'Because there are other things I want to do with my life as well.'

'Such as?

'Just let it go.' Holly's voice was low now, as they emerged from the shade of the grove.

'No.'

For a moment a warning bell pealed in his head. This was none of his business; there was no need for him to get involved in Holly's life choices. Yet he couldn't help it.

'I can see how much you want to pursue marketing, and use it to take Il Boschetto di Sole forward. I recognise that fire because I've felt it myself.' In his case it had been born of a determination to succeed, in whatever he undertook. For Holly it was a real passion, born of itself. *One life.* 'This is your life, Holly, take the risk. Go for it.'

'It's not that easy.'

The words ricocheted with an intensity that impacted him.

'It's no secret—you'll find out soon enough. My father is ill.'

'I am so sorry...'

Before he could say any more she waved a hand. 'It's OK. He has a long-term heart condition, managed with medication and a healthy lifestyle. But there is a chance he won't make old bones, and I want him to see his grandchildren. I want my children to have a shot at knowing their grandfather. Even more so now. I want my father to know the Romano dynasty will continue. I want him to see his grandchildren running around these lemon trees, watch the lemons grow.'

The words silenced him, because he could see her point, but... 'I understand that—I really do. But your father may live for years. And to have children you need...'

'A father for them. I know.' Her mouth took on a rueful twist.

'Also, having children doesn't preclude having a career.'

'I know that too. But I want to spend time with my father and I want to be here for my children. Full time.' The words vibrated with sincerity, even with love for these as yet unborn children. 'That doesn't mean I don't agree with women working—I do. But for me it's important to give my all to being a mother. I can always go for a career later on.'

She resumed walking, and as they emerged from the shade of the grove he could see an ancient stone chapel in the near distance.

Relief touched Holly's face as she pointed to the building. 'Now would be as good a time as any to show you the chapel. Then we can decide if we want the ceremony to take place there.'

The topic of her future was clearly closed.

CHAPTER TEN

As they approached the chapel Holly realised she had been so caught up in their conversation that she hadn't given a thought to the fact that this was her first visit to the chapel since her wedding fiasco. Not that she'd actually made it to the chapel then.

For a second her footsteps faltered. She wondered if perhaps she should have come here alone, to lay the ghosts of her nearly-wedding to rest. Yet somehow Stefan's presence made her feel better. His sheer solidity, his energy, reinforced the knowledge that it had been better to have the fairy tale shattered before the ceremony rather than after.

Graham had wanted to marry her for her family position, to have a job for life. Had never loved her. Their whole union would have been fake, built on foundations of quicksand.

As they approached the chapel an old familiar sensation of peace crept over her. The ancient stone walls… the arched door with its honeysuckle surround… It was a place she had come to countless times when life's complexities had overwhelmed her—when she'd been small and hurt by her mother's indifference, an indifference that had bordered on dislike. Somehow the pews had given her comfort, and she'd studied the stained-glass windows, marvelling that those red and green and blue sainted figures had looked down and seen centuries, hundreds of people coming in hope of solace.

'This is a beautiful place,' Stefan said softly as they entered, and she knew from the reverence in his tone that he could sense the history in the very air they breathed.

As she watched him walk around she felt a strange warmth that he shared her appreciation of this hallowed place.

'It's always been special to me. My go-to place when life throws a curve ball.'

'I get that, and I would understand if you don't want our wedding to take place here. If you want to wait for the real thing.'

'I'm not sure if I'll ever experience "the real thing". And somehow, because this marriage is for Il Boschetto di Sole, it feels right that we should do it here. This chapel must have seen countless marriages. Many of them will have been made for reasons of duty rather than love. Some of them will have been forced unions of misery and others will have been joyous.' As she'd thought *her* marriage would be. 'I think we should have the ceremony here. If you're good with that?'

'I'm fine with wherever we do it.'

'No doubt you'd prefer to have the ceremony in a boardroom, with an agenda and the deal written out carefully. *I, Stefan Petrelli, agree to marry you subject to the following terms and conditions.*'

Odd that she felt able to tease him, and his smile made her heart give a funny little dip.

Then his expression took on a serious hue. 'But really that is what marriage is—the ultimate deal between two people. You enter a pact to look after each other in sickness and in health. It's a deal. It's just a non-negotiable one that should last for life. Which is why I wouldn't enter it—I don't deal if I can't keep my side.'

'Does it bother you that we'll be standing here taking vows we know we won't keep?'

'No, because we both know that this is a one-year deal. It will be *With this ring I thee wed...for a year.*'

The phrase rolled off his tongue and she gave a sudden shiver. The enormity of those vows, even for a year, felt huge even as she reminded herself they weren't for real. They would be bound together for a year not by love but by legal necessity. Husband and wife. Any attempt to untie the knot before meant Il Boschetto di Sole would be forfeit.

'Is it bothering you?' he asked.

'A bit. I know we aren't lying to each other, but we are lying to all the people who will be watching.'

'Hah! Most of the guests won't give a rat's ar— bottom. And a large proportion of them will be laying bets on how long we'll last. Plus, how many people *really* believe the promises they make when they say their marriage vows? *Really* believe in the "ever after" bit of the happy-ever-after?'

'I'd like to think most of them do.'

'That is naïve. In today's age you would have to be an idiot not to consider the very big possibility that you'll end up divorced. Or that one of you will be unfaithful.'

Graham hadn't even waited to make his vow of fidelity before he'd broken it. 'Then why bother?'

'People figure it's a way of making some sort of commitment, but they know there's a get-out clause—they know they aren't really signing up for life. We've just agreed our get-out clause up-front. And I suppose some people get married because they want kids and see marriage as a natural precursor, the right thing to do.' He gestured around the chapel. 'For me, this wedding is the only one I will undertake. I know that. But you want the whole deal, and one day you might want to get married for real here.'

Holly shook her head. 'Right now it's hard to picture. I used to believe hook, line and sinker in the whole fairy tale. Now…not so much.'

'Because of the "complicated break-up"?'

'Yes.'

Holly hesitated. At some point they needed to discuss past relationships. Now seemed as good a time as any. No doubt the press would find out about Graham, and whilst she doubted it would feature in an interview, there might well be some coverage or commentary in the press.

'About that… It really was complicated. We were due to get married. Here, in fact. Then on my wedding day I found out he'd been cheating on me, so I cancelled the wedding.'

She looked down at the stone floor, traced a pattern with the toe of her foot. She didn't want to see pity or compassion in his eyes.

'That took guts,' he said at last. 'And in my opinion you did the right thing. If you tell me who he was I'll go and find him, bring him here and make him grovel.'

That surprised her enough that she looked up and met his gaze. She saw that his expression held nothing but a sympathy that didn't judge, mixed with an anger that she knew was directed at Graham.

'That's OK. I don't need him to grovel—it's over and done with. And, whilst I don't doubt your ability to make him grovel, you can't make him mean it.'

'I'd be happy to try.'

'It wouldn't be possible. In Graham's world he didn't do anything wrong.'

'How does he figure that?'

Holly hesitated. She'd never spoken to anyone about Graham's crass revelations. Yet here and now, with Stefan, she wanted to.

'The whole relationship was a con. Graham worked for my father and he saw a way to further his career. Marrying me would give him a direct line to the Romano wealth and prestige—a job on Il Boschetto di Sole for life, a house, prestige, social standing…yada-yada. He never loved me. I don't think he even liked me. But he pretended to and I fell for it. Hook, line and proverbial sinker. And the whole time he was sleeping with a "real" woman.'

'So what are you? An alien?'

All she could do was shrug and he shook his head.

'The man must be blind. Or stupid. Take my word for it. You *are* a real woman.' He leant forward, his expression intent and serious. 'You are beautiful and gorgeous and…hell, you are *all* woman.'

Shyness mingled with a desire to move forward and show him that he was a hundred percent right. To kiss him, hold him and…and then what? This was a business arrangement, and most importantly there was no future to this attraction except potential humiliation. This man liked variety.

But his words had warmed her, acted as a counter to Graham's betrayal, and for that she could say, 'Thank you. Really. I mean that.'

'No problem. I'm sorry you went through what he put you through.'

'On the plus side, I think I've learnt from it. It's shown me that love isn't the way forward for me.'

'Why? If you want love you shouldn't let one loser change your mind.'

'It's not that. Love made me blind.' And delusional. She should have learned from her parents' example;

love had warped their lives. Her father's love for Eloise had affected his whole life. As for her mother—she had loved her father with a love that had made her miserable, persevering for years in a doomed marriage in the hope that her husband would love her.

'It made me unable to see what sort of man Graham really is. I think I'd be better off in a marriage without love. Finding a good, decent man—a man who will love Il Boschetto di Sole, who has a love and understanding for the land, who is willing to make his life here. A man who wants children, who will make a good dad.'

Because that was more important than anything.

She broke off and narrowed her eyes at his expression, his raised brow. 'What?' she demanded. 'Am I amusing you?'

'No, but I think you're talking rubbish. This paragon of a man sounds boring, and the whole idea of a union like that would be soulless.'

'Soulless? Just because *you* need variety and a different woman every month it doesn't mean a good, decent man has to be boring or a union with him soulless.'

'Where would the spark be?'

'There would have to be an element of attraction, but that isn't the most important consideration.'

An element of attraction? Jeez. A sudden memory of their kisses filled her brain—and she banished them.

'Physical attraction doesn't guarantee a happy, stable relationship.'

'No, but I'm pretty sure it helps with the "happy" part of it.'

'You can have an enjoyable physical relationship without love. That's what *you* advocate, isn't it?'

'Sure, but only on a short-term basis.'

'Probably best if you stick to your relationship criteria and I'll stick to mine.' *And never the twain shall meet.*

'Fair enough. But don't go looking for this paragon on *my* watch.'

'Meaning?'

'Meaning don't forget that whilst we are married we will be on show. If you find a suitable man don't follow up until our divorce goes through.'

There was a hint of steel in his voice and she narrowed her eyes.

'And does the same go for you? Because *that* is something we haven't discussed.'

'Meaning?' His question echoed hers.

'Well, what *is* your relationship plan for this year? We've agreed this is a marriage of convenience, but I'd prefer it if you didn't see other women, no matter how discreetly.'

His expression solidified to ice. 'I have no intention of seeing other women. I'm not a fool either. It would hardly do my image any good. And even if I were guaranteed anonymity I wouldn't expose you to that sort of public humiliation. I'm not as unprincipled as you seem to think. Liking variety does *not* make me a cheat. Whilst we are married I'll be taking my vows seriously.'

For some reason the words seemed to ring through her brain, taking the whole situation from the realm of the surreal to cold, hard reality. *Vows.* They would be standing up and taking vows. In this very chapel. Looked down upon by the figures in the stained-glass windows, watched by a congregation seated on these pews. How on earth had all this happened?

Pull yourself together.

'Good. I'm glad that's sorted. Shall we go and meet with my father now?'

* * *

Stefan entered the cool confines of the Romano villa and wondered whether his mother had been a regular visitor or whether she and Thomas Romano had tried to fight their feelings for each other. There was so much Thomas could tell him, but he knew he couldn't ask.

Holly had made it clear that Eloise had hurt Thomas deeply, and he suspected the ramifications of that hurt had gone deeper than Holly had told him. In addition, Thomas was not a well man. So this visit needed to be polite but impersonal, kept to questions about Il Boschetto di Sole so that a fair split of the land could be devised.

He watched as Holly went forward to greet her father, saw the worry and the anxiety and the love in her blue eyes as she laid a hand on his arm, questioned him in a low voice.

Her father smiled, nodded and then moved forward to greet Stefan. 'Welcome to our home.'

'Thank you.'

He followed Thomas and Holly into a spacious kitchen. Though clean and sunlit it had an air of disuse, no smell of cooking lingered, and the surfaces were almost too pristine.

Holly glanced around and a small frown creased her forehead. 'Would you like a drink?' she offered. 'Tea?'

'That would be great.'

He noted that once she put the kettle on she went around and did a quiet check of all the cupboards. Her lips pressed together and her frown deepened.

Thomas Romano seemed oblivious to his daughter's actions, and instead focused on Stefan. 'So what do you think of Il Boschetto di Sole? I hope the staff were all helpful.'

'It is a truly beautiful place.' A place he knew his mother had loved...a place he would bring her ashes.

'Yes.' The older man sighed and then smiled. 'I understand from Holly that you wish to divide the estate between you?'

Holly approached the table, placed a tray with a teapot, delicate china cups and a plate of biscuits down. 'That is what Stefan wishes to discuss, Papa, but that need not be done today if you're tired.'

'I have already given the matter some thought.' Thomas turned his gaze to Stefan. 'I have looked at yields, at the economic and practical feasibility of where to draw the lines so that from a monetary viewpoint the split is as fair as can be. But there are other matters to consider. This place is a community, and I care about all the people who work here. Any split has to take their livelihoods into consideration.'

'Of course.' Stefan nodded. 'I understand that there are further considerations. I am sure there are places here that are meaningful to the Romanos.' He turned to Holly. 'I believe the chapel is important to you and I understand that—perhaps that should be included in your half? In return, I would like the Bianchi villa to be included in mine.'

The villa where his mother would have stayed.

Holly glanced at her father and Stefan pushed down a sensation of frustration. He did understand the idea of respect, but Holly was part of this too. Technically this was *her* decision to make.

'I have already included that in my proposal.' Thomas sipped his tea. 'I have also suggested giving you Forester's Glade. It's a place that your mother loved—Eloise said she found peace there, even when the decisions she had to make were hard.'

He grimaced suddenly and Holly leaned forward, her face twisted with worry.

'Papa?'

'I am fine, Holly.'

'No, you aren't. Have you been taking your medication?'

'Of course. I told you. I am *fine*.'

'I'll stay here tonight.'

'No.' Now Thomas's voice was authoritative. 'I do not want ill-founded rumours of my ill-health to circulate and I know how important it is that you and Stefan present as an engaged couple should.' He reached up and took Holly's hand. 'Truly. Holly, I am fine. But if it will make you feel better I will ask Jessica Alderney to come and stay.'

Holly twisted a tendril of hair around her finger. 'That *would* make me feel better. And I'll check in tomorrow.'

'Good. I will look forward to it. I have missed you; I am happy that soon you will be back here.' Thomas nodded to Stefan. 'Stefan, it was good to meet you. Please feel free to visit Il Boschetto di Sole any time. I look forward to your views on my proposal.'

'I am sure we can all come to an agreement.' Rising, he held out a hand, shook the older man's hand and turned to Holly. 'You ready?'

'Yes.' Not that she sounded sure, and her blue eyes were worried as they rested on her father.

'Go!' Thomas smiled as he made shooing motions with his hands. 'I will talk to you tomorrow.'

Holly moved over to kiss his cheek and then followed Stefan from the room.

As they headed to the car she stopped, turned to him. 'Would you like to go to Forester's Glade?'

He halted, touched at the question.

'It may be a while before you can head out here again.'

'I'd like that.'

Or at least he thought he would. The idea sent a skitter of emotion through him.

As if she sensed it, she slipped her hand into his. The gesture felt somehow right and he left it there, clasped firmly as they wended their way through another terrace of lemon trees, the fragrance as intense as earlier. Once through this they started to climb a set of steep winding stairs cut into the mountain face.

A glance at her face and he could see that anxiety still lingered in the troubled crease of her forehead. 'I think you're worrying too much about your father.'

'That's easy for you to say. I know my father. Before I went to London I made sure he took his medication, ate right and followed the doctor's orders. Now he's on his own I am not at all convinced he is doing any of that.'

'He looked OK to me.'

Holly shook her head. 'Nowhere near as good as he looked last time I saw him. I checked his cupboards and they are all full.'

'That's good, isn't it?'

'No—because they are full of unopened bags of pasta, unopened *everything*. I don't think he's cooked anything since I left. I think he's been getting take-aways and he's done a big clean-up before I arrived.'

'Surely that is his choice to make?'

'So you suggest that I sit back and allow him to jeopardise his health?'

Stefan considered her words. 'Pretty much, yes. Sure, you can advise him to take care, remind him, but other than that it is up to him. He's a grown man; he is also a man with huge responsibilities on the work front. I can't believe he is incapable of sticking to a healthy diet.'

'It's not incapability. It's habit. He's just used to someone doing it for him.'

'Then hire a housekeeper.'

'He doesn't want to do that. Says he prefers family

around him. Jessica Alderney is a friend—she's also a trained nurse and an excellent cook—but she isn't *family*.'

Stefan frowned. 'So you will live on Il Boschetto di Sole for life?'

Through duty. Do the right thing, marry her supposed paragon, have Romano heirs, look after her father. It was not his business—and who was to say she was wrong?

'You make it sound like a prison sentence. It isn't. *Look* at this place. Plus, my father is entitled to my support and my help. I love him and I have a vested interest in keeping him healthy.'

They came to the end of a small wooded copse and she stopped.

'OK. We're here. Forester's Glade—or Radura dei Guardaboschi.'

The view stopped his breath. The glade had an aura of magic, conifers, a babbling brook, meadow flowers, a waterfall.

'I always used to imagine sylvan nymphs lived here,' Holly said softly. 'My father used to bring me up here sometimes when I was small and I'd play for hours. Anyway, would you prefer if I left you on your own?'

'No. It's fine.'

Stefan hauled in a breath, inhaled the scent of the conifers overlaid by the meadow flowers, looked at the verdant greens mingled with the deep copper brown of the soil, the blue of the late afternoon sky. He wondered if his mother had come here to make the fateful decision to marry his father—whether she had done it because she had been pressured into it by her guardian, persuaded to do her duty because it was the 'right' thing to do.

In so doing she'd made a grave mistake. And he didn't want Holly to do the same. Before he could change his mind, he turned to her.

'My mother...' he began. 'I know you have doubts about her, and in truth I don't know the history between her and your father. What I *do* know, from what Roberto Bianchi said, is that he pushed her into marriage with my father for the sake of duty. Perhaps she stood right here and made the decision. And perhaps she figured it wouldn't be so bad. Maybe she was swayed by the idea of the pomp and glamour of being a princess. Perhaps she did want to rule—to be the mother of royalty. Perhaps she believed she was doing the best for your father. Roberto Bianchi would never have permitted them to marry. Maybe she did what she thought was right. Just like you are trying to do.'

As he talked they continued to walk through the glade. They came to a stop at the edge of a cliff and he sat down on a grassy tussock, waited as she settled beside him.

'There is a lot I don't know—will never know now—but what I do know is that her marriage was worse than miserable. All the possessions in the world didn't change that.'

He didn't look at her—didn't want to see her expression of dismissal or disbelief. He knew that many in Lycander did still believe that his mother had been at fault. Instead he focused on the horizon, on the feel of the grass under his fingers.

'She didn't complain, but I sensed her unhappiness, saw how my father treated her—he made no attempt to hide it. Perhaps their marriage was doomed because she didn't love him. Because she loved your father. Alphonse claimed to love her, but it seemed to me that he treated her like a plaything—a remote-controlled toy that *he* needed to control. If she didn't comply, made a mistake, it made him angry. I saw the bruises on her. I just didn't understand where they came from.'

He sensed Holly's movement, her shift closer to him.

Her body was close and so he continued, hoping against hope that she'd believe his words.

'So whatever her reasons for marrying him—doing her duty, doing what she felt to be right—it was a mistake. If she could have turned the clock back she wouldn't have made the same decision.'

'Maybe she would because she had you.'

The words cut him like a knife. 'No. I was the reason she was in my father's control—he had the power to take me away from her.'

He'd been the pawn that had ensured her compliance and in the end had brought her down. So it had all been for naught; she should have cut her losses long before.

'She loved you, Stefan. Be glad of that.'

Glad—how could he be glad when her loving him had cost her so much? *Enough*. This was not a conversation that he wanted or needed to have.

'Holly, just take heed. Live your life as you want to live it—you've got *one* shot. Don't waste it, or throw it away to do what is "right" for others.'

Holly sighed and he turned, saw the tears that sparkled on her eyelashes.

'What's wrong?'

'It's all so sad…'

A swipe of her eyes and then she shifted to face him, leant forward and kissed his cheek. The imprint of her lips was so sweet his heart ached.

'Thank you. For sharing.'

Warning bells clanged in his head. *Again*. A chaste kiss should not evoke an ache in his heart. Time to pull back—way, *way* back.

'You're welcome.'

A glance at his watch, a final look around the glade and he rose to his feet, stretched out a hand to pull her up

He noted the feel of her fingers around his, the jolt it sent through his whole body.

Make that time to pull way, way, *way* back. This marriage was a business deal, and he had no intention of blowing it with an injudicious sharing of emotion.

CHAPTER ELEVEN

HOLLY OPENED HER EYES, relieved to see that this morning she was firmly on her side of the pillow barrier. A quick glance over showed that Stefan's side was empty, and she wondered if he'd even made it to bed. He had cited work the previous evening on their return from Il Boschetto di Sole, and remained glued to his laptop for the duration.

Part of her had welcomed the time to reflect, and part of her had wanted to hold him, to offer comfort after he'd given her that insight into his parents' marriage.

Guilt and mixed emotions had swirled inside her. She had grown up believing Eloise to be evil incarnate, the harbinger of all her parents' troubles. Now that picture no longer held good; the woman evoked by Stefan had been a victim just as much as anyone else. Another victim of love and duty. Could Stefan be right? That sometimes following the dutiful path wasn't the right way?

No! Her situation was a far cry from Eloise's. Her father loved her, and she wasn't in love with anyone else… The choice to look after her father was made from love, not duty, and she wanted a family. Yet doubt had unfurled a shoot, and she swung her legs out of bed, determined not to contemplate it or allow it to flourish.

Showered and dressed, she emerged into the living area, found him sitting again in front of the screen.

A continental breakfast was already spread on the table and he glanced up, gestured towards it. 'Help yourself.'

As she ate, he pushed the screen aside and came to join her. 'Have you looked at the itinerary for the day?'

'Of course.' She sensed the question was part rhetorical, part designed to indicate that today was all about business. 'We're visiting a nursery, a school and a community centre. Are you feeling OK?' Surely he must feel *some* trepidation about the day ahead; the idea of putting himself out there to many Lycandrians.

'Of course,' he returned. 'I'm looking forward to seeing if Frederick is making a difference.'

The statement had an edge to it, and she wasn't sure whether he hoped his brother was succeeding or failing.

The rest of breakfast was a silent affair, only today the silence didn't feel comfortable, and later, when they left the hotel, although he took her hand it felt false—she would swear she sensed reluctance in his fingers, knew it was done solely for the sake of their charade.

The car drove them through streets that spoke of the rich elite that Lycander was known for, filled with colonial mansions, freshly painted terracotta villas, but gradually, as they proceeded, the surroundings became dingier, evidence of poverty more and more apparent in graffiti and an air of dilapidation. Yet there were signs of change: construction under way, the hum of lorries transporting building materials, rows of newly built houses.

Still, the contrast between the glitz and glamour of Lycander's centre and its outskirts was stark indeed.

Franco pulled up in a narrow street outside a ramshackle building that, despite its lopsided air, did attempt a sense of cheer. The walls were painted bright yellow, and a sign jauntily proclaimed 'Ladybirds Nursery'. Yet Stefan's face looked grim as they emerged from the car, stepped forward to meet Marcus.

'Does this building comply with *any* building standards?'

'Yes.' Marcus's voice was even. 'I know it doesn't look like much, but it is safe—and, as you can see, the staff have made an effort to make it look welcoming. The children are also looking forward to showing you the garden at the back. Feel free to inspect every centimetre of it yourself. It *is* safe or I would not allow it to be open.'

Stefan relaxed slightly, and his smile was in place as the nursery leader came out with a group of young children to meet them. A small pigtailed girl approached Holly, curtsied, and handed her a posy of flowers

Holly went down on her haunches to thank her. 'Thank you, sweetheart. What's your name?'

'Sasha.'

'Well, Sasha, these are beautiful, and we are really looking forward to seeing your nursery.'

'I love it,' the little girl confided. 'My big sister is really jealous, because it wasn't here when she was little. The teachers are really nice, and we have lots of fun. And it means my mum can go and work. "So everyone wins," she says.' She gave a hop of excitement. 'And we get lunch here and it's really nice. Me and my best friend Tommy are going to show you and the Prince around the kitchens. Is it fun being a princess?'

'Well, I'm not quite a princess yet. But I think one of my favourite things will be meeting people like you!'

Sasha looked up at Stefan, then back to Holly. 'Is it OK if I ask him something?' she whispered.

'Of course it is.'

Stefan, who must have overheard the whispered words,

smiled down at her. 'Go right ahead—what do you want to know?'

'Are you like a prince from the fairy tales?'

Stefan smiled, but Holly caught sadness behind the smile.

'No, I don't think I am. But I want to be a good prince if I can. I want to help people.'

The words, though simple, were sincere, and Holly knew with gut-deep certainty that he meant them. That this wasn't all part of the charade.

'Now, Holly and I would love it if you'd show us round.'

Sasha slipped her hands into theirs and they entered the nursery. The converted house, though small, had been subdivided into four rooms, each one brightly painted, its walls covered with children's paintings and letters and numbers. Boxes stored toys that, though clearly second-hand, were serviceable and clean; the children were a mix of shy and confident, tall and small.

'We set up as a voluntary place after the major storm that hit last year,' the leader explained. 'It was somewhere parents could leave their children safely whilst they tried to cobble their lives together…rebuild their homes. But now the crown is funding this nursery and others—not completely, and we do still rely on donations, but we can afford to pay our staff something and the children get one good square meal a day. Now, I think these children desperately want to show you round.'

Even as Holly focused on the children, admired their work, laughed at their jokes and answered their questions as best she could, she was all the time oh, so aware of Stefan by her side—his stance, his relaxed air, the way he treated each child as an individual.

Once in the garden, the children proudly showed off the vegetable plots, as well as the sunflowers that stretched towards the sky with an optimism that seemed to reflect this nursery. Out of the corner of her eye she saw a little boy come forward, urged on by the pigtailed Sasha. But he pulled back and the two engaged in a spirited conversation.

Stefan had spotted it too and he headed towards them, looked down at the little boy, and Holly saw sudden compassion touch his eyes.

He leant down and spoke with them both. The words were too low for Holly to overhear, but she saw the little boy's face light up, then saw Sasha and the boy high-five.

Later, as they prepared to leave, Sasha bounded up and wrapped her arms around Stefan's legs. 'I think you're a very good prince. Better than a fairy tale one. And you *did* help.'

'What did you do?' Holly asked, once they were in the car en route to their next visit.

'It's no big deal.'

'It was to the little boy. I saw his face light up.'

'He and his brother were trapped in a building during the storm. A beam fell on his leg and now he can't play football any more. Both he and his brother are ardent football fans. Sasha wanted me to help cheer him up. All I did was say he and his brother could be the mascots at the next game of their favourite team.'

'That *is* a big deal. For those kids it's a huge deal.' Warmth touched her at what he had done.

'Yes, but maybe the house they were in wouldn't have collapsed if it had been built properly in the first place.'

'Which is why there is a whole new housing programme under way, and new standards and regulations are now being enforced.'

'My father has a lot to answer for.'

Anger darkened his face and she could sense him pull it under control, contain it.

'I think your brother is trying to do just that.'

He opened his mouth and then closed it again. She could almost see him make the decision to close the conversation down. To close her out.

He said politely, 'I'm sure you are right. Now, if you'll excuse me, I want to sort out this mascot issue.'

Two weeks later

Stefan glanced at Holly over breakfast, saw that she looked a little pale, with dark smudges under her eyes, and wondered if she too found it hard to sleep every night next to that damn barrier of pillows, knowing how close and yet so far she was from him. But, difficult though it had been, he'd stuck to his resolve—made sure he kept a physical and emotional distance from her when they weren't in the public eye.

Every day he held her hand, looped his arm round her waist, inhaled the strawberry scent of her shampoo, and every day his libido went into overdrive—only to be iced as soon as they entered their hotel room.

'Are you all right?' he asked. 'You look tired. I know this isn't what you signed up for, but you've been incredible.' She truly had, and guilt prodded him that he hadn't thanked her before. He had been so busy closing any connection down that he had failed to acknowledge her efforts.

'I *am* tired, but I've enjoyed every minute of it.'

He raised his eyebrow. 'Even the TV interview?'

'Fair point. *Not* the television interview. That terrified me and I'm still not sure we pulled it off.'

'We did OK.'

Hours of coaching from April had allowed them to put forward a pretty credible performance—perhaps the 'L' word had sounded a little forced, but Holly had laughed it off, blamed her falter on nerves and how hard it was to declare emotion in front of a global audience.

'Are you sure it's not all getting too much? Especially with the wedding plans as well?'

'It's not too much. Seeing all the problems Lycander faces, meeting the people affected by the floods, by the lack of public funding over the years, but also seeing how people cope in adverse conditions, how they pull together is…humbling. It's made me realise what a bubble I live in at Il Boschetto di Sole.' She hesitated. 'It has also made me realise what a great job Frederick is doing and how much there is left to do.'

'Yes.' Stefan refilled his coffee cup. 'He is.'

Like it or not, Holly was correct: his older brother *did* appear to be doing a sterling job and Stefan had no issue in supporting that. He had appeared with Frederick at some official events, and had indicated his willingness to continue to do so. But despite that the couple of attempts he and Frederick had made to spend 'brother time' together had been disastrous.

Not that he had any intent of discussing that with Holly. Not her problem, not her business. In truth, it didn't need to be a problem. Their deal had not included the establishment of a brotherly bond.

Aware of her scrutiny, he cleared his throat. 'Do you need any input on the wedding plans?'

Holly picked up the final flakes of her croissant with one finger as she considered the question. 'To be honest, Marcus and his department have done loads of the work. But there are a few things we need to figure out. For example, we need a song.'

'Huh?'

'The bride and groom start the dancing at the reception— take to the floor to whatever "their" tune is.'

'You pick.'

'Actually, I thought maybe we could put a different twist on it.' Holly hesitated. 'Did your mother have a favourite song?'

'She loved jazz—she had a whole collection.'

'Perfect. We'll have a jazz band. That will set the right tone as well. And it will be wonderful in a marquee. Wait till you see the marquee—it is amazing. Just right to house the very impressive guest list Marcus has come up with, and the perfect backdrop for the wedding of a younger, returning royal.'

'Excellent. You truly are doing a great job.'

'So are you,' she said softly. 'You've won the people over—showed them that you want to bring about change just as Frederick does.'

A twinge of discomfort touched him. 'I do agree that change is needed, and as part of my deal with Frederick I will support his position, but remember this is all part of the deal. I am here to win my lands back, to regain my right to visit Lycander. No more than that.'

Holly frowned. 'I don't buy that,' she said. 'I saw you with that little boy at that nursery, and since then I've seen you interact with hundreds of people. You *do* care; you just don't want to admit it.'

'Don't kid yourself, Holly—and don't give me attributes I don't possess. I care about these people, but it isn't my responsibility to create change in Lycander or to undo my father's wrongs. That is down to Frederick. Once this year is out I will be returning to London and my life.'

How had this conversation got personal? Rising, he hooked his jacket from the back of the armchair. 'I've got a meeting with Marcus. Gotta run. I'll swing by and pick you up later for the luncheon with the charity commission.'

She nodded and he headed for the door.

Holly watched as the door closed behind him, leant back in the armchair and closed her eyes.

Get real, Holly.

Stefan Petrelli was a businessman. She must not try and imbue him with attributes he didn't have; he'd made it clear from the start that duty was an irrelevance to him.

A knock at the door pulled her from her reverie and she rose to open it, stepping back in surprise at the identity of her visitor. Sunita. Frederick's wife. Exotic, beautiful. Ex-supermodel. Fashion designer. Mother of the heir to the throne, three-year-old Amil.

'I am sorry to turn up unannounced; if it's inconvenient please say.'

'No. Come in.'

Pulling the door open, she stepped back and Sunita swept in on a swirl of energy and vibrant colour. Her dark hair was pulled back in a sleek high ponytail and her vivid orange and red tunic top fell to mid-thigh over skinny jeans.

'I thought it would be good for us to meet unofficially. I also know how hard it is to arrange a royal wedding, so I've come to offer my help. Though I won't be offended if you refuse it.'

'No. Your advice would be great. Really useful.'

'OK. But before we begin can I ask you something? I know about the deal—I understand that this wedding wins you half of Il Boschetto di Sole—but are you sure you're happy playing the part you're playing? Because if you aren't we'll cancel it.'

'Just like that?'

'Yes. Frederick and Stefan may be princes, but that doesn't mean they get it all their way.'

Holly couldn't help but laugh. 'No. I'm good with this. Really.'

'Good. There is something else I'd like to know. Has Stefan said anything to you about how it is going with Frederick?'

'You know that proverb about getting blood from a stone…?'

'Hmm… I also know the one about peas in a pod. Sounds as if they are more alike than they would care to admit. Frederick is being similarly reticent, but as far as I can tell their private meetings are a disaster. Enough that I think Frederick may bail on them soon.' Sunita wrinkled her nose. 'The problem is getting them to let go of the past—all those old resentments and feuds that Alphonse fed and nurtured and encouraged.'

Holly frowned. Perhaps she should stop Sunita there… But, damn it, she wanted to know more than Stefan had told her. All he'd said was that his mother's marriage had been miserable—he'd clammed up about what had happened after.

'It was awful for both of them when Alphonse divorced Eloise. You see, Eloise was kind to Frederick—tried to be a good stepmum—but as part of the custody agreement Alphonse refused to let her see Frederick at all. Frederick had already lost his own mother, and losing Eloise really got to him. Alphonse used that to pit Frederick against Stefan. And so it went on.'

Sunita sighed.

'Now they can't get past it. Even the Amil factor didn't work. I asked them to keep an eye on him and after an hour I went back, expecting them all to be in a group hug. But instead I walked in to find Amil happily playing in a corner and the two brothers sitting in awkward silence.'

'Surely they can discuss Lycander?'

'You would think so. But Frederick doesn't want Stefan to think he's blowing his own horn.' Sunita grimaced. 'Anyway, I'm out of ideas.'

Holly's mind raced, imagining a young Stefan and a young Frederick, both of them hurting and having that hurt exploited by their father. The man who should have supported and nurtured and cared for them had instead manipulated them, set them against each other. Stefan had been right. Alphonse *did* have a lot to answer for.

'I think I may have an idea…' she said slowly.

'I'm listening. And then I promise we'll move on to wedding talk.'

CHAPTER TWELVE

THE WEDDING TALK progressed over the next few weeks to the wedding day, which dawned bright and clear with just a nip of chill in the air as a reminder that autumn was well under way.

Holly gazed at her reflection, knowing that Sunita's expert help had provided the finishing touches to an ensemble that would hold up to any and all media scrutiny. Anticipation panged in her tummy as she wondered what Stefan's reaction would be as she walked towards him.

As a real bride would have done, she had opted to move to Il Boschetto di Sole for the past few days—to prepare, to ensure the groom didn't so much as glimpse the dress. Though she sensed that Stefan, unlike a real groom, had welcomed her removal.

The door opened and her father entered. A scrutiny of his face satisfied her that he looked well; Jessica Alderney was still in residence, keeping a strict eye on him, and he already looked the better for it.

'You look beautiful.'

'Thank you.'

'And, Holly, I wish to thank you for this; you are doing good thing for the Romano family—past, present and future. Of that I am proud, and you have my gratitude.'

The words warmed her soul, made it all worthwhile.

'Time to go.'

He held out his arm and she took it, tried to quell the butterflies that danced in her tummy.

She followed him from her childhood home, then paused on the threshold and blinked, nerves forgotten. There, in full glory, instead of the horse and carriage she'd been expecting, sat a pink limousine. 'Papa...?'

Thomas shrugged. 'Did you not order this?'

'No.'

It dawned on her that the only person who could have done this was Stefan. She gave a small chuckle and suddenly the whole ordeal ahead felt easier.

The afternoon took on a surreal quality as she climbed out of the limousine and smiled her well-practised smile at the selected photographers. Entering the chapel on her father's arm, she inhaled the scent of the fresh-cut flowers she'd chosen—a profusion of pink and white atop elegant stems.

The pews were filled with dignitaries and Il Boschetto di Sole staff. And out of the corner of her eye she spotted Sunita, bright and exotic in a golden *salwar kameez*, declaring her Indian heritage with pride, sitting next to Frederick, whose blond head glinted in the sunlight that shone through the stained glass. Amil looked adorable in a suit and bow tie.

Eyes forward and there Stefan stood—drop-dead, heart-stoppingly gorgeous—in a tuxedo that moulded his form emphasised the intensity of his presence, his lithe, muscular power and the deep grey of his eyes. The black hair was nearly tamed, but the hint of unruliness added to his allure

This man would soon be her husband, and she walked towards him now, watched by the world.

Remember Sunita's advice. Stand tall. Picture happy scenarios.

Il Boschetto di Sole in her father's hands. Stefan and
Holly posing for the camera with a tiny dark-haired baby
in Holly's arms. A girl. And they didn't give a damn…
were engulfed in love for their daughter…

Whoa—hang on a second. What was *Stefan* doing in
her happy picture? Idiot! Surely she wasn't stupid enough
to delude herself that this was for real? Yet the vision was
hard to shake…

At a gentle squeeze on her arm, Holly realised that she'd
slowed down, that people were looking at her askance.

Come on, Holly. It had been a blip—nothing more. The
important part of that happy scenario had been the baby.
Stefan was merely an unwanted intruder, sneaked in by
a brain that had been temporarily dazzled by this marriage fiction.

Reset button and resume walk.

She reached Stefan, kept the smile on her face, revelled
in the appreciative look in his.

Fake, fake, fake.

This was a show for the public—a term of the deal
he'd agreed with Marcus. The vows were a dream, the
solemnity of the words underscoring her hypocrisy, and
no amount of justification could quiet her conscience. All
she could do was tell herself that she would make sure
that some good came from this marriage—that it would
benefit Lycander and give her father Il Boschetto di Sole.

'With this ring…'

Stefan slipped the ring over her finger, and as the simple gold band slid over her knuckle she felt panic war with
disbelief. Fake or not, here and now, in this chapel, they
had pledged their troth. And, even though she knew that
the words did not bind them for ever, for the next twelve
months they were joined as man and wife.

'You may kiss the bride.'

The words seemed to penetrate the dreamlike fog of the past half-hour and she raised trembling hands to lift her veil—though a part of her wanted to keep hidden. Stefan's hands helped her, pushed the veil back and then cupped her face. His clasp was firm and full of reassurance, his grey eyes full of appreciation and warmth.

Fake, fake, fake, her brain warned her.

But then his lips brushed hers and sweet sensations cascaded through her body until, in a mutual recall of their surroundings, they both stepped back. He took her hand in his and they made their way back down the aisle, through the arched stone door around which honeysuckle grew, permeating the air with its scent and outside into the graveyard.

History seeped into the air from the weathered gravestones and the stone walls and spire of the chapel itself—a place that had witnessed generations of happiness and heartache. Here she and Stefan, Prince and Princess of Lycander, greeted their well-wishers until they were whisked off for photos.

Her realisation that these photos would go down in Lycandrian history threatened to call on her panic, but somehow she kept the smile on her face, remembered all the coaching, placed her hand on his arm and looked up at him in a semblance of loving wife, absorbed in the way he looked at her.

Fake, fake, fake.

But her awareness of him was, oh, so real, and nigh on impossible to ignore with their enforced proximity. His nearness played havoc with her senses. Each and every one was on high alert, revelling in the idea that for a year they were husband and wife.

As the hours wore on, through the reception and the four-course dinner, her head whirled. Gleaming cutlery clinked, conversation flowed, and the sound of laughter mingled with the pop of champagne corks. Dish followed dish—exquisite artichoke hearts, melt-in-the-mouth medallions of wild boar, crispy potato *rosti* and simple buttered spinach. The marquee glowed, illuminated by the warm white glow of fairy lights.

Once the food was cleared away, the jazz band started to warm up and Holly looked at Stefan.

'Are you ready?' he asked.

'As I'll ever be.'

And so they went onto the dance floor, to the smooth strains of a saxophone and the deep velvet voice of the singer as he crooned out the words. She'd hoped that dancing to jazz wouldn't be as tactile as to any other music, but in fact it was worse. The sensual sway of their movements, the to and fro, the distance and the proximity, messed further with her head.

Was he equally affected? Every instinct told her that he was. Each time he pulled her into his body she could sense the heat rising in him, see the scorch of desire in his eyes as they focused solely on her. When his hands spanned her waist, circling the wide belt of satin, she felt lighter than air—and yet heavy desire pooled in her gut.

Finally the first dance came to an end and they moved off the dance floor. She kept a smile pinned to her lips even as her head whirled. He walked beside her, coiled taut, and she knew his body was as tense as her own.

'How long until we leave for our honeymoon?' he asked, his voice a rasp.

She gave a shaky laugh. A laugh that tapered off as the word 'honeymoon' permeated her desire-hazed brain.

'About the honeymoon…'

'Yes. We agreed on Paris—nice and clichéd, plenty of romantic social media opportunities.'

Desire faded into a background hum as she met his gaze a touch apprehensively. 'There may have been a slight change of plan.'

Now an eyebrow was raised. 'Define "slight".'

'Actually, do you think we could discuss it later? People are watching us now and we need to mingle.'

Coward.

Perhaps, but it would be foolhardy to spark a potential argument now.

There was a pause and then he nodded. 'OK. I'll look forward to my surprise destination.'

Three hours and much mingling later, they were once more in the back of the pink limousine. Stefan handed Holly a glass of pink champagne—her first of the whole day. His too, for that matter.

'To pink limos,' she said. 'I haven't had a chance to say thank you. It's fabulous.'

'I'm glad you like it. I gather it is not, however, taking us to the airport so we can catch a plane to Paris?'

'No…' Holly took a deep breath and apprehension returned to her blue eyes.

As the silence stretched he took the time to study her. She had changed out of her wedding dress into her 'going away outfit'. A simple cream linen dress. Her hair now hung loose in all its golden glory, and she still looked every bit as beautiful as she had when she'd walked down the aisle, a vision in ivory satin and lace.

'You're going to have to tell me some time,' he pointed out.

She took another sip of champagne—presumably for fortification. 'We aren't going anywhere. We're staying here.'

Stefan closed his eyes and then opened them again

pinched the bridge of his nose and focused on keeping his voice calm. 'Why?'

'Because the past few weeks have all been about being in the public eye, being on show. I thought it might be nice to explore Lycander differently. I reckon it would look good to the public as well—fit well with the "returning prince" theme. What do you think?'

He thought she wasn't speaking the whole truth; there was something in the way her gaze had fluttered away from his for an instant.

'Wouldn't you like to go to Paris? Explore there.'

'One day I would, yes.'

Damn it. Maybe she didn't want to go there on a fake honeymoon; maybe she wanted to save Paris for when she could do the clichéd romance for real.

'But now you want to remain in Lycander?'

'Yes. I've realised that even though I have lived here all my life there are still so many places I haven't seen—and I think it will be fun.'

A study of her expression yielded nothing but apparent sincerity, and he did believe her. He recalled how she had described her exploration of London. But he suspected there was an additional ulterior motive, and wariness banded his chest at the idea he was being manipulated in some way.

Well, if he was then he'd never give something for nothing. He shrugged. 'OK. If that's what you want. We can find Lycander's equivalent of the Chelsea Physic Garden. But I want something in return.'

It was her turn to look suspicious, and her forehead creased as she sipped her drink and looked at him narrow-eyed over the rim of the glass. 'Like what?'

'Take the marketing role at Lamberts.'

'Jeez. Why can't you let that go? We've been through

it. There is no point—I will be taking up residence on Il Boschetto di Sole in a year.'

'I understand that; I am simply suggesting that this year you take the chance to do a job you enjoy—give it a try. It will be good experience that will help with Il Boschetto di Sole. One year. Where is the harm in that?'

Holly hesitated, twisting a tendril of hair around her finger. She considered his words and then suddenly she grinned. 'What the hell? You're right. Why not? I *can't* live on Il Boschetto di Sole during our marriage, and I *do* want to try marketing, and it *will* be good experience. I'll do it.'

'Good.' He raised his glass and a smile tilted his lips. 'To your new job.' And to his private hope that it would be the first step for Holly to veer from the path of tradition and duty. 'It's important to enjoy life—grab the good times whilst you can.'

This he knew.

And just like that the atmosphere in the limousine subtly changed. The air became charged with a shimmer of awareness—he'd swear he could almost see it—a pink glitter of desire. And he knew that really all their talk had simply been to put off an inevitable decision—a decision they had been headed for ever since he'd seen her walk down the aisle…ever since he'd lifted her veil and kissed her.

Holly stilled, her blue eyes wide as their gazes met and locked. Then slowly—so slowly, so tentatively—she shifted across the seat. The swish of her dress against the pink leather mesmerised him.

There was no need for words; instead he cupped her face in his hands and brushed his lips against hers, the movement so natural, so right, that he let out a small groan as her lips parted beneath his.

The kiss seemed timeless. It could have been seconds or it could have been hours before the limo glided to a halt

By then he was gripped with a desire so deep he ached, and he felt her answering need in the press of her body against his, the tangle of her fingers in his hair.

As they emerged, hand in hand, he tugged her towards the revolving door of the hotel, through the lobby and towards the stairs. Once inside their suite they didn't—couldn't—wait. His jacket fell to the floor and her fingers fumbled with the buttons of his shirt, crept underneath the material, and as she touched his chest, he exhaled a pent-up breath.

The words of their vows rang through his head: 'With my body I thee worship.' And without further ado he scooped her up and carried her to the bedroom.

Holly opened her eyes, turned to look for Stefan and saw the empty bed. Her languorous happiness started to fade and for a moment she clung to it, allowed herself the memory of the previous night. Laughter, joy, passion, gentleness... The swoop and soar of desire and fulfilment.

Her face flushed and she suddenly wondered exactly how to face him. But she had to—she had plans for the day...plans she was determined to see through.

Swinging her legs out of bed, she felt gratitude that he had discreetly exited, saving her an undignified scramble for clothes. Far better to face him clothed. Unless, of course, he had left because he was worried she'd request a replay. What if she hadn't measured up? Hadn't been woman enough? No—that was foolish. Last night had been magical—she knew it.

Yet that certainty dipped as she entered the living area. He looked so gorgeous and yet so remote that for a crazy moment she wondered if she'd imagined the previous night.

'Hey...'

'Hey.'

Misgivings continued to smite her. There was a grim set to his mouth, and his lips strained up into a smile that did not match the cool glint in his eyes.

'We need to talk.'

'Sure.'

His fingers drummed against his thigh and she could sense his frustration.

'Last night… I'm sorry… It shouldn't have happened like that.'

The onset of hurt began to pool inside her tummy, and she focused on keeping all emotion from her face and her voice. 'How *should* it have happened?'

'I should have checked that it was really what you wanted.'

'I think it was pretty clear what I wanted.'

'I meant in the longer term. We decided that we didn't want this relationship to become physical. Last night it did—without either of us considering the consequences.'

'We used protection.'

'That isn't what I meant. I meant the consequences to our marriage of convenience, to our deal.'

'So you regret last night?' Damn it, she hoped that hadn't been a tremor in her voice.

'No, I don't. But I do regret that we didn't figure out the rules first. Now we need to decide what happens from here.'

What *did* she want? Right now her body still strummed in the aftermath of the previous hours, and it was telling her in no uncertain terms that it really *didn't* want to give up that sort of pleasure.

'You said to me that you believe relationships with a time limit work—relationships based around physical fulfilment and a bit of sparkle over the dinner table occasionally. We could do that.'

'And *you* said that that sort of relationship wasn't for you. I think you may have mentioned "clinical sex".'

'Yes… Well, it turns out I may have been wrong about that. Turns out clinical sex is right up my street.'

Her words pulled the glimpse of a smile from him before the grimness returned.

'This isn't *about* that, though. The point is this is not the type of relationship you want and I knew that. So last night should not have happened. You are looking for a real husband, a father for your children, and I am *not* that person.'

'I know that—and I knew that last night. If I hadn't wanted to go ahead I would have said so. You are right that I want a real marriage and a family, a man who shares my values and beliefs. You don't—and I get that. But right now you are in my life and we *do* have some sort of attraction thing going on.'

She hauled in a breath.

'So last night happened and I don't regret it. As you said, the question is where do we go from here?'

Stefan has a point! yelled a voice in the back of her head. *This is not what you want—imagine the humiliation when he tires of you.*

I may tire of him.

Yeah, right. Dream on.

Fine.

'I think we should have a very short-term relationship— just for the honeymoon. Once we get back to London we'll live separate lives for the year.'

He hesitated, searched her face as if he wished he could penetrate her very soul. 'You are sure that is what you want?'

'Yes.' This was under *her* control—*she* was putting the time limit on it. This way she couldn't get hurt and she would get to replay last night. Win-win, right? 'But only if you do.'

'Oh, I *definitely* do.'

Finally his face relaxed into a grin that curled her toes and sent a thrill of anticipation through her entire body.

'In fact, why don't I show you *exactly* how much I want this? Want *you*.'

Temptation beckoned, but she shook her head. 'No can do. I have a plan for the day. We need to get going.'

'Get going to where?'

'Xanos Island.'

The smile dropped from his lips but she soldiered on. 'Sunita mentioned it. She said it's an amazing little island, completely secluded, with sand, rocks, caves—the works. I've figured out the tides, a boat awaits us, and we have the most amazing picnic ever.'

'Did Sunita say anything else about it?'

'Yes.' There was no point lying about it. 'She said Eloise used to take you there.'

'So you figured it was a good place to go to?'

'Yes.'

Because she thought the best way for him to let go of the past might be to revisit the good bits of it. He might not have had many good bits, but it seemed clear that he and Eloise had shared a few happy years before the divorce and its horrors. More than that, so had he and Frederick under Eloise's guidance.

'I thought you might like to revisit some of your good childhood memories. I know there may not be many of them, but that makes them all the more precious.' She hauled in breath. 'And it's not only for you—it's for me as well.'

'How so?'

'I told you that your mother broke my father's hear

when she married your father. But the repercussions went deeper than that. My mother loved my father and she couldn't deal with his relationship with Eloise. Couldn't deal with the fact that my father didn't really love *her*. So she hated your mother with real venom—and I was brought up to do the same. To me, your mother was the wicked witch incarnate and I never questioned that.'

It hadn't taken the young Holly long to figure out that the best way to win a crumb of her mother's attention, if not her affection, had been to insult Eloise.

'I'd like to make amends—go somewhere like Xanos Island and remember Eloise differently.'

Stefan met her gaze and then he nodded. 'Thank you. For feeling able to give her memory a chance. I truly don't believe she wanted to hurt anyone. And she wouldn't have wanted the fall-out to hurt *you*—I know first-hand how horrible it is to be a child caught in the web of your parents' destructive marriage. I'm sorry you went through that and so would she be.'

He rose.

'Xanos Island here we come.'

As the small red and white motorboat bobbed over the waves Stefan could picture his younger self, recall the sheer joy of being on a real boat, singing a sea shanty with the Captain and his mother joining in, the soft lilt of her voice helping him with the words.

But it hadn't only been the three of them singing—it had been Frederick as well. The memory, long buried, slipped into focus. His five-year-old self sitting on Frederick's lap, leaning over the side, safe in the knowledge that his older brother held him secure around the waist as he trailed his fingers in the water.

Enough. That had been then. Before the horror of the

divorce. Before Eloise's departure. Before his father's *'toughen Stefan up and make him a prince'* notions. Before the anger and the blame in his brother's eyes. Before the emotions he couldn't forget, followed by his brother's utter lack of support through his father's *'make Stefan a prince'* regime.

Hell, he was trying, but each meeting with Frederick was so damned awkward—there was a vibe of anger, of strain, that neither of them seemed able to circumvent. Not that it mattered. As long as they continued to pull off a public pretence of civility that was all that was needed. All that he'd signed up to.

The Captain steered the boat to a small harbour and Stefan followed Holly onto the wooden jetty, hauling the picnic basket with him, and soon they were crossing golden sands.

'It's magic,' Holly said as they came to a halt. 'It feels like it's a million miles from anywhere.'

The sea seemed impossibly blue and the waves lapped gently against the sands. Flecks of sunlight dotted the green fronds of the palm trees that dotted the beach.

'I think that's why my mother loved it here: the seclusion gave her peace. I remember the last time we came here...'

The scene was vivid. The present faded and Eloise seemed to shimmer in front of him, kneeling in the sand, making a reluctant Frederick apply sun lotion, helping build a sandcastle.

'Frederick ran off to explore the caves and I had a monster tantrum because my mother wouldn't let me go with him—said it was too dangerous. I lost it, but she didn't— she didn't even raise her voice.'

She never had... It had almost been as if she'd know their time together was limited.

'Instead she hugged me, told me that when I was older we'd explore the caves together. It never happened.' It was a promise she hadn't been able to keep. 'This is the first time I've been back since then.'

'Then let's go and explore now.'

'You sure?'

Holly raised her eyebrows. 'I'm twenty-four years old, and I was brought up on a lemon grove where I roamed wild. I'm pretty sure I can rock-climb.'

'Then let's go.'

As they clambered over rocks, discovered trickles of water and debated the difference between stalactites and stalagmites, he watched Holly, saw the lithe, sure grace with which she moved, the impatient pushing away of tendrils of blonde hair as they escaped her ponytail so that vibrant corn-coloured curls bounced off her shoulder.

As if she sensed his scrutiny, she smiled at him. 'You OK?'

'Yes.'

Somehow Holly had taken a bittersweet memory and created a new, happy one to blend with it. And he hoped that somewhere, somehow, his mother could see this, would know that he'd finally explored the caves.

For heaven's sake, Petrelli. Get a grip.

'Let's go eat—I've gone from ravenous to desperate!'

Once back on the beach, they unpacked the food: mini-quiches, tabbouleh salad, pork pies, tiny sandwiches, cheese straws and succulent Lycandrian olives, black and green and glistening in oil. They heaped their plates, sat back in the warmth of the sun and ate.

She shifted closer to him, turned to face him. Almost as if she had read his mind, she said, 'If Eloise could see you she'd be proud of you.'

The words cut him, threatened to destroy the warmth of the day, and as if on cue the sun hid behind a passing cloud.

Stefan shook his head. 'I don't think so.' If he'd been stronger, toughened up faster, jumped through the hoops his father had set, he could have saved her. *That* would have been something to be proud of.

'Well, *I* do.'

'Even if she would it wouldn't change anything.'

Not a single one of his achievements could change his mother's life and how it had panned out.

'The misery of her marriage, the horror of the custody battle, the fact that her love for me meant she suffered whatever my father meted out, her exile from Lycander...'

'That wasn't your fault. None of it.'

'If she hadn't loved me her life would have been a whole lot easier. Without me her life would have been immeasurably better.'

If he had been stronger, better, more princely, then her life would have been easier too. But he'd failed—or so his father had said. He had come in one day and announced the end of the regime. It was over and Eloise was gone.

In that moment, as he'd seen the cruelty on his father's face, Stefan had vowed that he would never be a prince— that as soon as he could he would follow his mother into exile. When he'd learnt of her death, in his grief and anger, he'd renewed that vow.

'I'm sorry.' Holly hesitated, then reached out and clasped his hand. 'Truly sorry. All I can say is please try to remember that she loved you and treasure the memories you have. I know she did.'

Stefan frowned, sure that alongside the compassion in her voice there was a strange wistfulness. As if she had a paucity of similar memories.

As if aware of it, she shifted slightly, turned to face the

sea, choppier now, with white crests on the waves looping and rolling in the breeze, casting a salt scent towards the shore along with their spray.

She'd said her parents' marriage had been embittered, and she had hardly ever mentioned her mother.

'What happened with *your* parents?' He kept his voice gentle, non-intrusive.

'My mother left when I was eight—went to Australia.'

'That must have been tough. How did they sort out custody?'

'They didn't. She decided to make a clean break; I haven't seen her since.'

Now she turned to him.

'I know it's awful that your mother suffered, and it breaks my heart when I think about it. But I also know that you are so lucky that she loved you. Because you see my mother never did—never loved me. My parents wanted a boy. Desperately. After Eloise left, my father knew he needed to get married—needed Romano heirs. He was upfront with my mother, told that he didn't love her, that his heart belonged to Eloise, but that he'd do his best to make her happy. Maybe if they'd had a brood of children they would have been. But it didn't happen, and as time went by they became desperate. For a boy. When Eloise had you I think it tipped my mother over the edge—made her feel a complete failure. She did everything; she went to herbalists, soothsayers, every doctor she could think of. I think she would have sold her soul for a child—or rather for a boy. When I turned up they were devastated. I've heard people talking about it.'

Stefan scooted across the sand, moved as close to her as possible and hoped his proximity would offer some comfort. The idea of tiny baby Holly, left unloved, desperate for care and love, made his chest ache.

'My father hired a nurse…tried to persuade my mother to take an interest. But she didn't. I think she couldn't. It was as though the sight of me turned her stomach. It always did and there's nothing I can do to change that. My father was different; his disappointment has never fully faded, but he has always shown me love and kindness and I will be grateful for ever for that.'

It explained so much about why Holly was willing to do anything for her father. Gratitude, a desire to make up for his disappointment in her gender and of course love. Confirmation, perhaps, that love gave power; if you accepted love then you had to give something back.

Next to him, she gave a sudden tight smile. 'Don't look so gutted—it could have been worse. My mother never physically hurt me, and there were plenty of staff around—they all looked out for me. And my father was amazing.'

She glanced at her watch.

'The tide is turning and the boat will soon be back for us. We'd better go.'

'Wait.'

Turning, he pulled her into his arms, rested her head against his shoulder, felt the tickle of her hair against his chin. For a second she resisted, and then she relaxed. He rubbed her back, hoped he could soothe her childhood pain.

They sat like that for a while and then she pulled back, touched his cheek with one gentle finger. 'We really do need to go.'

He nodded, rose and held out his hand to pull her up from the sand.

As they packed up the remains of their picnic a small voice warned him to take care. Holly had been rebuffed all her life by the person who should have loved her most and she was vulnerable.

But not to *him*, he reassured himself. Holly knew he wasn't a long-term prospect and she didn't even want him to be one. She'd been more than clear on that. But he knew that in this honeymoon period he wanted to make her happy, give her some memories to treasure.

They had a week—and he wanted to make it count.

CHAPTER THIRTEEN

HOLLY WOKE WITH a feeling of well-being and opened her eyes sleepily, aware of warmth, security and Stefan's arm around her. Her brain kicked in and computed the day. Already in countdown mode, she was aware that their honeymoon period was tick-tick-ticking away. But it was OK. They still had a few days to go.

Relief trickled through her and she closed her eyes— just as the alarm shrilled out and her brain properly kicked into gear, dissipating the cloud of sleep. She sat up.

Stefan made a small noise of disapproval, reached up and pulled her back down. The sleepy caress of his hands down her back caused the now familiar jolt of desire. But today she couldn't act on it. Instead she placed a gentle hand on his chest, leaned over and nuzzled his neck and then sat up again.

His eyes opened in protest.

'We have to get up,' she explained. 'Today we have somewhere we need to be.'

'Where?' Now alertness had come into play, and his grey eyes watched her.

Holly bit her lip. Part of her wanted to tell him, but another part suspected he'd refuse to go. 'I'd rather not say.'

Now he too sat up, leant back against the wooden headboard, and a frown grooved his forehead. 'I'd rather you did.'

Holly shook her head and plumped for honesty. 'You may not go if I do.'

'And you want me to go?'

'Yes.'

A pause, and then he shrugged. 'Then we'll go.'

'Thank you.' She dropped a kiss on the top of his head and grinned at him. 'I'm going to get ready.'

'Lumberjack look or suit?'

'Lumberjack is fine, and there won't be any reporters. Or I hope not.'

Now she frowned. Despite promises from the press that they would respect their privacy, April had been correct. Stray reporters dogged their steps. Not many, to be fair, but enough that they had taken to sneaking out through the back door of the hotel en route to quirky corners of Lycander, where they wandered hand in hand, eating ice cream, or savoury crêpes, chatting or walking in silence. But even then every so often she'd been aware of the click of a camera, the sense of being followed.

'OK. Let's get this show on the road.'

Swinging her legs out of bed, she headed for the bathroom, trying to soothe the jangle of nerves, her anxiety that she was making a monumental mistake—a massive overstepping of the bounds of their marriage deal.

Stefan looked out of the window of the official car, watching as the prosperous vista dropped away and the houses became progressively more dingy, the vegetation more sparse and scrubby, the poverty more and more clear. He realised they were headed to the now familiar outskirts— back to the suburb they had first visited, where they had met Sasha.

The car glided to a stop near the nursery, and once again the sheer contrast between life here and in the affluent city hit him anew. Roofless houses, patched over with tin, smashed windows... And yet a community resided here. Children were playing in the streets, looking at the cars with rapt interest.

Cars in the plural... Another car from the royal fleet was parked opposite.

The door opened and he watched with a sense of inevitability as Frederick emerged, flanked by two security men whom he waved away to a discreet distance.

The Crown Prince's expression mirrored his own—surprise mixed with resignation—and a sense of solidarity sneaked up on Stefan. Seconds later Sunita also stepped out, clad in a discreet dark blue dress. His sister-in-law waved cheerily and Stefan lifted a hand in an attempt at enthusiasm.

'Why are we here?' he hissed out of the side of his mouth.

Holly gave him a tentative smile, though her blue eyes shaded apprehensively. 'You'll see. Come on.'

Compression banded his chest and the sense that he had been manipulated fuzzed his brain as he considered his options. He could ask Franco to turn the car and rev it out of here. But wiser counsel prevailed—that would hardly back up the impression of brothers reunited. Whilst there were no reporters visible, he was pretty sure this meeting could hardly be kept secret.

A glance at Frederick indicated that he'd come to much the same conclusion, and he headed towards them as Stefan climbed out, no doubt propelled by a prod in the back from Sunita.

'Stefan,' he said formally.

'Freddy.'

Stefan couldn't resist. His brother had hated being called Freddy as a child, and the sense of being pushed into an awkward position had clearly sent Stefan straight back to childhood. Any minute now he'd find a pram and start chucking toys.

To his surprise, Frederick's face split into an unexpected smile.

'No one's called me that since you left,' he said. 'And, for the record, this wasn't my idea. At a guess, it wasn't yours either.'

'Nope.' *Damn right.*

'Then we've been ambushed.' Frederick turned and smiled affably at his wife. 'Perhaps you want to enlighten us as to why we're here?'

'Actually, this is Holly's show. I am merely her assistant— or accomplice, depending on how you want to look at it. Holly, over to you.'

Holly's show. The words pulled the band tighter round his chest. Since his father, it had never been anyone's show but Stefan's own. Warning bells clanged as he focused on her, watched as she straightened up, pushed a tendril of hair behind her ear and divided her focus between Frederick and himself.

'This community has been hard-hit. It was already in trouble and the storm made things worse. What you both have in common is a desire to right the wrongs and injustices your father committed and help make Lycander a better place. I thought maybe you could work together on this specific community—use the ideas and strengths you both have. Frederick, I know how much you care about education. And, Stefan, I know of your belief in social housing. Together you could build houses…schools. I know you are doing that throughout Lycander, but perhaps this could be the one place that represents Stefan's return to Lycander. If that makes sense. What do you think?'

She held her ground in the silence that followed.

Frederick glanced at his wife and Stefan could sense some sort of silent communication in progress. He suspected Sunita was issuing an escape route veto. Well, she had that right. Holly didn't.

In reality escape wasn't possible—this community *did* need assistance and he could provide it. But, right or wrong, the whole scenario didn't sit well with him. Holly had pushed him onto the moral high ground—was pulling his strings, pushing his buttons. *Find the cliché and apply.*

So it might be. But these people in this community had been pushed into poverty and destitution by the policies his father had instigated. His father had pushed buttons and pulled strings to cause dissension and unhappiness. He knew Holly's motives were good, that her aim was to help sow accord and not discord, and to achieve help for this place and the people who lived in it. Yet he couldn't shake the warning buzz in his head, the shades of discomfort.

But that was for later. Here and now, this was a project he believed in.

'I'm in.' He turned to his brother. 'But don't feel you have to do this—I can handle it solo.'

Impossible to guess the thoughts that were going through Frederick's blond head, but his face lightened into a smile. 'Actually, I think this *should* be a joint enterprise. I know it's your honeymoon, but do you want to stick around here for a bit and have a look? Bounce some ideas.'

One deep breath and then Stefan nodded. 'Sure.'

In unison, Sunita and Holly stepped forward.

'Grand!' Sunita said. 'Holly and I will take one car and you boys can have the other. Have fun!'

Holly paced the hotel room, anxiety edging her nerves as she wondered how it was going—whether this project would bring the brothers together. She wondered if she'd misread Stefan's body language, the sense of irritation at her perceived interference. Yet she couldn't regret it.

Her phone buzzed and she snatched it up, tried not be disappointed at the identity of the caller.

'Hi, April.'

'Holly. That's a *great* write-up on you and Stefan. That should definitely nail it with regard to everyone buying into the two of you.'

Huh?

'I haven't heard of the reporter but it's a fair article—she did well.'

Still not with it, she held her phone in place with her shoulder and pulled her laptop towards her. Pulled up the article April was describing in happy detail.

Oh, hell.

'April, I'll call you back.'

Disconnecting, she sank onto the armchair and started to read.

Love for Real? The Verdict is In.

As all of Lycander knows, last week Prince Stefan tied the knot with Holly Romano, and amid a complicated backdrop of wills and lemons, the big question has been: Are they in love for real?

Well, let's take a look at some of the evidence.

Exhibit One: The official interview done by April Fotherington —aka wife of Chief Advisor Marcus Alriksson—accompanied by the first official photograph.

Analysis: A little posed, a little formal, expressions a little strained. But who can blame them? It's hard to pose officially.

Verdict: Are they in love? Possibly...maybe.

Exhibit Two: The televised interview.

*Analysis: They talked the talk, walked the walk...
until it came to the L question. Then they stumbled,
but made a quick recovery.*

Verdict: Are they in love? Maybe, baby.

Exhibit Three: The wedding.

*Analysis: Definitely looking hot—but who
wouldn't in a dress like that?*

Verdict: The jury is still out.

So I undertook a little casual surveillance...

*Please note that I made no attempt to breach the
privacy of the honeymoon suite itself, but I am guilty
of a bit of ducking and diving whilst I followed the
newlyweds around Lycander.*

And so to Exhibit Four:

Holly's heart hit her boots as she skimmed the photos.

Herself in the palace gardens, looking up at Stefan, a smile on her lips and love in her eyes. *Jeez.* She looked as if she thought he was the best thing since sliced granary. Oh, and joy! There was a picture of them in a clinch. She was literally hanging off his lips. But it wasn't only that photo. The next was the killer. Her hand was on his T-shirt, brushing off a speck of dirt, and the goddamn look in her eyes was one of love.

She didn't need to read the verdict, but she did it anyway—just in case there was even a sliver of a possibility that she'd got it wrong.

Verdict: One loved-up princess...

*So, the best of luck to our new royals. Life gave
them lemons and it looks like Princess Holly is going
to make lemonade!*

Panic strummed every single synapse—how had it happened? This reporter had got it *right.* Somewhere down the line she'd fallen for Stefan. Fool that she was. He'd made it more than clear that he was no fairy tale prince and she'd been damned sure her fairy tale days were over. Yet somehow she'd done it again—fallen in love with a man who didn't love her back.

What to do? *What to do?*

For a start she had to make sure Stefan didn't so much as suspect the truth. If he saw this article she'd laugh it off, put it down to the light, her acting skills, sexual afterglow... anything but the truth.

Speak of the devil... She looked up as the door opened, braced herself, shut the laptop and rose to her feet.

'Hi. How did it go?' *Too breezy.*

'It went fine.'

His voice was even—not cold, but not warm, and the glint she'd become used to over the past days was gone. She'd been right—he was mad at her.

'Good—and I'm sorry.'

'For what?' He shrugged off his jacket and threw it over the back of an armchair.

'I know I forced your hand. I didn't think you'd go if I'd told you where we were going.'

Even as she focused on the words the truth whirled inside her head, made his coolness hurt more. *Love...* She *loved* him.

'It should have been my decision to make. I don't like being bulldozed or manipulated. But I do understand that you did it with the best intentions, and Frederick and I had a productive few hours. The community wins...brand Petrelli Princes wins.'

'That isn't why I organised it.'

'Then why *did* you?'

'Because I knew you and Frederick weren't bonding and I wanted to give you a chance to sort it out, to bring you closer together, to show you how much you have in common. I thought you could both let go of the past by doing something worthwhile together *now*. If you can let go of the past then you have a future.'

She could only pray that he didn't read the subtext she was seeing herself. Damn it, she wanted a future with this man. Wanted him to decide love was for him after all.

'The past makes us who we are,' he said. 'The past matters—you can't just let go of it. But you can learn from it.'

'But maybe sometimes the lessons we learn from it are wrong. Sunita told me that your father pitted you and Frederick against each other; it was Alphonse who fostered the dislike. You and Frederick can overcome that.'

His grey eyes darkened, and bleak shadows chased across them as he shook his head. 'If it were as easy as that perhaps we could. But it isn't. In any case, I don't want closeness with Frederick.'

'Why not?'

'That's not my way, Holly. I prefer to walk alone. I like the control it gives me to do what I want to do without answering to anyone else.'

The certainty in his voice was unassailable, and his words made her heart ache as she began to accept the futility of her love.

But maybe she could make him see reason.

'You can still have control and be close to others—you would still have choices.' *Deep breath.* 'I know how much seeing your mother suffer must have hurt you, and I know it must feel like it was your fault...that loving you resulted in hurt for her.'

'It didn't *feel* like that. That is what *happened*. Fact, not feeling.'

'But *all* love doesn't have to be like that. Your mother wouldn't want you to give up on closeness or love. I know that.'

'Then she would be wrong. She had one life, Holly. One life—and most of it was miserable because of her love for *me*. She was chained to an abusive man who used her love for me to humiliate her, to make her life hell. Her love for me gave my father power. Love gives power.'

Oh, God. As her brain joined the dots all she wanted to do was hold him, but as she moved towards him she saw him move imperceptibly backwards and she stopped.

'And your love for her…it gave your father power over *you*?'

'Yes.' His voice was flat. 'And he used that power. He made me pay dearly for every visit to my mother. He decided her love for me had weakened me, made me less "princely". So he devised a regime—a training programme. If I adhered to it, if I achieved his goals, I'd get time with my mother—as well as becoming a *real* prince, of course.'

The sneer, the bitterness, made her ache even as she was appalled at Alphonse's actions. It twisted her insides. The image of a young boy, desperately missing his mother, being put through such a regime made her feel ill.

'But even then he changed the rules. One day the regime was over. I'd failed and my mother was gone. Exiled.'

'But…*why*?' It seemed impossible to fathom how anyone could do that.

'He'd met his next wife. She wanted rid of Eloise. He wanted it to look as though she'd abandoned me and he was remarrying to give his children a "proper" mother. It worked for him. And love *still* gave him power—over both of us. My mother went without a fight because she was scared of what he might do to me. As for me, there was nothing I could do—I'd already failed her.'

'No!' The word was torn from her, and now she did move towards him—didn't care if he rejected her. She stepped into his space and put her arms around him. 'That's not true.'

But she could see exactly why his younger self had thought that—knew that deep down, despite his adult understanding, he still believed it. His body was hard, unyielding, no trace of the man she'd shared so much passion with, the man who had held her, whose arms she had woken up in these past three mornings.

'Just like it's not my fault that my mother didn't— couldn't—love me. That wasn't *my* failure. I was a child. So were you. You didn't fail your mother.'

She held her breath, and then hope deflated as he shrugged.

'Whether it's true or not isn't the point. I don't want closeness. Closeness leads to love. Love is not for me—I won't give anyone that power again. Hell, I don't want that power over anyone either.'

That told her. Any not yet formed idea of telling him of her love died before it could even take root. She could not, *would* not, repeat the past. He was right—the past was there to be learned from.

Her mother, her father, *his* mother, *his* father, had all been caught in the coils of unrequited love. It had caused bitterness and misery and she was damned if she would walk that path. Or do that to him. Because if he even so much as suspected she'd fallen for him he would be appalled, and she couldn't stand the humiliation of that.

She loved him—he didn't love her. She would not do what her mother had done: hang on for years, becoming progressively more bitter, hoping in perpetuity that he would miraculously change his mind and love her. The only path—the only *sensible* path—was to walk away. At speed, with as much dignity as possible.

Think.

She couldn't walk away from their marriage—ironically those vows *did* bind them for another few months—but she could change the terms of the deal. That was a language Stefan *did* understand. Because she couldn't have any sort of relationship with him—not now she knew she loved him.

'I don't agree,' she said simply. 'Love doesn't have to give abusive power. Look at Sunita and Frederick. Look at Marcus and April.'

'That is the choice they have made. It's not a choice I agree with.'

'And that's your right. Just like it's your right and choice not to engage with Frederick. But you're missing out. Yes, you won't get hurt, but you won't experience closeness either.' Another deep breath and she forced herself to continue. 'On that note, I think we need to cool it.'

His eyes registered shock, surprise and a fleeting emotion that looked like hurt, and for an instant she nearly changed her mind. But Stefan did not love her; he would never love her. Right now, she had to protect herself.

'Why?' he asked.

Another deep breath. 'There's an article about us.' Her gaze flicked to the laptop. 'It's on there, if you want to look.'

Bracing herself, she waited as he flipped the screen up, scanned the article. Then his grey eyes came up to study her.

Hold it together. She wouldn't, *couldn't* allow the humiliation of letting him know what a fool she had been.

'It made me realise that I *do* want the real thing one day—a real marriage with love. So what we are doing feels wrong to me. I want to call it a day now, instead of in a few days. No big deal, right?'

Stefan's expression was unreadable, though she could

see the tension in the jut of his jaw, the almost unnatural stillness of his body.

'No big deal,' he agreed, his voice without any discernible emotion.

No big deal. A hollow feeling of being bereft scooped her insides. She'd never feel his touch again, never hold him, never wake up in the crook of his arm, never walk hand in hand with him. *Never...* The word that rhymed with *for ever* and it meant the opposite. Her heartache deepened and her whole being scrambled to find some semblance of pride.

He must not suspect the truth.

CHAPTER FOURTEEN

STEFAN EYED HIS brother over the piles of reports that littered the table between them, tried to focus on the figures before him. Lord knew they were important. The community project had grown and developed over the past few days of discussion. Days when they had found common beliefs and causes, a mutual desire to help those less fortunate, to give something back.

Yet despite the importance of the documents on the table it took all his willpower to focus, to try and block the images of Holly that invaded his brain wherever he was.

It shouldn't matter—he shouldn't miss her so damn much. Shouldn't keep wanting to talk to her, tell her about the project. Shouldn't miss the warmth of her body next to his in the night. Shouldn't miss the sound of her laughter, the way she swirled a tendril of her hair, the tantalising *Holly*-ness of her.

Frederick closed the lid of his computer. 'I think we should finish up for today.' A hesitation and then, 'I know Holly is at Il Boschetto di Sole for a few days—I hope her father is OK?'

'He's fine.' His illness was a cover story to explain Holly's absence.

'Sunita's out for the evening. Would you like to come back

to the palace? Have a beer…spend some time with Amil. I know he'd like that.' Another pause. 'And so would I.'

Stefan opened his mouth, closed it again. He realised the idea appealed—that the idea of a return to the hotel where Holly's absence was like an actual physical pain didn't.

'That would be good. Thank you.'

Twenty minutes later he entered Frederick and Sunita's home, watching as Amil hurtled across the floor away from the nanny and into Frederick's outstretched arms with a cry of, 'Daddy!'

Stefan stood still, aware of a pang that smote him. A pang of what? Envy? Surely not—this was exactly what he *didn't* want.

Frederick thanked the nanny before she left and then grinned at his son. 'Today Uncle Stefan is here for your bath.'

Amil beamed at him and Stefan's heart gave a funny little twist. Twisted further as he ended up in the bathroom, sleeves rolled up, sitting by the tub where Amil sat, four rubber ducks bobbing in the water.

'Sing the song, Uncle Stefan.'

Stefan shook his head. 'I don't know it, Amil. I'm sorry.'

'Yes, you do. Eloise and I sang it to you in *your* bath,' Frederick said from the doorway, and started to hum.

The tune ricocheted around his brain…evoked a crystal-clear memory. Himself in the bath, surrounded by bubbles, a rubber duck in each hand, splashing in time as his mother and Frederick sang.

'"Five little ducks went swimming one day…"'

Soon he and Frederick were singing and Amil was splashing and moving the ducks around the bath. Finally Frederick called a halt, helped Amil out of the bath, wrapped him in a fluffy towel and carried him into the lounge.

'Help yourself to a drink whilst I put Amil to bed.'

'Uncle Stefan. Please read my book?'

Frederick hesitated, then glanced at Stefan with a rueful smile. 'Do you mind?'

'Not at all.'

And he meant it. So he read his nephew a book featuring a variety of farmyard animals and felt his heart tug again.

Later, when Amil was in bed, Frederick poured two glasses of deep red wine and heated up a casserole. He sat down opposite Stefan in the spacious kitchen as the scent of herbs filled the air. 'Can we talk?'

'Sure.' Though wariness touched him.

'I know the deal you made with Marcus. Support me and get your lands back. I went along with it because I knew you wouldn't accept the lands otherwise. But I have always been happy to restore them; they are yours by right. I want you to know that.'

Stefan shook his head. 'I don't work like that. Our father took my rights and my lands away—that was his right. I would like them back, but I have no wish to be beholden.'

'We're brothers. You wouldn't be beholden. It wouldn't give me any power over you. That's what you're worried about, isn't it? Giving anyone power over you. Me? Holly?'

Stefan froze. 'Holly has nothing to do with this.'

'Yes, she does. You made a deal with her too—a marriage deal. And now I think you care about her. Maybe even love her.'

'Of course I don't. I don't *do* love.' Inside him something twisted, turned, unlocked with a creak, opening a floodgate of panic.

His brother smiled. 'Famous last words, little brother. Sometimes love doesn't give you a choice.'

'There is *always* a choice.' And right now he chose to cut himself loose before it was too late to uproot love. Love that had already coiled around his heart, inserting insidious tendrils of weakness.

Whoa… *Love?* He *loved* Holly…? *Loved* her?

Frederick leant forward, his blue eyes arresting, his mien serious. 'This may be none of my business, but you are my brother. We shared a childhood…we shared an upbringing. I cared about your mother and I cared about you. But when Eloise left, when you still got to see her and I didn't, I was angry and I blamed you. Instead of becoming a better brother I switched off, insulated myself from all emotions and feelings, allowed our father to mess with my head. Like I know he messed with yours. I owe you an apology, Stefan; I didn't step up when I should have.'

Stefan could feel emotions long-buried begin to surface. The hurt he'd felt at losing Frederick's affection… the guilt of his belief that he'd deserved to lose it…their father's relentless pitting of brother against brother. But through it all he hadn't thought about how *Frederick* felt, how *he* was affected.

'Maybe it's time to put it behind us.'

He saw an image of Holly's face, heard an echo of her voice. *'If you can let go of the past then you can have a future.'*

'Go forward from here.'

'I'd like that.' Frederick took a breath. 'But there's something else I'd like to say. Our father messed with my head so much I didn't believe that I could be a good husband or father. Sunita and Amil showed me that I can—maybe Holly can show you the same. Don't let our father mess with your head from beyond the grave. If you love her, go for it—I promise you it will be worth it.'

Frederick paused and leant over and ruffled Stefan's hair. The gesture was ridiculously familiar.

'Lecture over, little bro, but if you need anything then let me know.'

Stefan stood up, unsure of what to say. He loved Holly—and now he had a choice as to what to do about it.

Holly looked up from her computer as her father knocked on the door, a look of concern on his face. 'Holly, Jessica has made dinner. It will be ready in half an hour—come eat something.'

'I'm sorry, Dad. I'm just not hungry. But you two go ahead.' Holly summoned up a smile. 'I'm glad it's working out with Jessica.'

'That is thanks to Stefan.' Thomas uttered the name with caution. 'It was he who spoke with me, persuaded me to talk to Jessica.'

'He did?' Holly looked up. She knew she shouldn't encourage the conversation—she was trying to forget Stefan—yet she wanted to know.

'Yes, he did. In fact my temporary son-in-law was quite vocal on the subject.'

'He was?' Holly tried to feel annoyed. Instead all she could summon was a picture of Stefan—the jut of his jaw, the intensity of his eyes, the gentle touch of his hand, his smile.

'Yes, and what he said made me think.'

Her father entered the room and sat down on the bed, just as he had when she was younger, studying for exams.

'I owe you an apology.'

'No. You don't.' Now she really *was* annoyed. 'And if Stefan told you that I hope you told him to get knotted.'

'He said nothing so discourteous and neither did I. What he *did* tell me about was about your job prospects at Lamberts. Something *you* hadn't told me.'

'Because it's not important.'

'Yes, Holly, it *is* important. You should have told me—but also I should have asked. Instead I assumed that you wanted what I wanted, that your wish was to live here with me, marry, settle down, have Romano heirs, and of course work here on Il Boschetto di Sole. I assumed all that and that was wrong.'

'No, Papa. It wasn't wrong. Our family has worked here for generations. I do want to work here—of course I do.'

'But it doesn't have to be *now*, Holly. You need time to spread your wings, see the world, travel. Yes, of course I want you to live here, settle down, but most of all I want you to be happy. I can look after Il Boschetto di Sole and I can also look after myself. That is *my* responsibility. I want to be here to see your children and I will do my best to do so. I am sure Jessica will help me do that.'

Holly stood up, moved over to her father and hugged him. 'Thank you.'

'Now, come and eat with us and tell us about the new job. I want to know all about it.'

Holly grinned at him, and for a moment her heart lightened. But before she could say anything more there was another knock on the door and Jessica popped her head round, looking flustered.

'We have a visitor.'

'Who?'

'Prince Stefan. I've put him in the lounge.'

Holly's heart jumped as her tummy went into freefall.

Her father rose to his feet and smiled. 'Go to him, Holly.'

'I can't. Tell him I'm not here—that I'm sick, have been beamed up by aliens… Anything!'

Her father shook his head. 'Do you love him?'

She flinched. 'Of course not. You know that this is a marriage of convenience.'

'Are you sure?'

Holly tried to hold his gaze, but couldn't.

'Love is nothing to be ashamed of,' her father said gently.

'I'm not ashamed.' Holly twisted her hands together, saw the love in her father's eyes and opted for the truth. 'But Stefan doesn't want my love. He doesn't want anyone's love. I was a fool to fall for him. All I want to do now is get over it.'

'Have you told him you love him?'

'No! And I'm not going to. There is no point in humiliating myself and making him feel bad. This is not his fault.' Unlike Graham, Stefan had not strung her along or pretended love—he'd been up-front. 'I don't want to be like you and my mother.'

Thomas closed his eyes for a moment, then opened them, reached out and touched her arm. 'Holly. Please do not let me and your mother's actions destroy your relationship or taint your attitude to love. Our mistakes, our issues, do not need to be yours. Stefan is not me, and you are not your mother. Give your love a chance.'

Holly looked at him and her own words to Stefan came back to her. *If you can let go of the past then you can have a future.* And his words, about the past being there to be learned from.

What if they were both right?

What if her father was right?

Maybe she *should* let go of her past and tell Stefan of her love. And if he rejected that love then she would learn from her parents and she would walk away, knowing she had done all she could to give love a chance.

'Thank you, Papa.' She dropped a kiss on his head and then, pulling up every reserve of courage, she headed for the lounge.

As she entered her heart pounded so hard it was a wonder her ribcage could cope. Her lungs certainly couldn't. Her breath caught in her throat as she saw him, standing by the mantelpiece, studying the array of photographs there, his whole body tense.

His fingers drummed his thigh as he turned to face her. 'Holly. We need to talk.'

What to say? What to say? And where to say it?

Not here. Somehow she wanted to be outside, under the sky, amongst the trees in the vast beauty of Il Boschetto di Sole.

'Shall we go outside?'

He nodded, and together they made their way to the front door and stepped out into the early evening, where the last rays of sunshine were giving way to the dusk. His proximity made her head whirl, and his familiar scent made her want to bury herself in his arms and burrow in.

Rather than that, she sought some form of conversation. 'So…um…how is it going with Frederick?'

'Good. We've come up with some pretty solid ideas that we're both excited about.'

'Good.'

Conversation dwindled after that as they walked through the garden of the villa and headed by tacit consent to the lemon groves, where the intense fragrance offered her the comfort of familiarity as they wended through the trees towards a bench. A breeze holding the first chill of the year blew and she gave a small shiver.

'Here.' He shrugged off the green and blue checked shirt that he wore over a deep blue T-shirt. Seeing his bare arms made her shiver with the sudden bittersweet ache of desire and the memory of being held. Perhaps she should refuse the shirt, but she couldn't. She wanted to feel the material that had touched his skin against hers.

'Thank you.'

They sat on the bench and she turned to him, knowing she needed to do it—take the plunge.

'I'm glad you're here. I need to talk to you. We left some things unsaid.'

The ghost of a smile touched his lips. 'Yes, we did. That's why I'm here too. To say…'

Goodbye? Had he discovered some legal loophole that would allow their marriage to be annulled?

'Could I go first? Please.' Before she bottled it.

For a moment she thought, almost hoped, he'd refuse, but then he nodded. 'Go ahead.'

After a deep breath she launched in. 'I wasn't fully truthful with you and I should have been. But before I say what I need to say I need you to know that this is not your fault.'

Come on, Holly.

'I love you.'

There—she'd said it. Admittedly whilst staring down at the slats of the wooden bench, but she'd said it.

She hurried on. 'I just wanted you to know. I don't want anything back…don't expect anything back. And please don't feel bad—I don't regret loving you.'

'Holly.' His voice sounded strangled. 'Look at me.'

She looked up, braced herself for pity, anger, sorrow, but instead saw a shell-shocked look of stunned disbelief succeeded by a dawning of joy, a light so bright, so happy, that her own heart gave a small cautious leap.

'I came here to tell you *I* love *you*.'

Happiness sparked, but she doused the joy, needed to know he meant it, that it was real and not an illusion.

'Don't say it because you feel sorry for me.'

'I would never do that. I do not feel sorry for you. I love you.'

'But just days ago you told me you didn't want love… didn't *do* love.'

'It turns out I knew absolutely nothing about love. I love you whether I want to or not, and it turns out I *do* want to.' He sounded almost bewildered. 'I love you and I want to shout it from the rooftops. I love the way you smile, I love the way you twirl your hair round your finger, I love your warmth, your generosity, your loyalty and how much you care. Loving you makes me a better person—a stronger person, not a weaker one. Maybe it does give you power over me, but I trust you not to abuse that power. I've been falling for you since the moment I laid eyes on you; and now you have made me the happiest man on this earth.'

Now he paused.

'As long as you're sure too. You're not mistaking love for duty? It's not for your father, or for Il Boschetto di Sole, or…?'

'No! This love is for real! I love you—I love how you bring out the best in me, make me strive and question and leave my comfort zone. You make me smile, you make me laugh, you make me feel safe, you encourage me and you make me so happy I can feel the happiness tingle through my whole body.'

He rose to his feet and pulled her up with him. He spanned her waist with his hands and twirled her round, and then he sank to one knee and took her hand in his.

'In this beautiful place—*our* beautiful place—will you, Holly Romano, stay married to me, Stefan Petrelli, for ever? To have and to hold, till death us do part?'

She beamed. 'Yes, I will.'

And as he stood and kissed her, she knew that they would fulfil each and every vow they had made with love and happiness. For ever.

EPILOGUE

STEFAN LOOKED OUT over Forester's Glade—Radura dei Guardaboschi.

'You OK?' Holly asked, slipping her hand into his.

'Yes. Really I am.'

They had just scattered his mother's ashes over the earth she had loved so much and a sense of peace enveloped him.

'I hope she is now at rest.'

Holly moved even closer to him, increased the pressure of her clasp. 'I wish I could have known her. I wish it could all have panned out differently.'

'Me too. But I know she would have been happy for me and I know she would have loved you. Not, of course, as much as I do, but she would have loved you.'

For a moment they looked out over the lush, verdant land, listening to the babble of the stream, the rush of the waterfall.

'I love you very much, Holly. And I am very proud of you. Especially for that award.'

'I'm pretty stoked myself.'

She'd won Global Marketing Trainee of the Year and she more than deserved it.

'But the wonderful thing is how much I love the work. And did you see my father's face when they handed me the prize?'

'I thought he'd burst, he was so proud.'

She nestled closer to him. 'I wouldn't have tried it if it wasn't for you.'

'Well, I wouldn't have such a great relationship with Frederick if it wasn't for you.'

His closeness with his older brother made him feel warm inside. He knew Frederick would always have his back and vice versa.

'I guess we work pretty well together, huh?'

'I guess we do.'

Turning, he pulled her into his arms and knew that this marriage deal was one that would last for ever—and it was the best deal he'd ever made.

* * * * *

COMING SOON!

We really hope you enjoyed reading this book.
If you're looking for more romance
be sure to head to the shops when
new books are available on

Thursday 27th March

To see which titles are coming soon, please visit
millsandboon.co.uk/nextmonth

MILLS & BOON

THE HEART OF ROMANCE

A ROMANCE FOR EVERY READER

MODERN

Prepare to be swept off your feet by sophisticated, sexy and seductive heroes, in some of the world's most glamourous and romantic locations, where power and passion collide.

HISTORICAL

Escape with historical heroes from time gone by. Whether you passion is for wicked Regency Rakes, muscled Vikings or rugge Highlanders, awaken the romance of the past.

MEDICAL

Set your pulse racing with dedicated, delectable doctors in the high-pressure world of medicine, where emotions run high an passion, comfort and love are the best medicine.

True Love

Celebrate true love with tender stories of heartfelt romance, from the rush of falling in love to the joy a new baby can brin and a focus on the emotional heart of a relationship.

HEROES

The excitement of a gripping thriller, with intense romance its heart. Resourceful, true-to-life women and strong, fearless men face danger and desire - a killer combination!

From showing up to glowing up, these characters are on the path to leading their best lives and finding romance along th way – with plenty of sizzling spice!

To see which titles are coming soon, please visit

millsandboon.co.uk/nextmonth

LET'S TALK
Romance

For exclusive extracts, competitions and special offers, find us online:

- MillsandBoon
- @MillsandBoon
- @MillsandBoonUK
- @MillsandBoonUK

Get in touch on 01413 063 232

afterglow BOOKS

Afterglow Books is a trend-led, trope-filled list of books with diverse, authentic and relatable characters, a wide array of voices and representations, plus real world trials and tribulations. Featuring all the tropes you could possibly want (think small-town settings, fake relationships, grumpy vs sunshine, enemies to lovers) and all with a generous dose of spice in every story.

♪ @millsandboonuk
📷 @millsandboonuk
afterglowbooks.co.uk

#AfterglowBooks

For all the latest book news, exclusive content and giveaways scan the QR code below to sign up to the Afterglow newsletter:

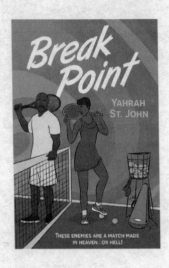